Posy: Book Two

Luna

By Mary Ann Weir

Table of Contents

1: Cuddles with Quartz

Quartz

Jayden kindly shifted and gave me complete control for Posy's cuddle session. I'd have to repay him somehow, but for now, all I could focus on was my mate's sweet self.

I couldn't say I was shocked by her reaction to the king and queen's disagreement; trauma didn't go away overnight - or ever - and we should have known that she'd get upset. The incident was a good reminder to me, my wolf brothers, and our boys why we were keeping the arguing to a minimum and walking away before our tempers made us loud and aggressive.

Now, lying on the living room rug in my own fur, I let Posy do anything she wanted to me because I knew she took comfort in it, even if it was *absolutely ridiculous* for an alpha wolf to be treated like a dog.

"I was so scared, Quartz," she whispered. "I thought he would kill her for talking that way to him. That's what my father would have done. No one ever argued with him, not even my mom."

Your father was probably abusive toward her, too, my love, I said. *He seemed like the type. I bet he even blamed his wife for what happened while the rogues held her.*

"My brothers said my mates could explain that." She rubbed the inside of my ears in that way I loved. "Will you tell me? What did James mean, they forced her?"

I debated for a moment, then decided no one would mind if I handled this one.

You remember what you and the boys talked about concerning mating? I waited until she nodded. *The rogues mated with your mom without her permission and without the mate bond. It was nothing like what you feel with the boys. They were mean and cruel and hurt her. It's called rape.*

Her eyes overflowed with tears as I spoke, and I licked them off her cheeks as they fell.

"Why?" her voice cracked. "Why would they do that to any she-wolf, least of all my mom? She was sweet and kind and gentle!"

I am sorry to say that there is a type of male in whom there exists a need to brutally control everything and everyone, to destroy anything sweet and kind and gentle. Now, add in the rogue factor. Most are vile and lawless, little more than gangs of mutts who don't understand family or love. That is why the king works to exterminate those that cannot be rehabilitated.

"But why would Father blame my mom? If they forced her, it wasn't her fault!"

4

Jayden was telling me something, and I listened as he explained the psychology of victim-blaming. It made no sense to me, but I tried to boil it down for Posy as cleanly as I could.

Your father was that type of male, too. Control without empathy. Destruction without sympathy.

She tilted her head as she thought about that, and I shoved my muzzle in her bared neck. Taking a deep inhale, I drowned in her chocolate-chip cookie scent. Compared to me, she was so very tiny, and it brought out every protective instinct I had.

I'd give every single inch of my blood-stained soul to keep this little one safe.

She'd stopped petting me while she was thinking, so I nudged her hand with my nose. She blinked, smiled at me, and began to run her fingers through my chest hair. I rumbled deep in my throat and laid my chin on her shoulder.

Do you know how she ended up with the rogues?

"Um, no. I didn't know anything about it at all until James told me. I thought Father was my father. Do you think it matters?"

No. I'm just curious. Packs are so secure and well-established now, thanks to King Julian and his father before him, that rogues don't dare attack or invade anymore. I wonder how they got their hands on her, that's all.

"I can ask my brothers. They might know."

It isn't important. Those it affected the most are dead.

"Quartz?"

Hmm?

"Do you think—" She paused and bit her bottom lip.

Just ask me, my love. There is nothing you can't ask me.

"Do you think it bothers the boys?"

What? Does what bother them?

"That I'm— That I'm part rogue?" She finished on a little sob, and my heart broke.

You are nothing of the kind. As soon as you mate with the boys, you will be the luna of Five Fangs, Earthshine, Great Rocks, Moonset, Dark Woods, and River Rapids. There is no other shifter alive today who is a part of six packs, let alone in such a high position. You are as far from a rogue as it is possible to get. Besides, being a rogue is more about the mindset than being packless.

"Wait. *Six* packs? I remember Ash mentioning Dark Woods was his former pack. Are those others the rest of the boys' former packs?"

The Moon Goddess still recognizes them, so I don't know if 'former' is the right word. However, once your first pup is born, they will dissolve and only Five Fangs will exist.

5

"First pup," she mouthed with wide eyes.

I smirked at her look of shell-shock. I could not wait to see her round with a pup, although I knew it was likely to be a few years. They were all so young, as Ash had pointed out, and wanted to live a little. My wolf brothers and I understood that and wouldn't pressure any of them - no matter how much we longed for it. Continuing our line was a primal need in a wolf, made even stronger by our alpha blood.

"The way moon magic works can be weird sometimes," she said at last. "Well, anyway, which pack belongs to who?"

Earthshine is Mason's. Great Rocks is Cole's. Moonset is ours. River Rapids is Wyatt's.

"Moonset. That's a beautiful name for a pack. I haven't been outside under the moon for a very long time. Does Five Fangs have midnight runs on a full moon?"

Of course. Is that something you look forward to, my love?

"Oh, yes! I can't wait!"

I chuckled as her enthusiasm made her bounce up and down and clap her hands.

"I love you, Quartz." She cradled my head in her hands and kissed me right between my eyes.

I love you, too.

"Can I pet your belly?"

I groaned, but gave in and rolled onto my back. Almost immediately, she found my sweet spot and my back leg kicked in reaction, which made her dissolve into a fit of giggles.

We spent nearly an hour together, snuggling and talking about anything she wanted to, before Wyatt came into the living room and scooped her up.

Granite, you need to stop interrupting others while they're loving on our mate, I grumbled.

Come on, Q, he said with a cheeky smile. *You know I never good at waiting my turn.*

Sinking to his level, I blew a raspberry at him.

6

2: Making Her Point

Wyatt

Much later, we were in bed waiting for our girl, who said she wanted to talk to us. She'd seemed so serious when she said it that we were all a little tense.

We knew she was down because we were leaving tomorrow, but we got the feeling that something more was on her mind.

She came out of *our* closet wearing one of Cole's white dress shirts - and nothing else. Well, I assumed she had panties on, but the shirt went to her knees, so she was fully covered either way. The sleeves were rolled up to her elbows and the top two buttons were undone.

Not nearly far enough, I mourned. *Not a hint of her perfect cleavage on display.*

What's cleavage, Wy?

Titties, Granite.

Ooh. I LIKE Posy's titties.

Me, too.

Without a word, she came over and stood at the side of the bed, then looked at us expectantly.

"Yes, princess?" Ash asked with raised eyebrows.

"Could one of you please pick me and put me on the bed?"

Rock-Paper-Scissors? Cole shot through the link.

We all nodded, not taking our eyes off of her as he counted 1-2-3. We each threw out a hand and glanced to see if someone had won. I crowed in victory and leapt off the bed, making our girl giggle.

I swung her up like a bride and went to place her in the middle when she shook her head and pointed her finger to the foot end. I gave her a curious look, but set her down where she wanted.

I ran back to my side and jumped in as Posy folded her legs demurely to the side. Once I was settled against the headboard with my brothers, I saw that her hair was up in a messy bun, there was a pencil behind her ear, and she held a clipboard.

An actual clipboard.

"Now, boys, as I said earlier, I have some very important things to discuss with you before you leave tomorrow, so please pay attention."

Oh, my Goddess, Jay moaned through the link. *She just needs a pair of those half-moon reading glasses to make all my sexy librarian fantasies come true.*

I was thinking naughty secretary, I admitted, *but that works, too.*

"I know Ash is going to fall asleep soon," she was saying, "so I'll start with the most urgent one first. That way, when he falls asleep, I can put the rest on hold until you get back. Sound okay?"

Like good little puppies, we all nodded.

"Number one." She unclipped a stack of cash from her clipboard and held it up. "I won four hundred dollars on a bet today. The queen hasn't paid up yet, but I assume she's good for it. I want to use it to host a birthday party for Tyler."

"There's— There's so much to talk about in what you just said," Cole murmured.

Ash and I giggled.

"Oh, don't worry. I didn't bet with *your* money. Emerson said he'd spot me if I lost, but since I won, it didn't matter. Anyway, Queen Lilah is going to help me plan it, but I don't know how much it costs. Will you loan me some if this isn't enough?"

"Of course, sweetness," Jay said for all of us. "We were going to do something, anyway, with the other betas."

"And you don't have to use your money. Save it for a rainy day. We'll cover it," Mason told her.

I don't think she knows too much about money, I linked my boys. *Like how much things cost and stuff. I mean, she's worried that some balloons, a cake, and a few decorations will cost more than four hundred dollars.*

And what did she mean, our *money? It's* her *money, too*, Cole sounded puzzled.

We need to set her straight on a couple of issues, money being one of them, Mason linked back.

"We need to have a talk about money when we get back from Tall Pines," he said aloud.

"You can make up your own list of topics for discussion." She raised an eyebrow and gave him a stern look. "Right now, I'm going over mine."

"Yes, ma'am."

"Thank you." She took her pencil from behind her ear, licked the tip, and checked off something on her clipboard.

I let out a quiet groan and folded my hands over my growing erection.

Ahh! This girl is going to kill me! Cole was also struggling, it seemed.

"Moving on to number two, which is related to number one. I checked with Peri first, and she said she's ninety-nine percent sure none of you will have a bad reaction to me asking this. For that tiny one percent chance, though, I'm letting you know it's about Tyler."

She paused and looked at us.

What's she waiting for? I asked.

To see if any of us are going to wolf out like I did when she asked about Ev the other night. Jay's tone was bitter.

Don't be like that, Ash told him. *She's being her usual considerate self and making sure you - and all of us - are okay before she brings it up. Be grateful, not sour, about it.*

"I'd like to know Tyler's story," she continued when we stayed silent. "Not tonight, and not because I'm being nosy. It's obvious that he went through something traumatic. When I first came here, Ash explained to me what triggering was, and I don't want to trigger Tyler with something I do or say if I can avoid it."

She bit her bottom lip, as if nervous we would say no.

I don't understand how her heart can be so sweet after what she's gone through, Ash said, *but I'm going to love it for the rest of my life.*

Me, too, we all agreed.

"Sure, little flower. How kind and thoughtful of you." Mason smiled, something he'd been doing a lot more lately.

Thanks to our little mate, Granite grinned, and I nodded.

Pink washed over her face at the compliments, making us *aww* at her.

"You know, I like this." She cocked her head to the side with a tiny smile. "I feel in control. Organized. Like I actually know what I'm doing." She laughed lightly. "Does that even make sense?"

"Of course it does, cutie," I told her. "We'll do this more often since it makes you happy and builds your confidence. Now, how many points do you have left? Ash's eyelids are drooping."

They are? he asked.

They are, we replied.

"Three more, but I can hold off on the last one. In fact, I'm deciding right now to hold off on it. So, number three, which goes into four. I'm ready for you to mark me, and I'd like to practice mating."

Shock silenced us for a moment.

"Thank you, sweetness," Jay said at last. "That makes us so happy."

"Practice?" My brain turned on again. "I get marking, but what do you mean by *practice* mating?"

"Um, well, ease into, uh, mating." Her eyes went to Mason, then flicked to Cole as red fired through her cheeks. "Like with clothes on? See how it goes? Just, you know, *practice.*"

She held the clipboard up to cover her face.

So she wants to do more kissing and touching? Is that what she's saying? I felt like I was about to come apart at the seams with excitement.

9

She already has. At least with me and Mase. Cole's grin made me grind my teeth.

Smug mutt.

It sounds like that's what she wants, but we'll clarify it with her later, Jay said, *because Ash is fading fast.*

I am? His voice was groggy and slow.

You are, we chorused.

"Wait a minute!" I squawked, making Posy lower her clipboard. "Tyler's birthday was ranked higher than marking and mating?!"

"Of course marking and mating are more *important,* but I said I was ordering things by urgency. Tyler's only going to turn eighteen one time, and it happens in two weeks."

At her sassy tone, my dick hardened a little more, and I grabbed one of my many pillows to cover it. My hands were big, but not big enough to hide *that* tent in my boxers.

"We understand, honey, and we can talk more about number four in the morning when we're all wide awake."

Hey, don't throw me under the bus, Ash grumbled at Cole. *I can't help the way I am.*

"When would you like us to mark you?" Jay asked her.

"First thing in the morning."

We finally get to mark our mate! Granite and I yipped at the same time.

"Okay, go to number five, princess," Ash slurred a little, a small snore buzzing through the words.

"I decided to table that for another time, remember? It wasn't a good idea to bring it up at bedtime anyway because you'll have strong emotions on it."

"Is it a time-sensitive issue?" Mason suddenly became alert. "Is it anything that affects your safety or health?"

"Uh, no and no. Just something I'm struggling with and want your opinions on."

"I can wake up if you need me to," Ash yawned.

Despite his words, his body moved from sitting against the headboard with the rest of us to lying flat on his back, his usual sleeping position.

"No, we'll talk later," she told him.

" 'K, cupcake. Gimme kisses 'fore beddy."

Posy put down her clipboard, crawled up next to him, and kissed him softly on the lips.

No fair, he mumbled. *Our first real kiss ... and I'm not ... awake ... enough ... to—*

And he was out.

10

Posy leaned over him to give Mase, then Cole goodnight kisses, and her shirt rode up, exposing the silky skin of her thighs and the barest hint of butt cheeks.

Jay let a few no-no words slip into the link, and Mase and Cole wanted to know why, so I sent them the image of our girl's sweet ass up in the air, and their groans echoed my own.

What I wouldn't give to plow into that right this second, I thought. *Grab her hips and pound balls-deep into her—*

Wyatt! my brothers yelled at me, and I realized I still had the link open.

Sorry not sorry.

They all three groaned again, and I snickered out loud, drawing Posy's attention.

She spun toward me with gleaming eyes. Wriggling halfway over Jay to reach me, she playfully smushed my face between her palms and made my lips pop out like a fish. She giggled, and Jay put his hands on her waist to hold her still.

Oh, Goddess, he groaned. *Take her, Wy, before she feels something that'll embarrass her.*

She wasn't embarrassed to feel my boner earlier, Cole smirked, *or Mase's.*

Okay, then before I embarrass myself, he hissed. *I don't want to come in my shorts right now, thank you very much.*

I ignored their little spat to focus on Posy as she whispered, "Good night, Wyatt."

Then her warm lips pressed against mine.

Oh, my! Posy's lips feel so nice, Granite cooed. *Is she soft and warm like this all over?*

I don't know. Let's find out.

Wrapping one arm around her shoulders and clamping the other over the back of her thighs, I dragged her off Jay and rolled until she was under me. She squeaked, but didn't protest or seem upset or uncomfortable. I deepened the kiss as I gathered her wrists in my hand and pinned them over her head, which drew her titties up. Her nipples stiffened into tight buds and poked into my chest, and something *else* hardened and wanted to poke her back.

Pull up shirt, Granite said. *I want to see between her legs.*

My free hand traveled up the back of her smooth thigh and slipped under her shirt, and my fingers found the edge of her cotton panties. Without thinking, I squeezed one round cheek and caught her moan in my mouth.

Be careful, Mase warned me. *Don't go too far without asking her.*

I broke the kiss with a growl.

11

Granite! Don't put ideas in my head.

It not me, Wy. The ideas already there. I just tell you to do them.

"Wyatt?" She sounded so hesitant and unsure, and I knew I went too far.

Releasing her hands, I propped myself up on my elbows to take my weight off of her and opened my mouth to apologize, but she started to speak first.

"Why did you growl at me?" Crystal drops filled her eyes. "Did I do something wrong?"

Bad Wyatt! Granite roared at me. *You made mate cry! Bad!*

I grimaced as his piercing volume rattled my brain.

"You didn't do anything wrong; *I* did," I explained gently. "I was growling at Granite, not you. I'm sorry."

Dropping my head, I kissed her forehead, then her cheek, and finally her lips again. She melted into me and twined her arms around my neck, pulling me down on top of her again.

"I'm too heavy," I murmured against her lips.

"I like it. I feel surrounded by your strength and warmth."

I no can wait until her warmth surrounds our d—

Listen, wolf, it's hard enough to control myself without your influence.

But just imagine, Wy. Granite's eyes rolled in bliss. *Her warm, wet, tight pussy—*

I rolled off of her and kept going until I hit the edge of the bed, then ran for the bathroom.

"Wyatt?"

"Sorry, cutie. Need to pee!" I called back.

I heard Jay talking quietly to her as I closed the bathroom door. Shedding my boxers, I dove into the shower and turned on the cold water.

\#

Posy

I stared at the bathroom door as Wyatt closed it behind him, but Jayden looped his arms around my waist, pulled me to him, and kissed my cheek.

"He's fine, Posy," he murmured, "but I'm not. I'm sad."

My surprised gaze flew to his dragon eyes.

"What? Why? I don't want you to be sad, Jayden!"

"You kissed Ash right next to me, then crawled over me to kiss Wyatt. Am I not worthy of kisses?"

My heart squeezed.

"Of course you are! I love you! I'm sorry! I didn't mean to make you feel—"

"Relax, Posy. I'm only teasing," he laughed and rubbed his nose against mine. "But I *would* like a kiss, please, if you're okay with that."

Closing my eyes, I leaned in and touched my lips to his, and his gentle response was exactly what I'd expected from him. A little hum vibrated out of his throat, and I snuggled further into the muscled planes of his chest. When we broke apart, I opened my eyes and stared at him, overwhelmed by the love filling up every empty place inside me.

Sometimes, I still have trouble believing these gorgeous, sweet, strong men are mine.

"Jayden?" I whispered.

"Hmm?"

"Can I hear you play the guitar sometime?"

"Sure. Anytime."

"Do you sing, too?"

"Um, yeah, but I don't know how good I am," he chuckled.

"He's great, Posy," Cole told me. "He's being modest."

"He sings all the time," Mason added. "He's being shy because it's *you*."

Pink streaked across Jayden's cheek bones, and my heart fluttered.

"Maybe someday you'll feel comfortable enough to sing something for me." I cradled his face in my hands and smiled. "But no pressure."

"How about a lullaby?" Wyatt suggested as he came out of the bathroom.

Looking at him over my shoulder, I saw his hair was slightly damp. Maybe he'd had a quick shower, too? He plopped back into his spot and cuddled up to my back, his arm going around my waist and shoving Jayden's down. Jayden didn't seem to mind, though, and squeezed my hip.

"It's been a long day for all of us, Ash is already out, and I'm beat." Wyatt paused to yawn. "Sing something soft and quiet, Jay."

"I don't know," he muttered.

Almost as if they planned it, the two of them snuggled in closer until I was sandwiched between them, but I wasn't uncomfortable. In fact, I liked being surrounded by their hard bodies and wrapped in their strong arms, their legs tangling up with mine and each other's. Wyatt's face was in the back of my neck, his warm breath tickling my ear, and Jayden's dragon eyes were inches away as he stared at me.

13

My own eyelids grew heavier as my muscles began to relax. Wyatt was right; it had been a long day, and tomorrow would be an even longer one.

"Good night, Posy. We love you," Wyatt whispered.

Then Jayden began to sing an achingly sweet song of simple notes and delicate lyrics. I tried to stay awake, wanting to listen to his mesmerizing voice, but the lure of sleep was too strong, and I drifted off into a dream about a joker and his queen.

3: Leaving Their Mark

Quartz

After Jayden sang our mate to sleep, the rest soon followed her into dreamland. Everyone except Garnet, who would remain on guard until the patrol changed at midnight. Then he'd end his self-appointed vigil and sleep, too. It was his nightly routine ever since we'd all moved into the alpha house together.

I was in the mood to talk for once. Jayden wasn't *quite* asleep, but close enough that I didn't want to disturb him, so I spoke with Garnet for the first time in a while. Our lack of communication wasn't because we were on bad terms, but because he was as talkative as his human half, and I was...

Well, I was what I was.

Are you happy, Garnet?

It took him a minute, but he responded.

More than I thought possible.

And Mason? I asked.

Same. Worried about Papa, though.

Mason suffers so much for no reason. I wish you would take control and end that problem one day.

You think I could? Garnet's laugh was a harsh bark. *Not even on my best day and Mase's worst.*

That was probably true. Mason Price was one of the most dominant, powerful shifters I'd ever met, nearly on par with the king.

Like *my* human half, he kept too much inside. Both he and Jayden were landmines rigged to detonate under a feather's weight. If they ever exploded, they would smash the world.

And Jayden thought *I* was dangerous.

Our mate was slowly helping them, for which all of us were grateful. The others tried, too, but our boys were stubborn. Mine because he didn't want to be a burden, and Garnet's because of his father.

Cuddled with our mate, Q?

Deep satisfaction made me grin.

Mm-hmm. She rubbed my ears and petted my coat. She prattled on about so many things, and her voice was as sweet as honey. She would cuddle with you, too. With any of our brothers. She loves us all equally.

I know. Someday soon. He nodded.

She is worried about the young beta.

A little brother, Garnet agreed, and I knew what he meant.

15

I had a feeling we would see River and his boy a lot more often now that our mate had taken him under her wing. Not that I minded. River was a baby in many ways, and Sid, who had a soft spot for pups, loved him like no other. We all did in our own way and were proud of the man Tyler was becoming in spite of everything his father did to him.

Seymour James was my first kill. When Jayden was only twelve years old, I took control and ripped that bastard to pieces. My only regret was that I did it in front of Tyler.

What can I say? I lost my temper.

After the dust settled, the alphas called a meeting and discussed what steps might have to be taken in the future to 'contain' me.

The wolves of the pack, however, looked at me with new respect. Nathan always tried to give a shifter a second chance, and Royal demanded a ton of evidence before an execution was carried out. I, on the other hand, had killed one who needed killing, and the wolves of Five Fangs appreciated the fact that at least one of the future alphas would dole out swift justice to those who deserved it.

Afterward, Jayden put me in a cage and kept me there, and it was only once we found Posy that I was able to break free of it. Thinking back, I was half-convinced that he subconsciously *wanted* me to. Before, I'd only ever been able to flicker in his eyes or underscore his voice without his consent. Since we found our mate, though, I'd fully taken the reins several times before he knew what was happening.

Hate to leave her tomorrow, Q. Hurts my heart. Garnet's words brought me out of my thoughts.

Yes. Mine, too. The babies will cry, I said of Sid, Topaz, and Granite.

Just because you and I won't doesn't mean we feel it any less.

I nodded and began to quiet my mind before sleeping. Then a touch of anxiety trickled into our bond, startling me. Like Mason, Garnet rarely shared his emotions.

What's worrying you, brother? I asked him.

Never be able to mate with Lark.

I winced. I'd realized that, too, the second I saw her. She was far too small. Even if one of our boys stayed human to help, which would be awkward and embarrassing to say the least, we could hurt her.

Or worse.

I remembered what happened in a California pack three years ago. The alpha had just found his mate, who was also a runt, and his wolf accidentally broke her neck while trying to mate her. He'd killed himself shortly afterward. None of the pack with alpha blood was old enough to step up, so the king had to get involved. Nyx told me all about it the next time they visited.

So, no mating Lark. No matter how small the risk might be, we would never chance it.

Do you think our brothers understand that? I wondered.

They do. They talked. I heard.

I had an idea, if everyone is willing. I said, then hesitated to share it.

Mate her in Posy's body and us in our boys'.

Of course, Garnet had already thought of the same solution. Although he was nearly mute except with our mate, he was smart, this wolf brother of mine.

Sid and Granite might not be able to handle it, I admitted with a chuckle, *and I have my doubts about Topaz, too.*

Granite huffed out a quiet laugh as I shared a certain memory through the link. Jayden was about sixteen at the time, and we were all in control of our humans' forms for some reason I'd since forgotten. Sid, Granite, and Topaz had an argument about jerking off of all things, which only ended when they decided to demonstrate their individual techniques on each other. Granite and I watched in fascinated disbelief. We didn't get involved, but we didn't intervene, either. Topaz had stopped when Cole commanded, but Sid and Granite ignored their boys' yelling and went all the way to the finish.

We wolves didn't care, but Ash and Wyatt couldn't look at each other in the face for a week afterwards.

The babies would go first, Granite said with laughter still in his voice, *so that you and I could make it up to her afterwards.*

Our boys will agree. They won't deny us the bond that we need with our wolf mate, I told him.

As if we'd let them, Garnet snorted, *but would Posy agree?*

That was the question, wasn't it?

Remembering our cuddle session earlier, I thought about how she'd stuffed her face in my fur and kissed my head between my eyes. She'd massaged my ears and rubbed my belly until one of my back feet kicked, her laughter like silver bells. Best of all, during her rambling, she'd told me she loved me over and over.

She'd agree, I said now with conviction. *In the future, though. Right now, she's barely ready to mate the boys.*

A flash of anger burned into me, and my low growl rumbled around the room. Jayden opened his eyes, which went right to Posy and scanned her sleeping form.

"Quartz?" he rasped. " 'S wrong?"

Nothing. A bad thought. Go back to sleep.

17

With a nod, he dropped a kiss on Posy's forehead and was out again.

He's dead, Q, and she is safe now, Garnet murmured. *No one will ever hurt her again. As for us, we can wait. For as long as it takes.*

Yes. I sighed and shoved the anger away. *We will wait, and we will keep her safe.*

Forever, he vowed.

Forever.

#

Jayden

As I was drifting off to sleep, I'd heard Quartz talking to Garnet, which was unusual because Garnet usually kept to himself and Quartz was, well, *Quartz.*

They were both turning into regular chatterboxes with our mate, though, and now they were jabbering away with each other.

I was happy, and I knew Mase would be, too, when I told him.

Quartz woke me up once when he growled about something, but said he was fine and Garnet wasn't worried about it. I didn't try to eavesdrop on their conversation, wanting them to talk freely about whatever they'd found to talk about, and I *was* tired, so I closed my eyes and went to sleep again.

Hours later, I woke up to sunlight gradually brightening the room and the sounds of slow, even breathing all around me. Sometime during the night, Wyatt and I had lost Posy, though, which brought a pout to my face. Instead of hugging our sweet girl, I had Wyatt half on top of me with his fluffy blond hair right under my chin and his drool making his cheek stick to my chest.

We weren't lying when we told Posy that he and Cole were snugglers at night.

Rolling my eyes, I shoved him off and over, then gave him my pillow when he whined in his sleep. He curled up around it with a happy little grunt.

Big baby. I rubbed the top of his head with an affectionate smile. *Surprised you still don't suck your thumb.*

Posy's scent was so fresh and rich, I knew she was still in bed, so I rolled over to see which of my brothers was the thief and found her and Ash locked in a heated kiss. He was flat on his back as usual, and she lay on his chest with her legs straddling his stomach and her fingers sunk into his wild curls. His huge hands spanned her ribcage and his thumbs swept back and forth just below the bottom swells of her breasts.

Smirking, I wondered if she had any idea of the pyramid growing in the sheets just a few inches below her ass.

The little noises she made caused the same reaction in me, too, and I sat up.

Can I join? I asked Ash as he broke the kiss.

Sure. She says she wants us to mark her now. You want to wake the others?

Let me get good morning kisses first.

Ash grinned and flipped them so she was on her back and his stomach was nestled between her legs. She looked over and saw me and smiled, her dimples flashing and making my heart sing.

"Good morning, Jayden," she whispered.

"Morning," I whispered back.

As Ash kissed his way down her throat, his morning prickles scraped her skin and it was turning a little pink. From the way she clenched a fistful of his messy hair and arched into him, it wasn't hurting her, so I left it alone.

Seeing as her lips were free, I decided to help myself and leaned down to kiss her. I couldn't get enough of that mouth and devoured her soft, warm lips while Ash left a damp trail down to her collar bone.

Wanting to make sure we weren't pushing her too far too fast, I ended the kiss and raised my head to see her pretty face. Her cheeks were flushed and her half-lidded eyes glittered, and I knew she'd look just like this when I eventually buried myself inside her.

"Tilt your head back, sweetness."

When she did, I kissed the other side of her throat, both Ash and I in search of that special spot to make our mark. The sexy shirt was now in our way, so I undid another button, and we pulled the fabric aside to reveal more of her creamy, satiny skin.

"Ash," she squeaked, then, "Jayden," and drew out my name on a long moan.

Not going to lie, that made me even harder, and I sat up on my knees, planted my hands on either side of her head, and kissed her on the lips again. Her free hand fisted into my hair and tugged gently, and I grew even more excited. Thrusting my tongue in her mouth, I coaxed her to play and nearly came undone when she swiped the tip of her tongue along the roof of my mouth.

Dude! Ash grunted. *Stop making her squirm! I'm so hard, I'm going to explode!*

You're contributing to the squirming, too, brother. Hump the bed if you have to. We can change the sheets later.

Shut up, Jay!

I grinned as I ended the kiss to let us both breathe.

Suddenly, her eyes closed, a heavy shudder ripped through her whole body, and she moaned louder than she had before. Glancing

19

down, I saw Ash's mouth sucking her throat near her ear - and he *was* humping the bed.

Right there, I told him, biting back a giggle.

Mm-hmm. Better wake the others.

I'm busy, I murmured and kissed Posy again. *They snooze, they lose.*

Cole and I are already awake, Mase said dryly. *Cole, wake Wyatt up.*

Why me? Cole muttered, but rolled off his side of the bed and walked around to ours.

"Wake up." He shook Wyatt's shoulder. "Or you're going to miss out on marking Posy with us."

"Wha? 'K. 'M up."

Is there an order we should do this in? I asked my boys.

The same as she marked us makes the most sense, I think, Cole pointed out, and we all nodded.

"Hey, why did you stop kissing me?" Posy opened her eyes and pouted up at me.

"We're going to mark you now, baby." I pecked the tip of her nose. "Is that okay?"

"Yes, please." Her dimpled smile melted my heart. "Do I need to do anything?"

"Just relax and enjoy the ride," Ash murmured against her skin.

Ride? You're the one riding the mattress, I teased.

She's so freaking soft and warm, I'm losing my mind, Ash groaned. *I'm going to come as soon as my teeth break her skin!*

"Ready?" he asked.

"Yes."

"I love you, cupcake."

"I love you, too, Ash."

She stiffened when his canines bit down, but only for a second. Then her eyes rolled back in her head, and we knew she was surfing the same waves of pleasure that we had when she'd marked us. It wasn't an orgasm, but it felt *real* good.

And she has four more marks to go, Cole smirked.

As he predicted, Ash came as soon as his teeth embedded in her neck, his long body taut and still for several seconds before he collapsed on her. He managed to finish the mark and lap up the blood, his saliva healing the punctures, then dropped his head on her breasts and panted.

"Ash," she breathed and wrapped her arms around his head and neck.

The smug mutt had the freaking audacity to wink at me as he rubbed his face into her round boobs, his mouth millimeters from one hard nipple straining against her shirt.

You weigh a ton! Mase barked. *Get off of her, you moose!*

With a groan, Ash rolled my way and pulled the sheet with him, probably to hide his wet shorts from Posy. I shuffled toward the headboard to be out of his way, and he rolled into Wyatt.

Grumpy pup that he was in the mornings, Wyatt scrambled over him with a scowl, then shoved him off the edge of the bed.

Ash's groan, and the loud thud when he hit the floor, made Posy worry.

"Ash?" she called out, her eyebrows puckering, and I reached down to smooth them out with my thumb.

"He's fine," I told her.

"I'm fine," Ash echoed from the floor.

"My turn, Posy," Mase distracted her, and she stared up at him with heart eyes.

He touched our mate as if she were a fragile kitten, and his rough hands were gentle as he cupped her face and kissed her.

"Mason," she breathed when he freed her lips. "I love you."

"You are my whole heart, little flower."

He buried his face in her neck, his hands clenched on either side of her pillow. When he bit into her, she dug her fingernails into his shoulders for a second, then sighed and smoothed her hands over the little crescent indents she'd left. Goosebumps broke out all over his skin as he hummed deep in his throat and licked away the blood.

When he pulled back, he stared down at the mark with a pleased smile.

"What does it look like?" she asked.

"Beautiful."

"No, I mean—"

"It's a replica of ours, sweetness," I told her. "A lovely full moon with two stars so far."

Her eyes bright, she pecked Mason on the lips before craning her neck to look up at me where I was still crouched by the headboard. Shaking my head at the silliness of my position, I scooted to hover over her as I had before. This time, I slid my hands under her shoulders and propped myself up on my elbows.

"I love you, sweetness," I said as I stared into her glittering blue eyes. "I'm so, so happy you're our mate."

She slid her arms around my waist and hugged me.

"I love you, too, Jayden, and I'm beyond happy that you all are my mates."

I smiled, then dropped my head to lay an open-mouth kiss on her mark. She hissed and shivered, and my smile stretched into a grin.

Okay, Quartz. Ready for this?

Permission?

Granted.

He dropped his canines and sank them into her soft flesh. Instantly, the moon magic danced between us and the mate sparks tickled my skin everywhere it touched Posy. She made a breathy little noise and her arms tightened around me, and Quartz retracted his fangs. Swiping his tongue over the wound, he cleaned up the blood, then handed control back to me.

Knowing how sideways this could have gone, I gave him my praise and thanks.

For our mate, he acknowledged. *Anything for our mate.*

I nodded, and he sank to the back of my mind.

Raising my head, I examined the mark and satisfaction filled me. A new link formed in my mind, and I prodded it to see if she could hear me yet. Either she couldn't, or she didn't understand what it was or how to open it.

"Posy, do you feel the mind link with Ash, Mase, or me yet?" I asked, kissing the corner of her lips.

Her eyes spaced out for a second, then she shook her head.

"It's probably an all or nothing thing," Mase guessed as he traded places with Cole. "Like when you marked us and each star showed up until you'd marked all five of us. Just like our mark is doing now."

"That makes sense," she said with a nod.

Cole cleared his throat, and I cut my eyes to him. He made a shooing gesture with one hand. I rolled my eyes, but moved out of his way and laid down on my side with Wyatt at my back.

Cole drew her closer, and his bear-like build enveloped her whole body until the only thing visible was a sweep of brown hair on her white pillow.

"Good morning, honey," he said and kissed her.

"Good morning, Cole. Did you have a good sleep?"

She rubbed her hands over his beard, which he kept at a long stubble in the summer. I wondered if she would be surprised when she saw how full he let it grow during the colder months.

"I did," he answered. "What about you?"

"Me, too. I've slept so well every night since I came here."

"Good. I'm happy to hear that. We all are." He kissed her again. "I love you, honey. For the rest of my life and with every beat of my heart."

"Oh, Cole." Her bottom lip trembled and tears gathered in her eyes, but she gave him a wide smile. "I love you, too. More than I could ever say in words."

He kissed the side of her jaw, then down her neck to the mate mark. He must have lost his hair tie in the night; his long black hair fell loose and created a curtain that thankfully hid his smug face, and I smirked as I shared that thought with my other brothers.

Posy is much more interesting to look at anyway, Wyatt linked me as his head plopped on my shoulder and his arm went around my chest.

Always. And why are you laying on me?

Just enjoying the show, and you're comfortable. And Ash took my pillows with him when he rolled off the bed.

Was pushed off, you mean, I scoffed.

Same same. Give me your pillow.

No, I already did. This one is Posy's, and you drool too m—

Posy gasped in pain, drawing our immediate attention. A second later, her face filled with bliss, and we both let out a breath of relief. Even knowing what it was and why, her being hurt for any reason was not something we would ever take lightly.

She arched her head back further and latched onto Cole's biceps until he finished and raised his head.

"Perfect," he whispered as his eyes found his star on her neck.

She giggled, then turned toward Wyatt.

"Best for last, right, cutie?"

"My fifth star," she murmured with love written all over her face.

He *finally* levered his heavy self off of me and reached for her, pulling her half over me exactly like he did last night, and kissed her senseless. She wiggled, trying to get closer to him, and my body reacted. I shimmied out from under her, which didn't help my growing problem any.

Wyatt! I just got calmed down! I complained.

You're welcome.

He pulled her flush against him, one hand on the back of her neck under her thick hair and the other hooking her knee to pull it over his hip.

Careful, Wy. Not too much too soon, Mase cautioned him the same as he had last night.

Wyatt's middle finger poked out of her hair, but disappeared quickly when Mase growled at him.

I knew the second Wyatt finished his part of the mark because Posy flung open the mate link.

Hi! Can you hear me? Can you? Are you there? Hello!

23

Slow down, precious girl. I chuckled. *Yes, we can hear you.*

With a squeal, she pushed out of Wyatt's hold and sat up on his stomach to clap her hands.

We did it! she cheered.

Wyatt sent us an image through the alpha link of her crossed eyes as she linked us, and we all chuckled. Ash finally got untangled from the sheet and knelt beside the bed to stare up at our girl. The rest of us crowded around her, and the degree of happiness flowing through the mate bond made me a little giddy.

How does my mark look? she asked.

As gorgeous as you, honey, Cole told her with a grin.

In her excitement, she bounced on Wyatt, and I raised an eyebrow as his eyes rolled back and the front of his boxers rose.

Not so fun, is it, little prick? Ash mocked him while smiling at our girl.

I'm going to go look in the mirror! she chirped.

Before she could slither off Wyatt, though, Mase looped an arm around her waist and hauled her to the other side of the bed.

"Allow me," he said.

Scooping her up, he carried her into her bathroom.

Wyatt, Ash, Cole, and I looked at each other for a second, then a mini brawl broke out as we all raced for *our* bathroom. Ash squeaked in ahead of us, closed the door, and locked it, leaving the three of us to grumble about the inconvenience of using a guest room for yet another cold shower.

4: Topic Five

Mason

"Okay, baby," I said, "where's your clipboard? We're ready to hear number five."

We sat around the table after breakfast, just hanging out until the king and his crew and our betas arrived, and I wanted to clear up any and all things that were bothering her before we left.

Just in case.

Don't be morbid, Garnet chided me. *Even if the whole pack attacks, we'd have no trouble destroying them.*

I'm not worried about us dying, I said with a frown. *But it's a delicate situation. If the king's plan fails, many innocents will be killed. In which case, we might not be in the best mental health to give our girl good answers or advice when we return.*

"Well, we talked a little bit about this topic before." She twisted her fingers in painful-looking knots. "Um, it's a difficult one. Are you sure you want to do this now?"

Please let it not be about mating, Wyatt begged in the alpha link. *I can't take any more cold showers! I've had three since yesterday afternoon.*

I'd be more prepared for it to be about her family, Jay said. *She was talking to Quartz about her brothers yesterday.*

Cole and Wyatt swore, and Ash grimaced.

With a sigh, I reached over, untangled our girl's fingers, and held her hands.

"Yes. Let's clear it up while we have the time," I told her.

"I don't want you to get mad at me," her voice grew quieter and quieter until it was less than a whisper. "I don't want to have bad feelings between us while you're gone."

"Little flower, no one is going to get mad at you."

As I kissed her forehead, I realized my voice had the audacity to turn into a croon.

Goddess, this girl is turning me soft.

Turning? Garnet snickered. *You already are.*

"No matter what you want to talk about," I told her, "we won't be mad at you or leave with bad feelings about it. I promise."

"So, um, I— I don't know how to feel about my brothers." She lowered her pretty eyes to where our clasped hands rested on her thighs. "The more I hear Lilah talk about what Luke did to help her and protect her from their alpha, the more upset I am."

She stopped talking, and Ash opened his mouth, but Jay shook his head at him.

25

She's not done yet. She's just gathering her courage, he explained.

Ash snapped his mouth closed.

"I don't want to—" She hesitated. "I don't want to *hate* James and Aiden, but I'm— I'm *mad* at them. I'm *so mad.*"

Shortly after meeting her, my brothers and I had made some quick decisions. This was one of them, so I knew exactly what to say.

"Posy, if you want to forgive them and build a relationship with them, we'll support you one-hundred percent. If you want to forgive them, but have nothing to do with them, same. If you want to be mad at them or hate them for the rest of your life, same. We will back you on whatever you want to do."

We'd also decided that, if the Briggs brothers so much as *looked* wrong at our girl, they were dead. She didn't need to know that part, though.

She didn't like that answer. Shaking her head, she raised her eyes to mine and frowned at me. Looking around the table, she paused for a few seconds on each of our faces.

"No. I want to know what you think. And I want the truth."

"Princess, this is your decision, not ours," Ash said. "Our opinions might sway you in a direction you otherwise wouldn't go."

"I still want to know. How do you feel about James and Aiden?"

Her hands squeezed mine tightly, and little tremors shook her shoulders.

"We *hate* them, okay?" Predictably, Cole broke first and spat out his words like bullets. "We *detest* them! You don't know how much control it took to stand there and let them hug you goodbye when, as both men and wolves, we wanted to rip them to shreds!"

Posy's eyes widened and her face paled, and I glared at Cole.

"He's not mad at you," I assured her. Lifting our clasped hands, I kissed the back of her knuckles. "Only your brothers. Never you."

"You probably didn't notice," Ash said, "but either Mase or Cole had their hand on Jay's shoulder the whole time, slamming him with alpha power. That's how bad Quartz wanted out to kill them."

"We both wanted the same thing," Jay admitted. "He knew it would have hurt you, though, and that helped some."

"Like Cole said before, the fact that your brothers *waited* and did *nothing*, not even helped you run away, is unacceptable." Wyatt shook his head. "Their decision was infuriating and makes no sense to us."

She turned her big blue eyes back to me.

"And you, Mason?"

"If any of us found out Dad was hurting Peri, we'd kill him," I said quietly. "Even when he was the alpha, we would have done everything and anything to save her, even if it meant our lives."

"But I think they were abused, too," she said in a sad little voice.

I didn't give a rat's rectum about James and Aiden Briggs, but seeing her bottom lip quiver broke my heart.

My brothers weren't in any better shape. Ash was whimpering, and the others were blasting their thoughts in the alpha link.

I can't believe she's so worried about those pricks, Cole muttered. *They don't deserve her forgiveness, let alone her love.*

Even if they themselves were abused, if it were me in her shoes, I would hate them, Wyatt said, *and I definitely wouldn't have been able to let them touch me, never mind hug me!*

If they were abused and manipulated their whole lives, they were not capable of making good decisions. Jay was the only one of us with some objectivity. *We only heard a small part of the story. Maybe they did try to help her escape. Maybe they did try to smuggle her out of there.*

Quit giving them the benefit of the doubt, Cole snapped. *They were wrong, and you know it!*

I'm not saying they were right, Jay replied calmly. *For Posy's sake, however, I'm willing to look at all angles of the issue. If she wants to repair her relationship with her brothers, we all need to be prepared to see them again. And you know darned well she will want us all to get along.*

That's a big if, I pointed out, *but Jay has a point. If she wants them in her life, that means they'll be in ours, too.*

"Mason?" Posy tilted her head to the side, her whole face a question mark.

"Just thinking about what you said, little flower." I gave her a tiny smile to reassure her. "Alpha Briggs made sure it was a bad situation all around."

She tugged her hands out of mine and stood. Even sitting, I was an inch or two taller than she was, which I found adorable. She put her arms around my neck and laid her cheek against mine.

"I don't know what to do," she whispered. "Just *tell me* what to do."

With a deep sigh, I wrapped my arms around her waist and hugged her closer.

"Don't do anything, baby. There is no time limit or expiration date on your feelings, whether it's ten weeks, ten months or ten years from now."

"Let your heart heal a little more before you make any big decisions," Jay added.

When she nodded, Ash came over and pulled her off of me while ignoring my glare.

Sliding his hands under her arms, he lifted her straight up until they were eye to eye, her shoes dangling two feet above the ground. With wide eyes, she clutched his biceps, which bulged like baseballs under her tiny hands. Their size difference was comical - and so cute.

Beauty and the Beast, I chuckled to myself, shaking my head.

"All right, princess, enough sad talk! Time for some fun." He gave her a quick kiss on the lips. "Let's do your hair!"

5: Beta Skirmishes

Posy

Ash spent about twenty minutes messing with my hair, and I ended up with two fat braids that led into a low bun at the base of my neck. I thought it looked very nice and told him so.

"Well, I *had* to get my hair fix in before I go, since I don't know how long it'll be before we're back." Smiling, he laid a big palm on my cheek as his dark eyes stared down at me. "I love you, Posy."

"I love you, Ash." I squeezed him in a tight hug. "I'll miss you."

"Me, too, princess. I'll think about you every second we're apart."

"Except when you need to concentrate." I pulled back a bit and shook a finger at him. "Don't get distracted, or something awful could happen."

He grabbed my hand and brought it up to his mouth and bit my finger!

"Ash!" My eyes widened with shock, which grew into something else as he wrapped his lips around my finger and began to suck it.

"Posy?" Wyatt called as he walked from the living room into the kitchen. "Are you done yet— Ooh!"

He ran over and swept me off the bar stool and away from Ash. Swirling me around, he gave me a toothy grin.

"So pretty! What a pretty, pretty girl you are!"

I giggled at his silliness and pecked his lips with a quick kiss.

"Is that all I get?" He stopped spinning us to pout at me.

I shook my head, my cheeks turning pink, and linked my fingers at the back of his neck to pull his face closer. The next thing I knew, his mouth was devouring mine.

I love you. I love you. I love you, he chanted through our mate link as his tongue slipped between my lips.

I love you, too, my fifth star.

Cole's voice and scent caught my attention. He was talking a mile a minute to the betas and sounded like he was right outside the kitchen. I wiggled in Wyatt's hold, wanting down because I was too shy to have the betas see me kissing one of my mates. At least, *that* kind of kissing.

Aw, Posy, Wyatt whined, but ended the kiss and put me back on my feet.

"The plants on her balcony need to be watered first thing in the morning every morning. Google says you have to water them

29

before it gets too hot," Cole said as he and four of the betas walked into the kitchen.

"I thought we were guarding, not gardening," Matthew muttered.

"I can do that, alpha," Tyler piped up. "No worries!"

"Always such a fawning goody two-shoes," Matthew sneered, then pitched his voice to mimic Tyler. " 'Yes, alpha, right away.' 'Anything for you, luna.' 'Your servant, your majesty.' Don't you *ever* get sick of kissing everyone's a—"

"Matthew!"

Instantly, all our heads turned to the doorway, where Mason stood with an impassive face and a cold glare.

"Home office. Now!"

"Yes, alpha."

My mates had a separate building where they each had an office, and also one they all shared here at our house. To get to it, Matthew would have to go past Mason. Tilting my head, I watched as Mason made the beta wait for ten seconds - which is a really long time when you're nervous or scared - before he turned sideways and allowed Matthew to walk by him.

I'll be back in a few, baby, Mason linked me, then followed Matthew down the hall.

Okay. When you come back, I'll give you kisses, I promised him.

In that case, I'll punish him quick!

I giggled, and turned to say good morning to the betas only to see Crew pull out his wallet and hand Emerson a twenty, which Emerson took with a smirk.

"Well, dang it," Crew grumbled.

"Did you bet on whether he would insult Tyler?" I asked, aghast.

"Oh, no, little luna bunny. That would be a dumb bet." Even Tyler snorted at Emerson's fake innocent look. "We bet on *how soon* he'd insult Tyler."

Ash threw back his head and laughed, and Wyatt snickered into his hand.

"I thought for sure he'd last until you left, alphas." Crew shook his head. "I should have known better."

"Well, I don't like any kind of bullying," I growled, "and I definitely don't like you guys bullying each other!"

"Hey, it's not us!" Emerson raised his hands, and Crew shook his head with wide eyes, his long bangs flying. "Matthew's the one who—"

"I don't see either of you doing anything to discourage it." I folded my arms over my chest and raised an eyebrow. "In fact, betting on it *encourages* it."

"Matthew doesn't know about their betting, luna." Tyler came over and patted my shoulder. "The other betas started doing it to cheer me up. It's a running joke. They've traded that one twenty-dollar bill between the three of them like five times now."

I looked up at him, saw the truth in his eyes, and nodded.

"All right, but if he bullies you again, he's going to answer to *me*."

"Oh, the horror." Emerson rolled his eyes. "What are you going to do, little luna bunny? *Hop* at him?"

Frowning, I motioned for him to lean down. When he did, I cupped my hand around his ear.

"Wyatt said he'd teach me self-defense, but I have other weapons in my arsenal to use until then." I whispered. "Don't test me, Em, or you'll find out how dangerous I am."

Straightening up, he burst out laughing.

"Little luna bunny, you live a life of delusion."

Okay, I said to myself with a shrug. *He asked for it.*

I ran over to where three of my mates lounged around the breakfast bar. Throwing myself in Cole's arms, I buried my face in his chest and sniffed. In an instant, Cole wrapped his arms around my head and shoulders, and Ash and Wyatt closed in on either side.

"What is it, honey? What's wrong?"

Pretend to be really mad at Emerson, okay? I said through our mate link.

Why? What's going on? Wyatt wanted to know.

I'm teaching him something. He didn't do anything, so don't really get mad, though.

Cupcake, are you playing a prank on him?

Maybe. Will you do it? Please, please, please?

What do we get if we play along? Cole asked with a little smirk.

Kisses if you do, and no kisses if you don't.

We'll do it, they chorused.

"Em is being mean," I said out loud and sniffed again. "He's making fun of me."

"*Emerson*," Wyatt and Cole said through their teeth, and a low growl rumbled from Ash's chest.

Oh, that's perfect, I praised them. *Thank you!*

Looking up through my eyelashes, I saw three pairs of wolf-lit eyes glaring at Emerson. With a tiny smirk, I looked over my shoulder

31

at the pure shock in his dark eyes. After a few seconds, he pulled himself together and slowly shook his head.

"You are one evil bunny, luna."

"Don't call our girl evil." Jayden breezed into the room. "She's smart enough to trick you *and* play my brothers. That's genius, not evil."

Sticking my tongue out at Emerson, I totally hopped like a bunny over to Jayden and jumped into his arms.

#

Mason

I couldn't count how many times I sat behind a desk and simply stared at my victim in utter silence.

A simple technique, but oh so effective.

I let Matthew stew for three whole minutes before I unclasped my hands and drummed my fingers on the desktop twice.

"Why are we having the same conversation for a second time?" I asked in a calm, quiet voice.

"Alpha—"

"I apologize." I raised one hand, and Matthew flinched. "By using the word 'conversation' and phrasing it as a question, I led you to believe I wanted you to speak. My bad. Allow me to correct myself. I've talked to you about this same issue before. Just days ago, in fact."

Matthew tilted his head to bare his neck, and it was only then I realized Garnet had underscored my voice.

Down, I commanded.

He disregarded your warning.

I am aware.

Since a hard warning didn't work, which was my father's approach, I'd try a soft talk, which was Dad's approach.

"Look, Matthew, I know Ev's death messed you up. I get it. I do. But Tyler had nothing to do with it. He was not involved in any way. Why do you keep taking your grief and anger out on him?"

Matthew rolled his shoulders, but didn't reply.

"He took the vacant beta position," I said. "He didn't take Ev's place. Stop making him pay for crimes he didn't commit. He's a good kid. If you take time to get to know him, you might find you actually like him."

That's the whole problem, Garnet pointed out. *Matthew doesn't want to open himself up for any more pain, and Tyler is too easy to like.*

I'm aware, I repeated.

"Your luna is starting to look at him as a little brother." I leaned back and folded my arms over my chest. "Every cruel word you say to him, each time you mock him, it hurts her, and I will not tolerate that any more than I'll tolerate your defiance and disrespect. Do you understand?"

"I understand." He stared at his shoes.

"Twenty extra laps each morning for the next week."

He blanched and let out a nearly silent whine, and I held back a satisfied grin. If there was one thing Matthew Rose hated, it was extra laps.

"That's for upsetting Posy twice since you've met her," I said. "For tormenting Tyler after my warning, you're my sparring partner for two weeks, to begin after we return from Tall Pines."

His jaw dropped and his light blue eyes widened in dismay. I raised an eyebrow at him, and he quickly snapped his mouth closed.

"Yes, alpha."

"Matthew, if you need to talk to someone about Ev—"

"I'm good, alpha."

Narrowing my eyes at him, I studied his face. Matthew was a good person, and a great beta. Losing his best friend had hurt him down to his soul.

"Alpha?" Matthew's voice brought me out of my thoughts. "Crew says the king and his party are here."

"Very well. Dismissed."

"Thank you, alpha."

After he left, I sat in my chair for a few minutes and thought about Everett Breckenridge's unfortunate demise.

I can only imagine what Matthew would do if he knew the whole truth, Garnet muttered.

Only we and our brothers know, I reminded him, *and that's the way we want to keep it.*

Posy wants to know. She will ask again when she remembers.

Cursing under my breath, I balled up one hand in a fist. That was *not* a conversation I wanted to have with her, but I wasn't surprised. Not after Quartz and Jay's reaction at dinner the other night when Ash mentioned it.

Maybe she'll get so distracted, she'll forget it. Garnet sounded more wistful than hopeful.

Pfft. I know our mate. She'll never forget, and she'll worm the truth out of us.

Better us than Jayden and Q.

Truer words were never spoken, I told him, then smiled. *Now let's go get the kisses we were promised.*

Yes! Garnet's tail wagged and his tongue lolled out. *Hurry, Mason! Kisses await us!*

Chuckling, I got to my feet and went looking for our girl.

6: Sibling Rivalry

Ash

Of course, the queen noticed Posy's mate mark right away, and she and Gisela made a big deal over it. Our girl's face turned redder and redder as they fussed, but she radiated happiness through our bond, so we didn't intervene.

Once Tristan and Ariel arrived, the king wanted Ariel to talk with him, Gisela, and Ranger, so he took them out the back door to the patio. Luke and Tristan trailed along with their mates.

Wyatt went to the parking lot, ostensibly to make sure all our gear was loaded in my SUV, but we knew that excuse was a blatant dodge of dish duty. Mase followed him with our betas, wanting to go over some last minute instructions where Posy wouldn't hear - and probably to chew Wyatt out. As for Cole, he'd gone to pick Peri up since Posy wanted her to spend the day.

That left me and Jay alone with our girl.

Careful not to mess up her hair, I took her face in my hands and kissed her slowly and thoroughly until we were both gasping for air. Leaning back, I studied her pretty blush and sparkling eyes and seared the image in my brain. I wanted to stitch it into all the memories we'd been creating with her, then throw them around me like a comforting blanket when I was missing her later.

Some of that feeling must have slipped into our mate bond because she reached up and laid both hands, one on top of the other, over my heart.

"I love you, Ash," she said. "I am right here and I always will be."

I bent down and kissed her forehead.

"Hey, since we're alone right now and it's calm and everything, Quartz would like to come out for a second."

We both looked over at Jay, who was scratching the back of his neck.

"He would like to hug you goodbye, Posy, if that's okay with you."

"Of course!" Her face brightened with a sunshine smile.

Is Quartz her favorite? I linked Jay with a grin. *I think she loves him the most out of all of us.*

What's not to love? Quartz himself snorted, and I realized Jay had already given him the reins. *But our mate does not play favorites. She loves us all, and she loves us all unconditionally.*

I nodded and moved away slowly enough to show him I was no threat. Going to the other side of the kitchen island, I dried the last few glasses as I thought about what he'd said. *Did* she love us unconditionally? She hadn't seen any of us at our worst yet, or even our negative sides.

Well, maybe glimpses, I admitted. *Still, it can't be unconditional if she doesn't know every part of us, can it?*

Ashy, you think too much. Sid rolled his eyes, which made me giggle.

I was putting the glasses I'd dried into the cupboard when Wyatt jogged back into the kitchen.

"All right," he said. "We are set to go. I just need one last kiss from our girl."

I didn't realize what he was doing until he was right behind Quartz, who held Posy like she was his lifeline.

"Wyatt, stop!" I yelled in a panic. "That's not—"

Too late.

I watched in horror as his hand landed on what he thought was Jay's shoulder and yanked him away from our mate.

Then all hell broke loose.

#

Mason

When Ash screamed, *Code Q!*, through the alpha link, I didn't waste any time asking questions and took off for the house at a dead run.

"Quartz is loose and pissed!" I yelled for the betas, then linked the whole pack to stay away from the alpha house until further notice.

Posy is in the kitchen with him! Garnet howled.

"Betas," I hollered, "keep Posy away from him, no matter what she says!"

"Tyler," Matthew shouted, "take the luna to her special room and keep her there until you hear otherwise."

"On it."

We could hear Posy's screams, Ash's shouts, and Quartz's growls getting louder, and we all put on an extra burst of speed, not that we weren't hurrying before. Leaping up the front porch steps, I flung open the door and raced inside, leaving the betas to follow.

I made it to the kitchen and found Quartz rocketing toward Wyatt where he lay in a still and silent heap on the floor. Red trailed down the wall behind him in a smear that led to the back of his head.

Ash, who was half-shifted, crouched in front of Wyatt, ready to take on Quartz. I would have given them even odds if Sid were enraged, but he wasn't and despite Ash's great strength and size, he alone wouldn't be a match for the empty-eyed deathbringer stalking toward Wyatt.

"DOWN. NOW." I pulled up every ounce of moon magic I had, drew all the alpha power I could from Five Fangs *and* my own Earthshine pack, and threw it all at Quartz.

It hit him like an invisible fist, knocked him down, and pushed him five feet across the room before he fetched up against the oven. I thought that might be enough to bring him back to his senses, but he only stood with a snarl and started toward Wyatt again.

Hustling in front of Ash, I roared at him to get Wyatt out of here, then linked the betas to find Posy. She was still somewhere nearby, if her ear-piercing screams were anything to go by, and I didn't want her to see what was about to happen.

Then the back door opened and a black missile slammed into Quartz's side, saving us all.

#

Ranger Hemming

"Code Q!" Beta Tristan suddenly barked. "In the kitchen!'"

Julian immediately tugged off his shirt and shucked off his shoes and let Onyx take over.

"What's happening?" Lilah asked with wide, frightened eyes.

Her mate was too busy shifting to tell her, so I did.

"Nothing good. You stay with me. Julian will handle this."

Opening the back door for my brother, I waited until Onyx barreled inside, then pulled the door closed again.

"What do you want us to do, Ranger?" Gisela asked.

I went over to Lilah and grabbed her hand and pulled her away from the door.

"Protect the queen. Alpha Jayden's wolf, Quartz, has gone off the rails for some reason," I explained quickly. "Once that happens, no wolf other than Nyx can take him on. Just keep everyone vulnerable out of their path of destruction."

Quartz angry, Coal fretted and paced back and forth in my mind. *Quartz angry for real!*

I know. Nyx will settle him down, though.

The sounds of wolves fighting grew louder and more intense, although Posy's screams faded to nothing, and I hoped someone had had the good sense to take her to another room and not left her to faint on the bloody floor.

"What's happening?" Lilah demanded.

"Julian probably—"

I was interrupted by the back door exploding into toothpicks.

Oops. Guess I should have left it open.

Two balls of fur, one pure white and the other midnight black, rolled around in a tangled mass as they ripped and tore at each other.

36

I put Lilah behind my back and shuffled her against the side of the house, and Gisela and Luke made a wall in front of us.

"Is that black horse of a wolf *Nyx?*" Lilah gasped. "But the white wolf is Quartz! Why are they fighting? I thought they were friends! Ranger, what's—"

"Yes, it's Nyx, and it may not look like it, but he's getting Q away from here so he can't hurt anyone. Just watch."

It might look like chaotic violence to others, but I could clearly see how Nyx was forcing Quartz closer to the forest. The two wolves fought and rolled until Nyx had them out of sight in the trees, leaving only fading yips, whines, and growls behind.

I turned to check on Lilah only for her to grab my shirt in her fists and pull me down so we were eye to eye.

"What is my mate *doing?*"

My mouth opened, but no words came out. I was too shocked by my sweet sister-in-law's sudden aggression.

"*Speak!*" she demanded.

"Woof!"

Gisela snickered, but Luke clapped a hand on my shoulder.

"Not wise, man. Trust me. Antagonizing her when she's already furious leads to nothing but regret."

"I didn't mean to," I said, holding up both hands. "It just came out."

"Ranger, explain why my mate is hurting his friend!" Lilah's eyes flashed with fire.

"He's *not* hurting him," I sighed. "He's *helping* him."

#

Beta Tyler James

As we all rushed into the house, Matthew deliberately kept in front of me, which was frustrating. How was I supposed to do my job from behind his back?

Is he trying to make me look bad in an emergency?

Him scared, River said in his soft baby voice. *Him scared Quartz hurt Ty.*

I rolled my eyes privately. I was the *last* person Matthew Rose would be worried about getting hurt.

Okay, Riv. Now you hush so I can focus. We need to find the luna and take her to safety.

Me help find luna! Me good boy!

Yep. You sure are.

As panicked and upset as I might be, I still had to use a gentle tone and kind words. If I got angry or harsh with him, or let him see my

37

panic, he would have a bad reaction, and I couldn't afford that right now.

We all burst into the kitchen, and Matthew, Emerson and Crew fanned out to loosely surround the alphas. I followed the screams into the dining room and found the luna hiding under the table. She had her knees drawn up to her chest and her arms over her head as she rocked back and forth and screamed.

Having a wolf like mine was not something I'd wish on my worst enemy, but it sure had taught me a lot, and I intended to put that knowledge to good use to help my luna.

I crawled under there with her and gave her a heads up on everything before I did it.

"Luna Posy, it's Tyler. I know you're upset and scared, and I'm here to help you. I'm going to put one arm around your back and one under your knees. I know you may not like that, but it's going to happen."

She didn't respond, and I didn't expect her to. I simply moved into position.

"I'm going to slide you out from under the table, then I'm going to pick you up. I won't drop you. You can trust me."

I had no idea if she heard me, but I hoped she did and could find comfort in a calm voice.

Riv usually did.

I hauled her out from under the table, then stood and reached down for her. She didn't fight me, for which I was thankful, and I lifted her up easily. She couldn't weigh even a hundred pounds, and carrying her tiny body was like carrying the kids at the O off to bed when they fell asleep over their dinner.

"I'm going to take you to your special room, luna," I murmured in her ear.

The second I had her up in my arms, her screams stopped, but little whines and whimpers took their place.

Grimacing at my luna's pain, I hustled us out of there and took the stairs two at a time.

#

Quartz

What was that idiot thinking? I grumbled. *He knows better!*

We were washing off the blood and dirt in the mountain stream. The cold water helped me calm down, but not as much as the fight with Nyx had. It had been a long time since I was allowed to cut loose, and I rarely had an opponent on my level.

Granite and Wyatt must not know Quartz had control, Nyx suggested.

I shrugged and swatted a paw in the air, as if I could swat away such rational thought as easily as a fly.

Probably he didn't, but I told him to stop doing that just the other day! He interrupts each of us with her. All. The. Time.

A brat, he agreed. *Granite a pup, Q.*

He's only a year younger. I rolled my eyes.

Years don't matter. He grinned. *Granite will be a pup forever.*

I rammed my shoulder into his leg, and he rammed me back, knocking me over into a shallow pool.

Monstrous freak, I muttered as I got back up and knocked into him.

Snow white princess.

We tussled a bit more before we climbed out of the stream and shook out our fur. Of course, he made sure to hit me with the hundred pounds of water flying out of his massive coat, and I had to shake mine out all over again.

We should get back. I frowned, not looking forward to our return. *The king is probably anxious to leave.*

Jul will wait as long as needed.

Yeah, but I need time to make up with my love before we go.

Nyx tittered at me, and I told him to shut up.

As we turned toward home, my thoughts went to the fallout I would face when we got there. I knew Wyatt was physically fine - Cole and Mason had linked Jayden that much - but he wouldn't link with Jayden, who gave up after half a dozen attempts to talk to him.

Jayden blamed himself. He kept mumbling about how he should have linked everyone that I was ascendant, instead of just telling the only person who was in the room. Honestly, I didn't understand his guilt on this one, but that was how my boy rolled.

It's a good thing the Moon Goddess paired him with me, I said to myself. *Everyone would walk all over him otherwise.*

I wasn't too worried about Jayden and Wyatt. They would make up quickly because neither of them could stand to be on someone's bad side.

Granite, though? I'd hurt his feelings.

Actually, 'hurt' was an understatement.

He wasn't talking to me right now, but Topaz told me that Granite thought I was playing when I'd told him to stop interrupting others' special moments with Posy or Lark. I was big enough to admit that I deserved *some* of the blame for that misunderstanding. I shouldn't have blown a raspberry at him, as it gave him the wrong impression.

Still, I had no idea how to heal the wound I'd inflicted on his soft little heart today.

Even worse than *that* headache was the dread boiling in my gut over how Posy was going to react.

Any ideas on how to approach my mate? I asked my best friend.

Posy soft-hearted, like Nyx's little mate. Posy will cry, and Q will hold and comfort and say sweet words and make promises.

She's going to be disappointed in me, I sighed. *That will hurt worse than any angry words or shouting.*

Well, then Q knows what to do next time, yes? The sudden alpha power in his voice made me drop my head and curl my tail under my belly. *Save anger for enemies, **not** brothers.*

Yes, sire, I muttered.

Why, Q? He nipped my ear to make sure I was listening. *Why is Q the way Q is?*

I don't know, sire. I shook my head with a heavy frown. *I'm working on it.*

Hmm. His voice went back to normal, and I knew we were good again. *Race?*

Stakes? I tilted my head in question.

Q loses, rides with Granite all the way to Tall Pines. Q wins, rides with Nyx.

Bet, I agreed with a fierce grin.

7: Talking it Out

Mason

I found Posy in her balcony garden, cuddled up in Tyler's lap as he rocked her on the wicker chair. Her arms were wrapped around her middle as if she were trying to hold herself together, and his chin rested on the top of her head while he stared into space.

I called his name in the beta link, and his eyes snapped to me. *Has she said anything?* I asked.

No, alpha.

Thanks for staying with her. I know she trusts you a lot.

Anything for my luna.

"Go take a break," I murmured as I lifted our girl into my arms. "The other betas are with Ariel in the living room, but if you need to get yourself together in privacy, you're welcome to use one of the guest rooms."

"Thank you, alpha."

After he left, I carried Posy into her room and laid on the bed with her. Reaching over her head, I snagged Mr. Nibbles and handed him to her, and she buried her face in his belly.

"It's all right. Everyone is okay. You're okay." I pressed my lips to her forehead. "I'm here. I've got you."

Not knowing what else to do, I rubbed my hands up and down her back and kept telling her everything was fine now. After four or five minutes, she lifted her head out of Mr. Nibbles' fur and looked up at me with wide, tragic eyes.

"Wyatt?"

"He hit his head, and it knocked him out for a few minutes." I paused to check in and make sure I was telling her the truth. At Granite's reply, I nodded. "He's all right. Granite healed him, and he's cleaning up in the shower now."

"But there was so much blood! I thought he was— I thought Quartz had—"

"I swear, he's fine, baby. Head wounds bleed a lot because the skin is thin over the skull. The damage always looks much worse than it is."

"I want to see him. I want to see Wyatt."

"Of course. Do you mind giving him a minute to pull on a pair of boxers?"

I tried to lighten the mood and knew I shouldn't have when she only nodded with a serious face.

"I don't want them all hating each other over this," she whispered. "Both Wyatt and Quartz were wrong, and poor Jayden is caught in the middle. What do we do?"

By the moon, I wanted to maim my brothers for putting her through this.

And over what? A temper tantrum on Quartz's side and a dick move on Wyatt's. And to subject Posy - *gentle, sweet* Posy - *to either, let alone both, was inexcusable! I'm going to kick their asses so hard—*

"Mason?"

I shoved my anger down and brushed the knuckles of one hand down the side of her face.

"Well, little flower, when any of the boys fight, Cole and I sit down and have a ... talk with them. Unless Cole was one of the combatants. Then it's just me. Anyway, I guess the question now is, do you want *me* to chew the two of them out, or are *you* going to?"

She stared at me for a few seconds, then something formed in those deep blue eyes that made me think of an angel.

Not those cute, fat, little baby angels, either. Oh, no. The kind of angel who has a big-ass bronze sword and rains holy wrath down on the wicked.

Oh, they are in trouble, Garnet giggled with glee.

They are, indeed, I agreed with a dark smirk. *Good luck, my brothers.*

Wyatt

Someone knocked hard and sharp on the alpha link. That was Mase's usual style, and I sighed.

Time for one of his famous talks, Granite mumbled, his eyes dull with misery.

You'd think I'd have it memorized by now, huh? Maybe he'll change it up on us.

Don't joke, Wy. We screwed up.

Yeah.

I sighed again and opened the alpha link. As usual, Mase didn't mince words.

Posy wants to see you. Are you decent?

Yes.

I'm bringing her to you now.

Fine, I muttered.

Wyatt.

I said fine!

His displeasure smacked into me, and I scowled, but stayed silent.

Granite was right. I'd screwed up.

Like one of my worst screw-ups ever.

It even worse than the time you accidentally shot Ash with an arrow. Or the time you wrecked Dad's brand-new Harley Davidson. Or the time you set Mama's kitchen on fire with—

Okay, I get it, Granite! I've had a lot of big screw-ups. Thank you for the reminder!

This time, though, my screw-up not only pissed off Quartz and terrified Posy, but also put Ash in danger, upset Jay, and gave Mase one more reason to be disappointed in me.

Taking Ls all around today, I thought as I rooted around in my dresser for a pair of shorts. *Deserve them, too.*

The bedroom door opened, and Posy's delicious scent flooded my senses and soothed me.

"I thought you said you were decent," Mase barked.

I had boxers on. What was wrong with that? I ignored him, stepped into my sweat shorts, and yanked them up.

As I tied the drawstrings, I glanced over my shoulder and saw Posy lay her hand on Mase's chest as she looked up at him. He nodded once, then left, closing the door quietly behind him.

I turned forward again and started to look for a t-shirt. Coward that I was, I needed another few minutes to gather my courage before I could face her. Grabbing a wad of fabric, not even caring whose it was or what was on it, I pulled out a shirt and slipped it over my still-damp head.

"Wyatt?"

It was amazing, really, what a small, soft voice could do to a guy.

Head hanging low, hands on my hips, I took a deep breath and closed my eyes.

"Posy, I am so so—"

"Wyatt, I love you."

My eyes flew open. Spinning around, I let my hands fall to my sides and stared at her. Her bottom lip quivered and her eyes were glossy, and my heart felt like it was going through a meat grinder.

"Can I hug you?" she asked.

Without a word, I opened up my arms, and she flew into them and gripped me tightly, as if she was afraid I'd disappear.

Truth be told, I was holding her just as tightly.

I could have lost this. I could have lost this by being stupid and selfish and bratty.

"Don't do that again," she choked into my chest. "*Please* don't. I can't bear to see my mates hurting each other."

"I'm sorry. I didn't mean to set him off," I whispered. Closing my eyes, I kissed the top of her head. "I didn't realize it was Quartz and not—"

"I know that. We all do. But you shouldn't do that to Jayden, either. You shouldn't do that to any of your brothers. I know it must be hard to share a mate, and I'm sorry it's a broken girl like me that you have to share, but—"

"I'm not. I'm not sorry." My arms tightened around her. "We are so blessed to have you. Don't run yourself down like that. And it's not hard to share. I know they'll take care of you and make you happy just like I would. I can trust them with you when you're not with me."

Sucking in a huge lungful of air, I let it out slowly.

"How often do I take you away from them?" I asked, not meeting her eyes. "Granite says a lot, and I'm wondering if he's right. He thought it was funny the first time we did it, and that influenced me to think it was, too. So we kept doing it. When Quartz said something about it yesterday, Granite brushed it off, so I did, too, but now I want to know the truth."

"You do it a lot, Wyatt." She pulled her face out of my chest and stared up at me, her big blue eyes wide and earnest. "Jayden never really says anything, does he? But Ash, Cole, and Mason growl at you. Don't you notice?"

I shrugged. Granite and I thought them growling at us was funny, too.

"Okay." She nodded. "Watch, please."

Then she sent me her memories of all the times I'd pulled her away from my brothers when they were loving on her. As more and more images flashed between us, my mouth fell open.

"*Really?*" I asked, feeling like a fool. "That often?"

"I love that you want to hold me and kiss me all the time, Wyatt. Can you please remember that your brothers want to do the same?"

I nodded, ashamed of myself.

"Will you do something for me?"

"Anything. I'll do anything you ask me to do," I vowed.

"You and Quartz can be mad at each other for as long as you need or want to, but don't be mad at Jayden. This had nothing to do with him. It wasn't his fault. He's caught in the middle and you *know* what he's like. He'll blame himself and rant at Quartz and worry to death over it."

"I'm not mad at him. I promise." I gave her a little smile. "I'll tell him that and apologize, too. I'm not really mad at Quartz, either. If the shoe had been on the other foot, I probably would have been just as angry."

Although I wouldn't have shifted, and Granite wouldn't have tried to rip Jay's throat out, I grumbled to myself.

Why would I try to do that to my brother? Granite tilted his head in confusion.

Exactly.

I took a step away from her and clamped my hands on her small shoulders, rubbing my thumbs over her delicate collar bones simply because I couldn't help myself. Leaning down, I met and held her eyes.

"I'm going to talk to *all* my brothers. I want to apologize and let them know I'll work hard to get better about it."

A brilliant smile lit up her face like sunshine, and the agonizing ache in my chest finally began to subside.

"I want you to know something, Wyatt."

"Yeah? What's that?" I raised an eyebrow.

"I am not disappointed in you. In fact, I'm proud of you for being willing to admit your mistakes and apologize for them. For being willing to change so this can work better between all of us."

Something fluttered in my stomach and brought a knot up into my throat. Knowing she was proud of me was sexier than that flash of her beautiful titties the other night.

Well, now, Granite said slowly, *I not go that far, Wy. Her boobies by far the sexiest thing ever—*"

Hush, wolf.

"You're proud of me?" I choked. "You're really *proud* of me?"

"It takes a big person to do any of that, so, yes, I'm proud of you." She leaned in and kissed my lips. "Very proud of you, my fifth star."

Lucky. That's what I was. So very lucky.

Some people spend their whole lives searching for what I had in front of me. A girl who believed in me. Who loved me even when I was at my worst. Who wasn't perfect, but was perfect for my own imperfect self. For us. My brothers and me. My family.

So yeah, I was probably the luckiest bastard in the whole world right now.

And she not even yell at us like Masey would have! Granite grinned.

Hush, wolf.

#

Jayden

Someone poked the mate link, and I knew it wasn't any of my brothers. They would have used the alpha link, especially after what happened.

45

I wasn't ready to talk to her, but there was no way I could ignore her. I opened the link and found her waiting patiently.

Jayden? Are you okay?

I am. Are you?

I want to talk to you in person, not through the link. Could you please come to our bedroom?

I closed my eyes. Acid boiled in my gut and bubbled up in my throat, and I swallowed hard to keep from vomiting.

I'm on my way.

Trudging up the stairs, I felt like I was moving through molasses. All my senses were dull and the world faded to white noise.

Is this how condemned prisoners feel walking toward the death chamber?

The bedroom door was open, and I glanced inside to see her sitting on the side of the bed, her hands clasped in her lap and her ankles crossed. She stared ahead, obviously lost in thought.

What words could I give her that would fix this disaster? I didn't know, but I had to think of some quickly. She was waiting.

Breathe, I reminded myself. *Breathe through the pain. It'll end or it will get worse. Either way, just breathe through it.*

Her attention went right to me when I stepped into the room. She wiggled like she was going to stand up, and I hurried over to her and dropped to my knees at her feet. My hands palm up on my thighs, I raised my face in humble supplication to my love.

"Posy—"

She gently laid her fingers against my lips and shook her head.

"I'm not mad. I'm not disappointed. I'm not scared of you. I was, however, terrified that you or Wyatt would get hurt beyond healing. If that happened, my heart would never recover."

I closed my eyes and kissed the fingers she still held over my mouth.

"Look at me, my beautiful dragon."

Dragon?

My eyelids flew up, surprised by both her tone and the endearment. I hadn't heard her use any with me or my brothers before.

And why am I a dragon, *of all things?*

"You are not to feel guilty about what happened." Her blue gaze was as stern as her tone. "You are not Quartz. You are *Jayden.* Jayden Carson, who plays guitar - acoustic, not electric - and sings us to sleep at night and reads a book a week. You are kind and sweet and a far better man than you give yourself credit for."

"Posy, I don't—"

"And I love you."

Whatever had been clawing its way up my throat for the past hour finally broke free, and I dropped my face into my hands and sobbed.

Her small fingers threaded into my hair and pulled my head to her lap. Craving her comfort, I crawled even closer, and she opened her knees so I could kneel between her legs and rest my head against her stomach. My arms went around her waist and I held on for dear life, hating the gut-wrenching noises coming out of me almost as much as I hated myself.

"It wasn't your fault," she whispered. "You didn't do anything wrong. I love you. I love you so, so much, my dragon-eyed mate."

She said those things over and over while massaging my head, and I slowly regained my composure and stopped crying like a pup. Pulling up the front of my t-shirt, I wiped my face on it. Then, with red cheeks and redder eyes, I let her help me up onto the bed. We lay wrapped together and facing each other for several minutes before she asked me a pair of questions that I didn't expect.

"Are you mad at Wyatt? Do you hate him?"

"Of course not," I said with a little frown.

"Could you tell him that, please? And do not apologize. I *forbid* you to apologize! You did nothing that you need to apologize for. But please let him know that you don't hate him and aren't angry at him."

"I can do that, sweetness." I nodded and gave her a shaky smile.

"Wyatt didn't realize how often he was interrupting. I showed him memories of all the times he did, and he was shocked." She laid one soft little hand on my cheek. "He wants to correct that, so we'll need to help him. Okay?"

"Wyatt was always the baby, and I guess I spoiled him a bit." I rolled my shoulders. "It's a little my fault that he's a brat sometimes."

"No, it's not. You spoiled Ash, too, and he's not a brat. Now." She took a deep breath, which reminded me to start breathing again, too. "May I please speak with Quartz? In his wolf form, if you're okay with that."

With a sigh, I slipped off of the bed and began stripping down, and Posy fled into her bathroom with a squeak. Any other time, I would have laughed at that, but I was a long way away from laughing about anything.

And, despite her kind words and sweet kisses, I knew I probably would be for a while.

8: Not an Auspicious Start

Quartz

As soon as I was back in my own fur, I lowered my head and tucked my tail under me.

"Don't even do that," Posy said as she came out of her bathroom. "You are not sorry. You meant everything you did."

True, I admitted.

I turned to face her standing tall and proud, which put us nearly eye-to-eye.

"Were you going to kill Wyatt?"

No.

"He was unconscious on the ground, and you were still going for him."

I wouldn't have killed him. I overreacted, but I wouldn't have killed him.

"What about Ash? What about Mason?"

I wouldn't have hurt them.

"Even though they stood between you and your prey?"

He wasn't prey. I—

Dropping my eyes to the floor, I felt a wire of shame burn through my belly. I'd gone too far. It was as simple as that.

I regret causing a ruckus. I regret hurting Wyatt's head and Granite's feelings. I regret upsetting both Jayden and you, especially since we're leaving today.

"I understand why you did what you did. What I want *you* to understand is that you can't literally go for the throat to settle disagreements. That can't happen. I mean it, Quartz. If any of you died, I would be crippled with grief for the rest of my days. On top of that, I'd be even more devastated to know that one of my mates was responsible. Can you understand that?"

Yes. I can.

"I love you. Even when you mess up, even when you're violent, even when I can't agree with what you're doing or have done, I love you. That does *not* mean you get a free pass to do whatever you want. Look at me, Quartz."

Raising my head, I met her gaze and held it. What I saw in her eyes made mine narrow in wariness.

"As painful as it would be, I would rather see you *dead* than watch you turn into one of those males who needs to brutally control everything and everyone. Who destroys anything sweet and kind and gentle." Her little hands curled up into fists at her sides. "Who uses his mate's devotion to break her again and again until she's absolutely ruined."

My heart shattered. Neither hitting nor yelling nor the silent treatment nor crying would have hurt as much - or been as effective.

Was that the path I was on? If that witch downstairs looked in her crystal ball, was that what she would see in my future?

If it is, I'm taking a new path, starting here and now, I promised myself. *I'll smash that future.*

My throat as narrow as a straw, I shuffled closer and humbly pressed my nose to one of her fists, and she opened her hand so I could nuzzle into her palm.

*I'll **never** become that kind of wolf, Posy. I swear it.*

"Good." Wrapping her arms around my neck, she buried her face in my ruff. "Now, my beloved wolf, I expect you to find time on your trip to apologize to Jayden and your brothers. Wyatt and Granite will also be saying sorry. Jayden, however, is forbidden to. If you catch him even *thinking* of apologizing, you remind him I said no."

I wasn't good at apologies, but I didn't want to disappoint her. No, I wanted her to be proud of me.

As proud as I was of *her.*

My dear little mate whose soft heart hid a core of solid steel.

\#

Ash

"Ash?"

I turned my head to see Jay standing in the doorway.

"She wants you."

"Me?" I raised an eyebrow.

"Yes, you."

I left the supervision of repairing our back door in Mase's hands and walked over to Jay. Clamping one hand on his rigid shoulder, I squeezed it gently and stood there until his eyes met mine.

Stop, I linked him. *You're on the 'everything is my fault' train again. Time to get off.*

He pinched his lips together until they turned white, then kind of deflated with a sigh. He gave me a little nod, which I returned before I released him and jogged up the stairs.

Following my nose, I found her in our bedroom. She had her back to me as she stared out of one of the wide windows.

"Princess?" I murmured as I stood just inside the door.

"Can you please close the door?"

"Sure."

I did, then took a couple of long strides until my chest was inches from her ruler-straight back.

"Are Cole and Peri here yet?" she asked.

"No. Peri's taking forever. They'll be another twenty or thirty minutes."

She turned then and studied my face for several long moments. I wasn't sure what she wanted to see, but I wasn't hiding anything from her. I had never hid anything from anybody, and I probably never would.

I liked being underestimated as the simple, easygoing alpha.

"Are you okay?" she whispered at last.

"Yeah. Not the first time I've stood between Wyatt and someone who wanted to kill him," I smirked, "or between Quartz and someone he wanted to kill."

"Are you sure?"

My smirk curled into a genuine smile and leaned down to place a kiss on her forehead.

"I'm sure, cupcake."

"Then," her voice quavered, and my smile dropped, "is it okay if *I'm* not okay for a few minutes?"

"Baby, you can be as not okay as you want for as long as you need."

"Mason is too mad, Wyatt and Jayden are too upset, and Cole's not here, so would *you* mind ... holding me ... while I ... cry for ... a bit?"

Oh, Goddess.

I had her up in my arms and cuddled on the bed before the first tear finished its path down her cheek. Tucking her head under my chin, I wrapped my arms around her neck and shoulders.

"Don't tell the others," she sobbed into my chest. "Just for a minute. I need to let it out just for a minute. Don't tell them. Don't tell them."

"Shh, princess. Cry all you want. I'm here." I pressed kiss after kiss to the top of her head.

"I'm ... so ... sorry."

"*Don't*, Posy. I mean it." I tightened my arms around her a bit, careful not to hurt her, but wanting her to know I was serious. "You have nothing to be sorry for. Let the pain out, sweet girl. Let it all out."

"I wish ... I was ... stronger—"

"You are one of the strongest people I've ever met. You know why?"

She sniffed and hiccuped into my shirt.

"Because ... I get up ... and I ... keep going?"

"That's right. You cry. You get up. You keep going. That's what makes you one badass bitch, baby."

That earned me a watery giggle which, after this morning, was far more than I hoped for.

Will she ever stop surprising me? I wondered with a grin.

Nope! Sid grinned, too. *We'll be oldie-old, and our mate will still be surprising us.*

I hope so, buddy, I said as I marveled over 'oldie-old' in my mind.

She will, he insisted in his earnest way. *Ashy?*

Yeah?

Do you think we could get some more kissies?

You know what, buddy? I think I can make that happen.

He shivered in delight, and I giggled, which caught Posy's attention.

"What is it, waffle?" she asked as she wiped her face on my shirt.

"Sid was asking— Wait." My brain finished processing her words. "*Waffle?!*"

"You smell like maple syrup." She moved so she could look into my eyes.

"Well, why waffle? Why not pancake? Or French toast?"

"I like waffles better than pancakes and French toast is too long to say." She shrugged. "Anyway, why did you laugh like that?"

"Sid wants kisses."

Her eyes widened and red crept across her cheek, but she reached up and framed my face in her palms.

"Well, I can't deny Sid his kisses, now can I?"

"No, ma'am, you cannot," I purred.

KISSIES! Sid shouted.

Then her lips touched mine and the world turned into pink fuzz and chocolate chip cookies.

#

Cole

We rode in silence, not even the radio on to help.

It's going to be a long drive, I thought.

Of course it is, said my very literal wolf. *Tall Pines is several hundred miles away.*

I closed my eyes as I counted to ten.

Jay ended up riding in the king's SUV, and Mase and I figured their wolves had worked out something between them.

Which is not a bad thing, I admitted as I looked over at Wyatt.

He was curled up in his seat and drawing, all of his focus on what he was doing.

51

"Wyatt, when did you start a new sketchbook?" I asked in a quiet voice.

"Couple days ago."

"Does your head still hurt?" Papa Bear butted in. "You shouldn't draw if your head—"

"No, Mase. 'S fine."

"Can I see what you're drawing?" I held out one hand.

With a shrug, he gave me his sketchbook, and I looked at his work with a smile.

What's he drawing? Ash and Mase linked me at almost the same time.

Lark, I said and projected the image. *When she was chasing butterflies in the field.*

"I think we all want a copy of this one when you're finished," I told Wyatt as I handed him back his sketchbook.

He took it without a word and turned his face to the window.

I sighed.

We knew from the first that today was going to be difficult. All of us - man and wolf - were sad to leave Posy, but Topaz, Sid, and Granite were taking it exceptionally hard. Sid shut down completely, and Topaz and Granite were whining and crying like pups who'd been left at the daycare for the first time. Garnet and Quartz were their usual silent selves, although not even they could keep their unhappiness from leaking into the bond between us.

Then, the 'incident' happened and added an extra layer of misery to an already bad day.

I'm glad I missed it all, although I'm sorry Mase and Ash had to deal with it on their own.

Now, Wyatt was both embarrassed and ashamed. Embarrassed that Posy had seen Quartz hand him his ass, and ashamed that he'd intentionally-unintentionally provoked Quartz when he knew how hard Jayden worked to control his wolf.

Or at least, that's what I thought he was feeling. He didn't want to talk to us, a sure sign he was more upset than angry. When he got angry, his fists were flying. When he got quiet, his heart was bleeding.

Such an auspicious start to a long journey, I grumbled sourly.

What is aw- aps- awpas-

Stop before you hurt yourself, Paz. I smiled a little. *It means lucky. Bright. Good. Fortunate.*

But it isn't, boss. Topaz tilted his head to the side, his almond-shaped eyes wide and unblinking. *Granite is upset and Quartz is grumpy and Wyatt and Jay are sad and-*

I know, Paz. It was a bad joke.

No way was I going to tell him I was being sarcastic. We'd had that conversation a couple of years ago and the most I could get him to understand was that sarcasm meant a lie to insult someone. He'd scolded me and told me, "Don't sarcasm again because that's just mean."

Very bad, he agreed now. *At least Posy got everyone calmed down enough to leave with no arguing. That was aw-pish-ist.*

He was right about that. We'd all ignored her red eyes after Ash warned us to, then she'd given us hugs and kisses and told each one of us the same thing: "I love you. Take care of yourself and your brothers."

Auspicious. I slowed it down so Topaz could hear the syllables. *And yes. Our mate is amazing.*

Of course she is. He nodded, then frowned. *You know what, boss? I don't like that A word. I will say good or lucky. You can still say it, though.*

Thanks for your permission, Paz. I rolled my eyes, but he wagged his tail, taking it as praise.

Welcome, boss!

Yep. It was going to be one long-ass drive.

9: Treasure in the Dungeon

Cole

About ten miles from Tall Pines' border, we found a dumpy motel that would work perfectly for what we wanted.

Since it was 9 p.m. and the place was dead, we were easily able to rent all of the vacant rooms.

Thank the Goddess for the red-eyed human running the desk. He took one look at our dangerous expressions and Mase's heavy tattoos and snapped his mouth shut. He swiped my card, handed over a bunch of keys, and turned the desk sign to closed.

Taking the biggest and cleanest room, we dropped our gear, and King Julian gave Gisela and Ranger the amulets that Ariel had prepared. After they put them on, they would have eight hours of nose-silence to snoop around.

"Unless you're a dragon, there is no such thing as true invisibility," Ariel had told us before we left.

That was more than I'd known about either dragons or invisibility, and I could tell that having a witch in our pack was going to be handy.

"The best I can do is hide your scent, which should work well enough for wolves if you go in after dark," she'd said. "You're on your own when it comes to keeping quiet, though."

The plan was for Gisela to take a stroll around the alpha house and offices while Ranger monitored the patrols to see if they had been switched up since Luke left. The rest of us planned to add details to Luke's map as they sent information to the king through the royal link.

Our spies left as the last of the daylight slipped below the horizon, and it didn't take them long to infiltrate Tall Pines territory. We had no need to alter the map, we quickly discovered. Luke's memory had been plenty accurate.

Seeing as the dining hall was only a mile away from the alpha house, the king told Gisela to check on the shifters that Halder had locked in there. In the meantime, Ranger found Halder hadn't changed a thing about his patrols.

"Is he dumb or arrogant?" I snorted.

"Maybe both," Ash said with a big grin.

King Julian's eyes flicked from Ash to me to Mase, and I knew he was debating which of us he'd use.

This was a part of the plan we'd been careful to keep from Posy. She would have worried herself sick if she knew one of us planned to sneak in, too.

In other circumstances, it would have been Jay. The king found it invaluable to have Quartz on the inside as his own personal agent of chaos. With Tall Pines, though, no one wanted to risk a killing spree with so many innocent lives at stake.

Besides, Jay was not in the right mindset. Same with Wyatt.

That left Ash, Mase, or me.

"Figure it out between yourselves," the king said, pointing at the three of us.

We immediately assumed the position, and Ash counted, "1, 2, 3!"

We all tied, so we prepared to go again.

"1, 2, 3!" Ash called.

"You guys never change." King Julian shook his head with a small smile.

"What?" I asked him. "It's the easiest and fastest way for us to reach an unarguable decision."

"Yes, it is," Mase agreed.

His smug tone made me look down to see he'd thrown paper while Ash and I had both thrown rock, and Ash and I groaned in defeat.

I could tell that Ash didn't like it any more than I did, but we had a long-standing agreement that Rock-Paper-Scissors results were indisputable.

#

Ash

Beta Gisela and Ranger returned a few minutes before midnight and filled us in on the last bits of information they'd gathered on their way out of Tall Pines territory.

From what Gisela could see through the windows, the shifters in the dining hall were not in good shape. We'd specifically asked her to look for the little girl and the pregnant woman that Julio had told us about.

"There was a pup who was pale and limp in her mother's arms," she reported. "She didn't look good, to be honest, so that might have been her. And I only saw one pregnant woman. She seemed okay. She might not be able to move fast, but at least she wasn't in labor."

"Good thing we brought the supplies," I said, gesturing to the huge backpacks waiting for Mase, Ranger, and Gisela.

They planned to hit the dining hall first and hand out enough food and medical supplies to get everyone stable enough to move, then one of them would lead them back here to safety.

The other two would repeat the process at the prison.

Once the Tall Pines shifters were here, the king would break their bond with Halder so that he wouldn't be able to link or command them.

Luke had made a roster of all the Tall Pines pack members. If he hadn't missed anyone, the shifters in the dining hall, plus those we had captured at Five Fangs, added to the number we believed to be in the cells would equal about sixty wolves unaccounted for.

Of that number, Julio had estimated forty were loyal to Halder without coercion.

Wolves whose end would come under our fangs. Sid was especially looking forward to killing any of them who had hurt pups.

King Julian gave Mase the last of Ariel's amulets, and we wished them happy hunting.

"Don't make me tell Posy that you got injured," I told Mase as I gave him a bro hug.

"Wouldn't dream of it," he snorted and clapped me on the shoulder.

Then the three of them headed off, and the rest of us sacked out to catch a power nap while our wolves held the watch. By that time, I could hardly keep my eyes open, but took a second to check on our girl.

Throughout the day, we'd been picking up on Posy's emotions. While we had loads of experience as alphas with keeping things out of a bond, it was all brand-new to her. We didn't mind, though, because it made us feel connected to her while we were so far apart.

There were a couple of times something caught our attention, but when we linked her, she said everything was okay. And the betas gave us a report every hour until she linked us to say good night right around the time we were settling in here.

Now, I held back sleep to sink into the mate bond, where I found the gentle rhythm of her breathing and steady heartbeat. The comforting sounds lulled me and, smiling, I took them with me into the darkness.

\#

Mason

"You smell that, Mase?" Ranger asked.

While Gisela led the dining hall wolves back to the motel, Ranger and I tackled the prison. It was a rectangular block building with one hallway going straight down the center and doors on either side. We'd found only two guards that we'd knocked out, not wanting to risk Halder feeling their deaths through the pack bond.

After dragging their bodies inside the prison, we propped them up in a corner by the door and searched them, smirking at each other when I found a ring of keys.

Now, as we approached the first cell door, Ranger was insisting that he smelled something unusual.

"I smell body odor, urine, vomit, and blood," I told him. "How can you smell anything else over that fugly fume?"

"How can you *not*? It's so strong, and it's making Coal crazy."

I had an inkling of what was happening and grinned despite the circumstances.

"Where's it coming from?" I asked.

"There." He pointed to a door at the end of the hallway on our left. "Smells like chocolate."

"Let's check it out."

We went over there, his steps quickening until he was almost running, and he wasted no time opening the lock and bursting inside.

In the corner of the cold, damp cell lay a plump girl with reddish-brown curls.

"Mate?" Ranger whispered.

He dropped to his knees next to her and gently rolled her onto her back and into his arms. She whined in pain, and he crooned to her as he tried to assess the damage. Her face was a mass of bruises, her breathing was shallow and sharp, and there was a bloody lump above her left temple.

"Hey, there, beautiful," he murmured. "Can you open your eyes for me? Can you hear me? Try to wake up, treasure."

She didn't respond and Ranger raised his face to me, a tear streaking from the corner of his right eye.

"Mase? What do I do? *What do I do, Mase?!*"

#

Ranger

"Straw ... berries."

The sweetest voice in the world filled my ears and my head immediately swiveled to look at the girl in my arms. One of her eyes was so swollen, it wasn't going to open anytime soon, but the other eyelid slowly lifted to reveal a chocolate-brown iris.

"Your scent," she breathed. "Strawberries."

"What's your name, little mate?"

"Junia."

"I'm Ranger. Ranger Hemming."

"King's brother?" Her one working eye widened. "Flattering."

"That the Moon Goddess gifted me with you?" I smiled. "Why, yes. Yes, it is."

57

The ghost of a giggle wheezed from her cracked lips, and she grimaced in pain. Coal was roaring something at me, but I could only focus on my beautiful mate's battered face.

"So glad. So glad ... I got ... to meet you."

She was talking like she'd already given up, and my heart couldn't take it. No way was I going to lose my mate! Not now, not ever!

"Hold on, Junia! Please, treasure. Can your wolf help at all?"

"Too many ... broken bits." The sorrow in her smile smashed my heart into a million pieces. "Do you think ... I might have ... a kiss ... Ranger Hemming? My first ... and last kiss?"

Swallowing back a sob, I pressed my lips to hers, careful of her split bottom lip, and savored the sparks dancing between us.

Mark her so I can heal her, idiot! Coal's screaming finally made sense. *Hurry up!*

"I'm going to mark you so my wolf can heal you," I told her.

She seemed to have used up all her remaining energy because she lolled her head in a weak nod.

Nuzzling my face in her bruised throat, I found the right spot, dropped my canines, and bit down hard. She gasped, then moaned weakly, and I kissed the tip of her nose.

Then Coal flooded her with power. Despite having alpha blood, I didn't have a pack behind me. If her own wolf was drained down to nothing, I worried Coal and I wouldn't have enough in us to save her.

My big brother, though, had an entire kingdom to draw on. I linked him for help - and Onyx sent it. The holy trinity of power zipped through me and into her, and she jerked as her wounds healed and her bones knit back together.

"Oh, I *will* be your first and last kiss, treasure," I assured her, "but there will be at least a million more in between."

10: *Those Left Behind*

Posy

The day my mates left, the betas stayed, along with Peri and Ariel, Tristan's mate. They kept me busy and distracted.

The queen and Luke went over to the medical center to visit with their cousins, who were steadily improving. They were all very worried about the twins' little sister, Junia, who was Queen Lilah's best friend. All anyone knew was that Alpha Halder had taken her after leaving Zayne and Zayden to be savaged by his minions.

Since Luke and the queen were still members of Jayden's Moonset pack, Crew could link them, and they gave him updates that he shared with us throughout the day. If the twins continued to get better, it looked like they could be released as early as tomorrow morning.

That was going to cause all kinds of problems. Zayne and Zayden were determined to return to Tall Pines and find Junia, and the queen wanted them safe here at Five Fangs while the king handled it.

I wanted to meet them, but I didn't want to get involved in the family drama, so I held back on asking one of the betas to take me over there.

Getting to know Ariel was fun, and she and Peri taught me how to do nails. I was okay with the filing and trimming, but was too nervous to try painting them until Emerson offered to let me practice on him first.

"It's just nail polish, little luna bunny," he said. "If you mess up, we use the remover and try again."

I got them looking fairly decent in the end. He actually liked the color and wouldn't let me take it off when I finished.

"Next time, we'll try decals," Ariel promised.

When she saw I didn't know what that meant, she borrowed Tristan's phone and googled some pictures to show me. I loved them. There were so many choices, anything you could imagine, and I pointed out a few designs I liked.

Next, she showed me acrylic nail styles, but I didn't like them at all. I decided I'd stick to my natural ones, but I did want to try the decals.

I can't mess those up too much, I told myself. *They're basically stickers.*

Peri convinced me to order the ones I liked, even though I told her I didn't know how to pay for them. I had the cash I'd won in our bet the other day, but how did you use that to pay online?

In the end, Tristan bought everything we put in the shopping cart, despite my protests.

"It's only twenty bucks." When I opened my mouth again, he shook his head and smiled. "Let me spoil you and my mate a little bit, luna."

I shook my head, ran upstairs, peeled a twenty off my betting money, and took it down to him.

"Luna—"

"Please, Tristan."

"No. I won't take it. Put it away."

"Luna," Ariel intervened, "could I borrow some of your clothes until I can arrange to get my own things? I'll pay you twenty dollars for the loan."

"Oh, you don't have to pay for anything. I have a ton of new stuff, way more than I need, and I'm happy to help—"

"And that's how Tristan feels right now." She gave me a gentle smile and made me take back the money.

I fiddled with it for a moment, then nodded and took her and Peri up to "shop" in my closet.

Which was a brilliant move because it gave Peri and me the privacy to find out how Ariel got tangled up with Alpha Halder.

"Bird shifters were hit very hard by the sickness," she began as we sat on my closet floor. "Of my whole flock, only my little sister, three cousins, and I survived. My eldest cousin was eighteen and took custody of the rest of us. We've lived together ever since."

Her eyes glittered with tears, and I knew she was missing her family.

"Maybe they can move here," Peri suggested.

"I can't ask them to uproot their lives and the store to move here any more than I can ask Tristan to give up his beta position and move there." She shook her head.

"Store?" I asked.

"The del Vecchio line carries the magic, so that side of the family has traditionally opened occult shops, and we're no exception."

"That's where you met Alpha Halder," I guessed.

"Yes. Two weeks ago, he came in while it was just my little sister Beatrix and me manning the shop. We could tell he was a shifter, which isn't unusual as far as our customers go, but we both sensed something was off about him. When he asked for a love potion, we knew it for sure."

"I didn't even know that was a real thing." My eyebrows shot up. "I thought it was something made up for stories."

"It's one of the evilest magics," she explained, "and even dark witches are hesitant to peddle it because karma always finds those who do."

"Do you think he wanted it for the queen?" Peri covered her mouth with both hands.

"If so, she got out just in time!" I gasped.

"Now that I know what's been going on, yes, I believe Lilah MacGregor was his target." Ariel nodded.

"So what happened next? Obviously, you didn't give him what he wanted," Peri said.

"We told him no and asked him to leave. He didn't like that answer."

Ariel looked down at her tightly clasped hands and her shoulders trembled.

"You don't have to tell us the details," I murmured and put my hands over hers. "He kidnapped you and took you to Tall Pines, and you've been his prisoner since."

"Me *and* Beatrix. Tristan let me use his phone yesterday to call my cousins. They're coming here as soon as they can. I left something brewing at the shop that needed attention, and Gelo's stuck in New York City helping a friend deal with a dark witch."

"Jello?" Peri and I echoed.

"*An*gelo. My eldest cousin. None of us could say his name right when we were younger, and he eventually decided that Gelo was more tolerable than Angie or Lo-Lo. If I hadn't told him the king of werewolves was personally handling the matter, he would have hopped a flight down here immediately."

"Are your other two cousins his siblings?" Peri wanted to know.

"One is. Sara is his little sister. Maria is our uncle's daughter. Sara has an affinity for water and Maria's an air witch like me. Beatrix has fire. If we had an earth witch, we'd be a full coven."

"What's Angelo's affinity?" I asked.

"The magic gene skipped him." Ariel shook her head. "So did the shifter gene. He's about as human as it gets, although he has healing power."

"But he went to deal with a *dark witch?*" I raised an eyebrow.

"He has a lot of specialized weapons," Ariel smirked, but it quickly faded. "I feel bad for him because all he's done the past six years is take care of us girls. I wish he'd find his mate, but he's convinced that, even if he does have one, he'll be rejected because no one wants to risk their kids turning out *normal*, to use his word."

"Well, maybe he'll find one here at Five Fangs," Peri chirped. "Do any of the girls have mates? Or are they not old enough yet?"

"No mates, but they're all old enough. Beatrix turned eighteen in March and Maria in April. Sara is twenty-one, same as me, and Gelo is twenty-four."

"I can't wait to meet them and your little sister."

"I hope she's all right." Ariel's voice suddenly clogged with tears. "I've been so worried about her. We haven't been able to link in days. My cousins tried scrying for her last night and found nothing. Gelo caught a flight out of La Guardia this morning. He's going to pick them up and then they'll all head here."

She stopped talking and swiped at the tears streaming down her cheeks, and Peri and I hugged her on either side.

"I'm sorry. I'm just so afraid that he— That she's—"

A tornado named Tristan burst into my closet and scooped Ariel up in his arms, shushing her and cradling her against his chest. She put her arms around his neck and buried her face in his throat.

"Take her to one of the guest rooms," I told him quietly.

He gave me a short nod and carried her off.

"Poor thing." Peri swallowed hard. "At least we know my brothers and the king will make sure Alpha Halder gets everything he deserves. I only hope none of them lose their temper and give him a quick, painless death. That doesn't fit his many crimes."

If my Q involved, it no be quick and it definitely no be painless, Lark purred. *And Nyx already planning to keep him alive for months and months.*

I shuddered. Although I understood, I hated violence and torture.

Lark, when they check in again, remind me to tell the boys about Ariel's sister, okay? Just so she doesn't get overlooked.

On it.

"I don't want to think about that," I told Peri and stood up.

Holding out a hand, I waited until she took it and pulled her to her feet.

#

Except for Em and Ty, everyone went home after dinner. Those two decided I needed to update my movie knowledge, so we spent the evening with the television and ended up falling asleep on the comfy couches in the living room.

When I woke up the next morning, they made breakfast while I showered. We'd just finished eating when Crew, Matthew, and Tristan showed up. Em and Ty disappeared soon after, and Crew explained it was their turn to catch some sleep. It was only then that I realized they'd stayed up all night to guard me, and planned to do the same thing tonight.

When I asked him where Ariel was, Tristan said she'd gone over to his place to spruce it up before her family arrived. She also wanted to make sure they had enough space, supplies, and groceries for so many guests.

Next, I called Peri, but she was on house-cleaning duty in preparation for her family's return from their vacation, and both Callie and Keeley Breckenridge had volunteered to help her.

Crew linked Luke for me to check on the twins, and we discovered Zayne and Zayden had been released from the hospital an hour earlier. Luke and Queen Lilah took them to the bigger guest house to sit on them so they didn't try to sneak back to Tall Pines.

So I was left to hang out with Crew, Matthew and Tristan. For something to do, Crew decided to introduce me to video games. He showed me what all the buttons on the controller did, and that was a lot to remember. Since he wanted me to try a driving game first, he put in one called Mario Kart.

It didn't take long for me to realize I sucked. I almost immediately got lost and looped a cul-de-sac ten times, which made Matthew and Tristan laugh hysterically.

Crew honestly tried to help, but only made it worse.

"I'm sorry. I'm too dumb to learn this." I laid my controller down and got to my feet. "I'm going to get a drink. Does anyone else want one?"

They all wanted something different, and I nodded as I memorized who wanted what. Before I left the room, the betas' eyes fogged over, and I knew they were linking each other.

"I'll come help," Matthew said and stood, too.

He draw short straw? Lark smirked.

Shrugging, I turned and headed for the kitchen.

#

Beta Matthew Rose

I knew the luna wanted anyone but me to go with her.

A luna and her beta, in this case *betas*, had to have a strong relationship. We would be working together closely on pack matters, and she needed to trust us as her guards. I'd be the first to admit it was my fault we got off on the wrong foot, but I wanted to fix things between us.

Before I could even open my mouth to begin apologizing, her phone rang. I headed to the glasses cupboard to give her privacy for her call, but her shrill, panicky voice put me on instant alert.

"Matthew? I can't. I *can't!*"

I hurried over to her, and she shoved her phone at me with trembling hands. Confused, I looked at the screen and read, "Alpha James Briggs."

Isn't that her brother? I wondered.

Shrugging, I accepted the call.

"Hello, Luna Posy's phone. This is Beta Matthew Rose. How may I help you?"

"Beta, is my baby sister happy and well?"

"Yes, alpha. You're on speaker, and she is standing here with me."

A long pause followed.

"Hello, Posy. Aiden's here with me on speaker, too. We understand and accept you not wanting to talk to us. I wouldn't want to talk to us, either, if I were you. We know we failed you in every way possible, and nothing will ever absolve us of that."

I looked at my luna and held the phone out to her, but she shook her head furiously. Her bottom lip quivered as her eyes glistened with tears.

"She's listening to you, alpha, but doesn't want to speak," I said.

"We love you, baby sister," came a new voice.

Other brother? asked Arroyo, my wolf. *The Aiden guy?*

Yeah, Roy, I told him. *He's the beta of the pack now.*

"It's been a week and we wanted to check on you," Beta Aiden continued, "I hope you're safe and those mates of yours are treating you well."

"She is and they are," I relayed.

"We've been making a lot of changes here at Green River." Alpha Briggs either wasn't concerned his sister was silent, or he'd expected it. "We tore down the alpha house. Neither of us could stand even stepping foot in it, let alone live in it. We're going to rebuild on the same site, and there will be lots of windows. No more dark rooms, baby sister."

Dark rooms? Was their father a photographer?

No. Roy shook his head. *Something bad. Dark room is bad. Luna hurts!*

He was right. Her obvious distress sent a sharp spike into my heart as her tears finally fell.

The alphas will notice that for sure, I grumbled.

Other betas, too, Roy agreed.

Right on cue, the five alphas, Tristan, and Crew bombarded me, asking what happened. I linked them all that she was on the phone with her brothers, and that I was there and would stay with her until she hung up.

64

The alphas' language made my ears burn, and I told them I was closing the link so I could focus on my luna. Crew and Tristan wanted to know if they should come to the kitchen, but I asked them to give me the chance to deal with it.

Thankfully, Emerson and Tyler were out cold, catching up on their sleep from last night in preparation for tonight. Otherwise, they would have been down here faster than a lightning bolt, and I'd lose this opportunity to make things right between us.

Holding out my free hand, I motioned Luna Posy closer, and she hesitantly shuffled over. I put my arm around her shoulders and, after a moment, she burrowed into my side.

So tiny! Roy murmured. *Why she shaking?*

She's scared, I think. And yeah, it's like holding a fragile little bird. No wonder the alphas were so fierce when they told us how careful we needed to be with her.

"Posy?" Alpha Briggs asked.

"She's crying a bit," I said.

"Aw, we didn't mean to make you cry. We're sorry. We want to stay in contact with you, but if it only hurts you, we'll—" Now Beta Aiden sounded like *he* was on the verge of crying. "We'll back off. We don't want to hurt you anymore, baby sister, even if it means we have to let you go."

The luna's little fists gripped my shirt tightly, and she trembled harder.

"Hold on a second, please," I told them, then leaned down to whisper in her ear. "What do you want me to say?"

She lifted her face to mine and her eyes were wide and tragic, although she wasn't crying anymore.

"I can't talk to them, not yet, but I don't want to cut them out of my life. I'm so confused. What should I do, Matthew?"

The alphas had told us that her father abused her and kept her locked in the alpha house for six years, but they hadn't said a word about her brothers. I had no idea what I was dealing with here, but I could tell it wasn't anything good.

"What advice did your mates give you?" No way was I getting in the middle if there was something more going on than I knew.

"That it's my choice. They wouldn't help me decide, even though I asked them to just *tell* me what to do."

Knowing my alphas, I didn't expect anything else.

"Okay," I said slowly. "How about we thank them for checking in and say you'll be in touch later? That's polite and noncommittal."

She dropped her forehead to my chest and nodded.

After I told them that, Alpha Briggs thanked me for being there for his sister and told her she could call them any time, day or night.

After hanging up, I laid her phone on the kitchen island, took a deep breath, and put my other arm around her. As I swayed us side to side, I wondered what was going on between her and her brothers.

Stressful, Roy grumbled.

Yeah.

When she finally stopped shaking, I decided to get some answers.

"Luna, what did they do to you?" I murmured.

"Nothing. They did nothing."

Then why she upset? Roy wondered. *If brothers do nothing, why upset?*

"You mean your brothers did nothing as your father hurt you?" I asked, aghast. "What, did they sit back and watch?"

"Once Aiden turned eighteen, they moved out and stayed away." She took a step back, and I dropped my arms. "Other than challenging Father for the alphaship, they did *nothing*."

I couldn't wrap my brain around that. Both of my brothers were older, mated, and settled into careers, but I still would do anything to keep either of them safe, to protect them, and I knew that they would do the same for me. To abandon them completely when they were vulnerable and needed help the most?

It was unfathomable.

Maybe brothers were hurt? Roy was struggling to understand, too. *Or maybe father stopped brothers from helping?*

Or maybe they're more their father's sons than anyone wants to believe, I spat.

"Luna, I swear, you will never be abandoned again. Even if something were to happen to your mates, your beta guards will never desert you. I know it might take decades to convince you, but we will— *I* will stand by your side until death takes me."

She squinted her eyes at me for a moment, then held out her hand. I took it - and was surprised when she used it to pull me down to her eye level.

"I haven't forgiven you for how you've been treating Tyler." Her eyes burned like blue fire.

"I understand, and I'm sorry. I apologized to Tyler, too." My smile was hopeful. "I'm going to be a better teammate from now on. That's what you told me to do, right?"

"Yes. That's what I *expect* you to do." She shook my hand and released it, then went over to grab a tray from one of the cupboards.

"Uh, luna?" I scrubbed one hand over the back of my neck.

"Yes?"

"Thank you."

Wow, that's almost as hard to say as 'I'm sorry.'

"For what, Matthew?" She glanced at me over her shoulder as she opened the fridge door.

"For giving me a second chance. For trusting me to help you when you needed it."

"I believe everyone deserves a second chance, but only one. That's all you get. *One*. Don't screw it up."

"I won't, luna," I vowed.

And that was a promise I knew I'd kill or die to keep.

11: Birds of a Feather

Posy

The queen, Luke, and the Maxwell twins joined us for lunch. I knew Queen Lilah had only brought them over to distract them from wanting to storm Tall Pines, but I was happy to meet them all the same.

I'd been linking with my mates on and off as they had time - same for the queen with the king - and we were all excited to learn that Ranger had found his mate.

Surprise of surprises, she was Lilah's cousin, Junia!

He'd found her in a prison cell in the wee hours this morning. Mason told me that, if King Julian hadn't helped with healing her, she would have died in Ranger's arms.

Cole told me that they rescued quite a lot of shifters, whom they moved to a safe place for food, treatment, and rest. They hadn't found Gamma Reuben or Ariel's sister yet, but he said they had more places to search and promised they wouldn't leave until they found them, even if it was only their bodies.

I still worried. I knew how easily Beatrix could be overlooked in the chaos, especially if she was in her bird form.

Who watches for a little goldfinch in the middle of a wolf fight?

According to Wyatt, my mates and King Julian were now trying to get an estimate of how many members remained inside the pack territory. He didn't tell me what they planned to do next, but I imagined it involved taking care of Alpha Halder and his bully boys.

Like I'd told Peri, I didn't want to think about how they'd punish him, even though I knew it needed to be done.

After lunch, we were all sitting at the table and chatting when Tristan jumped to his feet as his eyes glazed over.

"No, Ariel," he muttered.

"What's up, Tris?" Crew asked.

"Her cousins are here. They're picking her up and going over to Tall Pines to find her sister." Tristan clenched and unclenched his hands.

"Go with them," I said. "Tell them to come get you and go with them."

"I can't! My duty is here with you, luna."

"I'm giving you permission. Just go!" I insisted.

"It doesn't work like that," he argued, shaking his head.

"We'll go with them," Zayne and Zayden said in unison.

"Link her to pick us up," Zayne said.

"We know the territory and the pack," Zayden added.

"I don't want you to go!" Queen Lilah stood and gripped the table edge with white knuckles. "They almost killed you once! This time, they might finish the job!"

"Lilah, we're fighters. It's what we were born to do." Zayden leaned down and kissed her cheek. "Sorry, but that's our final decision."

"Sorry, Lilah," Zayne echoed and kissed her other cheek. "Ranger may be her mate, but we need to *see* Junie to know she's safe and well."

Luke put his arm around the queen's shoulders, and she sank into the comfort he offered her.

"Be careful, you two hellions," he told them.

"Ariel said her cousins accept your help," Tristan told the Maxwell twins. "Apparently, their flock has an alliance with the king."

"Who all is in her flock, anyway?" Matthew asked. "Do you need a second vehicle?"

"Besides Ariel and her sister, there's her eldest cousin Angelo, his sister Sara, and their cousin Marie. And they don't need another vehicle. Sara and Marie shifted to their bird forms and flew ahead. Angelo is going to pick them up along the way."

"Wait. Angelo? Angelo *del Vecchio* is her cousin?" Luke clarified.

"*Angelo del Vecchio!*" shouted Zayne, Zayden, and Crew.

I jumped, startled by their volume.

"How do you know him?" Tristan asked.

"You know him, too," Crew smirked. "You just don't *know* you know him."

"Well? Who is he?" Matthew demanded.

"He's better known as *Angelo della Morte,*" Luke said.

"Dude! For real? And he's coming *here*?" Matthew squeaked.

"What?" I looked at Crew. "What's that mean?"

"It's a play on his name. *Angelo della Morte* means angel of death," he said. "Angelo del Vecchio has gained a reputation in the supernatural community for taking care of those who ... don't want to play nicely with others anymore."

"What, like rogues?" My forehead wrinkled in confusion.

"Among others," Luke explained. "Vampires, warlocks, sasquatches. I even heard he took out a *dragon* a couple years ago, although I think that's an exaggeration."

"But Ariel said he's almost human," I said with a frown. "How does he stand a chance against shifters, let alone magic users?"

"Same way human hunters do," Zayne grinned. "Silver bullets when hunting wolves, garlic-soaked stakes for vamps, all that old-school stuff, plus the advantage of his cousins making him amulets for magical resistance and protection."

"And his reflexes are insane. He might not be a true shifter, but he moves like one," Zayden added.

"Then it's fortunate the king has an alliance with him, right?" I asked.

"It is, indeed," Crew agreed.

"Well, I don't like this," Queen Lilah sighed, "but at least you're going in with allies. I'll let Julian know that you're coming."

"Thanks, cousin," Zayne and Zayden again spoke as one.

Five minutes later, a huge silver SUV came roaring up the drive, and the twins flew out the door. I followed, which meant my three betas did, too, and the queen and Luke tagged along.

As Zayne and Zayden ran for the vehicle, the driver's side window zoomed down and a guy's head popped out.

"Which one of you is Tristan?" he snarled.

Everyone else stayed on the porch with me as Tristan went down the steps and confidently approached with his hand held out. The guy studied him with narrowed eyes for a moment before shaking his hand.

"Angelo del Vecchio."

"Beta Tristan Harrington."

"Take good care of my *piccola uccella azzurra* (little bluebird), Harrington, or you're dead."

"Of course." Tristan nodded gravely. "Can I kiss her goodbye?"

"The hell you asking *me* for?" Angelo snorted. "Going by the mark on her neck, I'd say you've done a lot more than kiss her."

Luke, Crew and Matthew laughed and Lilah and I giggled.

Then the passenger door opened, and Ariel jumped out, ran around, and flung herself in Tristan's arms. While they were smooching, Zayne and Zayden opened the back door and climbed inside.

Even from my spot on the porch, I could see Angelo was getting impatient and, knowing the cause, I wanted them to get on the road as soon as possible.

"I'm Luna Posy Briggs of Five Fangs," I called and waved my arm. "You can meet the rest of us later. Now go find Beatrix!"

His gray-green eyes, sharp as razors, studied my face for a moment, then he nodded.

"We'll be back," he promised, then rolled up his window.

Tristan kissed Ariel one more time. Then she dove in the vehicle and it zoomed off, leaving a tremendous cloud of dust in its wake.

"Whew!" Crew choked and gagged. "I know the alphas are against disturbing nature more than necessary, but they really need to get this mess paved."

I knew he was trying to be funny, but he was right. Everyone's vehicles, including my mates', were covered with dirt.

"Hey, I have an idea," I said as Tristan joined us. "Let's wash the cars."

"Luna, that's a lot of work," Matthew groaned. "The alphas should have parked in the garage instead of out here, anyway, so it's their own fault. And the rest of us can just take our vehicles through the car wash."

"But playing with water on a hot day is a great way to cool off. Buckets and hoses and sponges! It'll be fun!"

I smiled widely, showing my dimples, and the betas groaned while Luke laughed.

"I think so, too." At least Queen Lilah was on my side. "Let's change into some old t-shirts and shorts, Posy. Will you guys get the hoses and buckets set up, please?"

"Of course, your majesty," came three resigned sighs and one cheerful chuckle.

Giggling, the queen and I went back in the house to change.

#

Jayden

"Okay, boys." The king sat on the end of the motel bed, dangling his hands between his knees. "Wyatt, you stay human and search the alpha house. Hopefully, you'll find Gamma Reuben or Ariel's sister or, Goddess willing, both."

"Why me?" Wyatt whined.

"Because you're the baaaay-beee," Ash teased him, "and have the least experience."

"You're like three months older than me, dickhead!" He swatted at Ash, who danced out of the way. "And how can I gain experience if I'm constantly sidelined for having no experience?"

"He has a point," I admitted with a nod.

"Fine." King Julian rolled his eyes. "Rock-Paper-Scissor it between the four of you."

He pointed to everyone but me.

"Why's Jay automatically exempted?"

Cole smacked Wyatt upside the back of his head.

"You know why," he hissed.

As if I'd let anyone keep me out of a fight, Quartz purred.

71

"*Anyway*," the king went on, "sort it. As for the rest of us, we kill any wolf that attacks us. If we find Halder, take him alive. Nyx wants to have fun with him for a few months."

We smirked at each other, knowing *exactly* the kinds of things Onyx considered to be fun.

"What if he runs?" Mase asked. "Or isn't even there right now?"

"Do you think Tristan's mate could track him? She's a witch," Ash told the king.

"Which magic family is she from? What's her last name?"

"Del Vecchio."

"Son. Of. A. Bitch." King Julian grimaced. "She's a bird shifter, isn't she?"

"Your majesty?" Cole's question reflected all our curiosity.

"Yeah, she can track him, but we have another worry now." He scrubbed a hand through his hair. "If her cousin finds out his family's in trouble—"

His eyes glazed over as he linked with someone, and we waited patiently.

"Too late," he muttered as his eyes cleared. "He already knows and is on his way."

"Is that good or bad?" Ash asked.

"Good, but he is going to be so very pissed."

"Who even *is* this guy?" Cole demanded.

"Angelo del Vecchio."

My brothers and I looked at each other and shrugged.

"You know him by a different name." The king's eyes sparkled with amusement. "He also goes by Angelo Della Morte."

Son of a bitch, indeed.

12: Flock Together

Mason

The fighting was heavy in front of Halder's alpha house when the roar of a shotgun startled Garnet and me. Shifters rarely used guns, and we had no experience fighting with, or against, those who did.

Where did that come from? Garnet demanded as he tore out a wolf's throat.

Then the heavy ozone of magic scorched my nostrils, and I had a fair idea of who the new players were, even though I couldn't see them.

The shooter is Angelo della Morte! Cole yelled in the alpha link, confirming my hunch. *He's with Ariel, Zayne and Zayden Maxwell, and two other witches.*

Explains why wolves are suddenly exploding in green flames, Garnet said dryly.

The fight around me cleared for a moment, and I took the chance to locate the newcomers.

Standing in the thick of things, Angelo della Morte wore military-grade armor and bristled with weapons. Knives on the front of his vest. Pistols at his waist, underarms, and small of his back. A shotgun holster on either hip and tied down above each knee. Probably a lot more that I couldn't see.

You think he's as good as the rumors say? Garnet asked.

We watched as he took out three wolves with three shots and no wasted motion.

I think he's so good, he doesn't feel the need to prove it, I answered.

Ariel and her cousins fanned out behind him and hurled hexes, and it was clear that they'd fought together before - and more than once.

Two wolves I didn't recognize ran protection around the witches, and I figured they were the Maxwell twins. I made a note of their coat colors and patterns so we didn't accidentally go after them, and sent that info to my brothers through the alpha link.

Ash was the only one to acknowledge me as the rest were too busy fighting, and I could tell from his sour tone that he was still ticked he'd lost Rock-Paper-Scissors and was stuck searching the alpha house.

Too bad, so sad, I smirked to myself, and Garnet snorted. *Just find Ariel's sister and Gamma Reuben.*

I'm trying! This house is a maze of locked and hidden doors, he muttered.

Soon enough, only Halder's wolf, Ruby, was left snapping and snarling at Onyx, and the rest of us circled around the two of them. We

73

all knew the king was struggling to rein in his wolf. Onyx wanted to kill his enemy while King Julian wanted to take him alive.

After Onyx had Ruby backed against a giant tree trunk, the king took charge and shifted. Standing before the red wolf, he clenched his hands into tight fists and ordered him to shift, and Halder had no choice but to do so.

"On your knees, dog!" King Julian snarled with a blast of power, and Halder dropped to the grass like his legs had gone boneless. "Leo Halder, I officially strip you of all titles, positions, and recognition."

The king's unique triad of power rippled over my brothers and me. It would spread to every alpha in the kingdom and let them know Halder had been deposed.

"On a personal note," King Julian hissed, "for every hurt you have given my queen, I will repay you tenfold."

Then he drew back one fist and slammed it into Halder's jaw, knocking him out cold. Looking at us over his shoulder, he started issuing orders.

"Garnet, Topaz, escort this piece of filth to the prison and lock him in a cell. Zayne and Zayden, you're on guard duty. And Granite, *please* link Ash to bring me some shorts or boxers. I'm getting sunburned in places a guy should never get sunburned in."

Our chuckles came to an abrupt end at the sound of twin pistols cocking.

"No one moves or the wolf king dies."

#

Cole

Angelo stood in a perfect shooter's stance with a gun in each hand. Both of them were trained on the back of King Julian's head.

Behind Angelo, Ariel and the other two witches spun hexes in their hands while their eyes scoured the yard for further threats.

Boss, I thought they were on our side? Topaz was as confused as I was.

Just be ready for anything, I told him.

Quartz slunk around, trying to flank the guy, but Angelo was too good. He caught the motion in his periphery and one pistol moved to track Quartz's approach.

"All my ammo is silver coated, wolf," he said. "I have no beef with you, but I will end you just the same if you keep moving."

Quartz froze, but growled low in his throat.

"What are you doing, Angelo?" the king asked. "And can't you wait until I get some freaking clothes on? I don't like you staring at my naked ass while you're threatening me."

"Not funny, Julian. You know what else isn't funny? Coming back from solving a problem for one of *your* packs only to find that some mutt has stolen two of my *piccoli uccelli* (little birds) right out of my nest."

"No wolf of mine acted against you," the king told him.

"Which is why I haven't pulled the trigger yet. Now, where's my *bambina* (baby), wolf king? Hmm? *Where?!*"

"Here! I found her!"

Ash ran out of the alpha house, his hands cupped in front of him. The witches dissolved their hexes and ran to Ash, surrounding him and crooning to the little puff of feathers in his giant hands.

Interestingly, the Maxwell twins' wolves whined and also hustled over. Shifting in a heartbeat, Zayne and Zayden crowded closer, gently moving the witches out of their way.

"Mate," they whispered together.

Very carefully, Zayne lifted the fragile goldfinch and cradled her in one palm, and Zayden touched the tip of his index finger to her tiny head.

"She was in a cage in the kitchen," Ash explained. "I gave her some water, and she chirped at me, so I know she's alive."

"Mate, if you shift," Zayden began.

"We can mark you and heal you," Zayne finished.

"Is there a quiet place where we can take her?" Ariel looked at Ash.

"Sure," he said. "I found a couple of bedrooms that look clean and unused. I'll show you."

"Ash, grab us some clothes on your way back," the king instructed.

"Okay, sire."

I noticed that the youngest-looking of Ariel's cousins paused when she passed Halder's unconscious body. Her eyebrows drew together and her mouth tightened. The longer she studied him, the more emotion swirled in her eyes.

Oh, Goddess! He's not her mate, is he? Topaz whimpered.

No. I don't think so. She looks confused more than anything.

"Maria?" Ariel called from the front door of the alpha house.

The little witch tapped one finger on her chin, narrowed her eyes, and nodded as if she'd made up her mind about something.

"Your majesty, we need to talk about *that* later." She pointed at Halder. "There's something you should know about it."

"All right, Ms. del Vecchio. Find me at your leisure."

"Thank you."

Once the witches were in the house with the twins, some of the tension eased, but Angelo never took his eyes or his aim off the king. That made all of us antsy and especially Quartz, who was still growling deep in his throat.

"Halder's mine," Angelo growled. "I'm going to skin him alive for hurting my *famiglia* (family)."

"He'll be a guest in my dungeon until I tire of his screams." The king inclined his head. "But feel free to visit anytime."

Angelo's gray-green eyes scrutinized King Julian's face for another few seconds before he uncocked his guns and reholstered them. Then he moved closer and opened his arms to meet the king in a bro hug.

"I don't like you hugging my naked ass anymore than I like you staring at it," the king grumbled.

"Heard you found your queen. Congratulations." Angelo stepped back and dropped his hands to rest on the pistol butts at his sides. "She's welcome to your ass, naked or otherwise. You're not my type."

"Thank the Goddess for that." The king deadpanned, then grinned. "It's good to see you, man."

"You, too. Can I assume I'm finally going to meet the famous alphas of Five Fangs?"

"Yes. And later, their new luna."

"Oh, I already met *her*."

His smirk set me off. What did he mean by that? Was he implying something? I knew nothing had happened because neither Posy nor the betas had linked us, but I didn't like the way he said that or his little twisted smile.

Topaz growled in concert with my thoughts, and Angelo swung his head in my direction. Whatever he saw in Topaz's eyes made him raise both hands with his palms forward.

"You're lucky to be gifted with such a smart, beautiful mate."

His words and sincerity calmed me, but Paz didn't want him talking about Posy at all, even if he'd said something nice.

I don't like that he was near our mate, either, Topaz scowled.

I know, Paz, but what's done is done. Jeez, you're a jealous thing.

Of anyone other than our brothers? Yes! Yes, I am! he snarled, which made me roll my eyes.

Ash came back and passed out clothes. Thankfully, he gave each of us the right sizes. He, Wyatt, and Jay could interchange easily, so long as he didn't mind the legs being too short, but Mase and I could only swap with each other, and even his pants were tight on me. One time, I had to wear Jay's, and I'd split the whole backside out with the first step.

76

After he shifted and tugged on his shorts, Mase stepped up to Angelo and held out his hand.

"We know we're lucky. I'm Mason Price."

"Angelo del Vecchio. Good to meet you." He shook Mase's hand. "You've built quite a reputation in the short time you've been alpha."

"Thank you. These are my brothers. Ash, Cole, and Wyatt, and that's Jay's wolf, Quartz. Watch your step around him until Jay has the reins again."

None of us was surprised that Quartz hadn't shifted; he wouldn't until he was sure the king was out of danger.

"So you're Quartz." Angelo gave him a sharp nod. "I've been hearing about *you* for years now. Ever since you ripped a shifter into itty bitty pieces. Your human must have been what? Twelve? Maybe thirteen? Heard the bastard murdered his mate and beat his pup. "

He stared into Quartz's eyes, and neither blinked.

"I'll tell you a secret," Angelo stage-whispered. "I'd have done the same thing."

Quartz stared at him for a moment longer, then he snorted and handed control back to Jay.

13: Little Sister

Posy

Crew didn't give up on the video games.

After Zayne and Zayden left with Ariel's flock, he bustled me into the game room, and everyone else trooped along for something to do.

"When you went into the kitchen earlier, Matthew's real reason for going along was to give you a pep talk," Crew said.

"Really?" I looked over at Matthew with raised eyebrows.

"Yeah. Uneducated is not the same as dumb." Matthew's smile reached his blue eyes for the first time since I'd met him. "You're not *dumb*, luna. You just never learned how to do some things, and that's easy to fix."

"Thanks, Matthew."

"Just the truth." He shrugged. "And Mario Kart was probably not the best game to start with. Let's try Minecraft instead. It can be as easy or difficult as you want, and you can learn the controller while building."

Surprisingly, I loved it. Everyone joined in and we created for hours. Lilah and I made pretty flower beds around the house the boys were building. Then Crew, Tristan, Matthew, and Luke played on a different mode for a bit to show Lilah and me the survival side of the game. I had a lot of fun and got to know more about everyone, especially my three betas.

Matthew, for example, was nineteen and had two much-older brothers who'd raised him after his mother died in childbirth and the sickness took his father. He lived at the pack house and hated it.

"The only good thing about it is that Emerson lives there, too," he grumbled.

"Is it a bad place?" My eyes widened. "Do I need to go there and check it out? I've been wanting to ask about the orphanage, too. Are the people in charge nice or mean? Are these places good enough for my betas to live in?"

Matthew stared at me, then burst into laughter.

"Yes, luna. The alphas would not allow them to be bad places," Tristan assured me.

"Then why do you hate it, Matthew?" Luke asked before I could.

"It's too noisy." Matthew sobered up enough to answer for himself. "I like the quiet. There's not much privacy, either. I know most wolves like denning together, but I need personal space. And quiet.

Sometimes I think I could easily be a lone wolf, but I'd miss my friends and family too much."

"Well, Matthew," the queen spoke up, "why not move into your own place?"

"I don't see the point until I find my mate. I don't want to pick a place she'll end up hating," he said with a shrug. "I want her to be happy, and where we live isn't as important to me as it probably will be to her."

"That's so sweet!" I smiled, showing him my dimples, and he ducked his head. "And the orphanage? Is it a good place for Ty?"

"After the sickness," Crew said, "the former alphas and lunas helped many orphans find good families, and created the orphanage for those who couldn't go to a new home for whatever reason. They visit it frequently, as do your mates. The den mother is an older lady whose mate died in the sickness. Minding the little orphans gave her the purpose she needed to keep from succumbing to her grief and loneliness."

"And Ty wouldn't tolerate anything inappropriate happening there," Tristan added. "There are only six other kids at the O, so it's easy to keep track of them. If someone was being mean or abusive, Ty would put them in their place or tell the alphas."

I nodded, satisfied to hear that.

"What about you, Tristan? You have your own place?" Luke asked.

He replied that he had an apartment, but now that he'd found Ariel, he was on the hunt for a house.

"Once things settle down, the alphas said we could tour the pack territory and see what interests us from what's available." His smile radiated happiness. "Like Matthew, I'm not fussy about where we live, so long as I'm with her."

"Aw!" the queen and I cooed, making him duck his head with a little smile.

Crew also had his own place. His grandparents left him a stone cottage deep in the woods by a waterfall. From the way he talked about it, I could see how much he loved it.

"I'd like to see it," I told him.

"Of course. Anytime." He rubbed his hand over the back of his neck. "I've modernized the appliances and wiring and stuff, but it's crammed with my grandparents' antiques and books and oddities, and the location is isolated from the rest of the pack."

"Dude, it's a great location," lone wolf Matthew chimed in. "I want to find one just like it, if my mate agrees."

"But what do I do if my mate hates it?"

"Of course she won't hate it," I told him. "It's important to you, which will make it important to her, too. I mean, would you hate a place that *she* loves?"

"Oh. No. Okay, I see." He patted me on top of my head, mussing my hair. "There's a wise old soul inside you, luna."

"Stop," I whined and batted his hand away.

"Are you teasing our little luna bunny?" Emerson's voice came from the doorway.

Looking over, I saw he was dressed in black shorts and a white t-shirt, and his hair was damp.

"Good morning, sleepyhead!" Tristan called with a grin. "Are you hungry?"

"Yeah, but I can wait til Ty's down. He's finishing up in the shower now."

When Tyler joined us, we decided to have an early dinner. Emerson said he wanted to make something called lemon chicken piccata, and I was eager to learn a new recipe. He let me cut up the lemons, but that was it. While it simmered, he wrote out the recipe on a piece of paper.

"Now, if you like it, you can make it whenever you want." He handed me the paper.

Glancing at it, I saw that his handwriting was lovely, but I couldn't read it.

"Um, thanks, but what language is this?" I looked up at him.

"What do you mean? It's English, luna."

"Oh. Uh, okay."

My brow furrowed, I looked at the paper again. I could read the numbers, but the squiggles made no sense. I didn't want to bother him about it or look stupid, so I only nodded and used a magnet to hang the recipe on the refrigerator door.

Mates will help, Lark said. *Quartz and Garnet can read. Bet they know this kind of words.*

Okay. We'll ask when they get back. I don't want to disturb them with it right now. They're busy.

When I turned around, I ran into a wall. An enormous wall named Emerson. He put his hands on my shoulders, and I craned my neck to meet his eyes.

"Luna?" His voice was gentle and soft. "Do you know how to read cursive?"

"What's cursive?"

He took a deep breath, closed his eyes, and shook his head. When he opened his eyes, I saw something in them that I couldn't understand.

"I'll teach you," he murmured. "Ty doesn't know cursive, either, so you two can learn it together."

Oh, good. I wasn't alone in needing to learn this 'cursive' thing. That made me feel less dumb.

Not dumb, Lark scolded me. *Untaught. Remember what Matthew said?*

I nodded. Dumb was different than uneducated, and if someone wanted to teach me, I would accept with a grateful heart.

"Thank you, Em."

"Anything for you, luna bunny."

#

Beta Emerson Jones

Hours later, Ty and I were doing a quick reconnoiter of the downstairs, checking that all was secure and locked for the night, when eardrum-shattering screams broke the midnight silence.

Luna bunny! Cove screamed at me. *Go to luna bunny!*

How did someone get past us? I growled as fear sent my pulse into overdrive.

I bolted up the stairs, Ty hot on my heels, and we raced down the hallway. Throwing open the alphas' bedroom door, I let Cove rise to the surface and prepared to rip apart whoever had dared to hurt our luna, but found no enemy to kill - only our luna thrashing and screaming so loudly, it had to hurt her throat.

"Shh, it's a dream." Ty ran by my shocked self to her side of the bed. "You're safe in your house with your betas. Wake up."

EMERSON! TYLER! WHAT IS HAPPENING? WHERE'S POSY? ANSWER ME!

Alpha Mason's frantic bellow in the mind link made my brain rattle around in my skull, and poor Ty clutched his head and bent double.

Nightmare, alpha. We can't help her with you howling at us, I linked back.

That shut him up toot sweet.

"Luna, you're safe. You're not there anymore." Ty leaned over her, but didn't touch her. "Wake up, luna. You're okay."

I finally got Cove shoved back down and could move my feet. Going over next to Ty, I started to reach for her, but he stuck out his arm to block me.

"Since we don't know what she's dreaming about, we don't want to do anything that could add to the nightmare and prolong it. Best thing to do is keep her from hurting herself and talk to her. If you shake her awake, it'll scare her more and take longer for her to calm down."

81

I raised my eyebrows at him. How did he know so much about nightmares?

Has his own, Cove said thoughtfully as the kid continued encouraging our luna to wake up.

I knew what his father did to him as a pup, and understood why he'd have nightmares from that. He was so careful to keep his scars covered up, but I'd glimpsed a few here and there. I always wondered why he was so ashamed of them. Did he think we'd be disgusted? Tease him?

Matthew, Cove grunted.

Yeah. Matthew would, I agreed, *but he's trying to treat the kid better now. Still, I think I'd have to slaughter him if he ever picks on the kid because of his scars or his father.*

Have to beat Alpha Mason to it, Cove snorted, making me smirk internally.

Ty finally managed to wake Luna Posy, and she scrambled up against the headboard, panting and crying and shaking. She held out her hands to ward us off, and I knew she didn't recognize us.

Go fetch her stuffed bunny from her special room, I told the kid, and he took off like a shot.

"Luna, it's Beta Emerson Jones. You're safe. You're in your house. You're not there anymore. Beta Tyler James is here, too. We'll keep you safe."

I had no freaking idea what to do for someone having a nightmare, but I'd been watching and listening to Ty. Since it had worked to wake her up, I kept repeating what he'd said.

"Em— Emerson?" she stammered at last.

"I'm here." I kept my voice soft and low, like Ty had been doing. "Ty went to get your bunny."

"*I want my mates!*" she sobbed.

"I know, luna. I know you do."

"Can I—" She hiccuped. "Can I have a hug?"

"Of course." I sat on the edge of the bed and held out my arms. "Come here, little luna bunny."

That was all it took for her to snuggle up into my side and clench my shirt in her fists. She held on so tightly, as if she was afraid I'd disappear and she'd be left with no anchor to keep her safe in the storm.

I hesitated for a second, then put my arms around her.

Careful! Cove barked. *Luna bunny is FRAGILE! Don't break her!*

Yes, Cove. I rolled my eyes at him.

When the alphas first linked us about their special girl, I was skeptical. An abused girl who'd been locked away for six years? How was she going to handle five alphas *and* their wolves *and* be the luna for the second-largest and most powerful pack in the United States?

I wasn't sure what to think when I first saw her. She was tiny, and shy, and so very vulnerable, and my doubts resurfaced. Just one of our alphas was hard to manage, and this little thing was supposed to manage *all* of them? Then I accidentally scared her while introducing myself, and the stark fear in her big blue eyes made me want to slit my own throat.

In that instant, all of my protective instincts rose up, and not just from the burgeoning luna-beta bond. Everything about her made me want to wrap her up in bubble wrap and keep her safe from anything that could harm her.

And the more I got to know her, the stronger those protective instincts became. Same for my beta brothers.

That day at the pool when she cried because Tyler lived at the orphanage? Yeah, that smashed all our hearts good and proper. We knew she herself hadn't had a birthday cake or presents in years. No one had celebrated her precious self in so long, she'd forgotten she was worthy of being celebrated.

'Ash got me a present this year! A set of hair pins with the prettiest flowers! I didn't even ask *for them and he got them for me!'*

She'd said that with a dimpled smile and shining eyes, too, as if a few hair barrettes was some fabulous prize or rare treasure. And the *way* she'd said it - amazed that she hadn't had to ask for it, shocked that her mate had thought enough of her to give her a gift - had made me blind angry. Her golden heart deserved to be given anything it desired, not debased into thinking she was worthy of *nothing*.

She didn't want expensive and extravagant things, though. She delighted in simple pleasures. The tiniest things, like a few flowers and fairy lights on a balcony, made her happy.

"Luna?" Ty sat down on her other side. "Here's Mr. Nibbles."

He held it out to her, and she took it with a shy thank you, then crammed her face into the doll before snuggling against me again.

Ty, I'm going to link the alphas and let them know she's okay before they have an aneurysm.

Good idea. How about I make some hot chocolate? That might help her settle and sleep again.

"Luna?" I asked. "Would you like some hot chocolate?"

"Yes, please." Her voice was muffled by Mr. Nibbles, and Ty and I smiled at each other.

After he left again, I opened the link with the alphas and found a storm of anxiety, sorrow, and rage.

She's okay, I assured them. *She's tucked up with her bunny doll. Tyler is making some hot chocolate for her right now.*

I looked down and sent the image of her resting against my side with her arms wrapped around Mr. Nibbles.

It's her first nightmare since we found her, and we're not there to help her through it! Alpha Wyatt roared.

The next few words he ripped out probably turned the air blue around him.

I understand your feelings, alpha, I said, *but at least you know she's in good hands. We got her. Until you get home, you can trust that we got her.*

Thanks, Em, Alpha Jayden said. *It means the world to know we have such good and capable betas to take care of our luna in our absence.*

Of course, alpha. We all love our little luna bunny.

The alphas wanted to see her, so I just stared at her and let them watch her through my eyes. When she raised her wet, red face and looked at me, I could tell she knew I was linking, and was quick enough to know with who.

"I'm sorry for making you worry," she whispered. "I'm all right now. Em and Ty are with me, and Mr. Nibbles is making me feel better."

She picked up the bunny's arm and made it wave at them - and my heart almost stopped from an overload of cuteness. Then the alphas all started talking at once, wanting to know why she wouldn't link with them. I winced over the volume in my head and told them to pipe down.

If you're this loud when - if - she opens her link, you'll scare her! I yelled at them.

Yeah, that's right. The beta yelled at his alphas. But my luna will always take priority over anyone or anything else.

"Luna bunny, could you link with them? They're giving me a headache."

"Oh, yeah. I forgot I could do that now!" Her dimpled smile was a thing of beauty. "Thanks, Em."

I closed my link with them as she opened hers, and we sat together quietly as she talked with her mates. When Ty came into the room with a tray of mugs and set it on the nightstand, she sat up and away from me, although she still clutched Mr. Nibbles in one arm.

"Okay, I told them goodnight and closed the link," she said. "I think they're calm enough to function now."

"And are you?" I asked.

"I am. Thank you both so much for being here with me."

"Wouldn't want to be anywhere else, luna," Ty said as he handed her a mug. "My mom used to make it this way. I hope you like it."

"Yeah?" Her face lit up. "Mine, too."

I looked at the mug he gave me and saw dollops of whipped cream, which I never tried.

"I usually make it with marshmallows. Have you had that before?" I asked, and they both shook their heads. "We can try that sometime if you want."

"Sounds good," said luna while Ty nodded.

The three of us chatted about everything and nothing, and watching luna bunny and Ty giggle together was so cute. Whether he knew it or not, she'd claimed him as her little brother, which was proven when she began to gently tease him about finding his mate.

His cheeks flushed cherry red, and how could I resist joining in? Within seconds, even the tips of his ears were burning, and I laughed.

She and I were both very careful not to say Peri's name. While *everyone* believed it, and the attraction between the two was undeniable, no one wanted to jinx it. I couldn't believe the Moon Goddess would be so cruel, but why risk it?

I myself wouldn't have a mate. I'd known and accepted it years ago. While shifters in general were open-minded about homosexuality, many packs' priorities changed after the sickness. Alphas wanted to replenish their numbers; since gay male couples didn't make babies, they weren't welcome. A few alphas even went to the extreme of executing gays, although they called it 'weeding out the weak' or 'purifying the bloodline.'

Fortunately for me, my own parents weren't such Nazis.

Alpha Bellamy Jones only banished me from the Gray Shadows pack. Mom, also known as Luna Ivana Jones, hadn't argued. Like always, she followed everything her husband said like the good little puppet she was.

To be fair, they'd given me a choice before they'd kicked me out.

"Be as gay as you want to be, but you *will* produce pups," dear old Dad had demanded.

"How can I do that with a male mate?" I'd challenged him.

"You will reject him, of course, and take a female as a chosen mate!"

When I'd refused, he'd told me how worthless I was to him, taken me to my room, and made me pack my things. As he marched me through the house to his car, Mom hadn't even looked at me as I tried to talk to her. Then my father drove me to the border of the territory, stopped, tossed my duffel bags and my sixteen-year-old ass out of his car, got back in, and drove away - and that was the last contact I had with my birth family.

Thankfully, I eventually found my way to Five Fangs, where the alphas accepted and supported me from the very beginning. I could never repay their kindness and generosity when I stumbled into their lives. They gave me a pack, a family, a home, and, later, a purpose when they made me Alpha Cole's beta.

And now they'd given me a luna to love and protect.

A thought struck me and I glanced down at her. She had a hot chocolate mustache, but was unaware of it and couldn't figure out why Ty giggled every time he looked at her.

Both so sweet and pure, I mused with fondness. *I know Ty understands what gay is, but I doubt she does.*

To be frank, I quailed at the thought of explaining it to her.

Job for the alphas, Cove muttered.

I heartily agree. Let them tell our innocent little sister what it means.

Sister? he asked hopefully. *She can be our little sister now?*

That's right. We're claiming her as our little bunny sister, I told him with a smile. *Just like Ty is our little baby brother.*

Good. He paused, then unexpectedly added, *I am happy with this family we have built, Emerson. I love them all.*

My eyes suddenly stung, making me blink. Cove was rarely sentimental, and I'd trained myself not to be for my own emotional protection.

At least, I *thought* I'd trained myself. Yet, there I sat with wet eyelashes and a knot in my throat.

Me, too, Cove, I whispered. *Me, too.*

14: A Long Day

Cole

After we met Angelo, Mase and Jay took Leo Halder over to the prison, where Jay would stay to guard him until we came up with a better arrangement. The rest of us followed Ash back into the kitchen and he showed us the door he thought led to the basement.

"I got sidetracked when I saw the bird cage and realized Beatrix was probably in it," Ash said.

"How much of the house did you search?" I asked.

"Thoroughly? This ground floor and most of the second floor. There's one more floor and an attic to go."

"Angelo, you go with him and finish searching this place," the king directed. "Cole, you're with me. Wyatt, stand guard. I don't want us trapped down there. When Mase gets back, tell him to go check on the witches and the twins."

After Ash and Angelo left the room, I tried the door to the basement, found it locked, and kicked it open. The smell that oozed up from the blackness told us all we needed to know about what was down there.

I smell black magic, boss! Topaz growled. *Call witches.*

"Paz says he smells black magic. What do your wolves say?" I coughed, flapping my hand in front of my face.

"Granite says the same," Wyatt choked out.

"Nyx, too, and he scented a layer of something else, but he doesn't know what. He's never smelled it before," the king wheezed. "We need the witches to do some purifying."

"We will, and you're right," Ariel's voice came from behind us.

Looking over my shoulder, I saw her and her two cousins standing in the kitchen doorway. With the foul reek slowly filling up the kitchen, we knew they wouldn't come any closer, so we walked over to them.

"Black magic was used here," she continued, "and the 'something else' your wolf smells, your majesty, is an infernal being."

"Whoa. Wait. *Here?*" I swung my head around as Topaz went into high alert, both of us ready to kill something.

"What's an infernal being?" Wyatt yipped.

"A creature from Hell. A lesser demon, by the feel of it," said Sara, one of the witches.

"Well, where is it?"

"We know, and it is not here," the three witches crooned.

"MacBeth, anyone?" the king chuckled to himself.

I scowled at him, and he rolled his eyes.

87

"Chill, Cole. Whatever it was, it's long gone," he pointed out.

"Again, correct." Ariel gave him a quick nod. "We'll get to that later. Now, are you going down in that awful hole?"

"I need to know," he said simply.

"And there might be survivors," Wyatt added with more hope than expectation in his voice.

"Then let's not waste any more time." She looked at her sister witches. "Shall we, ladies?"

They all joined hands, and their power buffeted against us. The smell of lemon filled the kitchen and spread until I couldn't detect so much as a trace of the vile stench.

Nodding at each other, the king and I went down the stairs.

What we found in that basement made me wish there was a purifying spell for my memory. If there was, I'd ask those witches to bleach out everything I saw.

I wouldn't even care if it took a few brain cells along with it.

#

Ash

Gamma Reuben Ford was the only one King Julian and Cole found alive in the basement. They laid him right on the kitchen floor to assess his injuries before the king blasted him with power. Reuben sat up with a loud gasp, his hair sticking up as if he had been electrocuted.

"Hey, Rube. Let's go get cleaned up, yeah?" Wyatt said in a quiet voice, rubbing a hand up and down Reuben's back. "I'll help you get a shower while Ash finds you some clean clothes. Then we can get something to eat. How's that sound?"

Reuben opened his mouth, but only babble came out.

I went to the door and called for the witches, hoping they could make sense of this better than we could. When they ran into the kitchen, they immediately hustled over to Reuben, made him lie down again, and knelt around him.

A flurry of whispers later, Ariel put her thumb on his forehead, and his eyes rolled back in his head before his eyelids closed.

"Too much trauma." She rocked on her heels. "I put him to sleep, real sleep, where no memories will disturb him. Rest is what's best for him right now. Try to get some broth in him later."

Cole picked Reuben up in a fireman's carry, and I led him to another one of the guest rooms Angelo and I had cleared earlier. We got him in bed, then left him to his healing slumber.

After that, the king split us into teams, one per floor except the basement, which would be taken care of by him, Ariel, and Sara. As they worked down there, the rest of us went to our assigned spaces and washed the walls and floors with bucket after bucket of herbal water that Maria kept cooking up. My nose said the potion included lavender and rosemary, not my favorite scents, but it worked. I could feel the negative energy evaporating quickly.

It also helped rejuvenate me. I hadn't gotten nearly enough sleep last night. Add in the big fight today, and I was dragging. I knew the others were, too, especially Mase, who hadn't gotten more than a cat nap after coming back with Ranger, Junia, and the prisoners after dawn this morning.

While we were washing down the alpha house, Mason and Angelo cleared the pack's office building, which was only about five hundred feet away from the alpha house's detached garage. Then they cleared the garage while the rest of us washed down the office walls.

By the time everything had been cleared and purified to the witches' satisfaction, it was around eight at night. We trudged back to the alpha house, dog-tired and starving.

Thankfully, the twins and Beatrix had come out of their room at some point and made dinner and set the table. They'd left a note saying they'd already eaten and to enjoy the food, but not to disturb them.

The witches were not happy with that last part, and Angelo looked ready to storm upstairs, but the king said to sit down and eat and be grateful for their thoughtfulness.

"Thoughtfulness?" sassed Sara, the water witch and Angelo's sister. "While we worked our guts out, those bloody twins locked themselves in a bedroom with our baby cousin!"

"Well, she *is* their mate," Cole reasoned.

Wyatt and I giggled, which made her huff and cross her arms over her chest.

"You male wolves are so impulsive," she sneered. "All your testosterone-laden brains can process is find, mark, and mate, and do it as fast as possible!"

She says that like it's bad, Ashy. Sid blinked in confusion, and I grinned.

"When you find your mate, you'll understand," Ariel said with a pink blush. "The female can't help it anymore than the male can."

"I can assure you that *I* won't be dragging my mate off to a bedroom five minutes after meeting him!" Sara rolled her gray-green eyes, which were mirrors of Angelo's.

"Now, cousin, you should know not to say things like that!" Maria, the youngest and an air witch, shook her finger at Sara. "That's basically tempting the universe."

"We shall see."

89

"Tomorrow," the king interrupted their light bickering, "I want to assess where we stand. If everything looks good and safe, I'm going to have Luke bring Lilah here."

At the king's announcement, my brothers and I shared giant grins. That meant our girl could come, too.

"We need to be here for Ranger's induction as alpha," he continued, "which will probably also include Junia's luna ceremony. If I'm happy with the security here, I see no reason why my queen can't join us while we prepare for that."

"We couldn't agree more," I grinned.

"It's going to be a full house with all of us here," Cole pointed out. "We should assign spaces, especially if more people will be coming soon. We may have to take over the alpha office building and see about getting some beds and bedding over there."

"I can take care of organizing all of that," Ariel volunteered.

"Luke had his own house that might still be vacant," King Julian said. "I *think* Lilah said Junia lived with her parents, and I'm not sure if the twins did, too, or had their own place. I'll ask after dinner."

Ariel nodded.

"We're going to need more food and other supplies," Sara said. "I'll make a list, but I'm not fetching. Those ruddy twins can."

"Of course," the king agreed smoothly. "Since they know the territory and pack best, that is an excellent suggestion. Mason, you go with them."

Mase nodded in his stoic way as the king wisely ignored Sara's muttered, "Suggestion, my ass. That was an *order*."

"Should we bring the pack members back from the motel?" Wyatt asked.

"As soon as I deem it secure here. Once I do, you can link your gammas to load up the prisoners you have at Five Fangs and send them back, too." The king thought for a second, then looked back at Cole.

"When you're done eating, take some dinner over to Jay and let him know I'll relieve him in an hour. Angelo, you relieve me at dawn. We'll figure out the rest of the rota tomorrow."

"And just what am I supposed to do until dawn?" Angelo frowned.

"I don't know. Clean your guns or something."

"You can help me with the food list," Sara decided. "You'll be doing most of the cooking, anyway."

"You cook?" My ears perked up.

"Yeah. Why?" He narrowed his eyes at me. "Is there something wrong with that?"

"No, not at all, my dude. I'm just happy someone can really cook over the next couple of days. I'm horrible at it, and Wyatt's worse than horrible. Jay and Cole make basic stuff like sandwiches, which is okay, but gets boring fast. Only Mase and Posy can do real meals, and our girl isn't here."

"I see."

"Gelo does almost all the cooking when he's home," Maria chimed in. "When he's not, Sara and Beatrix do basic meals. Ariel and I are barred from the kitchen."

"Wyatt and Ash should be," Mase muttered.

Wyatt and I laughed with everyone else. We sucked and we knew it.

"Gelo mainly cooks Italian," Ariel told us, "because that's what we grew up with. If you have other requests, speak up now."

"Where should I start?" I rubbed my hands together with a grin and earned another round of laughter.

Let them laugh, Sid giggled. *We going to be eating good, Ashy!*

You know it, buddy.

91

15: And a Longer Night

Cole

Bedtime that night did not go well.

Wyatt was upset about Reuben, Ash and Mase were both dead on their feet, and Ariel had assigned us two rooms, not understanding what we meant when we said we shared. Even though we took over the bigger of the two, this room only had a queen-sized bed.

As soon as he saw that, Ash began to whine, which was unusual enough to make the rest of us stop and stare at him.

"What's wrong, Ash?" I asked.

"I don't like it. I want to sleep with my brothers."

"Jay, let's go get the mattress from the other room and drag it in here," Mase said. "Some of us can sleep on the bed and some can sleep on the floor."

"No!" Ash shouted, surprising us. "Want to be together!"

I moved closer to see his eyes.

Uh-oh, I linked the others. *Sid's in charge. Ash conked out somewhere between the dining room and here.*

Obviously, Jay snickered, *and not surprising since he only had four hours of sleep last night.*

I'll take Sid and Wy in the bed with me, I offered, *if you two don't mind the mattress on the floor?*

Sure. We'll get it set up.

Mase's voice was so tired, I grimaced. The best thing I could do to help him, though, was to take care of Ash's child-like wolf.

"Okay, little one. Come sleep with me," I said to Sid-in-Ash's-body. "Wyatt, you, too."

After we stripped down to our boxers, the three of us climbed into bed, Sid in the middle and Wyatt and me on either side. Sid dropped off almost immediately, despite Wyatt flailing around to get comfortable.

He did that for about half an hour. I wasn't surprised, considering the noise Mase and Jay made as they wrangled the mattress through the door and laid it on the floor, then went out again and came back with a stack of bedding and pillows.

After they got settled on the floor, Wyatt calmed down and I thought we were home free. I was just drifting off to sleep myself when terror jolted through the mate bond and jerked me wide awake.

Mase was already thundering at the betas, demanding to know what had happened to Posy.

Nightmare, alpha, Emerson linked us. *We can't help her with you howling at us.*

Sitting up, we all waited in silence. Well, except for Sid. He continued to sleep like the baby he was.

It seemed like forever before Em linked to tell us she was okay and sent us an image of our girl nestled against him with Mr. Nibbles in her arms.

It's her first nightmare since we found her, and we're not there to help her through it! Wyatt rumbled, then cursed himself hoarse.

I understand your feelings, alpha, Em said, *but at least you know she's in good hands. We got her. Until you get home, you can trust that we got her.*

Jay thanked him, and Em let us watch her through his eyes for a little bit.

"Why won't she link with us?" I asked after trying the mate link for the thousandth time.

"Ten bucks says she forgot," Jay chuckled.

"How can you *laugh* at this?" Wyatt was losing it. He had his fists clenched in his hair and tears in his eyes.

"Hey, it's okay." I reached over Sid to untangle his hands, then pulled him into a hug. "I know it's stressful, but she's not in any danger. She's with people who care about her."

I'm sorry for making you worry, Posy whispered through Emerson's link. *I'm all right now. Em and Ty are with me, and Mr. Nibbles is making me feel better.*

"See?" I told him and petted his head. "Look how she's waving the bunny's arm. Isn't that adorable?"

He nodded, but didn't say anything. Instead, he rested his head against my chest and lay there quietly.

When Em asked her why she wasn't linking with us, her answer made Jay grin.

Oh, yeah, she said. *I forgot I could do that now!*

For several minutes, we linked with her and reassured her that we loved her and that she hadn't bothered us, that we *wanted* to know when things like this happened. Finally, she said good night and blew us kisses, and I relaxed.

"Did he fall asleep like that?" Jay gestured to Wyatt, who still rested against my chest.

Wyatt shook his head, but didn't reply.

"Come on, Wy," I murmured. "Let's go back to sleep."

" 'Kay."

In hindsight, there were so many warning signs that I was ashamed of myself later for not picking up on even *one* of them. As it was, I didn't realize there was a problem until he wouldn't stop flailing around again. Usually, if something woke him or he got up to pee in the middle of the night, he fell right back to sleep.

"Wyatt, come snuggle in between me and Sid." I raised the sheet and motioned for him to come over. "Maybe that will help you settle."

He crawled over and wedged his back against Sid's side and wrapped his arms around my torso, then squeezed me too hard.

"Ouch!" I complained with a scowl. "Stop that. You're going to break my ribs!"

His arms relaxed, and he bent his head to kiss my side.

Confused by his behavior, I linked Mase and Jay and told them what was going on.

Wait. Did either of you—

"Sorry, Coley," Wyatt said before Mase could finish.

As soon as he called me that, we all knew.

Oh, Goddess, I groaned. *He's gone wolfy.*

Both babies out in one night. What are the odds? Jay sighed.

At least Sid hasn't been disturbed, Mase said groggily. *One at a time is manageable—*

A quiet whine interrupted him, and Sid began to flap one hand around as he unconsciously tried to find the rest of his brothers.

Without a word, Jay hauled himself up on the bed and slid in next to Sid. It was a tight fit, but if he didn't have someone on either side, Sid would look for us all night.

"I'll take Granite," Mase sighed. "You deal with Sid."

"You're exhausted. Jay and I can handle this," I tried to tell him.

He ignored me as he walked around to my side of the bed.

"Dude, really," I looked up at him, "we can—"

"*Let me have my baby brother, Cole!*" he growled.

Rolling my eyes, I got out of bed so he could reach Granite.

"Yes, Papa Bear," I smirked and ignored his glare.

#

Mason

I picked Granite up like a toddler, and he immediately wrapped his arms around my neck and his legs around my waist.

"Shh," I murmured and laid my cheek on his fluffy blond head. "Everything's going to be okay, Gran."

"You just want *him* because you can carry Wyatt's body around like that, but not Ash's gargantuan self," Cole teased with a grin.

"I could *absolutely* carry Ash if I wanted to," I grunted, "but Sid only needs babying and comfort. Granite needs help."

"I know that, Mase," he said in a soothing tone. "Humor wasn't a good idea. Sorry."

I waved off his apology and waited until it looked like they had Sid calmed down. Then I left the bedroom and carried Granite to the oversized rocker-recliner in the living room.

Sinking down in the soft cushions, I cuddled him in my lap and slowly rocked us back and forth. Dropping kisses on top of his head, I waited until I felt his breathing and heartbeat even out.

"What's wrong, Gran?" I whispered.

"Wyatt's heart hurts. It hurts *so bad*, Masey."

Taking a deep breath, I let it out slowly, upset at myself for missing the signs.

How could I be so blind and careless?

You're tired, Garnet sighed. *Give yourself a break. And you're not the only one with eyes. Cole should have noticed. He was right there with him.*

I know, but I still let him down.

You didn't, but now you can help him get back up.

Wyatt's dad, Alpha Shawn Black, was one of the best people to ever live. His passing left a scar on all our hearts, but it destroyed Wyatt. For nearly a year, he spiraled deeper and deeper into darkness.

And none of us saw it.

By the time we realized that he'd dropped the reins completely, leaving Granite in charge, he was sunk so deep into his subconscious that no one, *not even his own wolf,* could reach him. While that was awful and horrifying on its own, having Granite running the show was worse.

Imagine a toddler's mental and emotional capacity in a pre-teen's body that could turn into a few hundred pounds of deadly werewolf, and you'd have a fair idea of what those six miserable days were like.

Thank the Goddess we were able to bring him out of it before he spiraled any further - or Granite got them killed.

Of course, it happened again, but we knew what we were dealing with by then. Over time, we taught ourselves what to look for, what worked, what didn't, and how to help and support without overwhelming him. Ash even came up with a term for it - going wolfy - that had made Wyatt laugh, which had been Ash's goal.

The severity and frequency of his episodes lessened as the years passed. Although he still had lapses, none ever lasted longer than a day, and most only for a few hours.

When was the last time? I asked Garnet.

Right after Thanksgiving last fall. William was in the clinic with pneumonia, and Wyatt was babysitting Winnie.

And Winnie fell down the stairs, I recalled, *and broke his arm.*

Wyatt had felt so guilty about that, he went wolfy for a couple hours.

Looking down at him now, I wanted to cry. I hated knowing he was in so much pain that he hid because he couldn't take it anymore.

"Why does it hurt, baby brother?" I asked Granite. "Is it because of Posy's nightmare?"

"Some. And he misses her. And Gamma Reuben got hurt bad because we sent him here. And—"

"And?" I coaxed after a few moments.

"Q is mad at us," he whispered.

I sighed.

Wyatt Black was a funny, brash, vibrant, crude, daredevil dickhead that got on someone's last nerve at least twice a day - and few realized how easy it was to bruise the battered heart beneath the show.

"Well, yeah," I agreed, "he is, but you know what?"

"What?"

"He still loves you."

Granite raised his head from my chest and stared up at me with wide, innocent eyes that glittered in the moonlight.

"He does?" he whispered.

"Of course he does." I smiled down at him. "Once he calms down, Quartz will talk to you again and you two can make up."

"I did a dumb. That's why he's mad."

I nodded, wondering if he was asking me or simply processing through what had happened.

"Are *you* mad at me, Masey?"

"Me? No, I'm not mad."

"Promise?"

"I promise." Knowing Wyatt rarely remembered anything of what happened when Granite was fully in charge, I leaned down and kissed his forehead. "I love you, Gran. You're my baby brother."

"I am *not* a baby, Masey!" He glared up at me and pouted his lips.

"You'll always be the youngest of us," I explained. "That makes you the baby."

"And I'm a boy!" Now his face beamed with a smile. "That's why you call me baby brother, right?"

Goddess, this kid. Garnet rolled his eyes, but his smile was pure affection.

"Yeah. That's why. Now, I need you to be brave, okay?"

"But Masey, I don't want to! I want to talk to you."

And now we were back to a pout.

"You can link me anytime and you can come out again when Wyatt *isn't* struggling. This is not healthy for either of you, and you know that. Besides, it's getting late and I'm really tired."

"Okay, I'll do it." He nodded his head rapidly. "Masey needs me to be a good boy and be brave."

"That's right, but you know what?"

"What?"

"You're *always* a good boy, Gran."

The brilliant smile that broke over his face was one I would never get out of Wyatt, which made me treasure it all the more.

"I go sleepies after, 'kay?"

"Okay. I know you're tired, too. It's way past bedtime for little wolves."

"Yes." He nodded solemnly. "Nighty-night."

"Good night, baby brother."

He closed his eyes and laid his head on my shoulder. I pushed my foot on the floor to set us rocking again and waited for Granite to 'be brave,' which basically meant to convince Wyatt he needed to come back to the real world.

I had almost drifted off when I felt Wyatt's whole body tense.

And now for the difficult part, Garnet grumbled.

16: Exorcizing Demons

Wyatt

I kept my eyes closed and prayed I'd disappear.

By the moon, I hate myself sometimes.

"Stop beating yourself up."

Under my ear, Mason's chest rumbled with his deep voice, and his arms tightened around me a little bit.

He didn't say anything more, and I didn't feel like talking, either, although I knew he wouldn't let me get away with that for long.

The sigh I let out came from the bottom of my soul.

"Want to talk about it?" he asked.

"Why? I'm sure Granite told you everything." Like Posy, my wolf couldn't keep a secret for anything.

"I'd like you to tell me yourself."

"Just a bunch of dumb stuff," I muttered.

"It's not dumb stuff if it hurts you."

I didn't answer, but Mason had more patience than I *ever* would. He rocked us and rubbed my back and waited.

"I miss Posy," I brought up the easiest issue first.

"Yeah. It's hard being away from her. We'll see her soon, though."

"I'm still struggling with how much I hate what she went through." My hands turned into tight fists. "She shouldn't have panic attacks. She shouldn't get so scared. She shouldn't feel worthless. She shouldn't have nightmares."

"I know." He took a long, deep breath and let it out slowly. "I find comfort in knowing that she's healing. It's slow progress, and there will be steps backwards, but remember the day we met her? Compare that to how she reacted after Quartz attacked you. Yes, she panicked while it was happening, but after she calmed down, she handled it like a queen."

"True. I half thought she'd completely shut down."

I snuggled more into Mase's side, wanting comfort for what I had to say next.

"Reuben almost died because of me," I whispered as guilt racked me.

"*Not* because of you. Someone had to come deliver the papers to sever our alliance. No matter who you or I or any of our brothers sent, they would have been hurt. The person to blame for that is not you."

We rocked in silence for a bit until I could admit what hurt the worst.

"Quartz is mad and Jay's upset."

"Yeah. Granite said you did a dumb."

I snorted. That was Granite, all right.

"I didn't realize the extent of it until Posy showed me. I'm sorry, Mase, for doing that to you so often. And I want to tell Q sorry, too, but he won't link with me."

"What's Jay say?" he asked.

"Well, I haven't linked with him." I squirmed internally. "At first, he tried a bunch of times, but I ignored him, and now I'm too ashamed to link him."

"Why don't you find some time tomorrow and the two of you have a face-to-face conversation? I think that would be best."

"Yeah." I nodded, then squeezed my eyes shut. "I'm sorry. I know I keep letting you down."

He tensed and stopped rocking us. Hugging me hard, he bent his head and spoke softly in my ear.

"I want you to listen to me. Are you listening? You better be. You are *not* a burden. You are *not* a disappointment. You are *not* letting me down. You are my baby brother—"

"Mase—"

"And I love you."

And that was all it took to open the floodgates.

"I'm sorry. I'm sorry," I muttered over and over as I sobbed.

"Shh. You have nothing to be sorry for." He started rocking us again and rubbed his cheek on the top of my head. "I love you. Your brothers love you. Your mate loves you. Your family loves you. We're all here for you. And not because we *have* to be, but because we *want* to be."

I dripped snot and saltwater all over him for a few minutes before I got myself together. He must have realized the storm was over because he handed me the box of tissues from the side table. I didn't know whether I should mop him up first or myself, and he solved my dilemma by grabbing a wad of tissues and swabbing his chest.

After I blew my nose and dried up my face, I went to stand up, but he caught my shoulders and tugged me back down, then reclined the chair.

"You're staying here, baby brother," he said on a yawn. "I'm too exhausted to move, and I want you with me. We'll talk more tomorrow. For now, just go to sleep."

Shrugging, I made myself comfortable, pushing at him until he gave in with a sigh and moved where I wanted him. Once we were both settled, he started petting my head.

I didn't know why my brothers couldn't leave my hair alone. Any time they were being affectionate, the first thing they did was pet my head or give me a soft noogie.

I'd *never* admit it, not even under torture, but I loved it.

We lay there quietly, listening to the unfamiliar noises the house made, and I knew he was on the edge of sleep and only waiting for me to drop off first.

"I don't want Posy to know," I whispered. "Not yet. I'll explain to her, but not yet."

"You have nothing to be ashamed of, and she won't see you any different. You *know* she won't. But, yeah, wait until you're ready. When you do, we'll be there for you."

"You always are."

"And we always will be, baby brother," he promised and kissed the top of my head.

With a tiny smile, I snuggled closer and closed my eyes.

#

Cole

An almighty roar rattled the whole house, jolting me from sleep.

"Who pissed Mase off so early in the morning?" Ash asked in a groggy voice.

"I don't know, but we better find out before they get killed."

I leapt out of bed to find a pair of shorts and noticed Jay was gone. By the light coming from the windows, it was just after dawn, which was early for Jay to be up and about.

"Where are the others?" Ash asked as he rolled out of bed and hunted for his own shorts.

"It was a bad night," I said. "You fell asleep and left Sid in charge, then Wyatt went wolfy."

"Oh, no. Why?"

"I don't know. I was busy with Sid, and you know how Papa Bear gets about Wyatt. He carried him off, and I assume they fell asleep together somewhere."

"Did he call him baby brother?"

"And growled at me when I told him I had it covered." I rolled my eyes.

"He's going to be such a good dad," Ash smirked at me as we hustled out of the bedroom and clamored down the stairs.

Yeah, he was, which was interesting considering how Papa treated *him*.

He gets it from Mama, Topaz piped up. *He's more like her than Papa.*

100

I nodded in agreement. Mama was one of the greatest moms ever. So was Wyatt's. After our mothers had died in the sickness, Mama and Mom took Jay, Ash, and me into their homes and hearts without hesitation and cared for us as if we were their own.

"Since we don't hear any sounds of a fight," Ash said, "I think everyone might still be alive."

"Hmm. Wonder if someone tried to take Wyatt from him?" I guessed.

When we made it downstairs, I found I was partially right. After he woke up, Jay had gone looking for Wyatt and found him sacked out in the living room with Mase. He'd gotten Wyatt awake because Quartz wanted to apologize to Granite and Wyatt.

Not in front of anyone, though. That's not how Q rolled.

So Jay had taken Wyatt to the kitchen to talk, and Mase had freaked out when he woke up without his baby in his arms.

"Now that we're all awake," King Julian paused to glare at Mase, who only raised an eyebrow, "I think it's a good time for the witches to share some knowledge with us. Ariel, I trusted you when you told me not to worry about the lesser demon Nyx scented, but I know it's connected to what Cole and I found in the basement."

"I *said* we needed to talk to you about what you have locked up at the prison," Maria said.

"What—"

"Um, wait." Cutting the king off, Wyatt raised his hand as if he were back in school. "I'm going to need coffee first. *Lots* of coffee."

"And maybe some clothes, too?" Angelo scoffed, then glared at Mase. "You as well. Why are you two running around in just boxers, anyway? There are ladies present."

"Oh, we don't mind the show." Sara rested her chin on her hand as her eyes ran up and down Mase's body.

"Private property signs are all over us," Wyatt waved his hand between him and Mase. "Keep your hungry eyes off, witch."

"Honey, if you're putting perfection on display," she eyed his cut chest and abs with a smirk, "I'm going to admire it."

Wyatt opened his mouth to retort, probably crudely, but a blushing Mase grabbed his elbow and pulled him toward the stairs.

"He seems better," I murmured to Jay as they disappeared up the stairs.

"He, Granite, and Quartz had a good talk. Quartz hated knowing he caused Wyatt to go wolfy."

More like, you *hated it and Quartz hated that you were upset*, I thought to myself.

But whatever worked to clear the air between them. That was all that mattered.

# #

Jayden

"What we found in the basement," Cole paused and swallowed, then shook his head. "Wolves don't act like that."

We sat around the table after a simple breakfast of cereal and fruit - and Wyatt's precious coffee. After last night, we *all* needed a couple of cups, and I wasn't complaining about how strong he'd made it.

"What do you mean?" I asked Cole.

"There were half-mauled body parts and others without a mark on them. All were in various stages of decomposing, some as fresh as a couple of days and others so old, they were shriveled mummies."

"No intestines or internal organs anywhere," the king picked up. "No eyes, either. Blood coated the floor and splattered up the walls. I'd estimate about seven or eight total bodies' worth of parts."

Hmm. Cole's right, Quartz murmured. *No wolf, not even rogues or feral ones, wastes good meat like that.*

I grimaced at the 'good meat' comment, but admitted he was right.

"Julian, after Ariel told me that you smelled a lesser demon, I looked through the basement," Angelo said. "I didn't see any evidence of diabolical activity or rituals that would have summoned any kind of demon to this plane. I think it just used the basement as its pantry and playground."

"So there's a lesser demon working with the wolves here." The king crossed his arms over his chest and leaned back in his chair. "How do we find it?"

"I saw it when we arrived," Maria said.

"I smelled it with the one who locked me in the cage," Beatrix said from where she was squished between the twins.

"Halder?" The king's eyebrows rose. "Or one of his wolves?"

"It was the same wolf who kidnapped us and brought us here." She fiddled with her fingers, and Zayne and Zayden cuddled her closer.

"The same wolf you have locked in your prison," Ariel clarified.

"Can you please give us a simple yes or no?" I asked.

"Good luck with that." Angelo rolled his eyes.

"Straight, plain English, ladies," the king scowled. "Is Leo Halder working with a demon?"

"No, he's *possessed* by one," all four witches chorused.

Possessed? Quartz's ears perked up. *Never killed a demon before. Should be a good fight.*

"Luke MacGregor said Halder was planning an insurrection and sowing seeds of rebellion against the king," I said, tuning out Quartz's blood lust. "A possessed alpha with a pack at his command is terrible enough, but imagine if he succeeded in taking the crown."

"I'd rather *not* imagine that, thank you," King Julian said dryly.

"So it's a demon making Halder act like this?" Wyatt asked.

"We learned that his behavior began to change about a year ago," Mase said. "Could he have been possessed all that time?"

"Sure. A year is nothing to a demon." Sara shrugged.

"How did he get possessed?" Ash asked.

"Yeah, how does that happen, anyway?" Wyatt chimed in.

"We can take a peek inside his head after we exorcize the demon and find out," Sara said. "And it can happen in lots of ways. Might be a consensual contract or a forced invasion."

"Let's get the demon out and see what Halder has to say," Cole suggested. "If he didn't consent, that's one thing, but if he did—"

He left us to finish his thoughts, which Quartz was more than happy to do in vivid detail.

"If he survives the exorcism, you can interrogate him all you want." Maria shrugged.

"It could kill him?" I asked.

"He might not have enough mental landscape left to reclaim."

"I'll take that risk," the king decreed. "He knows he's a dead wolf, anyway. The only way he lives is if the demon, not him, committed the crimes."

"Very well. We'll need one of you to assist." Sara looked around the table as her eyes assessed each of us.

"You used me before." Angelo shrugged. "Why not now?"

"First, I doubt *we* will be able to banish it," Beatrix said. "A lesser demon with a year to nibble on a soul, plus the souls it consumed in the basement? Without an earth witch, we'll be lucky to draw it out. Banishing is going to be up to you."

"Second, you're too close to the air, even if you don't shift," Ariel told him. "We need someone more grounded. Like Bea said, if we had an earth witch to complete the coven, it wouldn't be a problem. For now, though, wolves are a good second best."

"I'll—" The king started.

"*NO!*" my brothers and I cut him off.

"You're too valuable," Angelo voiced what we were all thinking. "If something goes wrong, the whole kingdom might be affected."

"We'll do it," Zayne and Zayden offered.

"Thanks, mates," Beatrix smiled at each of them, "but we want *that* one."

Surprisingly enough, she pointed to me, and Quartz stirred with interest.

"Mase and I are more powerful," Cole said, "and Jay's younger than us. Let one of us do it."

"You *are* more powerful, but his wolf has an unlimited supply of something we need. Yours doesn't." Maria turned and gave me a sweet smile.

"And what's that?" I questioned, suspicious about what they wanted from Quartz.

"Unbothered brutality."

#

Mason

"I don't like this," I muttered.

"Me, either," Cole said from beside me.

We both felt the same way, that it should be one of us at risk and not our little brother. It was ingrained in us to protect the younger ones.

The girls and Jay stood in a circle around Leo Halder's limp form where it lay on the grass in the front yard. The witches had described how they'd draw on Quartz's unlimited supply of "unbothered brutality" to literally rip the demon out of Halder's soul, then Angelo would send it back to the infernal plane.

With a sigh, I crossed my arms over my chest and frowned. Angelo stood on my other side, a sleek black rifle in his hands and a pair of pistols snug in holsters under his arms.

"What are we waiting for?" I asked him.

"High noon. Sunlight is lethal to infernal creatures," he explained. "If it somehow escapes the circle and I miss it, the sunlight will slow it down and eventually kill it."

As we waited for the right moment, I watched Jay. He flexed his fingers and shuffled his feet a few times.

He's nervous, Cole linked me.

We all are. We've never dealt with demons before, I told him. *Or with any magic other than moon.*

We're making an alliance with Angelo, he said. *In case this happens again, I want a combat expert in the occult on hand.*

I nodded. Having Ariel in the pack was going to come in handy in the future. Not only would we benefit from *her* magic and knowledge, but also Angelo's.

I wonder how he's going to deal with her and Beatrix living so far away from him, I replied. *Same with Maria and Sara.*

The Moon Goddess knows best, Garnet told us before Cole could reply. *The flock and the pack were obviously always destined to entwine.*

"What should the rest of us do?" Ash interrupted our silent conversation.

"Wait and watch," Angelo said with a shrug. "The *piccoli uccelli* (little birds) will do their job, then I'll do mine. You stay out of it since none of you know what you're doing."

"Alpha Jayden, don't let go of us," Sara said as she took one of his hands and Ariel the other. "No matter what."

"I won't let go."

"It's important." She gave him a stern look. "If you do, we could die or be sucked into the infernal plane with the creature."

"I won't let go," he repeated, Quartz underscoring his voice a little and taking it to a darker timbre.

Sara nodded, and she and Ariel joined hands with the other two witches to make a circle around Halder. As they began to chant, the heavy scent of magic stung my nostrils.

I tried to link Jay, but he was either blocking it to concentrate or the witches had locked down communications.

Garnet? Can you tell how Q is doing?

He's fine. My wolf rolled his eyes at my worrying. *You know combat of any kind doesn't bother that bastard.*

I grunted in acknowledgement.

As the witches chanted, the air around Halder began to shimmer. His body jerked a few times, then went dead still. The witches seemed unaffected, but Jay dropped to his knees. He managed to keep holding the girls' hands, but his eyes rolled back in his head, and I barely restrained myself from barging over there and yanking him away from them.

Wyatt's impulse control wasn't so good.

"Jay!" he shouted and lunged forward.

"Don't!" Angelo caught him by his shoulders. "If you interrupt the circle, there'll be a backlash! Now behave or leave! I can't babysit you and be ready to kill this thing!"

I went over to Wyatt and stood next to him, giving Angelo a sharp look for putting his hands on my baby brother. Cole and Ash joined us, and we waited with clenched fists and impatient scowls.

After a few minutes, a dark and vile substance began to ooze from Halder as if his very pores were ejecting the creature. It stank of evil and something else I'd never come across before.

"Is that what the infernal smells like?" Cole asked Angelo before I could.

"I guess. I don't smell as keenly as you do. Julian, is this what your wolf noticed in the kitchen?"

"Yes." The king nodded, but never took his eyes off Halder.

The ooze began to solidify into a misshapen ball that grew four bumps, each of which slowly formed into limbs.

"Time for me to go to work." Angelo dropped to one knee and lifted the rifle butt to his shoulder. "Don't break their circle or bump into me."

Agonized screeching hurt our ears and we covered them with our hands. A gray skull rose from the center of two limbs and dull red eyes glowed deep inside the sockets above the hollow nose.

"Now, Angelo!" Ariel shouted.

The witches dropped each other's hands, the smell of magic faded, and a single shot rang out right as the ooze creature stood on its stumps of legs. The bullet flew straight through its heart and exploded out its back. The goo splattered everywhere on the grass, burning it black, but the scorching sun quickly began to evaporate it.

"Clear!" Angelo called, and my brothers and I ran to Jay.

Wyatt reached him first and checked him over, fussing until Jay waved him off. He helped him stand, and Jay turned his head to crack his neck on one side, then did the same on the other.

"That was intense," he said when we gave him curious looks.

"Are you in pain? Anything hurt?" King Julian asked.

"Nope. Just feel a little disoriented, like I rode a roller coaster upside and backward," he grinned.

"That's about right." Angelo smirked as he looked at Jay. "You did good, wolf. I puked my guts out the first time that they used me in a circle."

"He's still alive," Maria's voice broke the silence, and we all turned to see her and the other witches crouched next to Halder's motionless body. "He's not going to be in any condition to talk for a long time, but he's alive."

"Where do you want me to put him?" Angelo asked, nudging one of Halder's boots with his own.

"I'm not comfortable with him anywhere but in a cell." King Julian scratched his beard and looked unconcerned.

"He may look fine physically, but he's a bloody mess inside." Sara stood and brushed her pants off. "He has a long road to recovery and will need lots of rest and nourishing food. An overheated jail cell with only a thin mattress on the floor and no fresh water isn't good enough."

The other three witches agreed with her, and I could see we were going to have a fight on our hands if we threw him back in his cell. They had a lot more compassion than we did.

106

"He's staying locked up until I can talk with him and get to the bottom of this," King Julian said with Onyx lighting his eyes.

If Posy were here, what solution would she suggest? asked Garnet, the sly dog.

Whose side are you on, anyway? I grumbled.

Whatever side would please our mate. As you should be.

That's playing dirty, Garnet.

But, "We can make the cell more comfortable for him," is what I said aloud.

Both the king and the witches were good with that, so I helped Angelo carry Halder's dead weight back to the prison where, in my opinion, he belonged.

#

Ash

After we improved Leo Halder's cell to the witches' satisfaction, the king asked us to do a sweep of the territory while he took one last, thorough look through the alpha house and offices. Splitting up into three-person teams, we each took a section of the pack lands, checked it out, and reconvened back at the prison to check on Halder.

He was still sleeping, as Ariel had predicted he would be, and we left him to it.

It was close enough to dinner time by then that we all went up to the alpha house for a meal and found the King of Werewolves making grilled cheese sandwiches and tomato soup.

"We need to get those groceries and supplies," he said as we trooped in the back door. "Twins, you're on shopping detail after we eat."

"Beatrix is coming with us," Zayne and Zayden said at the same time.

"Of course." The king nodded as he flipped a sandwich. "By the way, as soon as I got your all-clear reports, I contacted Luke and told him to bring my queen to me."

"Posy can come, too, right?" I started to hop up and down.

"She's already on her way." King Julian smiled. "Your betas are in a convoy with Luke and Lilah."

"Excellent!" Wyatt threw his fists into the air.

We all started to link our girl, excited and talking over each other.

Guys, guys! she laughed. *I'm happy, too, but I can't understand you when you all talk at once. Emerson says we're about three hours away.*

We talked to her until the car ride started to put her to sleep, then told her how much we loved her and that we'd see her very soon.

Jay brought up where we were going to sleep tonight if our girl was with us since the set-up we had already wasn't working. Our unique arrangement often presented a problem when we traveled, and we'd had to come up with creative solutions in the past. This time was no different, except our mate's comfort took priority.

"Between the alpha house, Luke's place, and the twins' house, Ariel found everyone a space except for Matthew and Crew," I said. "If we give Ariel back our two rooms for them, that would leave the alpha office building completely empty. Let's take it over."

"Conference room," Mase said. "Biggest room there."

"We can move the table and chairs out, get three king mattresses, and put them together on the floor," Jay said while nodding. "Since it's a completely interior room, we won't need to get blinds or curtains, and there's a full bathroom right across the hall."

"I think that's the best solution," Cole agreed.

"Perfect!" I jumped up and down in my excitement.

"Let's go buy them now," Wyatt said. "And let's not forget sheets and pillows. Especially pillows. I like lots of pillows."

"We know," we all chorused, and he stuck his tongue out at us.

Zayne and Zayden gave us directions to a store and we were off. We got what we needed and paid the manager a good wad of cash to have his truck driver follow us with the mattresses. We got everything set up in the conference room, including Wyatt's multitude of pillows, and then we went up to the alpha house to wait with everyone else.

To kill time, my brothers and I settled down to watch a movie in the living room with the king, the witches, Zayne, and Zayden.

"What are you watching?" Angelo asked, as if our choice would determine him staying or not.

After a few minutes of scrolling through the horror section, Cole clicked on *Prey for the Devil*, and Angelo frowned and shook his head.

"Too scary for the Angel of Death?" King Julian teased with a smirk.

Angelo flipped him off, said he was going to do some meal planning in the kitchen, and left the room. Chuckling, the king rested his head back on the couch and propped his feet up on the coffee table, and his foggy eyes were all the evidence we needed to know he was linking his lovely lady.

Ten minutes into the movie, I realized Angelo had the right idea. The movie had an interesting premise, but was just a rehash of other exorcist movies. Bored now, I started throwing popcorn for Wyatt to catch in his mouth and wasn't paying much attention to anything else.

Fortunately, Sid was.

Ashy, something up with the witchies!

Lifting my head, I looked over and saw Sara and Maria slowly turn in unison toward the east. Their eyes began to glow with an eerie light, which made Sid pace anxiously.

Witchies are scary, Ashy!

They won't hurt us, buddy. Magic is new to you, to both of us, which can make it seem scary. Since Ariel's going to be in our pack now, we'll be around it more and can get used to it. Then it won't be scary anymore.

"Gelo!" Sara shouted. When he popped his head around the doorway, she said, "Go shower and put on fresh clothes. And no weapons! You want to make a good impression, not be intimidating."

"What? Why? What's going on?"

"Our mates approach," they chorus in a monotone, which weirded Sid out again.

"If your mates can't handle meeting me as I am—"

"Gelo," Maria cut him off in a gentle tone, "*your* mate approaches, too."

17: Risks and Rewards

~Three years ago~

Emerson

Wretched cheap boots, I thought as I trudged toward the well-lit diner on this lonely stretch of road. *My feet are freezing!*

I could sense I was near a pack, so I didn't dare shift. Cove might be mistaken for a rogue instead of a lone wolf. We were strong and had gotten tough surviving on our own during the last year and a half, but we couldn't take on a patrol of warriors intent on killing a rogue.

I'd heard about an enormous pack formed out of what remained of five others after the sickness decimated them. Since every alpha had declined my request to join, I had decided to head north and see if Five Fangs would be more open-minded.

Which was how I found myself outside Roger's Diner at dusk on an early October evening. Looking through the windows, I saw the place was nearly empty except for a big table at the back where some guys were cutting up.

When I first saw the diner, I'd hoped I could get a job there; my cash was running dangerously low, and I needed those new boots before winter hit. Seeing the guys inside, however, I hesitated with my hand on the door. If they were humans, I wasn't going to have a problem. If they were shifters, they'd smell that I was, too, and who knew how that would go down?

I studied them a little closer. There were six of them, and they all looked about my age or a little younger. I was fairly sure they were shifters, since they were taller and much more built than normal human teen males. As they stole food from each other, they laughed loud enough for me to hear outside and seemed so happy and carefree, it made me jealous.

Try, Cove encouraged me. *They don't look mean.*

They're probably shifters. It could be dangerous.

I'm lonely, Em. You are, too. Try. Please?

I sighed. Neither of us were cut out to be lone wolves. We missed having a pack, the bond it brought, and friends.

All right, but if we get killed, I'm blaming you.

Going inside, I heard a little bell jingle over my head, and the smell of wolves went right up my nose. Definitely shifters, then. I scented both alpha and beta blood and felt a ton of power, which told me at least one of them already led a pack.

110

Swallowing hard, I stepped further inside, and the man at the serving counter straightened up from his newspaper.

"Hey, kid," he said over the noise of guys mucking about. "Sit anywhere. When you know what you want, flag me down."

"Uh, a cheeseburger would be great." Before he could turn away, I added, "I was wondering if you were hiring at all. I can wash dishes, bus and wait tables, clean, and even cook a little."

"You a lone wolf?"

And he's a shifter, too. Great. What have you gotten me into, Cove?

"For now." I gave him a curt nod. "I heard about this pack called Five Fangs and thought I'd see if they might need a beta. I can tell I'm close. How far off am I?"

"You want Five Fangs? You found it." The man nodded his head toward the guys in the back. "First alpha is here with his beta and the other four alphas-to-be. You picked the right night for a cheeseburger, kid."

First alpha? Four alphas-to-be? I'd never heard of such things.

The noise behind me came to a dead stop, and I lifted my chin before turning around. All six guys were staring at me with a variety of expressions except for one. *His* face was as blank as a snow-covered field as he stood up and started walking over to me. Preparing for a fight, I let my backpack drop to the floor and flexed my fingers.

He came to a stop three feet in front of me and narrowed his gray eyes as he stared at me. The power radiating off him made me want to take a step back. It was dead hard to hold my ground and his gaze, but I did.

So he's the alpha.

He was an inch or two taller than me, although I had a broader frame. My size had saved me in the past, but right now I was basically skin and bones under my layers of clothing. It had been months since I'd had a stable job and a safe place to sleep, and the weeks of hiking and scavenging had taken their toll.

"Why'd you get kicked out of your pack?" he asked after studying me for another minute.

Not every lone wolf is made from being banished by their alpha. I could have been born in the wild, or orphaned, or half a dozen other scenarios. He'd guessed correctly, though, and I didn't bother to ask how.

"I'm gay."

Dude did not react. At all. After a few seconds, he tilted his head slightly to the side.

"And?"

"There's no 'and' to it." I shrugged. "I'm not willing to take a female as a chosen mate when I turn eighteen. I want my Goddess-given mate, even if that means I can't make pups to replenish a pack. My father, the alpha of Gray Shadows, refused to accept that."

His expression remained impassive as he stared at me.

"You have beta blood."

It wasn't a question, but I still gave a quick nod.

Then his eyes whited out as he linked someone, probably the guys behind him, before returning to normal.

"Alpha Mason Price." He held out his hand.

"Emerson Jones." I took his hand and shook it.

"Come meet my brothers and my beta." Looking at the man at the counter, he said, "Roger, bring him some food. Lots of it, too. From the look of him, he could use it. Put it on our bill."

He turned and headed back to their table as my cheeks turned dull red. I hated charity, but by the moon, I was hungry!

For a second or two, I debated whether or not to follow, but Cove reminded me that we'd wanted to see what Five Fangs could offer us. Since the Moon Goddess had kindly delivered us into the alpha's lap, I could hardly back out now.

When I reached their table, Alpha Mason pulled out a chair and gestured for me to sit in it.

"This is Emerson Jones. You heard the rest."

"Gray Shadows, huh? You're better off away from that pack of pussies," said a black-haired guy who looked my age. "Cole Barlow. Welcome to Five Fangs."

He stuck his hand out, and I reached across the table to shake it. The rest introduced themselves, and I kept my cool despite being surrounded by six gorgeous, powerful guys.

The close bond of the alpha and alphas-to-be was almost tangible, but confusing as well. Alpha Mason had called them brothers, but none of them resembled each other, and they all had different last names.

Despite their friendly welcome, I couldn't lower my guard. Two months ago, things had been looking promising at Cold Moon, too, until I met the luna.

That bitch! Cove snarled as my smile faltered at the memory. *Should have killed her!*

And had the whole pack on our tail as we ran. I rolled my eyes at him, then figured I'd better see if I would have a crazy luna to deal with here.

"Do you have a luna, Alpha Mason?" I asked, flicking my eyes to his face.

"No, we don't."

"Goddess, I hope we don't have to wait too long after Wyatt turns eighteen." Ash wiggled in his seat, sending his dark curls flying wildly. "I can't wait until we find her! I'm going to love her so much!"

"She's going to be so sweet." Cole's green eyes softened. "As sweet as honey."

"Wait until she finds out there's five of you," Beta Matthew muttered into his soda. "Poor girl."

"It'll be fine." Wyatt waved one hand. "The Moon Goddess said so."

I looked around at their faces, torn between concern and confusion.

Are they crazy?

"No. We're not crazy," Jayden chuckled while Wyatt giggled and Ash roared with laughter.

Oops. Said that out loud.

Cole explained that the Goddess had appeared to them in a dream several years ago. Although not related, the five of them were as close as brothers, and she'd explained that multiple mates would only tear them apart right when the new pack needed them to be tighter-knit than ever.

"So she said she was going to gift us with a mate to share," Jayden continued the story. "When our first pup arrives, it will finish solidifying Five Fangs and dissolve our individual packs."

"She said we're going to have to be very patient, but she has the perfect girl for us." Wyatt's smile grew dreamy.

"You're going to have to work hard on the patience thing over the next three years." Cole shot him a dark glare.

"I can be patient! I can have all the patience in the world if it's for our mate. *You're* the one who needs to work on your temper."

As the two bantered, I chuckled. I liked these guys. I hoped I had a place here.

I hope so, too, Cove whispered. *I like these wolves.*

You're talking to their wolves?

Yep! He bounced around in my head. *Two are funny. Two are silly babies. One is quiet, but nice. The other does not speak. He is grumpy.*

Alpha Mason's wolf?

No, Jayden's. The others say not to bother him.

Then don't bother him. As Cove went back to talking with the other wolves, I asked myself if I should take the chance with this pack. *They know I'm gay and won't be a pup-making machine, so that shouldn't be an issue. They're going to need four more betas, and I'm strong, fast, and dependable.*

My enthusiasm suddenly ground down to nothing. If they offered me a beta position, I'd have to dedicate my life to protecting their luna. What if she turned out to be as horrible as the one at Cold Moon? Could I do that?

As my mind whirled, I sat in silence and bit my bottom lip, and a hand came down on my shoulder.

"Chill, my dude," Ash advised me with a smile. "Just eat and enjoy the moment."

So I did. Before I knew it, I was scarfing down the best cheeseburger I'd ever had in my life and laughing hysterically as Wyatt shoved a French fry up each nostril and mocked Cole over something.

"All right, Emerson Jones, the boys want to keep you." Alpha Mason stood up, pulled out a pocket knife, and moved closer. "If you want to join Five Fangs, give me your hand."

"You're inducting him into the pack right here and now?" Ash squeaked.

"Why wait?" the alpha shrugged.

They're either really good or really bad judges of character, I chuckled silently.

I think good, Cove yipped happily.

"Papa is *so* going to give you an ass-chewing," Cole warned him.

"He gives me an ass-chewing every day, anyway." Alpha Mason shrugged. "Might as well do something to earn it for once. Besides, I don't need *anyone's* permission. He gave up that right when he handed me the reins of both Great Rocks and Five Fangs."

Making my choice, I stood up and held out my hand. The alpha slit my thumb, then his own, and smashed them together. Moon magic danced between us and, just like that, I was a member of Five Fangs.

As everyone took turns giving me a bro-hug, my chest burned. One hot tear streaked from the corner of my eye, and I swiped at it with a red face, ashamed to be caught acting so soft in front of my new alpha and pack members.

"Hey, it's okay," Jayden said quietly and reached up to pat my shoulder. "Everything's going to be all right now."

"Yeah, dude, you can relax." Wyatt grinned. "You're home."

#

~*Present day*~

Posy

"I think I'd like the stones to go all the way around."

The queen and I had slept a good bit as Emerson drove Jayden's SUV and Luke kept him company in the front seat. Once we were awake again, we started talking about wedding ring designs for my mates. Queen Lilah shared her idea to incorporate the stones their wolves were named for, and I loved it!

"Because a circle represents forever, right?" I smiled at her. "And their wolves are mine forever, too."

"It's a charming way to include their wolves, which will flatter and please them," she agreed.

I couldn't wait to sketch out my ideas and see about having the rings made. The betas had agreed to help me and keep the designs secret from my mates. They were going to love them; I just knew it!

"All right, everyone," Emerson said. "We've crossed into Tall Pines territory. Another thirty minutes should see us at the alpha house."

The queen squealed and I bounced in my seat. We reached for our bags simultaneously and brought out brushes and started to straighten up our hair. I'd missed Ash doing mine for me; the only style I could really do was a high ponytail. Knowing they'd want to pet my hair, I ended up brushing it out and leaving it down.

As soon as Emerson brought the car to a stop, the queen flung her door open and was off to find the king, Luke following close behind her. I was super excited to see my mates, too, and unbuckled my seat belt only to notice Emerson hadn't moved. I could see his dark brown eyes in the rear-view mirror. They swirled with emotions, but the only one I recognized was fear.

"Em? What's wrong?"

"I, um." He swallowed hard and met my eyes in the mirror, then whispered, "I smell my mate."

Joy bloomed in my heart, and I clapped my hands.

"That's great, Em! Come on! Let's go meet her!"

"Uh, about that." He rubbed the back of his neck and dropped his eyes. "Yeah. Never mind. I'm ... going to stay here for a bit."

"What? Don't you want to meet your mate? I'll go with you if you want."

"No, that's okay. Thanks." His shoulders curved down and his voice turned to a husky whisper. "You go ahead, luna bunny. Go to the alphas."

He worry she going to reject him? Lark tilted her head, as confused as I was. *Any girl lucky to have Em as mate. Cove a good wolf and Em a good man.*

I shook my head, not understanding what was wrong, but determination filled me. He was going to meet his mate, even if it was kicking and screaming.

Scowling, I opened my mouth, but my mates started linking me.

Where are you, princess?

Cutie! We need your hugs and kisses!

We missed you, sweetness.

Honey, we're dying to see you.

Little flower? Is everything okay?

Um, guys? I interrupted them. *Emerson is having a ... problem. He says he smells his mate, but won't get out of the car.*

They were silent for a long moment.

Posy, Emerson is gay, Cole said at last. *For his own reasons, he kept it a secret from most people, but if he's found his mate, the truth is going to come out now whether he wants it to or not.*

Okay. And? I asked, worried for my friend and not understanding the issue.

Sweetness, do you even know what being gay means?

No, not really.

He likes boys, Mason said in his blunt way.

Do you mean like as in the way you five like each other? Or—

No, honey, Cole cut me off. *Like as in the way we feel about you and you feel about us. He's attracted to males, not females.*

So, he's scared because he doesn't want anyone to know about the gay?

Ash giggled for some reason, but Mason and Jayden agreed that was probably the case.

What should I do? I want to help him.

Convince him to get out of the car, sweetness, Jayden said, *and the mate bond should do the rest. We'll explain 'the gay' to you later.*

Who might his mate be? I asked. *Would that information help me convince him?*

Uh, cupcake, we're pretty sure it's Angelo del Vecchio, unless the witches are all screwed up, which they might be because I don't know if Angelo is even gay. If they did *mix things up, the only other guy it could be is—*

Is who? I coaxed when Ash fell silent.

Leo Halder, he whispered. *No one else is here. The rest of the pack is at the motel, in our prison, or dead.*

Oh, no. The Moon Goddess wouldn't be that cruel, would she? To give a teddy bear like Emerson a mate like that monster?

To be fair, the boys had explained to me that Leo Halder was possessed by a demon. No one, however, knew how he'd gotten possessed or how much he'd participated in willingly.

116

Okay, definitely don't use any of that to convince him, I told myself, then linked my mates once more. *Give me a few minutes of quiet, please, then I'll be out. I promise.*

I closed the link on their whining, wiggled between the two front seats and over the console, and sat next to Emerson. Taking one of his giant paws in both of my hands, I tugged on it until he looked at me.

"My mates explained that you like boys. I don't understand the gay completely, but why are you upset for people to find out? You're still the same Emerson. You're still my beta and friend."

"Being gay cost me everything once before," he mumbled. "My family, my friends, my birth pack. I don't want to go through that again. If I lost Five Fangs and all of you, I—"

He stopped talking and drew in a deep breath.

"Why would you? I support you, your alphas support you, and I'm sure your brother betas do, too." With a tiny smile, I squeezed his hand. "No one here is going to turn their back on you for being who you are."

"But what if he rejects me? What if the Moon Goddess made a mistake and he isn't gay or she gave me a girl? What if—"

"What if he doesn't?" I cut him off. "What if she didn't? What if this ends up being the best day of your life? What if you find a kind of happiness you never thought possible?"

Getting to my knees on the seat, I dropped his hand and grabbed his bulging shoulders and shook him. Well, *tried* to shake him. He was a big, solid guy.

"You're going to love him and he's going to love you and what anyone else thinks of that isn't going to matter. Now go find your mate, Emerson Jones!"

#

Wyatt

All of us gathered in front of the Tall Pines alpha house as vehicles began to come up the drive.

The first to park was Tristan's Jeep, and he and Tyler bailed out quickly. Tristan because he wanted to get to Ariel faster and Tyler probably because Tristan's old-man driving had made him antsy. Tristan ran over to Ariel and picked her up and kissed her senseless. Tyler, on the other hand, stayed at the Jeep and looked around curiously, and I figured he was waiting for the other betas.

Waiting for his luna, Granite corrected.

Matthew's truck was the next one to arrive, and he and Crew jumped out and stretched, then joined Tyler. They stood chatting for a moment, then turned to watch as Jay's SUV came up the drive with Emerson at the wheel.

117

"Mmm!" Sara took a deep breath in through her nose. "My mate smells like rain!"

Maria bounced up and down and clasped her hands under her chin, reminding me of Posy when she got excited, and my heart squeezed. I'd missed her so much the past couple of days.

Only a few more minutes, Granite yipped as he danced around in my head.

"Mine smells like lavender!" Maria squealed.

"What about mine?" Angelo asked.

"We don't know," Sara retorted. "We can only smell our own."

"But we can *sense* that your mate is with them," Maria said kindly.

His hands reached for the pistol butts at his waist. When they didn't find them, they clenched into fists and dropped to his sides.

"You can't smell your mate?" I asked him.

I could smell our girl, but she hadn't gotten out of the SUV yet, and my brothers and I were trying to wait patiently. Talking with the del Vecchio flock helped to distract me.

"He doesn't have a bird spirit, so *no,* he won't be able to smell his mate. Don't make him feel bad for it!" Sara snapped at me.

"We're not even sure if he'll feel the mate bond or the sparks," Maria said much more gently than her sassy pants cousin.

"Bro! That sucks!" I clapped a hand on Angelo's shoulder and squeezed in sympathy. "How will you know who's your mate then?"

"Not sure." He reached for his guns again, and his empty hands fell to his sides. "Not sure how any of this is going to work. Maybe they're wrong about it all, and maybe they're right. I've learned to roll with it. You can't fight fate, anyway. That bitch always wins in the end."

"Amen." I grinned and dropped my hand.

"Alpha Wyatt, which one is mine, please?" Maria reached over and tugged on my sleeve, her hazel eyes smiling up at me.

"Um, I don't know? I'm not the Moon Goddess." I scowled at her.

Posy was linking us, and I wanted to concentrate on her. She said something was wrong with Emerson, which was why they were still sitting in his SUV. My brothers were getting it under control, though, and I knew I'd see our girl in a few minutes. That gave me enough patience to focus on what this itty bitty witchy at my elbow was yammering about.

"I know that, you silly puppy! My mate is the one with midnight black hair right there!" She pointed her pinkie finger at Matthew.

Granite let out a hurt woof at the 'silly puppy' comment, but I figured the poor girl didn't deserve any more payback than having Matthew as her mate.

"That's Mase's beta, Matthew Rose. Good luck, tiny." I patted her head and she pouted up at me. "Go say hi."

With a happy squeal, she took off across the yard at a dead run. Thankfully, Matthew was quick, both in intelligence and reflexes. I saw it in his face the second he realized his mate was hurtling toward him. His bright blue eyes grew wide with surprise, then joy, and he grinned and held out his arms to catch her.

"What's my mate's name, please, alpha?" Sara asked, which was much more polite and subdued than *anything* I'd heard out of her mouth since I'd met her. "He arrived in that black pick-up truck with Maria's mate."

I looked where she was pointing to see Crew with his nose up and his nostrils spread wide. Although his usual calm expression never faltered, I could see his eyes glowing with wolf-light.

"Crew Myers. He's Jay's beta."

"Thank you, Alpha Wyatt." She inclined her head, then began to walk gracefully across the yard.

"Is she bipolar?" I asked Angelo out of the side of my mouth.

"She's a water witch. Everyone thinks it's the fire witches that are the hardest to deal with, but it's really the water ones. Fire is always going to burn and you know it. You just adjust for how high and hot the flames get. Water, though?" He let out a low whistle. "Think of the ocean and how it can go from becalmed to hurricane in a heartbeat, and that's a water witch."

"Out of curiosity, what about air and earth witches?"

"No experience with earth witches. I've heard they're the most calm and easygoing, but also the most powerful. It takes a lot to get them to lose their temper, but when they do, they wreck everything. The *piccoli uccelli* (little birds) want to find one so they have a full coven. That's been on their radar for a couple of years now. Anyway, as for air witches, can't you tell anything from meeting Ariel and Maria?"

"Not really." I shrugged. "Jay and Mase probably have it figured out, but I don't pay enough attention. And I've only talked to either of them for maybe ten minutes in total. I *did* notice that they're both very kind."

"They *are* kind and crazy intelligent, but flighty as the birds they shift into. What my grandpa called book smart and life dumb. They get upset rather than angry, although they can be pushed too far. When that happens, watch out. Maria especially likes to throw things, and she doesn't need her hands to do it."

119

"Ha ha ha!" I laughed as I envisioned the future with witches in the pack. "Tristan would never purposely do anything to make Ariel angry, but Matthew is going to have some interesting times ahead."

"What about this Crew guy? Is a water witch going to be too much for him?"

"Nah. He's about the most zen guy you'll ever meet. Ha ha ha! I remember one time, I accidentally set his shoe on fire and dude just took it off and casually threw it into the fire pit. Didn't even get mad at me. Ha ha ha!"

Angelo looked over at me with furrowed brows.

"How do you accidentally set—"

"To be honest, I don't even know." I shrugged and made an 'oh, well' face. "Things like that happen around me *all* the time."

"Your poor mate," he muttered.

"Speaking of," my heartbeat accelerated as she *finally* got out of the vehicle, "here she comes!"

With that, I took off, aware that my brothers were running with me.

#

Angelo del Vecchio

If they thought about it at all, my cousins believed I was straight. Or at least, I thought they did. With witches, it was hard to know. They saw so much, but could be blind little bats, too.

And sometimes, just the 'little bats' part.

I never had any magic. Not even a fizzle. No one could tell me why.

I never got my animal spirit when I turned twelve, either. Again, no one could explain it.

Nothing like this had ever happened before in our recorded family history.

I was a glitch. A dud. A botch. A defect.

My family worked hard to convince me otherwise, but I knew the truth.

To make it up to them, I decided to become the flock's protector. I learned anything anyone was willing to teach me, studied languages and ancient texts, and became an expert in as many forms of combat as I could. I lived in the gym the rest of my time, hardening and strengthening my body and taking my cardio to the next level.

When there was no one left in the flock to teach me anything, I sought out others, in both supernatural and human communities, and trained with them. Guns of all kinds, swords, knives, fists, teeth, feet - I learned to fight with anything and everything.

My plan was going fine until I realized I liked guys more than girls. I'd never really paid attention to girls, too busy with everything I wanted to accomplish, but hormones kicked in eventually. For about a year, I wrestled with the decision to come out. Some of the older members of the family were very traditional, and I feared they might see it as yet another defect in Angelo Joseph del Vecchio's faulty wiring.

After the sickness swept through our flock, I was suddenly alone with four little witches looking up at me with devastated eyes. Expressing my sexual preferences dropped right to the bottom of my priority list. There was no one left to come out to, anyway.

As the girls got older, they teased me about finding a mate, and I told them it wasn't going to happen. A couple of years ago, Ariel and Sara ganged up on me and demanded to know why I thought I wouldn't have a mate, and I made up some lame-ass excuse that neither a shifter nor a witch would want someone who might give them 'normal' babies.

They'd let up after that, for which I was grateful, but I sometimes caught them staring at me with knowing eyes.

Freaking witches.

I was brought out of my depressing thoughts when the new arrivals began to move forward. One fire-haired girl broke away from the massive man she was walking with and sprinted ahead. She was breathtakingly beautiful, and I wasn't surprised when Julian caught her in a bear hug and swung her around and around.

It's good to be the king, I smirked to myself.

Since my little *streghe* (witches) ditched me, I was left to the process of elimination to find my mate.

I let my eyes go first to the guy who'd been walking with the queen. Honestly, he was gorgeous, but the dude's dominance echoed in every long stride. When Gisela collided with him and he let her tackle him down to the grass, I breathed a sigh of relief and stopped watching.

Good. Being submissive is not in my nature.

Looking around, I saw a blond kid. He was a real cutie, no doubt, but he was *young.* I didn't think he was even eighteen yet, but knew he was a Five Fangs betas. Maybe he just had a baby face? Regardless, I hoped it wasn't him.

I may be a glitch, but I ain't into that daddy's baby boy kink.

A field of blue fabric blocked my gaze. Shocked, I realized I'd been so fixated on finding my mate that I hadn't even noticed this guy's approach. Yet here he stood, a foot in front of me, his wide shoulders level with my eyes - and I was *not* a short guy.

Careless, Gelo, and careless can get you killed.

Irritated with myself, treacherous hope, and everything else now, I grabbed the dude's arm, intent on shoving him aside so I could find my *piccoli uccelli* (little birds) and *make* them tell me who my mate was.

"Can you please move your giant carcass?" I growled. "I want to—"

Tingles in my fingertips turned to sparks that spread up my arm. Slowly, I turned my eyes to where my hand gripped his hard bicep.

"Find."

The sparks weren't going away. If anything, they were getting stronger.

"My."

My eyes traveled up his arm to his shoulder, then the base of his throat.

"Mate."

Looking up at his face, I fell into a pair of dark brown eyes.

"So, uh, you're Emerson, my mate. No, I mean, I'm Emerson, my mate. No, sorry, *you're* my mate. So, ah, yeah." His thick eyelashes fanned down for a moment, then he opened his eyes and tried again. "Um, hi?"

Oh, yeah. A smile spread across my face as pink streaked across his. *This one is mine. All mine and mine alone.*

And the world would burn before I ever let him go.

18: Practice

Posy

Leaving Emerson to make his own decision, I jumped out of the car and let my eyes roam the area for my mates.

I wasn't surprised to see them sprinting toward me in a little pack. They all wore giant smiles, even Mason! That made me so happy to see; he was usually stone-faced, even with his brothers.

I dropped my bag and ran to meet them. In seconds, I was squished in a group hug as all of the octopuses tried to get a tentacle around me. After they'd each had a chance to hug me, Ash used his height to pluck me out of the mass of limbs and sat me on his hip like I was a child.

"We missed you, cupcake! Did you miss us even a little bit? You didn't link with us very often."

Hearing the uncertainty in his voice, I grabbed two handfuls of his curls and tugged him closer, then kissed him until I needed air.

"I missed all of you *so* much," I said as I drank in his delicious scent. "I thought about you all the time. I didn't link because I was afraid I'd interrupt what you were doing. What if I distracted you while you were in the middle of a fight? I couldn't bear being the reason you lost focus and were hurt."

"Makes sense, I guess, but I missed your sweet voice. Did the betas take care of you?"

"Of course they did." I kissed his jaw. His five-o'clock shadow pricked my skin, and I pulled back and rubbed my nose. "Itchy, waffle!"

"*Waffle?*" Cole and Jayden chorused as Wyatt snickered and Mason snorted.

"He smells like maple syrup." I shrugged.

As I looked down at them, I realized how high up I was. I swung my wide eyes back to Ash.

"Is this what it's like to be so tall? Is this how you see the world all the time?"

"Yep! You want to be even taller?" His dark eyes snapped with mischief.

I wasn't sure what he meant, but I trusted him. Every day, I was growing more and more secure in the knowledge that none of these boys would deliberately hurt me or allow me to be hurt.

Still, the ground was already a long, long way down.

"Okay," I said hesitantly.

"Ash." Mason's voice was loaded with warning, and Ash rolled his eyes at him.

"Relax, Papa Bear."

Papa Bear?

That made me giggle, but as Ash suddenly swung me up on his shoulders, my giggles turned into a shriek.

Although his hands held my calves tightly, I was scared and clung to his head. My pulse sped up, my lungs weren't working right, and my whole body shook.

"How's the view, princess?" Ash chuckled.

With a whimper, I pried my death grip from his head and made grabby hands at the first person I saw, who happened to be Mason. He held his arms up for me, but I was too frightened to jump.

"Put her down, Ash. She's panicking."

"Shit!"

"Language!" Cole snarled.

As Ash crouched down, Mason slid his hands under my arms and pulled me to him. I wrapped my arms around his neck and my legs around his torso and held on tightly.

"I'm sorry, Posy." Ash patted my shoulder. "I didn't mean to scare you."

I nodded, but didn't take my face out of Mason's throat.

"You're okay," Mason whispered in my ear. "You're okay."

He rubbed one hand up and down my back while his other arm slid under my bum to support my weight. Then he walked around with me until I calmed down.

"I'm sorry," I murmured. "I don't know why I get so stupid sometimes."

"Oh, my little baby, you're not stupid. It's not stupid to be afraid of something."

I decided to agree to disagree with him on that one. Lifting my head, I laid my palms on either side of his face and stared into his serious gray eyes.

"Junia told the queen that you helped Ranger rescue her." I tilted my head with a tiny frown. "You sneaking into Tall Pines at night was not part of the plan you shared with me."

"I know, but we had reasons for not telling you." Mason dropped his forehead to mine. "Mostly, we didn't want you to worry. I wasn't in any real danger. Between us, Ranger, Gisela and I could have handled nearly anything short of a full-pack attack."

"Good. I'm glad you can take care of yourself. I'm proud of how dependable and responsible you are. I'm sure Ranger knew you had his back so he could concentrate on his mate."

"I don't know about that." Pink skated across his cheekbones.

Oh. He's not used to compliments. I need to remember to give him some more often.

"Well, I do." I smiled, then leaned in and kissed him.

He angled his head and slid his tongue along the seam of my lips until I opened up. As he deepened the kiss, his hands cupped my bum cheeks. He squeezed them, and a funny little noise slipped out, surprising me. Mason grinned against my mouth, though, so I figured the weird sound was okay.

After he broke away, he stared into my eyes with a bright smile that I returned.

"Posy, are you okay now?" Wyatt touched my elbow.

Tearing my eyes away from Mason's handsome face, I met Wyatt's sparkling blue eyes.

"I'm fine," I promised and held my arms out to him.

He looked at Mason, who gave him a short nod, then took me in his arms and cradled me against his heart.

"Did you do what you said you were going to do?" I stretched up to whisper in his ear.

"I did." He nodded and his eyes grew solemn. "Granite and I talked to Quartz, and I apologized to all my brothers."

A big smile breaking across my lips, I threw my arms around his shoulders.

"I'm so proud of you, my fifth star!" I squeaked and squeezed him hard.

"Be proud of me, too, Posy! I found Ariel's little sister!" Ash stood in a superhero pose - fists on his hips and chest puffed out. "I rescued her from the birdcage she was in."

"Good job, waffle!"

He grinned and brushed my hair behind my ears, then kissed my nose.

"Do you forgive me for scaring you earlier?" he asked.

"Of course. You didn't do it to be mean." Still wrapped around Wyatt, I leaned up and gave Ash a quick kiss.

"Are you okay with more than one of us touching you at a time?" Wyatt asked, shuffling me in his arms to a more comfortable position.

"Of course I am. You're all my mates. Jayden and Ash kissed me at the same time the morning that you marked me, and it nearly blew my mind!"

My happy smile faltered when I thought of something, and my breathing became sharp and short.

"Wait. Is that bad? Does that make me bad? Father— Father said I was a bad girl. Father said bad girls were whores and sluts who—"

I couldn't get any more words out for the panic clogging my throat.

125

"Stop, Posy." Wyatt bounced me up and down and pushed my face in his neck. "I only asked because I wanted you to be comfortable. We love touching you, and we love that you don't mind more than one of us wanting to touch you at once. You are not bad. It is perfectly normal to want your mates and vice versa."

"You mean it?" I breathed.

"Yes, and if anyone ever *dares* to call you a slut or a whore, I will end them. You are a good girl. The goodest good girl in the world, and I love you."

"I love you, too." I kissed his mate mark, and a hard shudder rippled through his body.

"Forgive us, Posy." Cole stroked my hair. "We've been reunited with you for five minutes, and we made you panic twice."

"No, it's my fault. I'm sorry," I told him as I snuggled into Wyatt's chest, so embarrassed that I wished I could crawl into his skin.

"Honey, you don't have anything to be sorry for."

Drawing my face out of Wyatt's neck, I turned my eyes to Cole and hesitated at his red, tense face.

He angry at Alpha Briggs, not you, Lark said. *I no think he ever get mad at you.*

Knowing her words were true, I unwound myself from Wyatt and reached for Cole. He gathered me up in his arms as Wyatt stepped back. Stuffing his face in my neck, Cole's long stubble rubbed against my skin and made me quiver, and I let out a shaky breath.

"There's nothing to forgive. Ash was being playful and Wyatt asked a question. I love you all so much. Thank you for being patient with me when I act stupid or panic over dumb things."

"Like Mase said, you aren't dumb or stupid."

He kissed my mate mark, making tingles explode down my spine, and that funny sound came out of my mouth again.

"I'm sorry," I muttered, squirming with embarrassment. "I didn't mean to make that noise."

He raised his head and grinned at me.

"Are you kidding? I love your moans. We all do. Moan as often and as loudly as you want."

Still red-faced, I turned the conversation to him.

"The king told Queen Lilah that you went with him to deal with some nasty things in the basement, but were able to rescue Gamma Reuben." My eyes searched his, looking for distress or trauma.

"It was pretty nasty." He agreed with a nod. "I'm just glad we got there in time to get Reuben out alive."

"How is he?"

"The witches put him into a deep sleep. Sort of like a coma, from what I can tell. Once his body heals, they'll wake him up and work on his mental and emotional health."

"I'm sorry you had to deal with that," I whispered and pecked his cheek. "And I'm proud of you for holding it together so you could help the king and rescue our gamma."

"It's my job, but thank you, darling girl. Your heart is so sweet."

"It is, isn't it?" Jayden laid his head on Cole's shoulder and stared into my eyes. "Our sweet-hearted sweetheart. You're beautiful inside and out. You know that?"

Feeling bashful, I dropped my eyes to the ground, but Jayden slipped his fingers under my chin and lifted my face to meet his twinkling eyes.

He's so flirty! It makes my insides squirm!

He flirts because he know that, Lark smirked. *Flirt back, girl!*

"Hug me, dragon?" I pooched out my bottom lip and gave him puppy dog eyes.

"Oh, my Goddess." He grimaced and laid his hand over his heart. "You can't, Posy. You can't use those eyes."

I wanted to giggle, but forced myself to hold it in and made my eyes bigger.

"Come here," he groaned and held out his arms.

"Bwahaha!" I cackled and jumped from Cole's arms to his.

That was hardly evil, Quartz linked me, his eyes rolling. *He would have hugged you without the theatrics.*

I know that, Quartz, I stuck my tongue out at him. *I only wanted to play with him a little bit.*

You mean play him. We need to work on your manipulation skills, little one.

Oh, yes, please! Just think of all the havoc I could cause with a few tricks!

Goddess, what have I done? he sighed.

"What are you and Quartz talking about behind my back?" Jayden's eyebrows drew together. "The two of you working together in secret cannot possibly end in anything other than tears for someone."

Quartz and I shared a smirk before I threaded my fingers through Jayden's thick, wavy hair. I had discovered that I loved playing with my boys' hair, and they didn't seem to mind at all. Well, I hadn't really messed with Mason's yet, but I was going to!

"Don't worry about that, my dragon. Anyway, Quartz told Lark he helped exorcize a demon. Were you scared?"

"It wasn't much of a risk with the witches there." He shrugged, although I could see in his eyes how pleased he was that he and his wolf had been chosen to assist. "They did all the work and needed Q more than me. I hardly did anything."

"It was still very brave. I'm proud of you, Jayden."

"You're so kind to praise us even though we did nothing special or beyond what's usual for us."

"It's honesty more than kindness."

Smooshing his cheeks together with my fingers, I chortled at his squishy, deformed lips, then kissed them.

By the time we separated, pink gilded the clouds as the sun began to set. Looking around, I saw we were the only ones still outside, except for Emerson and Angelo, who seemed frozen in place.

"Should we do something?" I pointed to them. "They're just standing there staring at each other."

"How come they're not kissing? Or at least hugging?" Ash tilted his head, as if a different angle would change what he saw. "They're not even talking!"

"I think they're both in shock," Jayden snickered.

"Leave them." Mason shrugged. "They'll figure it out.

"Come on, Posy," Cole said as he took my hand. "Let's go in."

"Wait a minute. I need to grab my bags."

"I'll get them," Mason volunteered. "I see your purse on the ground. What else do you have?"

"I can—"

"Please, little flower. Let me."

"Okay," I gave in. "My gray duffel bag is in the back of the car. That's all. Thank you! "

As he walked back to the SUV, Wyatt claimed my other hand, and Jayden and Ash led the way to where we were staying for the night. Mason caught up to us before we reached the building. Before going through the door, I glanced back and grinned.

Emerson had his fingers in Angelo's hair, and Angelo held Emerson's face in his palms.

They're so cute! I squealed to myself.

Then Wyatt tugged me inside.

"Welcome home!" He half-bowed and swept his arm forward. "Well, it's not home, but at least we're together."

"That's all I need for any place to be home." I stretched up and kissed him on the cheek.

Grinning, he leaned down and kissed me on the lips, making me feel warm and tingly all over.

Cole led me to an interior room that was probably a conference room on a normal day. Right now, though, a bunch of mattresses and pillows took up most of the space.

"We had to improvise, and this was the best we could do on short notice," Mason explained as he set my bag on the floor by the door, then dropped my duffel beside it.

"We remembered a night light!" Ash proudly displayed a plastic plug-in shaped like a unicorn before he went over to a receptacle and plugged it in. "Ta-da!"

"Thanks! It's so cute!" I clapped my hands.

"There's a bathroom right across the hall, and we put one in there, too," Jayden said. "Sorry you have to share with us."

"Oh, that's fine. I'll sacrifice having my own bathroom if it means I get to be with you."

"Aww!" Ash, Wyatt and Cole said together.

We made our individual trips to the bathroom and changed into night clothes. At least, *I* did. The boys just stripped down to boxers like usual, although they put on fresh t-shirts. They were sorting out sleeping positions when I came back.

I watched them for a moment as I gathered myself. Taking a deep breath, I let it out slowly, then cleared my throat.

Five pairs of eyes swiveled to me. Twisting my hands nervously, I stood before them and told myself I could do it.

"Posy? You all right?" Jayden asked.

"I, ah, I want to tell you something."

"Sure, cutie. You can tell us anything," Wyatt assured me.

"Um, well, if you remember, I said I want to practice mating." Fire lit my cheeks and painfully spread over my whole face and down my throat. "So, uh, I'm ready. To practice."

They didn't say anything for a moment, just stared at me with wide eyes.

"So, um, after you told us that, the five of us had a talk." Mason scratched the back of his neck. "We agree that you should practice with Jay first."

"Did you—" I didn't want to believe it, but I knew my mates. "*Did you Rock-Paper-Scissor it?!*"

"No!" they all howled and looked outraged.

I tilted my head and gave them a 'Really?' look, which made them shuffle their feet.

"We thought about it, okay?" Wyatt admitted. "In case we couldn't reach a decision, that was our back-up plan."

"However, we came to a better conclusion," Cole said. "We realized that Jay has the best control, so he can be trusted to stay gentle and actually notice when - if - you're uncomfortable or ask him to stop. The rest of us can join in slowly if it works to do so, or wait and try again later if it doesn't."

Wracked with nerves, I nodded and my face turned even hotter. Ash came over, wrapped his arms around my shoulders, and tucked my head into his torso.

"It's awkward for us, too, Posy," he murmured. "We've never done this before, either, so don't be embarrassed. We'll figure it out together, okay?"

I nodded again and hugged his waist.

"Why don't we wait a little longer?" he asked. "You're uncomfortable already, and we're all still standing up with clothes on."

I bit my lip. I wanted this; I really did. I loved them with all my heart and wanted to be as close to them as possible in every way. My shyness was killing the mood, though.

"I can strip for you if that'll help you relax," Wyatt offered.

I gulped at the images popping up in my head, then heard the distinct sound of him getting slapped upside the head.

"Stop, Cole! You legit hurt my brain!"

"What little there is!" Cole snarled.

I couldn't stop the laughter from slipping out, and some of the tension in the room eased.

Jayden came over to stand next to me and Ash. He brushed his knuckles down my cheek, and I was captured by his dragon eyes.

"Hey, sweetness." Reaching out his left hand, he linked his fingers with mine. "Come to me, please?"

I stumbled as I left Ash's embrace, and he grinned. Still only touching my fingers, he leaned down and brushed his lips against mine.

"Posy," he murmured with his mouth still on mine. "I'm going to pick you up, okay?"

"Yeah," was the best I could do.

He scooped me up, and I flung my arms around his neck and held on tight as he started walking.

"I won't drop you," he promised.

"I know that, but you giants don't understand how far away the ground is from up here."

Breathing out a soft chuckle, he put his knee on the mattress and settled me against the pillows, then stretched out next to me. We laid on our sides and faced each other.

"I could stare into your eyes forever," I admitted with a shy blush. "They're beautiful."

"Thank you. Yours are, too. They make me think of the ocean."

"Oh! That's right!" Excitement brought a smile to my lips. "You said you wanted to visit the ocean. I do, too! Do you think we could go sometime?"

"Sure. We'll plan a vacation after we get home. Right, brothers?"

"Of course," they chorused.

"Although all of us running around shirtless in our swim trunks might be too much for you, honey," Cole teased me. "We'll probably need to buy you a bag of ice to cool down."

He wasn't wrong, but Wyatt interjected before I could say anything.

"*You're* going to be the one needing ice after seeing Posy in her bikini. You'll have wet dreams for a week."

Smack!

I turned my head to see Wyatt rubbing the back of his head with a fierce frown.

"For real, Cole, you're giving me brain damage!"

"How could anyone tell?" Cole snapped.

Jayden cupped my cheek in one hand and turned my face back to his.

"Look at me, sweetness."

I met his eyes and held them as his head came closer. Then his mouth touched mine, and my heart fluttered. When he licked my bottom lip, I opened up, and his tongue darted in.

His mouth was so warm and soft and addicting, and the smell of him - not only the mate scent of roses, but also the pure smell of *boy* - made my stomach tighten and my heart race.

Both of our chests were heaving by the time he broke away from my mouth.

"I like your kisses."

"I like yours," I admitted with a light blush.

"Is it okay if I take my shirt off?" he asked.

"Yes, please."

He leaned away enough to tug his t-shirt over his head and throw it on the floor. His eyes held mine as he settled next to me again.

"Is it okay if I take *your* shirt off?"

Take my shirt off? Then he'll see my scars!

He see them soon, anyway, Lark pointed out in her practical way. *And they saw your back first day.*

I know, but I hate them. They make me ugly.

No, no! Show you survived what tried to kill you! she argued.

Mine only show I was weak enough to be broken.

"Posy?

"Um."

"Hey, it's okay," he reassured me. "We'll get there. Here. Touch me. I'd like that."

131

He laid my hands on his chest, and I forgot my worries in the flurry of sparks leaping between us. His skin was velvety soft, but the muscle under it was rock hard. I skimmed my fingers across his collar bones and down to his chest, then hesitated at his nipples. I really wanted to touch them.

"Go ahead," he purred.

So I did. I rubbed my fingertips over the dark beads, and his body jerked. Worried, I quickly pulled my hands back.

"I'm sorry!"

"No, no, sweetness. I wasn't expecting it to feel so good." He caught my wrists and drew my hands back to his chest. "Do it again, please."

Well, I wasn't going to say no. I touched him again and delighted in the shivers that raised goosebumps on his skin.

"Can I kiss them?" I whispered.

"Baby, you can do anything you want to me. *Anything.*"

Timidly, I brought my lips closer and dropped a kiss on each one. He hummed, which encouraged me to lick them, too. Growing bolder, I drew one between my lips with gentle suction, then did the same to the other.

"Oh, my Goddess," he muttered.

I smiled against his skin.

"That feels amazing." He rubbed his hands up and down my sides. "Do you think you'd like me to do that to you?"

The thought of his mouth on my skin made my nipples painfully hard, and a heavy throb began between my legs.

Making a decision, I lifted my head to meet his gaze.

"You can take my shirt off. Just don't—" I closed my eyes and sucked in a deep breath. "Don't be disappointed."

"Baby, disappointed is something I'll never be with any part of you."

His face dipped into my neck and he laid an open-mouth kiss right on my mate mark, then kissed his way down my throat until he reached my shirt. One by one, he slipped my buttons free and left a trail of kisses in their place. His fingers ran down my stomach and sides, and I knew he felt the scars, but he didn't stop or comment.

As he peeled back my shirt, all I could think was, *I wish I'd worn a sexier bra.*

He didn't seem to mind plain white nylon, though, if the fixed stare was anything to go by.

"Sit up for a second, sweetness."

When I did, he slid my shirt off my shoulders and down my arms. It joined his on the floor, then his clever fingers found my bra clasp and unhooked it. I swallowed hard, but he didn't remove my bra.

Instead, he helped me lie down again, the fabric loose against my chest but still covering everything.

He kissed the upper swells of my breasts, making me arch up breathlessly. As I did, he slid the straps down my arms with his palms and the cups fell away. Slipping my hands free, he flung my bra across the room, then lowered himself on top of me before I could panic about him seeing my girls.

Sliding his hands under my shoulders, he laid his chest against mine and nuzzled his face against my collar bones. His warm breath tickled, and I shivered under him.

"I wanted to know how they'd feel against me," he whispered in my ear. "Is this too much?"

I couldn't speak, too awed by the feel of his weight and strength on top of me, not to mention the million sparks exploding everywhere our skin touched.

"Posy? Is it?"

"No," I murmured. "How *do* they feel?"

"Like two warm, squishy pillows. I love them."

I smiled and blushed at the same time, and he suddenly sat up with his knees straddling my hips. Feeling exposed, I crossed my arms over my chest, my face growing redder by the second.

"You're beautiful, little mate."

The tips of his fingers trailed over my shoulders, down my arms, and across my stomach. Whenever they encountered a scar, they stopped and caressed it, then continued their journey. His gentle touches were undoing me; my unease faded and I dared to look at his face.

Those dragon eyes reeled me in as they always did.

"Don't be afraid, baby. It's me. It's your mate. Take a deep breath of my scent." Once I did, he pecked my lips. "There. See? It's just me. Just Jayden."

I smiled and reached up to run my hands over his chest and abs, forgetting that would give him a clear view of my girls. He only stared at them, which made it easier, but a rush of moisture suddenly gathered between my legs and startled me.

Oh, please, not my period. Not now, I prayed.

"Can I touch them?" His eyes were riveted on my chest.

Distracted by what was happening down south, I nodded.

His fingers stroked the undersides of my breasts, then up over the nipples. They seemed to fascinate him, and he swirled his forefingers around them until they were rock hard and thrumming. I squirmed as my insides tightened, and I thought I'd die if he didn't put his mouth on me soon.

"Kiss them," I begged.

"*Thank you.*"

He leaned down and drew the left one into his mouth. He sucked it lightly at first, then harder, and the pleasure nearly blinded me. Now I was *really* wet down there, and my whole lower region throbbed painfully.

Worried, I clutched his shoulders.

"Um, Jayden, I think something's wrong."

"What's wrong?" he asked with a nipple caged between his teeth.

"There's— It's— Um." I felt like crying.

Sensing my distress, he sat up, his knees still straddling my hips.

"Sweetness? Do you need a break or want to stop?"

"No, but I think I got my period," I said in a rush.

He frowned and shook his head.

"That's not possible. Heat replaces it as soon as you meet your mate. Remember? We talked about this."

"Then why am I all wet," I dropped my voice to a whisper, "*down there?*"

"Uh, so, your body is getting ready for me. It's doing what it should be." He laughed lightly, but I didn't think he was laughing *at* me. "You scared me for a second."

"How, um, how is that getting ready for you?"

"Remember what Wyatt said about you getting nice and wet so we could slide inside you easier?" Red stole across his cheeks. "Hasn't that happened before? Like when we kissed or touched you?"

"Yes, but not as much as what's happening right now."

"That's because you're more aroused right now. You want me, don't you?"

"Yes."

"Will you trust me?" He laid his palm against the side of my face and swept his thumb over my cheek.

"Of course."

"How do you feel about taking your shorts off?" he murmured against my skin.

"Can I keep my panties on?" I asked with wide eyes. "At least at first?"

"Sure."

"Then okay."

Once he had my permission, he quickly stripped them off me and tossed them to the growing pile of clothes on the floor. He left his boxers on, which I appreciated. Despite what we were doing, I wasn't ready to see *that* just yet.

134

With a sweet smile, he laid me on my back and propped himself up on one elbow beside me.

"Open your legs a little for me, sweetness."

I did what he asked, and he slid his hand into my panties and between my thighs to cup me there.

"Whoa!" I gasped and gripped his forearm with one hand, the other curling into the sheets.

"You're okay," he whispered. "It's just me, remember?"

For several minutes, he simply held me like that, his hand still as he kissed me, his tongue delving into my mouth.

"Jayden," I moaned when the kiss ended.

"I'm going to touch you more deeply now," he whispered. "Is that all right?"

I nodded, incapable of speech.

His hand slid lower and his fingers parted my folds, and I held his forearm a little tighter. As his mouth nibbled its way down to my breasts, his fingers explored carefully, but thoroughly.

Then his thumb bumped against my hard nub, and I nearly jumped out of my skin.

"Too much?" he asked against my breasts.

I shook my head.

"You sure?"

"It feels good," I choked out.

Finally letting go of his forearm, I moved my hands to his biceps and clung to him.

"Want me to go on?"

"Yes," I breathed.

More comfortable with his touch now, I didn't jerk when he pushed one finger deep inside me, but I did let out a breathy noise. He held his finger there for a few seconds, then pulled it out slowly and just as slowly slid it in again. He did that a few times before adding a second finger and swirling his thumb against the little nub he found earlier.

My lower belly fluttered and tickled, making me squirm. As his fingers dove in and out, his thumb rubbed harder and faster, and the need beat stronger, the heat building up to fever pitch.

As his hand worked its magic, he licked my nipples like a cat lapping up milk. My stomach coiled tighter and tighter under his busy mouth and fingers, and my breath turned to short, sharp pants.

All at once, the feeling in my core spiraled toward something frightening.

"Jayden?" I quavered, my voice shrill with uncertainty.

He raised his head and met my eyes.

"Let it happen, Posy. Go ahead and fly."

135

Stuffing his face in my neck, he sucked my mate mark at the same time he gently pinched my nub - and that was all it took. I shot off into the sky with his name on my lips. Bumping back down to earth slowly, I let out a tiny whimper, already missing the sensations he'd caused and wanting to experience that again and again...

Tiny kisses rained down on my face and warm hands slid under me to pull me flush against a hard body.

"Shh. You're okay, precious girl," whispered a voice I loved. "Our sweet, precious girl. *Our Posy.*"

19: Pleasure

Posy

As I tried to catch my breath, Wyatt's whisper-hiss broke through my daze.

"Can I go next? I want her. I *need* her. Pass her to me, please!"

Smack!

"By the moon, Cole, you do that one more time and you'll regret it."

"Chill, idiot! She's setting the pace, *not* you. Don't rush things."

Sudden doubt struck me. Were they getting impatient? Unhappy? Or maybe they didn't want me now that they heard how embarrassingly loud I could be or saw all the scars. Despite what they'd said, maybe I *was* acting too much like the slut and whore my father always called me.

Whimpering, I clung to Jayden and tried to hold back the panic.

"Stop, Posy," Ash said in my ear. "Get those thoughts out of your head. It's making us upset to hear them."

Yikes.

I didn't realize I had the link open between us and closed it quickly, my face burning.

"I want to tell you something," Ash went on. "Are you listening? I never saw anything so stunning in my life as you having your first orgasm."

"Is that—" I swallowed. "Is that what you call that?"

"Yep." He gathered my hair up in his hands and began to braid it. "Did it blow your mind? It looked like it did."

I buried my hot face in my hands, and he chuckled as his nimble fingers worked.

"You did great, Posy." Jayden's calloused fingers scraped over my skin, making me arch with pleasure as they trailed down my side.

"You, too. I never imagined anything like that." I took my face out of my hands to smile up at him.

"Thank you, baby." He touched his forehead to mine and smiled softly. Then he raised his head and looked at Ash. "Where'd Cole go?"

I felt a little anxiety stir. I wanted all my mates near me.

"Bathroom to get a hair tie," Ash told him, and I relaxed again.

"And I'm back." Cole joined us and handed Ash the hair tie. "Here you go."

"Thank you," I said with a shy smile.

Leaning down, Cole cradled my cheek in his palm and pecked my forehead as Ash finished my braid and tied it off.

"Okay, princess." Ash patted my bum, which made me squeak. "Are you okay to keep practicing, or are you ready to stop?"

"Is it getting late?" Looking over my shoulder at him, I asked, "Are you too sleepy?"

"It's just after nine and I'm wide awake, princess."

"I— I'd like to keep practicing, if everyone is okay with that and it's not too much or too hard for anyone?"

"Oh, it's hard, all right, cutie." Wyatt draped himself over Ash's side to run his fingertips down my cheek.

"Yeah, and I can feel how hard it is since it's jabbing me in the back!" Ash scowled. "Get off of me!"

"What do you mean?" I asked. "What's jabbing you?"

"Come find out, Miss Curiosity." Wyatt wiggled his eyebrows at me and smirked.

Did I dare? Swallowing hard, I peeked up at Jay to find him staring down at me. His eyebrows quirked up, and I knew he was asking if I wanted to. When I nodded, he smiled and slid me closer to Ash, which made me giggle.

Ash looped an arm around my waist and pulled my back tight against his torso, then rolled onto his other side and squished me between him and Wyatt. Draping his arm across my collar bones, he rested his chin on my shoulder and began to kiss my ear and cheek and neck.

As for Wyatt, his hands roved everywhere, his rough palms scraping over my sensitive skin and making me squirm. Ash hissed as I wiggled against him, but I knew I wasn't hurting him. *Something* hard poked my thigh, which made me both blush and squirm again when I understood what it was.

"Shoot," Wyatt mumbled. "I've been dying to touch you and now that I can, I'm not going to last five minutes. I came twice just watching and listening to you with Jay."

"Came? Where did you go?" I thought he'd been there the whole time.

"Ha ha ha!" He laughed like I'd tickled him. "Came as in got off, cutie. Busted a nut. Shot my load. Squirted the juice. Climaxed."

"For Goddess' sake, Wyatt," Cole grumbled.

"Um. What?" I asked.

"Wyatt's bragging that he had two orgasms already," Jayden explained.

"How many are you supposed to have?" I asked.

"As many as you can or want." Ash laughed. "Ha ha ha! He probably has pup-making juice everywhere."

"Semen, Posy," Mason said in an annoyed tone. "It's called semen. For the love of the moon, all of you stop saying pup-making juice!"

"They're just jealous, Posy." Wyatt beamed at me. "Ready to see what they're so jealous of?"

I hesitated. Even though I was the one lying there with my girls on display, even after Jayden had touched me so intimately, the thought of one of the boys naked made everything suddenly seem much more serious. I didn't know why, but it did.

"Well, Miss Curiosity?" One of Wyatt's wandering hands found my hip and squeezed gently.

"I'll still be in control, right?"

"Oh, baby, of course. It's whatever you want. No pressure. Being here with you like this is all I need. If things go further, okay. If they don't, okay again."

Silently, I considered his words as his hand stroked up and down my thigh.

"All right."

"All right what? Say the words. I don't want to screw up now with a miscommunication."

"May I?" My skin was going to be permanently crimson after this.

"May you what? Tell me."

"Stop teasing her, Wyatt," Mason growled.

"I want her to voice her—"

"May I see what they're jealous of?" I got out before an argument could erupt. "Pretty please, Wyatt?"

A second later, his boxer shorts flew through the air, and I closed my eyes automatically. Taking a steadying breath, I opened my eyes and gave myself permission to look *down there* - and my mouth went dry.

It's so big.

My brain got stuck on that fact, and I couldn't stop staring.

"You look like you have questions, cutie." Wyatt smirked a little. "You can ask us anything, you know. We're not embarrassed. We've lived with our bodies all our lives, so it's nothing new to us."

"Oh. Well. Um." I cleared my throat. Where was I supposed to begin? "You're sure this isn't painful? It looks painful."

"It's not painful, I promise." Wyatt tucked his hands behind his head and his eyes dropped to my chest. "I wonder if it's similar to how your nipples feel when they get hard."

Crap. I forgot he can see all that!

139

I wanted to cross my arms over my breasts, but he was showing me everything he had, and fair was fair. Besides, he was just as curious about my body as I was about his.

"Then a little painful," I admitted, "but in a good way."

"Yes," he agreed. "And when Jay touched and kissed them?"

"Hmm. Nothing but pleasure." I took a deep breath. "What is the pouch below it?"

"It's called a scrotum," Ash answered before Wyatt could. "A slang word for it is ball sack. It holds two testicles that create the pup-making juice."

"Semen," Mason sighed.

"Is the ... scrotum ... full of the juice all the time?" I asked.

"No. It's an on-demand thing," Wyatt said.

"Thank you both for explaining everything so calmly and simply." I smiled at Wyatt, then glanced over my shoulder and met Ash's brown eyes. "It helps me to not be completely mortified."

"No need for any degree of mortification." Ash ran a hand up my stomach, his fingers skating along my skin. "Do you want to touch it? Wyatt won't mind at all, will you, Wyatt?"

"I'd be *very* happy if you touched me, baby."

Turning my head back, I looked at Wyatt's lazy smile, then trailed my eyes down his chest and abs to where he stood tall and proud.

"Do you want me to help?" Ash asked quietly.

I bit my bottom lip, then nodded. Ash moved us until I was on my knees with his giant body engulfing me from behind like a warm blanket. His arms came around me and guided my hands around Wyatt's throbbing shaft.

"Say stop whenever it's too much, princess."

As soon as my fingers made contact, Wyatt's penis pulsed and twitched, and he threw his head back in his pillows with a grimace.

I froze.

"I hurt you?" I gasped.

"Naw, baby," he groaned. "Feels good. *Really* good. More, please."

Ash ran my hands down, then up, and I paused at the top. It was such an interesting shape, and there was a little hole in the tip.

"Is that where the pup-making juice comes out?" My eyes darted to Wyatt's face.

"Semen," muttered a resigned voice.

"Yeah, and if you keep rubbing me like that, you'll get to see it happen in a minute."

"I thought it comes out when you're inside me?" This was confusing.

"Yeah, but you can make it come out in other ways," Ash said, "like jacking off."

I blinked rapidly for a few seconds.

"Jacking off?"

"It's called masturbating." Mason seemed to want me to know the right terms for everything. "What you did to me on the couch and what you're doing to him right now."

"Only he usually does it with his own hand," Cole muttered.

"So do you!" Wyatt laughed.

"Oh." I thought for a second, then nodded. "I want to see it come out. Come on, Ash. Show me."

Wyatt groaned again and closed his eyes tight, and Ash's chest shook with laughter against my back.

"Did I say something wrong?" I asked.

"No, cutie," Wyatt said through gritted teeth.

"Here." Ash kept one of my hands rubbing up and down, but moved my other hand under Wyatt's scrotum. "Massage his ball sack while stroking him."

It was squishy, but held what felt like two eggs inside that Ash showed me how to fondle. A low, rough sound vibrated through Wyatt's chest as I did, and I smiled a little, happy I was pleasing him.

"Those are testicles," Ash said. "People call them balls or nuts or a ton of other slang terms."

Oh! So that's what balls are.

"Got the hang of it now?" He pressed a kiss to my neck. "Think you can do it on your own?"

"Yes, I've got it."

"So, ah, is it okay if I hump your ass while you jack him off?"

I froze as I tried to work out what he was asking me.

What does he want to do to my bum? I asked Jayden through the link. *What is hump? Will it hurt?*

Jayden burst out laughing.

"That was abrupt, brother, and you could have worded it better," Mason snapped. "She probably has no idea what that means. And don't say ass!"

"Ash, you took her attention off me!" Wyatt complained at the same time. "Posy, ignore that moron."

"Ash wants to rub his penis against your bum," Jayden said as he got his laughter under control. "It won't hurt."

"Do you remember what we did on the balcony the other night?" Cole chimed in. "When I held you up against the wall and rocked against you? That's all it is, honey, but you can tell him no if you don't want to."

141

"Oh." I breathed a sigh of relief. "Okay. We can try it, but you'll stop if I don't like it, right?"

"Yes, princess. Your word is our law."

"I'm sorry you have to keep reassuring me. I just—"

"We'll reassure you as often as you need to hear it," he promised. "Just say stop at any time you're not comfortable, okay?"

"Okay."

He slid my panties down my thighs and paused when I gasped. "All right, princess?"

I nodded.

Then a hard rod slid between my bottom cheeks, and my eyes nearly exploded out of their sockets in my shock at both the sensation and the realization that he was naked now, too. His fingers gripped my bum and kneaded it as he slowly see-sawed back and forth.

"Ash," I moaned low in my throat.

"I take it you like?" he whispered in my ear, his chest brushing my back with every movement and his breath hot on my neck.

"Hmm," was the best I could do.

Wyatt jerked his hips up, and I noticed my hands had stilled on his boy parts.

"Please, Posy, please don't stop," he begged.

How could I say no to that?

I went back to rubbing and massaging him and, as Ash's slow thrusting picked up pace, so did my hands. Wyatt's penis seemed to grow harder the more I stroked him, and he clenched his fists into his pillow.

"Faster," he gritted. "Go faster."

I did as he asked and watched in amazement as his ball sack tightened and convulsed before white stuff shot out of the little hole in the tip. It came out so fast and so forcefully, it almost hit me in the face!

Startled, I jerked back, which made Ash groan harshly and bury his face in the back of my neck. Hot liquid gushed between my bum cheeks and slid down my thighs, and I realized he'd shot out juice, too.

He came just from rubbing against my bum?!

"Thank you for letting me experience that, princess." He kissed down my back, his lips following the long lines of scars and making me shiver. "It was amazing."

"Same." Wyatt sank into the mattress with a content and relaxed grin. "Incredible. Your little hands are magic. No wonder Mason didn't last long on the couch."

"I lasted longer than you did," Mason snorted.

"It isn't a competition," I reminded them both.

142

"Yes, it is," they disagreed in sync.

"Here, Ash," I heard Jayden murmur, then felt a warm, damp cloth swiping over my bum and between my legs and looked over my shoulder at Ash with wide, curious eyes.

"Shh, princess. I'm just cleaning up my mess. Did Wyatt get anything on your front?"

I looked down and saw some of Wyatt's pup-making juice on my hands.

"A little." I held them up for him to see. "Did I mess up? Am I not supposed to touch it?"

"It happens." I felt him shrug against my back, then he reached around me and wiped my hands clean. "You didn't mess up anything, and it's fine to touch it."

"It gets everywhere, baby," Wyatt tittered.

"Especially with *you*," Ash retorted as he finished what he was doing and uncurled himself from me. "You horny dog."

"What's horny?" I asked as I flapped my hands to dry them.

"Never mind," Mason grumbled. "Come over here to me and Cole now, little flower."

Clamoring over Wyatt's limp body, I launched myself into his open arms. He snuggled me in between him and Cole, who rolled onto his side and dropped kisses all over my face and down my neck. As I giggled, Mason looped an arm around my stomach and scooted closer so my side was flush along his chest and stomach.

"Posy?" Mason's deep voice was almost a physical caress. "Do you remember me saying that I wanted to repay the favor?"

"Yes," I breathed.

"Do you feel up to that right now? If you're tired or just done with this, that's okay, too."

"I'm not tired, and I, uh, I don't know that I'll ever be 'done' with this." I giggled.

"Would it be okay if I tried something different than Jay did?"

"Different how?" I tilted my head and stared up at him.

"I want to put my mouth where his hand was."

I was too surprised to answer for a few seconds.

"Is that ... clean? Healthy? I don't know what to say," I mumbled.

"It's fine." He chortled and brushed his nose along my jawline. "But I'm a little nervous. Obviously, I've never done it before, and I might mess up. I'd really like to try, though, and I promise I'll make it up to you afterward if it doesn't go well."

He was making himself vulnerable by admitting his nerves, and that made it easier for me to agree.

"I'm sure you can do it, Mason. Let's try."

"Thank you, baby."

He separated my legs, then knelt between my raised knees. Very carefully and slowly, as if I were made of glass, his big hands caressed the inside of my thighs. He slid his hands closer to where I ached and throbbed, then used his thumbs to part my soft folds. He paused and glanced at me, making sure I was okay with this, and I nodded. Giving me a soft smile, he dropped to his stomach and buried his face in my wet heat.

His mouth went right to my hard nub, and I dissolved into moans of pleasure as he sucked gently. Flinging out my hands, I reached for something to hold onto. Fortunately, I had Cole to help out. He threaded his fingers through mine and held them above my head. As Mason stuck his tongue in where Jayden's fingers had been, Cole kissed me deeply, his tongue making love to mine.

Little moans bubbled out of my throat in a steady stream, which seemed to encourage both of them. Their mouths grew rougher and Cole's hold on my hands tightened. Just as I thought I needed to take a breath or die, Cole lifted his lips and trailed kisses down my chin and throat, then sucked on my mate mark.

His mouth should be illegal.

Mason very gently bit down on my nub, and I squirmed so much, he laid one thick arm across my hips to hold me still.

His mouth, too.

I could feel Mason's lower half moving in the same rhythm Ash's had when he was "humping" me and wondered if Mason was doing that to the mattress. I almost giggled at the thought, but Cole's lips were on my breasts, distracting me.

When he suddenly latched onto my nipple and sucked it, I went up in flames, unable to hold out against two mouths suckling me in my most sensitive places. My eyes rolled back in my head and I couldn't even get their names out, just a wordless scream, as I drowned in tides of ecstasy.

Cole released my hands and moved his to cup my face and kiss me. Then he laid his head on my chest and wrapped his arm around me under my breasts.

Mason sat up on his knees and stared down at me with hooded eyes as his hands lightly rubbed my thighs.

"That's called eating you out, baby girl," he explained. "Although I think you heard Wyatt call it going down on you. Did you like it?"

Blushing furiously, I nodded and covered my face with my palms. He chuckled and grabbed my wrists to pull my hands away.

"Don't hide that gorgeous blush. We like seeing it because we know we put it there," he smirked. "Now that you know how we can

144

pleasure you and you us, are you more comfortable with the idea of mating? I know I am, now that I'm sure I can satisfy you, and I think the others feel the same, don't you, boys?"

"Yep."

"Yes."

"We worried about it, sweetness," Jayden said.

Sometimes it was hard for me to remember that they were as new to all of this as I was. They seemed so skilled compared to me. I didn't know anything, and they seemed to have all the answers.

About their own bodies, Posy, not yours, Lark snickered. *You going to have to tell them what you like and what you not like. All they know is, if it make you moan, it good.*

"I'm more comfortable, yes," I agreed. "I feel like I left Jayden hanging, though. He gave me an orgasm and I gave him nothing."

"I came in my shorts right after you did," Jayden admitted. "It's easy to make a guy come. We've all done it just by *looking* at you, so you don't really need to worry about it."

"Oh. Okay. But let me know if you need more. Will you? All of you?"

"Sure, honey, but like Mase and Jay said, it's not going to be a problem." Cole kissed my shoulder.

Suddenly, a huge yawn snuck up on me. I was more tired than I'd thought.

"Wore you out with two orgasms, hmm?" he teased. "We'll have to work on your stamina."

"Don't tease her," Mason rumbled as he laid down next to me. "Go to sleep, darling."

"Yeah. We'll clean up in the morning." Cole snuggled his face into my girls. "Wash the sheets so we have fresh ones to practice with again tomorrow night."

"But you didn't, um, come," I said, worried that he and Mason had been left out.

"Yeah, I did. While watching you with Ash and Wyatt. The way your boobies jiggled and bounced sent me right over the edge."

I felt his grin against my skin and rolled my eyes before turning my concerned gaze to Mason. His gray eyes softened as he ran his fingertips along my jaw.

"Like my brothers, I came in my shorts, too, little flower." He brushed his lips against mine.

"So you *were* humping the bed while eating me!" I narrowed my eyes at him.

"Eating you *out*," he corrected, then kissed me again. "And yes, although the delicious taste of you alone would have done it."

"Eww!" My face screwed up in disgust. "You didn't really *eat* that stuff, did you?"

He exploded with laughter, as did the others. Cole laughed so hard that he bent double and dug his face into my belly.

I didn't think it was funny, and I didn't understand what they were laughing about, but joy rose inside me and brought a smile to my lips.

Not even two weeks ago, I was completely alone and resigned to a slow and pain-filled death. Now here I was, surrounded by laughter and safe with my mates, who loved and cherished me above all things.

Thank you, Moon Goddess. I'll never doubt you again. I will treasure every day with these boys and take care of their precious hearts with all of my strength.

"I love you, Posy," Cole said around the last of his snickers. "Good night."

"I love you, too, Cole. Good night."

He kissed me, then turned me toward Mason. As had become our nightly routine, I was passed around to all of my mates for kisses and good nights and I love yous.

"Sweet dreams, Posy. I love you." Mason kissed my lips, then my mate mark.

"I love you, Mason. Good night."

He handed me over to Wyatt and Ash. As they snuggled me between them, they took turns kissing me and whispering how much they loved me.

"Good night, waffle. Good night, my fifth star. I love you."

Finally, I ended up back where I started.

"Sleep well, baby. I love you." Jayden bumped my nose with his, then kissed me.

"I love you, my dragon." Smiling, I curled up against him and laid my head on his shoulder. "Good night."

"Would you like a song?"

"Yes, please, if you don't mind."

"As you wish, sweetness."

And I fell asleep listening to him sing about kissing under the light of a thousand stars.

20: Il Mio Orsacchiotto

Emerson

Fighting the urge to fidget, I made myself stand still as I waited for my mate to introduce himself.

He's so pretty! Cove squealed.

He *was* pretty, especially his eyes. They were so pretty, in fact, that they made my heart flutter every time I looked into them.

But no wolf? Cove asked.

Nope, no wolf. Maybe he's part of Ariel's flock.

I didn't know who else he could be. The majority of the Tall Pines pack was in a secure area, and the rest of them were in our cells.

Birdie? I don't smell birdie.

Yeah, I know, I said. *Curious.*

Curious, he echoed me, making my lips twitch a fraction. *Why doesn't he tell us his name?*

Not sure.

My mate's face was completely blank. No emotion whatsoever. None. Nada. Zilch.

Sorry, Cove. I raised my chin and forced down the sudden knot in my throat. *I think— I think he might reject us.*

Doesn't want us? Tears built in his eyes, which didn't help me fight my own. *Why? We are not bad.*

I don't know why, Cove.

He whimpered, and an unrivaled pain ripped through my chest. I wanted to run into the woods and howl to the night sky, but every shifter in the area, including my luna, would hear and know what happened.

Disturbing the king, queen, and my alphas? Meh.

Making my little bunny sister cry? Unacceptable.

Wonder if there's a bar nearby? I grumbled to myself. *I might have to find out how much human liquor it takes to knock a werewolf out.*

"Hey, are you okay?" asked my mate, his hand still on my arm. "You look like you're in pain. I can heal you if you're injured?"

Oops. Guess my face is showing too much.

Swallowing hard, I tried to smile like it didn't matter, but that wasn't happening.

"No. Sorry. My wolf is—"

Destroyed? In agony? Shattered?

"Upset," I settled on, "that you're rejecting us. Listen, I need to check in with my alphas, but then you won't need to see me again—"

"*What?* Hold up!"

147

His fingers dug into my bicep before I could take a single step, and his eyes and face suddenly showed a rainbow of emotions. Shock, worry, fear, amazement, and maybe even a little caring?

I shook my head.

My imagination. I mean, he doesn't even think I'm worth knowing his name.

"I'm not rejecting you," he scowled. "I've been waiting my whole life for you! Hell if I'm going to let you go when I finally found you!"

He wants us? Cove hiccuped, then suddenly brightened. *Maybe he didn't hear you before?*

"I'm Emerson Jones."

My mate nodded, and I waited.

Maybe he doesn't know how to introduce himself? Cove tilted his head to the side.

I doubt that, but here goes.

"Um. What's your name?"

"Oh, Goddess! I assumed you knew who I was. I'm Angelo." Frowning, he dropped his hand from my arm and rammed his fingers through his hair, making it stand up in wild stalks all over his head. "Why did you think I was rejecting you?"

"I don't know." I dropped my gaze to the ground. "You were standing there with a blank face and not saying anything."

"Actually, I was steeling myself for *you* to reject *me*."

At his words, my eyes flew back to his.

"I'm a glitch." He shrugged. "A shifter who can't shift and has no animal spirit. A witchborn who has no magic beyond a little healing power. I was sure you wouldn't want me."

Hearing that description, my brain finally put the pieces together.

"Angelo *della Morte*?" I whispered. "My mate is the Angel of Death?"

"And *my* mate is the most handsome man I've ever met."

My face lit on fire at the compliment, and a surprised smile bloomed on his lips.

"You're blushing," he murmured.

Of course, that made my face burn worse.

"So cute!" he chuckled.

Laying his hands on either side of my face, he stroked his thumbs over my scorching cheekbones. I shivered as tingles flitted over my skin, and the wonderment in his eyes as he stared at his hands told me he was feeling the same thing.

"Is it okay if I touch you? I can stop if it makes you uncomfortable." He gave me a crooked smile. "You can touch me whenever you want."

Taking him at his word, I did what I'd been longing to from the moment I first saw him. I slid my trembling fingers into his messy hair and played with the thick strands.

It's every bit as soft as I thought it'd be.

Soft fluff! Cove yipped, which made me roll my eyes at him.

Ever so slowly, I leaned down and pressed my lips to his forehead, and sparks exploded under my lips. I heard his sharp inhale and was thrilled to know he was as affected as I was.

"Hey! No fair. I want to kiss you, too!" he laughed. "Come down here. How tall are you, anyway? I'm five eleven and the top of my head is barely even with your chin."

"Six six," I mumbled as I messed with his hair.

He wants our kisses! Leave the fluff and kiss mate! Cove growled.

Calm down. I'm working up my courage, okay?

Now, Em! Want our first kiss!

"Have you kissed anyone before?" I asked, my cheeks again growing hot with embarrassment at my lack of experience.

"No. Even though I believed I wouldn't have one, I wanted to stay faithful to my mate."

"Oh, thank the Goddess," I breathed. "Me, too. I have *no* idea what I'm doing."

"Want to figure it out together?"

"Oh, yeah."

"Then come down here," he smirked.

So I did.

\#

Angelo

One time, maybe two years ago now, the fae king asked for help to relocate a phoenix that built a nest too close to a pixie colony. Fortunately, I was able to convince the fire bird I meant no harm and only wanted to find a safer place for her babies. While I carefully packed each egg for transport, embers rained down on me as she hovered anxiously overhead, her wings shedding sparks like a welding torch.

Touching Emerson was exactly like standing under that fretting phoenix, only minus the pain. Warm flares tingled everywhere our skin made contact, and I wanted more. I wanted that sensation *all* over me.

149

When our lips met, nothing in my adventurous life could have prepared me for the feeling of utter *rightness* that settled in my soul.

"Wow," he gasped when he drew back.

"Yeah," I agreed.

Struggling to get my breathing back to normal, I looked around. We were alone out here and, except for the stars overhead, it was pitch dark.

"Want to go inside? You can share my room if you want. I'd like that, but no pressure. If nothing else, we can talk and get to know each other until we fall asleep."

"You're okay with everyone, with your flock, knowing about us?" he asked.

"Of course. They won't judge, and they probably know, anyway. You'll find out that there are few secrets when living with witches."

We started walking toward the alpha house as we talked.

"I'm excited to meet your family and introduce you to mine."

"Tomorrow," I said. "I want you all to myself tonight. Besides, Sara and Maria found their mates today, too. There'll be no separating them for a while."

His fingers brushed mine, and I wondered if he wanted to hold my hand. Taking the initiative, I slid my palm in his. He froze for a second, then threaded his fingers through mine.

"I've been tuning everyone out since I got here." He looked down at me with raised eyebrows. "Who's matched with whom?"

"Sara with Crew and Maria with Matthew. Oh, and yesterday, Beatrix with the Maxwell twins."

"Hmm. That's all my beta brothers now except Tyler, and he turns eighteen on the eighth." He smiled. "Garnet, who is Alpha Mase's wolf, believes the pack and the flock were always destined to entwine. Based on all these mate-matches, I think he's right."

"The Goddess works in mysterious ways," I agreed.

"There's something important I need to explain." He began to swing our linked hands between us. "I don't know how a flock is structured—"

"Loosely," I snorted. "There's no one leader. Everyone pitches in as needed. It's messy and leaves a flock ripe for attack, but bird shifters can't fight their avian nature, which is why I appointed myself as our flock's protector."

"Oh. Well, do you understand how a wolf pack is structured?"

"Yep. I've been Julian's friend and ally for several years now, and I've spent a lot of time with the royal pack. I know Five Fangs is a little different with five alphas, five betas, and five gammas, but it's basically the same hierarchy, right? Who are you beta for?"

"Yes, and Alpha Cole. Do you know that a beta's primary duty is to his luna? Even the alphas can't override that. I know this isn't what a mate wants to hear, but protecting Luna Posy will always come first. Even above myself. Even above you."

I breathed a sigh of relief. He *understood*, thank the Goddess.

"It's the same for me. Even now that they have mates, I am dedicated to the girls' safety, and that won't change. They are the last of our flock, and some of the few bird shifters left in the whole world. The sickness hit our kind especially hard, nearly to the point of extinction. Only the foxes had it worse."

"Yeah, we heard that. Very few foxes left." He stopped walking to stare down at me. "After the royal pack, Five Fangs is the largest, most powerful one in the U.S. You and your flock will be well protected with us."

"I can do my own protecting," I snorted, "but yeah, it does make it easier for me to accept that all my *piccoli uccelli* (little birds) have flown the nest. They sometimes worried about being separated when they found their mates. Now none of us have to be."

We started walking again, and I heard him muttering to himself. Was he getting nervous about staying in the same room with me?

"What's wrong?" I asked.

"Fireflies." He pointed toward the treeline behind the alpha house. "Cove wants to chase them, but don't worry. I told him you wouldn't want to do something like that. He's ... pouting a bit."

"Why wouldn't I?" I tilted my head. "I want to meet Cove, and chasing fireflies with him sounds like fun. Besides, I've hardly had any exercise today and could stand to burn off some energy."

Since I don't want to assume we'll burn it off in bed tonight, I thought and bit back a wicked grin.

"Um." Emerson scratched the back of his neck. "Cove isn't sophisticated or articulate or mature."

"If he's part of you, I'll love him."

And he freaking blushed *again,* which delighted me.

"Will I be able to talk with you while you're in wolf form?" I asked.

"Cove and I will both be able to hear and understand you, but not reply. Not until I mark you or the alphas induct you into the pack."

"Why don't you mark me now? I want to be able to fully communicate with both of you."

Emerson's brown eyes widened at my words and he gulped, making his Adam's apple bob.

"What did I say wrong?" I frowned.

151

"Marking is a permanent thing for wolves. You'll be tied to me until I die."

"Stop thinking I'm going to reject you!" I scowled. "Why would I reject the Goddess' gift when I prayed for you? When I *begged* for you?"

Seeing tears in his eyes made my breath catch. What had my mate endured to make him so emotionally vulnerable?

"I am keeping you forever, Emerson Don't-Know-Your-Middle-Name Jones." I dropped his hand and wrapped my arms around his waist. "I want to know everything about you, and it's going to take me the rest of my life to learn it all."

His heart thudded fast under my ear as he speared his fingers into my hair, and I grinned into his chest. I didn't think there was anything special about my poorly trimmed mop, but he sure seemed to like playing with it.

Maybe it's a wolf thing to pet your mate.

"It's Theodore," he whispered. "Emerson Theodore Jones. And I believe you. I want to keep you forever, too, Angelo."

Theodore. Adorable. And perfect for the teddy bear hidden inside his hulking body.

"Well, go ahead and mark me, *il mio orsacchiotto* (my teddy bear). We've got fireflies to chase."

"Do you speak Italian fluently? Your accent is sexy as sin. And what did you call me?"

"Yes, thanks, and I called you my teddy bear."

When red flooded his face, I laughed and squeezed my arms tighter around him.

"It's going to hurt," he warned me as he continued to pet my head, "but only for a few seconds. Then it should get better."

"I've been stabbed, burned, shot, and clawed. I think I can handle a wolf bite." I rolled my eyes.

He took a deep breath, then lowered his head and pressed his lips to my jaw. Kissing his way down my throat, he hummed a little, and I knew he was feeling the same knee-weakening sparks I was. His mouth touched a spot right below my earlobe, and I sucked in a sharp breath as goosebumps rose up on my skin.

"There?" His voice was deeper and rougher.

I couldn't speak, but my soft moan must have been answer enough. His canines pricked my neck, then stabbed in like twin knife points. He was right about it hurting, but I'd expected way worse. I'd *experienced* way worse.

Then the pleasure seeped in and spread through my veins like venom, heating me up from the inside out, and another little moan vibrated from my throat.

His tongue lapped at the wound, and I wondered if he was cleaning up the blood.

Can you hear me, Angelo? I heard his voice in my head.

Yep. Should I send a jolt of healing to the mark or leave it? Does it hurt?

No.

Then no. My saliva sealed the punctures and now it looks like a tattoo.

A tattoo of what? I asked.

Cove.

"And I get to meet him now, right?" I said aloud.

"Um, sure," Emerson said and stepped out of my hold.

Curling one arm behind his head, he grabbed the back of his t-shirt and tugged it over his head - and I stopped breathing as a whole lot of tanned skin and hard muscles suddenly came into view.

"Are you teasing me, Emerson?" I demanded.

"What? No!" His head popped out of the fabric, and his wide eyes showed confusion.

Is he teasing, or is he just that innocent?

"*Orsacchiotto* (teddy bear), you have to know how lickable you look without your shirt on." I had to reach down and adjust myself.

"*Lickable?*" If his eyes grew any wider, they were going to pop out of their sockets.

He has to be teasing, I told myself. *No guy his age can be that innocent. How old is he, anyway?*

"Yeah. You look like sex on a stick. Watching you strip is making me painfully hard."

Red bloomed on his cheeks and spread down to his throat and the center of his chest.

All right. It's official, I smirked to myself. *My new favorite thing is making Emerson blush.*

"Sorry! I wasn't teasing you, I swear, but I only brought along so many clothes. This was supposed to be an overnight trip."

"I don't understand. Connect the dots for me."

"Cove is a big wolf. If I don't take my clothes off first, they'll shred when I shift. I guess I could borrow some from Alpha Cole or Alpha Mason if it bothers you."

"No, it's good." I crossed my arms over my chest and raised an amused eyebrow. "Strip away."

Frowning, he kicked off his slides, then tucked his thumbs in his shorts and slicked them down his long, long legs. His hands went to the waistband of his boxers, and he paused.

"Um. Can you?" He made a twirling gesture with his index finger.

153

Well, hell. He really is that innocent.

"Oh. Sure." I turned my head. "Sorry if I made you uncomfortable."

He didn't answer, and I hoped I hadn't upset him. Then a new voice chirped in my head, and I realized he hadn't responded because he was shifting.

Look, mate! It's me! It's Cove! I'm so happy to meet you, mate!

Turning back, I saw a gorgeous wolf standing before me. His nose was about on level with my belly button, and his coat was a mix of tan, white, gray, and a little red.

"Well, hello there." I put a hand behind each ear and began to rub them. "Aren't you gorgeous?"

The wolf shivered under my touch and words, and pure happiness radiated into the new bond between us.

Thank you, mate! You are gorgeous, too!

Chuckling, I slid my hands through his silky coat to scratch his ruff.

"Cove," I said, "I'm sorry I don't have an animal spirit for you to bond with. There's just me in here."

It is okay, mate! I will make you happy!

"You can call me Angelo or Gelo."

Yes, mate!

Sorry, Emerson cut in, *but he'll probably continue to call you mate. Like I said, he's unsophisticated and immature.*

"He's precious," I corrected.

Cove's tail waved like a windshield wiper on high, and his upper half sank to the grass with his front legs stretched out in front of him.

"What is he doing, *orsacchiotto* (teddy bear)?" I asked Emerson.

Inviting you to play with him. You don't have to. He'll be satisfied if you just watch him run around for a bit.

"No, no. I'm not missing this opportunity. You want to play, Cove?"

Yes, mate! Chase fireflies?

"Oh, my darling, I'd love to!"

21: Decisions, Decisions

Posy

"Pass the butter, *orsacchiotto*," Angelo murmured to Emerson. We were all eating breakfast around the dining room table when Angelo's quiet request sent the four witches into a fit of giggles.

"That's adorable!" Beatrix squealed.

"Aw, what a cute nickname!" Ariel laughed.

"*Orsacchiotto?*" Sara raised her eyebrows. "Really, Gelo?"

"Well, he's as big as a bear!" Maria giggled and bounced on Matthew's lap. With a groan, he grabbed her hips and held her still, and a pretty pink blush dusted her cheeks.

I know what that's about, I thought, smug in my new knowledge.

"You called him a bear?" Cole asked as he looked from Emerson to Angelo.

"A *teddy* bear," Ariel and Beatrix corrected him in unison.

Emerson turned bright red, and Angelo chuckled as he half-stood and kissed Emerson's forehead. Emerson growled, looped his arm around his mate's waist, and dragged him onto his lap. Then he buried his face in Angelo's back.

The queen and I joined the witches as they cooed and giggled at the couple.

I'd declined sitting on any of my boys' laps, even though they'd all offered, because I didn't want it to look like I was favoring one of them over the others. Seeing their sad faces when I shook my head, I decided I'd work out a rota later. For now, I sat between Cole and Mason and across from the others.

Speaking of, I looked over at the three musketeers and grinned. Both Wyatt and Ash's eyes were currently riveted on my plate, and it was obvious they were only waiting until I was done before trying to beat each other to my leftovers.

Mischief stirring in me, I stood and scraped my eggs on Wyatt's plate and my bacon on Ash's. Their jaws dropped, and I giggled as I plopped back into my chair.

"Posy!" Wyatt pouted.

Ash looked outraged, although that didn't stop him from gobbling down my bacon. Giggling, I covered my mouth with my palm.

Everything's a competition with these guys.

Bright with cheerfulness, I looked at Jayden and found him staring at me. The heat in his dragon eyes lit my cheeks on fire, and the longer he stared, the more my insides tightened. I felt my panties grow damp, which made my whole face burn red, and his lips twitched into a little smirk.

Bad dragon! I linked him. *Do you know what you're doing to me?*

Oh, yeah, sweetness. I most certainly do. His smirk hiked up higher. *After last night, all I can think about is making you moan and squirm under me again.*

Slamming the link shut, I ducked under Cole's arm and buried my hot face in his stomach.

"Posy?"

He sounded alarmed at first, then a quiet chuckle told me that Jayden, the rat, had linked him what was going on.

"Oh, hey. Leo Halder is awake," Ash said suddenly, and I sat up again. "Tyler is helping him drink some water and wants to know what he should do next."

"We'll go check on him," Ariel said.

Kissing Tristan's cheek, she stood, and her sister witches scooted off their mates' laps, too.

"We're coming along," Zayne and Zayden spoke together.

"We don't need any help," Sara told them as she leaned down and kissed Crew's forehead. "We can manage on our own, thank you."

"Actually, you can carry some things for us," Beatrix told them with a sweet smile.

They grinned and stood and squished her between them. I giggled, knowing that was probably going to be her default position for the rest of her life.

And she looks ecstatic about it, I thought with a grin.

Sara linked her elbow with Maria's and tried to tug her along, but Maria clung to Matthew's shoulders.

"One more kiss from Puppy," she begged.

Matthew smiled smugly at Sara, who rolled her eyes and left them to it.

"Puppy?" Queen Lilah snickered.

Inspired, I turned to Mason, who was still shoveling down pancakes. Before I could open my mouth, though, he shook his head.

"No."

"You didn't even look at me," I pouted.

"Because I am not going to fall victim to those big blue eyes. The answer is no."

With a huff, I turned to my other side, where Cole was taking a sip of his coffee. He turned to me, and I smiled widely.

"Cole—"

"Absolutely not, Posy."

156

"But I have nicknames for all my mates except you two." I pooched out my bottom lip.

"Keep thinking." He cupped my face in one hand and swiped his thumb over my lip. "Come up with something on your own rather than steal someone else's nickname, shortcake."

"Shortcake?!" I squeaked. "I'm not short!"

"You are."

"Am not. You're just enormous."

"You're short, Posy," Wyatt said.

"You are." Ash nodded with solemn eyes.

"Nuh-uh. *You* don't get to say anything." I pointed at Ash and ignored Wyatt. "You know you're not normal. *I* am normal. Look at Maria. She's my height."

"She's three inches taller than you, sweetness," Jayden unhelpfully pointed out.

I frowned. I couldn't do anything about my height.

"It's okay, Posy." Wyatt gave me a smile. "We love you no matter how tall or short you are."

I returned his smile as Cole rubbed his hand up and down my back.

After the witches and the Maxwell twins left, the queen said she wanted to go to her house to pack some things. The king directed Luke and Gisela to go with her, and they left, too.

The rest of us moved to the living room, where King Julian brought up the issue of Leo Halder.

"Ranger and Junia will be returning with the Tall Pines pack by evening, and those who were at Five Fangs are already on their way. I need to interrogate him and make a decision today."

I was sharing a love seat with Mason, who had me tucked under his arm and pressed into his side. I squiggled my fingers into his ribs to get his attention, and he cut his eyes down at me.

"Are the gammas coming with the Tall Pines wolves?" I asked.

"No, they're in charge of the pack until we send the betas home later today."

"Then the betas will be in charge until you return?" When he nodded, I asked, "How are the Tall Pines wolves getting here?"

"The gammas set them up with some of our pack vehicles."

"Oh." I stretched up to kiss his jaw. "Thank you for explaining."

He smiled, which made me happy, and I tuned back into the conversation to hear Wyatt ask a question I'd wondered, too.

"Do you think he's innocent?"

157

"How innocent can you be if you agree to host a demon?" King Julian snorted.

"A demon can force itself into someone's soul through trickery and coercion," Angelo said. "Their hosts were unwillingly or unwittingly and never had a choice."

"I want to throw him in my dungeon and be done with it," the king grunted.

"You may need to defer this decision to someone else, wolf king."

"I *know* I'm too close to the issue. So you are. Same with Ranger, the Maxwells, and probably these betas now that they're mated to the witches." King Julian studied each of my mates' faces. "What about you guys? Can any of you be unbiased?"

"After what I saw in the basement?" Cole shook his head slowly. "Don't think so."

"And what happened to Reuben isn't something I can forget," Wyatt muttered.

"Seeing the condition of those pups got Sid all worked up," Ash admitted. "He and I are so in sync that separating his emotions from mine is almost impossible. I could try, but I can't guarantee any degree of objectivity."

"Mase?" The king raised his eyebrows.

Mason was silent for several long minutes as he thought, then he shook his head.

"No."

He didn't offer reasons or justification, but I knew he would have thought it out before he gave his answer.

"Jay?" the king asked.

"Maybe. Quartz is very angry, though, so there's a chance he'll sway me or simply take control and rip Halder's throat out."

"Problem solved, if you ask me," Angelo muttered.

"None of you think he's worth a chance to redeem himself?" I asked with a frown.

"That's not what we're deciding, sweetness," Jayden explained in a gentle tone. "We're trying to determine who among us is able to talk to him without our feelings getting in the way and influencing us."

I dropped my eyes to clasped hands as I thought about his words.

"Well, regardless of who interrogates him," Cole said, "if we find out he worked with the demon, the outcome is simple. If we find out he was coerced, things get a lot more complicated."

"He can't ever be an alpha again," the king said, "and he can't stay here at Tall Pines. I can't induct him in the royal pack, nor would I want to. Lilah would see him too frequently. Anyone have suggestions?"

"Most alphas would worry that he'd try to take over," Jayden pointed out. "With his history, they'd have good reason to."

"And if he happens to be more powerful," Cole said, "the alpha won't be able to *make* him submit."

"Exactly." The king sighed. "So where might a pariah have a chance at acceptance? It would need to be a strong pack with a powerful alpha, and one whose members are open-minded."

Everyone fell silent, their faces drawn in concentration.

I myself thought the answer was obvious.

Maybe they no want to admit it, Lark suggested. *Saying it out loud makes it real.*

"I'll talk to him," I said, "and you all know the best place for him is Five Fangs."

Chaos erupted around me.

Wyatt, Ash, and Cole were the loudest, although the betas weren't much quieter. Mason gathered me up on his lap and pushed my face in his neck, his thick arms wrapping around me as if he could hide me from the world.

Jayden, smart boy that he was, linked me instead of trying to be heard over everyone.

I agree that our pack is probably the best placement if he's innocent, which is a huge if, but why do you want to talk to him?

I was surprised by his calm question when everyone else was bellowing their disapproval.

I'm pretty sure I'm the only one here who doesn't want to kill him and for sure won't kill him, I gave him half of my reasons.

It could be dangerous, sweetness. However small a chance it may be, he could hurt you, and none of us are willing to take that risk.

Link Ty and see what he thinks about Mr. Halder's condition. If he's so weak he needs help getting water, I can't believe he's in any shape to attack me.

Hmm. Wait a minute.

Smiling into Mason's neck, I let myself relax in my mate's tight hold, certain I was going to win this one.

Ty says he's as weak as a kitten, Jayden admitted reluctantly.

See? What could possibly happen? Ty's there. And I can take Emerson along, too. I don't think he has any stake in this, other than knowing his mate would like to kill the guy, but I think he can separate himself from that.

Jayden was quiet for several long minutes. As I waited, I tuned in to the boys' wolves, curious to know what they were feeling. As Jayden had said, Quartz was in a rage, which was not unusual, but I was surprised to find Sid in the same condition. Granite and Topaz were more worried about their boys than anything. As for Garnet, he was sunk deep in Mason's mind, almost too deep for me to reach, but I could sense his fury.

I linked Mason to ask why. I could understand Quartz, because that was his default state, and Sid because of his love for pups. But what reason did Garnet have to be so angry?

Halder sent his wolves after the queen, which endangered you at the diner, Mason replied. *Then he sent wolves to invade our pack, which endangered you on our run. Why wouldn't he be angry?*

All right, Posy, Jayden linked before I could respond to Mason. *Here's what I propose. Ty and Em do not leave your side. If Halder shows any sign of aggression, they will kill him on the spot. If the worst happens, you shift into Lark and run straight back to us. You will keep the link open with us the whole time. These terms are non-negotiable.*

Thank you, dragon!

Just because I agreed doesn't mean the others will, he snorted.

I'm pretty sure you can sway them with your 'non-negotiable' terms, I said dryly.

The rest of my mates and the betas had calmed down enough for Jayden to get their attention. As he told them what we'd discussed, I stayed tucked in Mason's throat. I wrapped my arms around his neck, drew in deep breaths of his campfire scent, and kissed along his jaw.

He took in a deep breath, making me rise and fall with his broad chest. Feeling daring, I laid an open-mouth kiss on his mate mark and gently bit it.

"*Posy,*" he rumbled, and I felt him growing hard under my bum. "Don't think your kisses will influence my decision."

"Of course not."

With a secret smile, I kissed my way up to his earlobe, then sucked it into my mouth and swirled my tongue around it. He shifted me on his lap with a muffled groan, then lowered his head to whisper in my ear.

"Do that in bed tonight and see what happens."

Blushing heavily, I buried my face in the center of his chest, and he chuckled before rejoining the conversation around us.

A thought struck me and I considered the wisdom of it. Was the information I wanted worth the reaction I might get? Deciding it was, I nudged my link with Quartz.

He opened it right away.

I want to ask you a question about Leo Halder, and I'd like your answer to be as simple and straightforward as possible. Can you do that without losing your temper?

160

Yes, he said after a minute. *For you.*

When you were exorcizing the demon, what did you see inside Leo Halder?

He blinked, startled, and I wondered what he thought I was going to ask.

Fire. Blood. Darkness. Pain. And—

I waited as he wrestled with his conscience. He'd seen something that he didn't want to tell me, but I knew he would in the end.

Regret, he admitted. *Despair. Hopelessness. Resignation.*

When he fell silent, I gave him a sweet smile as thanks.

"I'm coming, too," I heard Angelo say in a gruff tone.

What's going on? I asked Lark, hoping she'd been paying more attention than I had.

They agree to Jayden's terms, Lark caught me up. *Gelo wants to tag along.*

"I don't need a hit man lurking around while I'm interrogating a prisoner." I raised my head and looked at him.

"You can't *interrogate* anyone, Luna Posy," King Julian teased with a grin. "You're too nice and soft to *interrogate* someone."

"Interview then," I said with a shrug.

"Angelo will act as another guard, little luna bunny," Emerson explained, "not a hit man."

"I'll have you and Ty. Why do I need another guard?"

"Better safe than sorry. If something happens, Angelo has more experience than any of us with the supernatural in general. It only makes sense."

I studied his serious face and solemn brown eyes and saw only concern. He wasn't trying to trick me into getting his mate close enough to the enemy to kill him.

"Okay," I sighed and turned to Angelo, "you can lurk, but stay out of sight."

"So where do you want to do this interview?" Wyatt asked. "You're not going to the prison."

"Why not?"

"It's foul and not a place you need to see." Jayden frowned.

He was usually the first to give in to me, but I could tell he wasn't going to budge on this one.

And I'm not all that interested in hanging out in a jail cell, anyway.

"How about his office?" Ash suggested.

"How about the front yard?" I raised my eyebrows. "It's shady under the trees, and the heatwave has finally broken. Fresh air and sunshine and—

161

"And Angelo will have a clear shot if something goes wrong," Cole muttered.

I huffed and rolled my eyes at him.

"Honey, you are far too willing to find good in him. It may blind you to the truth."

"I think that's better than all of you, who are far too willing to believe there is *no* good in him."

#

"Has he said much?" I asked the Maxwell twins.

After escorting Beatrix back to the alpha house, they returned to help Emerson and me rearrange the lawn furniture. Angelo had disappeared as soon as we came outside, but I knew he was lurking somewhere nearby.

Probably in a perfect shooting position, I thought sourly.

"He asked about some of the pack members," Zayne said, "and he—"

"He cried when we told him who died," Zayden picked up when Zayne stopped talking, "and when we told him what he did to Lilah and Junie."

I tapped my chin with an index finger as I thought.

"The bad shifters, the ones who were Leo's by choice and not coercion, how long were they in your pack?"

"A few months," the twins said in unison.

"We don't know where they came from," Zayne said.

"They weren't vetted by Luke or our gamma, yet suddenly they were in our pack," Zayden added.

"Who's the gamma?" I asked.

"No one now. It *was* Marcus Romano, who disappeared about eight months ago. After that, there was a new guy named Rafe, but Q—"

"The king killed him," Emerson cut Zayne off and gave him a look. "Luna bunny, should I go fetch Tyler and Halder now?"

"Tyler can't do it by himself?" I raised an eyebrow.

"Better safe than—"

"Yeah, yeah." I waved on hand. "Go ahead. I'm going to grab some drinks and snacks. I'll meet you back here."

He nodded and trotted off, and Zayne and Zayden walked with me up to the alpha house and trailed after me into the kitchen. Opening the fridge, I pulled out a pitcher of lemonade, then searched around until I found a tray and two glasses.

Hmm. What do we have that would be good with lemonade?

Rooting around in the cupboard, I found some shortbread cookies and grabbed them, then scooped up two bananas from the fruit

162

bowl on the counter. Arranging everything on the tray, I went to pick it up, but Zayne beat me to it.

"Thank you." I smiled.

"I've never heard of a prisoner being interrogated over lemonade and cookies before," Zayden smirked and shook his head.

"Well, it's really for me, but it would be bad manners not to offer him some." I shrugged. "And the king said I can't interrogate him, so I'm calling it an interview."

"The king said you can't? Then what are we doing if you're not allowed to—"

"Not *that* kind of can't," I tried to explain. "He meant it as in, I'm not *capable* of interrogating someone."

"Oh." They both chuckled.

Zayne carried the tray as he and Zayden walked me to the little outdoor area we'd set up.

"Need anything else, luna?"

"No, I think I'm set." Sprawled on the chaise lounge, I had my feet up with the tray on the little table by my elbow.

They snickered at me.

"What?" I whined. "I might as well be comfortable, right?"

"You're something else, Luna Posy," they chorused and grinned down at me.

"What was he like before everything went downhill?" I asked.

"He was a good alpha," Zayne said with a sad look in his eyes. "Stern, but fair. Strict, but not mean."

"Did he change suddenly or gradually?"

"At the time, we were all like, 'Oh, alpha's having a bad day' and brushed it off," Zayden said, his eyes narrowing as he thought. "Then every day started to be a bad day. It didn't *seem* sudden, but I think it must have been."

I thanked them, and they went looking for Beatrix. Not two minutes later, Em and Ty pulled up in Ash's SUV. They got out, and Ty opened the passenger side back door and held it as a man half-crawled, half-rolled out. I knew Leo Halder was the same age as Luke and King Julian, but his hunched shoulders, lined face, and gray-tinted skin made him seem like an old man.

Once the trio reached me, Leo went to sit down and lost his balance. Ty and Em each grabbed an arm and held him steady.

"Easy," Ty murmured as he helped Leo sit.

Then the betas stepped back to flank his chair, silently standing guard. As Em crossed his beefy arms, Ty took out his phone and fiddled with it for a second. When he looked over at me and nodded, I knew he was ready to start recording.

They'd tried to explain the process to me - how Ty would use an online meeting program so the people gathered in the living room could hear and see everything - but I'd tuned most of it out. Technology wasn't something I understood very much about. I only learned how to send texts on my phone two days ago.

"Hello," I said quietly. "I'm Posy Briggs, luna of Five Fangs."

Leo Halder raised his head and blinked his nearly black eyes at me several times, his surprise clear as day.

"Leo," he rasped at last.

"Your throat sounds dry. Would you like some lemonade?"

He nodded, and I took a glass from the little table and held it out to him. He reached for it with both hands, which shook with fine tremors, and took it carefully.

"Thank you," he murmured.

I waited until after he took a sip before I spoke again.

"Cookie? Banana?"

"Banana, please."

I passed him one and took a cookie for myself. Nibbling on it, I savored the rich buttery taste as he ate his banana. When he was done, he laid the peel on the grass next to his chair.

"More?" I asked him.

"No, thank you." He took a deep breath and let it out slowly. "Why are you being so nice to me? Did the king send you to soften me up before he comes to torture me?"

"How do you know *I'm* not going to torture you?"

"Please," he scoffed. "You don't look like you couldn't hurt a fly."

"Come on, Leo." I shook my head. "We both know that real torture has nothing to do with physical pain."

"True enough. Point to you."

Typical guy. I took a sip of my lemonade to stop myself from rolling my eyes. *Everything's a competition.*

"Which pack are you from?" he asked after a few seconds of silence.

"Green River."

He swung his head and stared at me with squinted eyes.

"You said your last name is Briggs. Is Alpha Kendall Briggs your father?"

"He was my mother's husband, but he was never my father," I admitted quietly.

"Yeah." Leo nodded. "I met him at a conference of alphas, oh, maybe five years ago. I wasn't impressed. I can't imagine that he's any better at being a father than he is at being a decent person."

"He isn't any kind of person now. He's dead." I set my glass down and folded my hands on my lap. "My mates killed him."

His eyebrows flew up, and his dark eyes rounded with unspoken questions, so I told him a bit about what happened. As I did, five boys sent me a wave of love, which I returned gratefully.

"I'm glad you got out before he killed you," Leo murmured when I stopped talking. "I'm also glad he's dead. That was one shifter who didn't need a demon to be an unspeakable bastard."

"Speaking of demons, how did it happen, Leo? How did you get possessed?"

"It was such a dumb thing." His hands scrubbed over his face, then sunk into his black hair. "Such a dumb thing to eat more than a year of my life and kill and torment so many of my people."

"Would you like to tell me about it?" I asked quietly.

He let out a deep breath, then the words poured out of him as if a plug had been pulled.

"My friend, Alpha Alphonse Riggans of the Blue Rock pack, asked for assistance in clearing some alligator spirits. They'd been leaving the bayou and encroaching on his territory. I put my beta, Luke MacGregor, in charge and took a squad of my best boys to help my friend. I figured we'd be back in two or three days with no problems. Goddess, was I wrong."

The story he told next was going to give me nightmares.

He explained how, in between the pack territory and the bayou, there's a group of sinking houses that have been abandoned for decades. During the fight, a pair of gator spirits waddled inside one of those houses, and Leo followed. He killed them, then investigated the closet they were guarding.

Instead of the nest he expected, he found the remains of a wooden trunk filled with a bunch of books and papers and stuff. There was a small velvet box, too, that he opened to find a beautiful ruby pendant on a gold chain. He said it glistened in the dim light and seemed to pulse like a heartbeat.

Since his wolf is Ruby, he thought it was a sign to take it, so he picked it up by the chain and thought about resetting it into a ring. The house chose that moment to shift under his feet, and the pendant whacked him in the face, one of the sharp facets cutting him.

I glanced over at him to see him touching a small, white star-shaped scar on the left side of his jaw.

"Next thing I knew, my head was filled with a new voice, one that was neither man nor wolf," he said. "You know how it feels when you shift and hand control over to your wolf? Like she's driving and you're in the backseat along for the ride? It was similar, only I couldn't regain control like I can when Ruby is being stubborn."

165

He shook his head and clenched his hands into fists.

"Like an alpha command, a demon is impossible to disobey," he muttered. "I was forced to watch everything it did while wearing my body, and there was nothing I could do. I couldn't fight it, I couldn't overpower it, and I couldn't command it. I was a prisoner inside my own head."

"What about Ruby?" I tilted my head, curious about how a demon affected a wolf. "What did he do?"

"The demon couldn't control him quite as well, but it kept him locked down. Ruby tried to protect me. Tried to take the psychic damage for me. I think he's in worse shape than I am right now, but the one witch said we'll both recover with time."

He let out a dark chuckle that made me frown.

"That is, if Angelo della Morte doesn't end me first. I knew the demon made a bad choice involving the del Vecchio flock, and I wished no harm to any of those witches, but I have to admit, I hoped it would attract the Angel of Death's attention. I just wanted to die."

Getting to my feet, I stood in front of him, framed his face between my palms, and stared into his dark brown eyes for a long moment. He didn't move, didn't even seem to be breathing, and I finally dropped my hands and stood straight.

"And you still do," I murmured.

His lips trembled as he pressed them together and his gaze dropped to the grass.

"How can I live with the memories, with all the blood on my head?" His voice cracked and a tear slid from each eye. "Even more important, how can I ever make this right? What could I possibly do to make up for all the evil these hands have done?"

There were still plenty of questions that needed to be answered. Why had the demon been so obsessed with Queen Lilah? What happened to the ruby pendant and that trunk of stuff in the sinking house? Still, I knew what decision was the right one.

He's coming home with us, I told my boys.

Honey, wait a minute—

We should talk first, cutie—

Uh, princess, I don't think—

*I **said**, he's coming home with us. My word is your law, remember? So make it happen. And that's the end of it.*

Yes, luna, Mason smirked, and the humor glazing his voice told me he accepted and agreed with my decision.

And if Mason did, the others would, too.

It good to be luna, Lark chuckled.

It's good to have my mates' trust and respect, I corrected her.

22: For Real

Posy

Much, much later, my mates and I were in our bed and Jayden had his hand between my thighs.

Sucking one of my nipples, he rubbed his thumb against my nub until my heart tried to beat out of my rib cage. I desperately wanted to catch what I was chasing, and he made sure I did.

"Jayden!" I cried out, clinging to his shoulders.

"Why does Jay always get to make her come first?" I heard Wyatt whine through the fog in my brain.

Jayden huffed in annoyance, gathered me against him, and rolled us so I was on the edge of the mattress and as far away from the others as I could get. I giggled at him, and he smiled.

"Um," I bit my lip and dropped my eyes to his chest, and all those hard ridges and lines distracted me.

"What is it, sweetness?"

"I don't want to practice anymore."

"All right. Give me a second to calm down and—"

"No, I don't want you to calm down. I want to—" I let it out in a rush. "I'm ready for real now. Not that *that* wasn't real. I mean, I'm ready to go on, if you are. Are you?"

I shut my eyes as my face caught on fire. Then a kiss landed on my nose, and my eyes popped open. Jayden smiled at me, his dragon gaze full of fire and want.

"Yes, I'm ready, too."

"And I'm okay to take my panties off now," I told him. "Although they didn't seem to be in your way before."

"Well, they'll be in the way of what we're going to do next, so let's take them off."

He hooked his thumbs in the waistband and zipped them down my legs in two seconds, then tossed them to the floor where he'd flung all the rest of our clothes earlier.

He laid me on my back before propping up on one elbow to see every inch of me. Under his hungry gaze, the throbbing returned to my core, and I pressed my thighs together to make it stop.

"What *are* we going to do next?" I asked.

His eyes swung up to lock with mine while his hand traveled down, down, down to where I ached. I opened my legs again, craving his touch.

"Remember how Wyatt explained it? I'll put myself in here." He eased two fingers inside me again, making me moan. "It might hurt at first. If it's too bad, tell me and I'll stop."

167

"Will it—" I frowned when he withdrew his fingers. I wanted to tell him to put them back, but wasn't that bold. "Will it get better?"

"Yeah, baby. I'll make you fly again," he promised.

"All right. I want to do this, and I want *you*."

He stared at me in silence, then leaned down to kiss me slowly and deeply.

"I love you, Posy."

My heart skipped a few beats.

"I love you, too. So, so much."

He slipped off his boxers, then crawled on top of me and started to wedge his thigh between mine. When I realized what he wanted, I eagerly spread my legs wider. He chuckled softly and slid his hips into the channel I'd made for him.

"Ready, my love?"

"Yes!"

He hooked a hand under my knee and hiked my leg over his hip. Then something big poked me, and my eyes rounded with wonder. It touched my entrance and went in only half an inch before it stopped, but it was enough to startle me.

"No, baby. Don't tighten up." He touched the tip of his nose to mine. "It's me, remember? It's Jayden, loving you in every way there is to love you. Relax, sweetness. Just relax."

Clinging to his words, I inhaled a lungful of his lush scent and my muscles loosened almost immediately.

I love the smell of roses, especially—

I cried out as pain jolted through me. It both stung and burned, and tears filled my eyes.

"I'm sorry. I'm sorry, darling girl. Give it a minute. Let your body adjust."

An eternity passed with his forehead on my shoulder and something enormous buried inside me.

"Sweetness? Is it better?"

I wiggled a bit to see and was happy to find the pain had faded.

"Yes," I told him.

He raised his head, and our eyes met and held. Very slowly, he drew his hips back, then carefully brought them forward again. At first, it burned a little, and I had to bite the inside of my lips after each of his strokes. I'd endured much worse for nothing, though; I could stand this if it led to the pleasure he'd promised.

After a few more unhurried thrusts, a new kind of burn began. Somehow, he knew when it happened. His smooth and tender rhythm steadily increased speed until I was panting again.

"Jayden?" I gasped.

168

"Goddess, you're tight!" he groaned, tipping his head back. "So damn tight! It feels amazing!"

He felt amazing, too. Everything he was doing to me felt amazing. I never knew my body could feel anything like this. I wanted to tell him that, but all that came out of my mouth was his name on a long, low moan.

"Jaaaayden!"

He groaned again, then braced his hands on either side of my head, rose up to hover over me, and drove in deeper. Soft cries escaped my lips every time he hit this one spot, and he was quick to figure that out.

"Get ready, little bird," he panted. "You're going to come with me."

Balancing on one hand, he reached between us and furiously rubbed my nub, and I couldn't hold on any longer.

"*Jayden?*"

"Fly, baby," he bit off as he pumped into me hard and fast.

I rocketed into the sun like a phoenix blazing across the sky. When the fire burned out, the wind buffeted me around like a feather, carrying me far away. Tears skated down my cheeks and I didn't understand why I felt so lost.

Then my beloved's voice drew me back to my nest. Back to my home.

"Shh. I'm here. I've got you, precious girl. You're okay. Sweet, sweet Posy."

I came to my senses to find Jayden lying on his back with me sprawled on top of him, his arms wrapped tight around my head and shoulders. Shaking hard, I hugged his neck and sobbed, and he pushed my face into his throat.

"Call on your wolf to heal the soreness," he whispered.

I didn't need to call Lark, though. She'd already done it, and I'd never felt better in my life.

"Let me clean you up, sweetness."

"I've got it, Jay," Cole murmured. "I'm going to wash you a bit, okay, baby?"

I nodded, then he gently wiped a warm wet cloth on my thighs and between them.

"I'll be right back, Posy. I'm going to clean up, too," Jayden said.

I didn't want to hear that. I felt vulnerable and needy.

"No," I whimpered and clung to him.

"Okay, okay," he murmured and stroked my hair.

"I'll get you a washcloth for now, Jay," Ash said from across the bed.

"I'm sorry for being selfish," I whispered.

"No, baby, don't be. I feel vulnerable right now, too."

"You do? But you were perfect." I stared into his beautiful eyes.

"Thank you, sweetness. You were, too." His smile was just as beautiful as his eyes. "I will never, ever forget that."

"Me, either," I said on a yawn, which made him chuckle.

"Sleep if you want to," he whispered and pecked my nose.

Languid and boneless, I drifted in and out of sleep to the lullaby of my mates' hushed voices.

"That was beautiful, man."

Jayden's chest vibrated under my ear as he told Cole to shut up.

"No, seriously," Cole said. "I couldn't have done that half as well. Thanks for making our mate's first time so good."

"Mmm. Not like I did anything I wasn't going to do anyway."

"You're going to make love to her like that *every time*?" Wyatt sounded incredulous.

"Why mess with perfection?"

"But it took forever," Wyatt whined. "It'll be dawn before I get my turn!"

"Listen, five minute wonder, it's about *her* pleasure, not yours," Jayden said.

"I know that, and it will be, but maybe I can go before you next time. I'll never make it if I have to go last every time."

"Get better at controlling yourself," Mason advised.

"He spent ten minutes just *talking* to her!"

"Something you should be good at, Motor Mouth!"

Jayden laughed so hard that he jiggled me off his chest, and I rolled until I bumped into Cole's side.

"Hey, honey."

His arms snaked around me and dragged me against him, then he stuffed his nose in my hair to take a deep inhale. I knew he was savoring my scent because I was doing the same thing with him.

That deep throb woke up between my legs again, and I debated if I should do what I wanted to do. Jayden had made me fly and I yearned to do it again, this time with Cole.

Decision made, I looped my arms around Cole's neck, then reached up and took out his hair tie. All that thick, black hair fell around his face and I tangled my fingers in it, greedy to play with the silky strands.

He groaned as his hands went to my bum and squeezed, pulling me closer to his big body.

I didn't really know how to ask for what I wanted, what I *needed*, but I gave it my best shot.

"Cole," I breathed, "will you love me now?"

"Oh, honey." His fern-green eyes widened. "I am so sorry, but I'm going to need to calm down *a whole lot* before I can do that like Jay."

"Why do you need to do it like Jayden?" I pouted. "You're Cole. Cole is Cole and Jayden is Jayden."

"He set a high bar. I don't want you to be disappointed."

I could feel his excitement in the hardness swelling against my thigh and knew he wasn't hesitating because he was uninterested. That gave me a jolt of confidence.

"How could I be disappointed if it's you loving me?" I tilted my head, puzzled.

He stared into my eyes for a second, then lowered his mouth to my throat. When he lightly nipped my mate mark, sparks zipped through my veins and made me shudder and squirm against him.

"You're dangerous, you know that?" His lips brushed my skin with each word. "I can't tell you no for anything."

I lost interest in talking when he kissed me like it was the last time he'd ever get the chance to do so. Urgent and needy, his tongue explored every bit of my mouth, and his rough hands slid up and down my back.

"Are you sure?" he whispered in my ear.

"I'm sure," I whispered back.

That seemed to be all the reassurance he needed. He shucked off his boxers, then slipped one hand between my legs. His mouth worked its way down to my breasts and tormented them with hard sucks and soft nibbles.

"Cole," I moaned and tightened my thighs against his busy hand.

With a wet pop, his lips left my nipple. He opened my knees, then settled his hips in place and braced his elbows on either side of my head.

"Tell me if I scare you, honey. Goddess, I hope I don't scare you."

"I will, but you won't."

With a clenched jaw, he pushed himself in, going slow as his thick girth stretched me. When he was all the way inside, he paused and kissed me.

"You feel incredible." His pretty green eyes widened and sparkled with wonder.

"So do you," I murmured.

Grinning, he began to move at a slow, easy pace that lasted all of thirty seconds before he ramped up to jackhammer speed.

For a second, I was shocked, unable to believe anyone could move that fast. My body loved it, though, and the tingling knot in my core turned into a desperate craving for more. I reached up and hung on to his arms.

Hungry moans tore from my throat, embarrassing me with their volume, but I couldn't hold them back. Cole was making me feel so good and it didn't seem like he'd be stopping any time soon, which made me *very* happy.

"I'm so sorry, honey," he ground out. "I can't be slow and gentle."

His apology frustrated me. Didn't he know that I wanted it like this? That I needed it?

Probably not, since it his first time, too. Lark rolled her eyes. *Tell him what you like.*

"Harder!" I pleaded, gripping his arms like a lifeline. "Harder, Cole!"

"Oh, baby. Whatever you say."

He reared back, hooked his elbows under my knees, and drew my legs up to his shoulders. Pressing forward, he slammed into me harder and faster than before. In this new position, my breasts bounced like crazy. He must have enjoyed that because his hooded eyes stayed glued on them.

Strangely enough, his staring only tightened the knot of tension building in my belly. I *liked* his eyes on me.

As if he couldn't help himself, he cupped one of my breasts with his hand, never losing his rhythm. When his thumb scraped over my taut nipple, I threw back my head with a moan.

He got a little rougher then, exciting me more. Pushing his upper body forward more forcefully, he curled my lower half up off the bed, and something started to slap into my bum with every quick thrust. It startled me at first, but it kept hitting the right spot and the longer he went, the tighter the knot twisted in my core.

"I love you," he growled.

I wanted to answer, but his fingers left my nipple and slipped down to find my little nub, and that was all it took. The straining knot burst into a thousand strings, and I cried out for him.

He was still going, but frantically now, and I wondered if that meant he was close to his own release. I got my answer when he stopped, threw his head back, and groaned deep in his throat.

After a few seconds, he rocked back on his knees with his long, black hair falling in his face.

"Are you okay?" he demanded. "Posy, did I hurt you? Did I scare you?"

"Mmm."

"Posy!" he barked.

"She's fine, dude," Ash answered for me. "Floating down from cloud nine. Wait a second for her eyes to stop spinning."

Cole let out a relieved breath and eased my legs down.

"I love you, too, Cole," I whispered when I could breathe again.

Still on his knees, he grinned down at me and gently massaged my hips.

"You're gorgeous, honey, especially like this. Naked and sprawled out and very well loved."

Fire lit my whole face, but I figured I could admire his sweat-beaded body if he was looking at mine.

"Ahem!"

I turned my head and saw Ash smirking at me. Embarrassed to be caught staring, I sat up, wrapped my arms around Cole's hips, and hid my face against his firm stomach. That wasn't the best move because now his sticky boy parts were pressed into my breasts, but he didn't seem to mind.

"Cole?" I raised my head. "What kept hitting my bum?"

"Probably my ball sack." His ears turned red. "Did it bother you?"

"Um, definitely not. It was—" I didn't know how to describe it, so settled for, "Mind-blowing."

"Good. It definitely blew my mind, too," he grinned.

"Can I have my mind blown?" Ash asked.

"Only if you return the favor," I teased, surprised at myself for being bold enough to do that.

"Of course, princess."

With a little smirk, Cole moved from between my legs and plopped down between me and Jayden. Ash took that to mean it was his turn and slid in against my back so that my spine rested against his chest. His arm wrapped around my collar bones so that his hand could cup my opposite shoulder, and he flipped us so we were lying on our other sides and now faced Mason.

"I love you, cupcake." His free hand squished and kneaded my bum cheek.

"I love you, too, waffle."

He chuckled, then bent his head down to whisper in my ear.

"Can I take you from behind?"

Electric shocks jolted through me at both his hot breath on my skin and the image created by his words.

173

"Like what you did last night?" I turned my head to see his dark eyes.

"Mm-hmm, only this time, I'll be inside your vagina instead of between your sweet cheeks."

Everything inside me clenched tight, and I couldn't catch my breath.

"Yes."

Before I finished the word, he stopped massaging my bum, wrapped his hand around my thigh, and lifted my leg. Then he carefully entered me, and I nearly passed out from the pure pleasure of his long, broad penis pushing into me inch by inch.

"Ash!" I cried out, loving the feel of him, *all* of him, sinking deep inside me.

"Goddess, you feel good! So, so good, baby!"

My only answer was a moan as all unnecessary brain functions shut down. With both hands, I gripped the arm he had slung across my upper shoulders and held on tight.

His pace became frenzied after the first few slow thrusts, and I couldn't keep up with him. He stiffened and groaned deep in his throat while my core was still spiraling tighter.

When he lowered my leg, I fisted my hands into the sheets and pushed my bum into him, desperate to find the intense pleasure that seemed to be just out of my reach.

"Posy?" he murmured and nuzzled his face into my neck. "What is it, princess? Did I hurt you?"

"Please, Ash," I begged with tears streaming down my cheeks. "*Please!*"

Opening my eyes, I saw Mason staring at me with concern.

"I don't think she finished," he told Ash in an urgent tone. "Help her!"

"What? How?"

Ash sounded upset, but my desperate need for release made it impossible for me to comfort him. I mewled like a kitten and ground my bum against him.

"I don't know. Rub her button?" Mason suggested.

"Keep moving even if you're soft," Jayden said. "She needs the friction."

"Play with her nips," Cole instructed.

"No, suck on her mate mark," Wyatt said.

Panicking, Ash took *all* of their advice. His mouth covered my mate mark and sucked hard, his fingers rubbed the nub inside my wet folds, and one hand kneaded my breast. As he bucked his hips against my bum, his penis once more grew thick and hard.

"Thank the Goddess for that," he mumbled.

174

Lifting my leg again, he rammed back inside me.

With a hoarse cry, I stretched my arms up and over my head and speared my fingers into his thick curls. My breasts danced all over my chest until two big hands caught them. I locked gazes with Mason as he stroked his thumbs over my hard nipples.

With Ash pounding into me from behind and Mason massaging my breasts, it was no surprise I exploded seconds later. A few more thrusts from Ash and he finished, too.

Then he buried his face in my throat, and I felt hot tears slide down my skin.

Oh, no. Oh, Goddess, what have I done?

My own tears fell as shame filled me. I'd let my mate down and made him feel awful about his first time.

"I'm so sorry," I hiccuped. "Ash, forgive—"

"No, no, no, angel! That was my fault. It's *you* who needs to forgive *me*."

"But I took too long and ruined it!"

"You didn't ruin anything, princess. It's our job to make sure you're satisfied, no matter how long it takes. I was clumsy and impatient and didn't pay attention to your needs." He sighed. "Talk about being mortified."

"No need for *any* degree of mortification," I repeated his words from last night.

"I'll do better next time, I promise."

"Me, too." I never, ever wanted to make one of my mates cry again.

"Oh, cupcake, you were perfect. I loved how it felt to sink my dick into your wet heat, and I love squeezing your soft, squishy ass—"

My breathing picked up and I squirmed against him again.

"Are you going to come just from listening to me?" He laughed so hard, he folded over.

Fire flooded my cheeks, and Mason pulled me into his arms.

"Don't be embarrassed," he murmured in my ear. "Each one of us has come in our shorts more than once just listening to your sweet moans and breathy noises. It's natural and normal, okay?"

I nodded and kissed his hard pecs, making him groan. Something had awakened inside me, some hunger that made me ache and yearn for more pleasure from my mates, even though I'd just made love with three of them.

"Posy?" Mason's thumbs tilted my head to meet his gray eyes.

"Mason," I gasped and pushed up to kiss him full on the lips.

I'm sorry! I linked him as my mouth ravaged his. *I'm ashamed of myself for being so ... lustful.*

That's also natural and normal, he linked back as he took control of the kiss and slowed it down. *Your body wants to complete the mate bond with all of us. Are you okay with that? If not, we can stop. Wyatt and I can wait however long you need us to.*

No! Please don't stop. I thought I might die if he did. *And yes, I want to.*

You want me? You want me to love you? Right now?

"Yes, Mason! Right now!"

I grabbed his face, shoved his head up, and bit his mate mark.

With a low growl, he flipped me onto my stomach, then pulled my bum up, spread my legs, and plunged into me with one heavy thrust.

"Mason!" I shrieked in both surprise and excitement.

He chuckled and gripped my hips tightly as he delved deep inside me.

Every stroke hit the right place, and orgasm after orgasm ripped through my body as he pistoned into me like a machine. Loud moans vibrated from my throat, and I was embarrassed until I heard his deep, husky voice making similar noises.

He went for a long time, slamming into me increasingly harder and faster, until my arms shook from holding myself up. Thankfully, right before they gave out, one of the boys shoved a pillow under me. I screamed Mason's name as he pleasured me three more times before he was finally spent, then his sweaty chest collapsed against my back, and we fell to the mattress.

I love you, little flower, Mason linked me.

I love you, too.

Every part of me quivered as we panted together. His big body felt delicious on top of me, but he must have thought he was too heavy; he rolled onto his side and pulled me with him so that my back was against his chest.

"Did you enjoy that, baby?" he crooned. "Do you like being mounted from behind and rode until you can't remember your name?"

I could only nod, so satisfied and sensitized that words were beyond me.

"Mmm. I did, too. So, so much." His voice dropped to a mere breath of sound. "I want to do that again and again and again until we're both raw from it."

A little hiss escaped me, and my bum ground against him without any input from my brain. He was growing thick and hard again, and I shivered in anticipation.

"I've been waiting very patiently, Mason Andre Price, and it is now my turn." Wyatt slid his hands under me. "Posy, may I *please* have you now?"

176

Craving my fifth star, I nodded, and he eased me out of Mason's arms and into his own.

"This time, I am going to be balls-deep inside you when I come," Wyatt muttered as he reached between us.

I latched onto his shoulders as he rubbed his tip against my opening and slipped it in. Then he withdrew and pushed back in. Just his tip. Over and over.

Growing frustrated, I frowned and lightly sank my fingernails into his shoulders.

"Okay, cutie?" he snickered.

"More," I begged. "Please. Wyatt, *please.*"

He grinned and pushed himself all the way in, and I moaned. Grabbing my hands, he held them above my head and threaded our fingers together, then began to rock his hips.

The whole time he slid in and out of me, he whispered in my ear. Most of the words flew by me like butterfly wings, but I caught a few.

"I liked watching your titties bounce while Mase drilled you from behind."

Titties? Drilled?

"Your pussy is so tight. So warm and wet and tight."

Pussy? What does a cat have to do with anything?

"Wyatt?" I whimpered.

"Take it, baby. Take it like a good girl."

His tongue should be illegal, too.

A tidal wave was cresting and would drown me any second. The intense need and want for release overwhelmed me, and hot tears slid from the corners of my eyes into my hair. I whined his name again as my toes curled.

"You want to come, little baby?"

"Yes! Yes, Wyatt!"

If I thought he was going fast and hard and deep before, it was nothing compared to what he was doing now. He sucked hard on my mate mark, and lightning scorched through every vein until it hit my core right where we were connected. At the same time, he gathered both my wrists in one hand and moved the other to find my overly stimulated nub.

Two strokes of his fingers later, the wave broke over me and stars burst behind my eyes.

"That's it, cutie," he gasped. "Squeeze that tight pussy around me. Milk me dry of every last drop."

I blanked out for a while after that, surfing the endless swells of euphoria under his heavy weight. I could hear my mates talking as if from a distant shore.

177

"For Goddess' sake," Mason grouched, "did you *have* to talk dirty to her? You shouldn't have said pussy. Or titties. Or, well, *any* of it."

"Ha ha ha! Did listening get you hard again, brother?"

"I think hard is going to be the default state for all of us for a while," Jayden chuckled.

Wyatt laughed, too, and finally released my hands.

"It's not like *she's* going to say those kinds of words, are you, cutie? You're too pure and proper to talk like that." He nudged my nose with his. "You liked it, though, didn't you?"

Suddenly shy, I squeaked and buried my face in my hands, which made him chuckle.

"Get off." Mason shoved his shoulder. "You're squishing her."

Snorting, Wyatt rolled over and pulled me with him. His arms stayed locked around my waist as he settled my legs between his raised knees.

Suddenly exhausted, I laid the side of my face against his chest and closed my eyes. My overused muscles quivered and stung, and my limbs turned boneless and weak.

"Posy?" he whispered.

"Mmm?"

"I love you."

No matter how many times I heard any of them say that, it always made my heart flutter.

"Love you, too," I whispered back. "My fifth star."

Mason leaned over and kissed the tears from my temple.

"You made her cry?" he asked Wyatt in a tone that would have made me pee my pants if it were directed at me.

"In a good way," Wyatt promised. "Right, Posy?"

I yawned.

Chuckling, he started to rub my neck. A pair of hands stroked up my legs and massaged my lower back and hips, and someone else's fingers kneaded my shoulders.

"Don't stop," I begged them. "Feels *good*."

"Better than mating?" Wyatt joked.

"Right now it does."

Chuckles erupted around me.

Their strong hands were magic, and I was on the edge of falling asleep when I heard Cole's exasperated voice.

"Okay, Jay and I want her over here with us now. You three have hogged her long enough."

"She needs this," Ash argued. "Wait until we're done, then you two can go with her while she soaks in the bath. Fairs?"

"Fairs," Cole agreed

178

23: Alpha and Luna

Posy

I woke up with Wyatt's face smashed into my neck as he spooned me from behind tightly enough to be my second skin.

"Wake, cutie?" he muttered, then made a noise as he blew some of my hair out of his mouth.

I giggled, which I supposed was answer enough.

"Mmm. Good."

He gathered my hair up in his hand and draped it out of the way, then cupped my breast and squeezed it gently. Dropping kisses on my back and shoulders, he hummed in approval when I wiggled back into him, and I sucked in a breath in anticipation as I felt him growing hard against my bum.

"Ash is standing outside the door, baby," Wyatt whispered as his hand left my breast and headed south. "He wants to know if he can join us."

"Why is he there and why is he even asking?" I turned my head to look into Wyatt's eyes.

"He's embarrassed after last night and has an idea he wants to try, if you're up for it."

Oh, my heart.

Waffle, you come in here right now! I linked him.

The door creaked open and my super-tall mate slunk in. His cheeks were pink and he didn't meet my eyes.

"Get in this bed right now." My voice started out stern, but ended in a breathy whine as Wyatt's fingers found what they were looking for.

Swallowing hard, Ash shed his clothes and crawled in, lying on his side so that we were eye to eye.

"What is this about?" I raised my hands and sank them into his dark curls as we stared at each other.

"So I want to try again with just the three of us. If you're willing. Wyatt said he'd help if I mess up again."

"Huh?"

Yeah, that was the best I could do with Wyatt's busy fingers stroking in and out of me.

"We'll swap in and out, Posy." Wyatt stopped to suck on my earlobe before continuing. "Like a pinch runner in baseball. Ash will bat first. When he shoots off too early, I'll sub in and finish the game."

"I knew I should have asked Jay instead of you!" Ash's eyes filled with tears, wrenching my heart. "At least he wouldn't make fun of me!"

179

"I wasn't!" Wyatt protested and sounded truly affronted that Ash thought he was making fun of him. "I was trying to explain it in a way she'd understand without being crude, which is what you always accuse me of being!"

"Both of you, stop." I used my hold on Ash's hair to draw him closer and kissed him gently.

"I understand that you're sensitive about the issue, and you feel vulnerable." I kissed him again. "Wyatt didn't mean it like that. Just because he talks all cocky doesn't mean he has any more experience than you do."

"Actually, I do," Wyatt said in a stage-whisper. "I've watched *videos*."

With a sigh, I reached back, ripped the sheet away, and slapped his bare thigh.

Hard.

"Ouch, Posy!"

"Take it like a good boy," I rephrased his words from last night.

"Oh, baby girl, do you know what you're saying?"

I could hear the grin in his voice and felt him growing even harder against my bum.

"Um, not really," I told him, then gave my attention back to Ash. "And just because Wyatt makes jokes doesn't mean he feels any less vulnerable. You should know by now that he uses humor to cover up his deeper feelings."

Ash's big brown eyes stared at me before a small smile twitched the corners of his lips up. Then those lips were on mine, massaging them open for his tongue to raid my mouth and relearn every crevice.

Pulling me away from Wyatt's warm bulk, Ash dragged me under him and kissed his way from my jaw to my breasts, where he stopped and spent several long moments giving each one love and attention. I wriggled under him, clenched my fist in his curls, and moaned as he sucked and nipped his way to my belly button, then further south.

When he opened my thighs and spread my outer folds wide with his thumbs, Wyatt undid my fingers from Ash's hair and pinned my hands over my head. He loomed over me and kissed me senseless while Ash's mouth dove in down below.

A low moan vibrated out of my throat as pleasure burned my insides like fire.

Wyatt's mouth released mine and moved to suck on my mate mark right as Ash's tongue flicked and swirled my nub, and I dug my toes into the bed as I panted and writhed beneath my mates.

180

"Ash!" I whimpered. "Wyatt!"

Wyatt lowered his head to my breasts, caught a taut nipple between his lips, and gently bit down. At the same time, Ash wrapped his soft lips around my nub and sucked hard.

Come, cutie. Come hard for us.

With a loud moan, I did as Wyatt demanded and fell apart at the seams, my body going as tense as a piano wire.

Still riding the waves of pleasure, I was only half aware of Wyatt releasing my hands and moving aside so Ash could hover over me as he settled his thighs between mine. Then he sank his whole length inside me with one solid stroke, and I grabbed his shoulders with a gasp.

"Did I hurt you, princess?" he whispered. "Please tell me I didn't hurt you. Wyatt, I told you that was a bad idea. Why do I listen—"

"No, Ash." I shook my head. "You didn't hurt me. I'm just so *full*. So full of *you*."

A little timidly, I wiggled my hips, wanting him to move, and watched as his eyes rolled back a bit.

"Please, Ash," I whispered.

He knew what I wanted, what I *needed*, and he didn't disappoint. He built his rhythm quickly and was soon pounding into me, his breath as hot and heavy in my ear as mine was in his.

Together, we spiraled higher and higher, and I chased the pleasure that glittered just out of my reach.

Then a thumb made contact with my aching nub and stroked it up and down at a rapid rate, and I finally came, starbursts exploding behind my eyelids.

Ash pumped into me a few more times before his long body went taut and he groaned deep in his throat. Collapsing on me, he nuzzled his face in my neck and laid an open-mouth kiss on my mate mark, sending shivers all through my body.

"I love you, Posy," he whispered.

"I love you, Ash," I whispered back.

I glanced over at Wyatt. His hand was sliding up and down his hard length, and stark hunger burned in his silvery-blue eyes.

"Cutie, can I—"

"Yes," I moaned. "Please, Wyatt!"

He didn't waste any time. Swapping places with Ash, he slid into me with a heavy groan and went right into the fast, hard pace he'd used last night. Wrapping my legs around his waist, I grabbed his forearms and held on as his hips drove forward again and again until I cried out his name.

"Good girl," he panted, still hammering into me. "Now give me another one."

"I don't think I can," I whined, so overly sensitized that his breath on my neck felt like a blow torch.

"Give me another one, baby," he demanded in a stern tone. "Ash!"

Ash's long fingers found my nub and went to work, moving as fast as Wyatt's hips, and I was done for, coming so hard that the world faded to black at the edges of my vision.

"Wyatt!" I screamed.

"That's my good little girl."

He suddenly stilled over me, his arms bulging with veins and his head tipped back as he groaned. After a few seconds, he leaned down to kiss me tenderly, then plopped onto his back, rearranging me on my side with his heavy arm draped over my collar bones and my bum snug against his boy parts.

"I love you, Wyatt," I murmured, still trying to catch my breath.

"I love you, too." His fingers stroked my upper arm, gently tracing the deep scars there.

"Join us, waffle." I held out my arms, and Ash's big, sticky body was pressed tight against mine before I finished my sentence.

"Posy," he whispered as he buried his face in my boobs and hugged my waist. "Sweet Posy."

"You were great, Ash," Wyatt murmured. "See? I told you that you could do it."

Reaching around me, he ruffled Ash's messy curls, and Ash giggled.

My heart swelled so much, I feared it might burst.

Goddess, I love these boys.

#

Jayden

While Wyatt was helping Ash with his "experiment," the rest of us sorted out several things.

First, we decided to induct all the new mates into the pack during Posy's luna ceremony. Now that we were fully mated, we could hold it whenever we wanted, and it would be the perfect time to add new members since the majority of the pack would be there.

Zayden and Zayne surprised us by asking to join Five Fangs so that Beatrix could stay with her flock. We explained we had no beta positions open, but they weren't interested in being betas, despite their blood. They planned to be Angelo's apprentices when they weren't busy with whatever pack jobs we assigned them.

When the del Vecchios realized they'd all be able to stay near each other, the witches immediately started the process to move their business. Mase told them about the empty lot next to Roger's Diner that they could have for a song, and Cole added that the pack had its own construction crew that would build a shop to their specifications.

I offered to contact a company to pack their personal belongings and their business, and Beatrix said she and her mates would go supervise the move, as the twins had no job in our pack yet. The betas had to return and take charge of Five Fangs until my brothers and I were done here; since none of their mates wanted to be separated from them, it was the perfect solution.

King Julian was going to install Ranger and Junia as alpha and luna after lunch, then we'd be free to go home, too.

As the betas and their mates got ready to leave, a little hiccup appeared when no one knew what to do with Leo.

And yes, I was starting to think of him as Leo and not 'Halder' or 'the bastard,' despite Quartz's grumbling.

Mase had texted the betas a list of properties available in Five Fangs' territory, and they planned to pick out their homes after they returned. That's when we got stuck on the Leo issue.

My brothers and I knew that, if Posy had her way, he'd move into the alpha house, and that was *so* not happening.

"I don't think the pack house would be a good idea," Tyler spoke up, "so what about the O? There's loads of room, and I'd be there to keep an eye on things."

He'd be around pups who are already vulnerable, Cole linked Mase and me.

He didn't willingly hurt the pups here, I pointed out.

Even knowing that, Sid would have a fit.

Conceding the point, I told Ty that wouldn't work.

Emerson and Angelo, who'd been having their own silent conversation, nodded at each other, then Em raised his hand like an overgrown schoolboy.

"Yeah, Em?" Mase gave him the floor.

"He can stay with us, at least at first. You know which house I'd like. It has dozens of rooms and loads of wilderness around it for running and de-stressing."

And Angelo would be there to end him if he relapses into ... bad habits, Cole linked, making me frown.

We're supposed to be giving him a second chance, I reminded him.

And I'm onboard with that. With certain precautions in place should things go sideways.

I rolled my eyes, but let it go. He'd slip up soon enough, and Posy would find out that he held a grudge against Leo. By the time she sorted him out, he'd be singing a different tune.

"Are either of you interested in that property?" Mase asked Tristan and Matthew.

"Which one is it, Em?" Tyler asked as Tristan and Matthew consulted their mates.

"That old Victorian monstrosity near the Moonset-Dark Woods border."

Tyler nodded, and Matthew and Tristan said Em was welcome to it.

"Great. That's settled." Mase nodded. "It may need some work, so let us know if you want a hand. We'll send painters around once you're ready for them. If I remember right, the outside needs a fresh coat. Get together with McFlynn about what colors you want."

"Thank you, alpha."

"Can we tour the properties before we decide?" Beatrix asked, looking from Emerson to us.

"Of course." I smiled and clapped a hand on Emerson's shoulder. "Em just knows that house. He's been in love with it since he first saw it."

"You're going to love it, too." Emerson squeezed Angelo's hand.

I chuckled. The poor guy looked dazzled by Emerson's brilliant grin, which was a rare enough sight, and I hoped Angelo was wise enough to treasure it.

#

Posy

The combined alpha installation-luna ceremony went smoothly, and the Tall Pines shifters welcomed their new leaders with hope and cheerfulness. I had a good feeling about the pack's future, especially with Ranger and Junia at the helm.

We left soon afterward because we all just wanted to be home. The king and queen had decided to stay a few days and see Ranger and Junia settled in. That meant Luke and Gisela stayed, too.

As for the betas, they and their mates had left before I got out of bed this morning, and my cheeks flushed red as I thought of why I started the day so late.

Lost in my delicious memories, I was startled when Ash brought the SUV to a halt. Raising my head, I looked out the window and saw we were home. Contentment and peace settled around me like a blanket, and I sighed with happiness.

184

At least until I saw two strangers sitting in the rocking chairs on the front porch.

After the five-hour drive home, all I wanted to do was shower and crawl into bed.

One of the men, who was built like Cole and sported more tattoos than Mason, came down the porch steps with a broad grin, and I felt my boys' excitement. Whoever he was, they were glad to see him.

The dark-haired man also came down the stairs, but stood off to the side as Cole, Wyatt, and Ash swarmed over to the tattooed man with happy shouts of, "Dad!"

Jayden stayed and opened my door for me, giving me a hand out, then Mason came around and the two of them looked at each other for a second. Jayden gave him a short, sharp nod, then joined my other mates.

"Come, Posy," Mason muttered. "Let's get this over with."

I was confused and concerned, but I took his hand when he held it out, and he led me toward the dark-haired stranger.

"So you're finally home." The man's tone was sharp and he looked angry.

I glanced up at Mason to see his face had closed up and his eyes were gray ice. I didn't know who this guy was, but it was clear Mason didn't like him.

"I can't believe you left the gammas in charge!" hissed the black-haired man.

Wow. Who is this guy and why is talking to his alpha in such a disrespectful way?

And why was Mason letting him get away with it?

"It was for less than twenty-four hours, and what would you have had me do?" Mason bit back. "You and Dad were out of town, and we needed the betas at Tall Pines for a short time while we helped the king."

"Always touting your relationship with the king!" sneered the man. "And who is this girl? A stray you brought home to entertain you until you find your mate?

As the man's gray eyes fixed on me, I cowered behind Mason, wadding up the back of his t-shirt in my fists.

"She *is* our mate," Mason said and squared his shoulders. "Posy, this is—"

"Your mate? A scrawny, weak runt of a girl? Tell me you're joking."

Tears slipped from my eyes as I buried my face in Mason's back. Is this how everyone would feel about me? If this one pack member already hated me, how would the rest feel?

"She is our mate and your luna, and you will show respect!" Mason thundered, Garnet rich in his voice.

He's mad, he's mad, he's mad, I chanted in my head and clenched my fists tighter. *Someone's going to get hurt!*

He not mad at you, Lark reassured me, *and this shifter deserve some hurt! How dare he insult alpha and luna?!*

"Ha!" the man scoffed. "I could accept her more easily as your whore than your mate!"

At those words, Mason Price lost his temper.

#

Cole

Mase took Posy over to Papa, not because he wanted to, but because he knew Papa would be angry if he didn't greet him and introduce our mate to him first.

The rest of us ran over to greet Dad, although I kept my eye on the trio by the porch steps. Papa and Mase's relationship was rocky at best and nuclear at worst.

It's all Papa's fault, Topaz grouched. *He hurts Mase so often and over nothing.*

I know, Paz. I just hope Posy doesn't get caught in the crossfire.

Don't let that happen, Cole, Topaz growled with a rough burr.

Assuring him I wouldn't, I half-listened as the three musketeers chatted with Dad, who was all ears to hear about Posy as well as what happened at Tall Pines.

Three musketeers, I smirked to myself.

Posy had called Ash, Wyatt, and Jay that the other day, and it had stuck with Mase and me. When I asked her why, she said it was because they were so close in age and were usually together.

And it was true. We were all very close, but those three went out of their way to be physically near each other. Jay and Ash had grown up together after Jay's parents adopted Ash at age two, and Wyatt fell in with the two of them as soon as they started school.

"Mom and Mama are going to want to meet her ASAP. You know that, right?" Dad said with a huge grin. "They'll want to help her plan her luna ceremony."

"How about a picnic tomorrow afternoon?" Ash suggested. "Bring Peri and the horde and get it all over with at once."

"That might overwhelm our girl," Jay disagreed. "Let's ask her first."

"Well, Per's birthday is Wednesday, so if nothing else, she can meet the family at the party," Dad pointed out.

"That would be better," Jay said. "Don't you think, Cole?"

186

Hearing my name drew my full attention to their conversation and my eyes away from Mase and Papa - which turned out to be very bad timing.

"*KNEEL BEFORE YOUR LUNA.*"

A mighty blast of alpha power hit us and we all - even Dad - fell to our knees and bent our backs under the immense weight of Mase's fury.

Goddess, that boy is powerful, I grunted, my nose inches from the grass.

Mase mad, Topaz fretted and paced in my mind. *Garnet mad, too.*

I know, Paz. Papa did something dumb, and fifty bucks say he insulted Posy.

No bet, boss. No bet.

24: Show Down with Papa

Mason

I have a beast inside me that I keep under lock and key twenty-four seven, and it is *not* my wolf.

Garnet is nothing to manage in comparison to the rage that bubbles and stews in my gut like a toxic sludge.

Except for Posy, everyone around me was on their knees, and I couldn't bring myself to care that I was being unfair to Dad and my brothers.

All I could focus on was the miserable, cruel bastard crouched at my feet.

"*I HAVE HAD ENOUGH!*" I roared.

Grabbing my father by his throat, I dragged him to his feet and squeezed hard enough to make him choke as he pried at my hand.

"I have tolerated your verbal abuse for years!" I shook him a little. "But for you to disrespect and deny our Goddess-given mate? That I will *never* tolerate!"

"Mase—" he gasped.

"I no longer recognize you as my father."

"Ma—"

"If you disrespect your luna or any of your alphas - *including me* - again, I will punish you as I would any other wolf under my leadership! Speaking of leadership, if you think I'm undeserving of the title of alpha," I leaned in so we were nose to nose, "challenge me for it."

"Mason—"

Keep pushing us, Papa, Garnet murmured in my mind. *Nothing would give me greater pleasure than to put you in your place good and proper.*

"*Alpha* Mason!" I snarled, Garnet's snarky comments fueling the rage. "Let me make it undeniably clear to you, Mr. Price. You are not welcome in my life. If you want to talk to me outside of official functions, make an appointment with my office and then only to discuss pack business."

I dropped him to his feet and almost - *almost!* - stepped back, but the rage still burned like a bonfire inside me.

"And one more thing. *Never* call our mate a whore again."

Drawing back one huge fist, I knocked him out cold, then stared down at his crumpled body.

Serves him right, Garnet smirked.

And felt damn good, I replied with a satisfied grunt.

#

Posy

After Mason finished yelling at his father, he punched him, and Mr. Price fell to the grass without a sound.

I folded my hands over my nose and mouth and stared at my mate's back with huge eyes. Little tremors shook my body, and I fought to keep my breathing even and normal.

"Posy," he said without turning around. "Are you okay?"

"Yes," I whispered.

"I'm sorry I scared you."

"I'm not scared of you," I hedged.

I couldn't lie to him; I *was* scared. Violence and aggression would probably always scare me, but I wasn't scared of my mate.

He probably thinks I am, though, I worried. *He still hasn't looked at me.*

"Listen, I'm going for a run to burn off some of the anger. Don't worry about me. I'm fine and I'll be back."

He ripped off his shirt and stepped out of his shoes.

"Wait!" I called out and raised my hand, but stopped myself from touching him. "Can someone go with you?"

He paused and looked at me over his shoulder, then made eye contact with someone behind me.

"Quartz feel up to it?" he rumbled.

"After being cooped in a vehicle for five hours? You know he is." Jayden sounded like he was grinning.

Seconds later, two piles of clothes were left behind as Garnet and Quartz took off into the woods at breakneck speed.

"Well, luna," said the tattooed man, "what a lovely first impression you must have of your new family."

The boys snickered as the man grinned.

"Hello. My name is Nathan Barlow. This guy's father." He slung an arm around Cole's neck and pulled him into a noogie, Cole's head nearly hidden in his beefy arms. "But I consider all of the boys my sons. You can call me Dad."

"I'm Posy. Posy Briggs. Nice to meet you." I knotted my fingers together behind my back and didn't meet his eyes.

Dad didn't seem anything like Mason's father, thank the Goddess, but I wasn't taking any chances after what just happened. I kept my gaze firmly on the grass.

Cole escaped his dad and came over to wrap his big arms around my shoulders and hold me close against him. Still shaking a little bit, I happily snuggled into his comforting embrace.

"Honey, are you okay?"

"Did I cause that?" I asked into his sternum. "Was that my fault?"

"No, Posy. That was long overdue, and Mase didn't go nearly as hard as I'd feared. I thought we'd be picking pieces of Papa out of the trees."

"That would hurt Mama, and Mase loves her too much for that," Dad disagreed. "She's why he held back all these years, you know."

The boys chatted for a bit with Dad, but I didn't bring my face out of Cole's shirt. Finally, Mr. Price started to stir and Dad sighed.

"All right. I think I better get Papa off your lawn before Mase gets back." He slung Mr. Price up in a fireman's carry, then walked to his car and settled him in the backseat. "I'll see you all on Wednesday for Per's birthday. Come over anytime after five."

The boys called out their goodbyes and Dad started his car, which was loud and rumbly and made me jump.

Cole laughed softly as he swung me up in his arms.

"I could use a snack before bed," he said. "How about you? Want some ice cream?"

I nodded and hid my face in his throat as he carried me into our house.

#

Mason

The next morning, my brothers and I had a ton of work to catch up on and a dozen places to go. We were going to Rock-Paper-Scissors who got to work out of the home office when Matthew linked me that I had a nine a.m. appointment.

I linked him back to reschedule it, but he replied that the person said it was "urgent and dire," so I gave in, albeit with a scowl.

Informing my brothers of that fact restored my good humor, and I accepted their dark scowls and middle fingers with a smirk. I was elated to stay home with our girl, who had assigned herself laundry detail for the day.

We'd protested, telling her we could do our own, but she pointed out that she would be doing hers, and it wouldn't make much difference to do a few loads of our travel clothes.

"Besides, it will give me a job and make me feel useful while you're working."

How could we argue with that? My brothers and I - even block-headed Wyatt - understood she wanted a purpose, wanted to feel like she was contributing, even though we all longed to spoil her rotten.

So we gave her hugs and kisses and left her in the laundry room after breakfast.

I sorted some things out in the home office while I waited for my appointment. According to the calendar on the desk, it was the only one of the day, and I wanted to get it over with so I could clear away the paperwork that had accrued in our absence.

Goddess knew there was enough of it on a regular day. Let it collect for three or four days, and it quickly became overwhelming, especially when certain people - *ahem, Ash* - tried to hide it in drawers rather than take care of it.

I was working away when *his* scent drifted into the room and three sharp knocks at the door soon followed.

Oh, no. What does he want? Garnet groaned. *Did he not understand a word you said yesterday?*

We'll play nice until he doesn't.

And then? my wolf wanted to know.

Then the office might get trashed. There may be a little screaming. And possibly some blood.

Good, Garnet grinned.

"Enter," I said, and the office door opened.

My father came in with a closed look I knew all too well.

"Have a seat, Mr. Price." I waved a hand at the chairs in front of my desk. "What can I do for you?"

"You're not seriously going to keep calling me—"

"I'm dead serious. Now why did you come here?"

"Hmpf." My father sat down on a chair and crossed his legs, his hands folded on his knee. "All right. I'll tell you why. Last night, I did a little digging on that mate of yours. Did you know her mother cheated on her husband with a rogue? *A rogue!* And poor Alpha Kendall Briggs was stuck raising that girl as his daughter."

"You know nothing about the situation. Don't listen to rumors and call it the truth."

I clenched my hands into white-knuckled fists under the desk. He was being civilized, though, so I had to be, too.

No matter how much I longed to beat him to his knees.

"How do you know she won't end up being an adulteress like her mother?" he asked with raised eyebrows. "When she starts popping out pups, how will any of you boys know that they're yours?"

"Our girl is as sweet and innocent as a flower and would never cheat on us." I hesitated to tell him, but the information was nothing that could harm Posy. "As for her mother, she was kidnapped and raped by rogues, and Posy was the result."

"How do you know she isn't playing you all?" he demanded.

"Drop the subject," I ordered. "Next topic on your agenda, or have you run out of venom for today?"

191

"What's with all the witches being inducted into the pack? Did you vet these people?"

"They're mates with our betas. I'm not separating mates." I rolled my eyes. Seriously? This was the 'urgent and dire' concern? "Besides, you know it takes all five of us to agree to induct people into the pack. It wasn't my decision alone."

"But they're *bird shifters*! Do you have any idea what mutant babies a blend of shifters might produce?" He shuddered.

What, is he picturing wolves with wings? Garnet chuffed, amused. *Or birds with teeth and furry ears?*

"They will be members of the pack," I assured him, "and under our protection."

He stared at me for a long time, his gray eyes as cold and unblinking as my own. Finally, he shook his head slowly from side to side.

"You are such a disappointment, Mason. This pack will fail under your weak leadership."

His words were like black pitch being splattered on me. Sure, I could ignore or forget them, but they left a stain. A dark and indelible stain.

The door burst open and slammed against the wall, shaking me out of my grim thoughts, and my eyes surveyed the tiny, quivering figure standing in the doorway.

"It's time for you to leave, Mr. Price."

#

Posy

I didn't mean to eavesdrop on Mason's appointment, but when I picked up Mr. Price's scent in the hallway, I couldn't hold back from checking on my mate. I leaned my ear against the wooden door and heard them talking about the witches, but it wasn't until I heard his father say that Mason was a disappointment that I let my emotions get the better of me.

Flinging the door open harder than I intended, I forced myself to square my shoulders rather than hunch them, then told Mr. Price that it was time for him to leave.

Mason's eyes locked with mine, and I saw both amusement and admiration in his gaze. It made me want to smile, but I was stiff and nervous and couldn't. As if he knew that, he stood and turned his eyes back to his father.

"If I am such a disappointment, blame yourself." He shrugged. "Your cruel words shaped me into what I am. And now, as my mate said, it's time for you to leave."

Mr. Price also stood, and Mason walked around him to loop an arm around my waist.

"I trust you can see yourself out, Mr. Price," he said, then tugged me along with him.

"We're just going to leave him in your office?" I asked.

"Yep. Don't worry. He'll leave when he realizes I'm not coming back."

As soon as we got to our bedroom, Mason picked me up by the back of my thighs, then buried his face in my throat.

"Thanks for the rescue, little flower," he murmured against my skin. "And I'm sorry if I scared you again."

"I'm not scared." I stroked his hair back from his forehead. "You did the right thing."

He inhaled deeply and slowly, then let it out in an explosive rush that ended in a vulnerable little whine, something I *never* thought I'd hear from my highly controlled mate.

"What's wrong with me, Posy?" he whimpered. "Why can't he love me the way a father should?"

He sounded so broken, and my chest burned. How dare his own father hurt him like this!

"There is *nothing* wrong with you!" I gripped the side of his head and pulled his face up so I could make eye contact with him. "I don't know why some people are so cruel and toxic, but I want you to listen to me. There is *nothing* wrong with you. Can you hear me? You are a loving, kind, considerate man, and I love you so, so much!"

Tears flooded his gray eyes. The iceman was melting, and I could finally see the deep chasm of hurt he hid under all the frost.

As I dropped little kisses everywhere I could reach, I opened my link with the rest of my mates, all the betas, and all the gammas.

Mason is taking the rest of the day off.

Wait. He's supposed to—

He's taking off, I interrupted Matthew. *Sort it out. End of.*

Then I closed all the links except for my mates.

You sound just like Mase, Ash chuckled. *Is he rubbing off on you?*

What happened? Cole asked the more practical question, which I answered.

His father was the appointment.

Oh, hell. Do you need one of us to come home? Jayden wanted to know.

Um, no, but what are some things he likes to do? He needs some de-stress time.

Well, he could bend you over the desk and bury himself balls-deep in—

193

WYATT! Three voices shouted.

My face burned red, but my core tingled in anticipation. Even though it was embarrassing to hear him say it, the thought made my panties damp.

Yeah, you're right, Wyatt said with a grin. *Better wait until I get home for that, cutie!*

Wyatt, Cole warned.

Try a video game, Jayden suggested. *He hasn't played in a long time, but he used to like it a lot.*

Which game? I asked.

Gran Turismo or Halo or Call of Duty, Ash said without hesitation.

But I don't know how to play anything except Minecraft. The betas taught me while you were at Tall Pines, but I'm garbage at the other one we tried.

Ask Mase to teach you, Ash said. *He'll like that, and those are - well, were -some of his favorites. Like Jay said, he hasn't taken time to game with us in forever.*

Thanks, my loves. Be safe and see you soon.

They said their goodbyes and went back to their jobs, and I began on my plan to help Mason relax.

Kissing his cheek, I ran my hands over his taut shoulders and massaged them, kneading the tight muscles and rubbing my thumbs over his collar bones.

"Mmm, feels good, baby," he mumbled and tightened his arms around me, still holding me off the floor.

When he shoved his face in my neck and bit down on my mate mark, I shuddered and arched into him.

"Mason," I moaned as his big hands cupped my bum and squeezed.

Okay, bed first, I decided, *then video games.*

25: Happy Birthday, Peri!

Posy

We came back from Tall Pines Monday evening, and Tuesday was ... busy ... after Mr. Price's visit.

Which is why I woke up Wednesday morning in a panic. I hadn't had a chance to get Peri a present for her party tonight.

"Wyatt?" I ran my fingers through his fluffy hair, trying to wake him up from where he lay half on top of me.

"Mrph," he muttered sleepily and snuggled his face further into my breasts.

I smiled, loving these morning moments with him. He was such a grumpy little bear when he first woke up.

"What did you guys get Peri for her birthday?"

"Arpd."

Giggling, I slid my hands under his jaw and tilted his face up. "What was that, my fifth star?"

"AirPods," he groaned groggily and didn't bother to open his eyes.

"What are they?"

"Like headphones with no wires."

"Is that from all of you, or did you each get her something?"

"Mase new laptop, Cole concert tickets, Jay roller skates, Ash an expensive-ass handbag."

"Roller skates?"

"She wanted 'em."

"What can I get her?"

"Dunno. Cutie, lemme sleep." His closed eyes screwed shut even tighter.

Knowing a lost cause when I saw it, I let his face drop back to its pair of soft pillows. He nestled in with a contented hum, making me smile.

The door opened and Cole came in.

"Time to get up, you two," he chirped. "Breakfast is ready!"

"Help, Cole! The grumpy bear is squishing me!" I held up my arms and made grabby hands. "Save me!"

Laughing, Cole put his hands under my arms and pulled me out from under Wyatt's solid weight, then picked me up and held me against his chest. His short beard scraped against my skin as he buried his face in my neck and dropped little kisses everywhere my nightshirt left bare.

"My hero," I murmured and wrapped my arms around his neck and my legs around his waist. "Good morning."

"Good morning, my lovely girl." He carried me toward my bathroom. "Need to freshen up before we go downstairs?"

"Yes, please. Cole, I know it's late, but I want to get Peri something for her birthday. Any ideas?"

"Let me think about it. You want someone to run you to the store after breakfast?"

"Yes, please."

"Such a polite baby." He kissed me before setting my feet down on the cold bathroom tile. "See you downstairs in a minute."

"Are you going to wrangle Wyatt out of bed?"

"Oh, yeah. Highlight of my morning," he grumbled.

I giggled and gave him one last hug before pushing him out and closing the bathroom door.

#

Now that I was fully mated to the pack's alphas, I could link all the betas and gammas. Jayden had explained that I would be able to link any member after I was inducted into the pack at my luna ceremony. I was looking forward to being able to link Peri, Callie, and Keeley. Although we all had phones and Peri had set up a group chat for the four of us, linking was much faster, especially in an emergency.

I wouldn't call my current predicament an emergency, but it was an issue.

Cole had given me a few ideas for Peri's present, but now I needed to get to the store to buy something. The boys spent breakfast moaning about the dreaded paperwork that waited for them, so I didn't want to bother them.

I could ask one of the flock, but Beatrix and her mates had already left to supervise the move to Five Fangs, and the others were picking out their new homes with their mates.

Emerson and Angelo had already selected their house and would probably be free to take me, and I was comfortable with Emerson. Angelo? Not so much. He could be scary.

You thought Em scary, too, at first, Lark murmured sleepily.

And he can be, but never with me. I don't know if that's true with Angelo.

What about Ty? she suggested.

Ah ha! I brightened, then frowned. *He doesn't have a vehicle, though.*

Your mates can loan him one, or he can get one from pack fleet.

Fleet? I asked, not knowing that word.

Garnet say it a group of vehicles anyone in pack can borrow.

Like a library book?

Sure. Lark snickered at me, and I rolled my eyes at her.

196

While I was talking with my wolf, the boys finished eating and were all looking at me.

"What?" I asked.

"I said, Wyatt, Ash, and I have been summoned to Mom and Dad's to help set up for tonight," Jayden explained. "Do you want to come along, or stay here?"

"Um, actually—"

"Mase and Cole will be holed up in the home office clearing out the paperwork backlog," Wyatt told me, "so you won't be here alone if you want to stay, but it'll probably be boring."

"Well—"

"That's right, princess. You should come with us. You can meet Mom and Mama." Ash bounced his left leg up and down as he grinned at me.

"I—"

"And you can—"

"Let her speak," Mason cut Wyatt off. "You two keep interrupting her every time she goes to answer!"

The three musketeers apologized, and I nodded at them.

"I want Tyler to take me shopping for a gift for Peri," I said. "If he's not busy and, um, wants to, and if he can, uh, borrow a vehicle."

"He'll do whatever you want him to," Cole assured me with a soft smile, "and he can take Jay's. Right, Jay?"

"Sure." Jayden shrugged. "Ash or Wyatt can drive us over to the parents' place."

"Here, baby." Mason took a plastic card out of his wallet and handed it to me. "Until we can get you a card of your own, you'll have to use one of ours. Get her whatever you want."

"I have money." I put my hands under the table.

"Take it, Posy. Everything that is ours is yours, too."

"But it's not my money. I didn't do anything to earn it." I shook my head and dropped my eyes.

I heard him get up, then felt my chair being pulled back. Next thing I knew, he was on his knees in front of me with his hands tilting my face up to meet his serious gray eyes.

"We didn't do anything to earn it, either. Not really. We are wealthy because we got lucky with the investments we made with our inheritances."

"Investments?" I tilted my head. *Another new word.*

"Yes. I invested mine as soon as I turned eighteen. When the others saw the profit margin in my portfolio, they agreed to invest theirs, too."

"Profit margin? Portfolio?" *All new words.*

"I'll explain another time in as much detail as you want, but for now, trust me when I say we have more money than we know what to do with. Last year, we netted nearly $5 billion."

"Five billion!" I gasped.

"Yep." He nodded.

"A billion. A *billion* dollars? Billion as in with a b?"

"Yeah, baby. We're billionaires."

My head spun as I stared at him.

"We wanted to provide for our mate and pups and just happened to be more successful than we could have ever dreamed. So *please* spend the money, baby. We invested it for you, even if we didn't know you yet."

I plucked the plastic card from his fingers.

"I'm still not comfortable with thinking of it as *our* money," I told him.

"When we first saw how much we made, we couldn't believe it, either." He pecked my cheek. "Get yourself something pretty to wear tonight, little flower. So many things have gotten in the way of our lives recently that we haven't had a chance to spoil you the way we want to."

"I'm spoiled enough just to be with all of you."

A chorus of *awws* filled the room, and I hid my red face in my hands.

#

Jayden drove me over to the orphanage in his SUV as Ash and Wyatt followed behind in Ash's SUV. Tyler was waiting for us on the sidewalk when Jayden came to a stop and got out. They spoke together for a few minutes, did that bro-hug guys do, and went their separate ways. Jayden went to Ash's vehicle and Tyler slid in behind the steering wheel next to me.

"Ready, luna?" he asked with a smile.

"Ready! Was Jayden threatening you?"

"Oh, no, luna." He buckled up, then put the SUV in drive. "He was telling me that my first paycheck as beta was deposited in my account this morning."

"Good! Now you have some money to spend, too. Although I can spot you if you need. Mason gave me his card."

"Nice! Now we can run away to Bora Bora."

"Bora Bora? Is it a store?"

He laughed.

"No, luna. It's a place. Get your phone and google it. It's my dream vacation destination."

After I pulled out my phone, he spelled it for me, and I surfed pictures as he drove, my jaw dropping in amazement.

"I never dreamed such a beautiful place existed," I murmured.

"You should get the alphas to take you. I don't think they've gone anywhere as a group since before Alpha Mase graduated high school."

"Jayden and I *were* talking about going to the beach, and the others agreed we could take a vacation. I'll have to talk to them about Bora Bora."

Tyler came to a stop outside a shop with a sign reading, "Stella's."

"All right, luna. Let's start here. It's an eclectic little place, so you might find something unique."

"What's eclectic mean?"

"A wide variety of things."

"Is it a shifter shop?" I asked.

"No, but Stella's aware of us. Her granddaughter is the mate of Gamma Rio."

"A human mate?" My eyebrows flew up. "Isn't that unusual?"

"Yeah." Tyler jumped out of the SUV and came around to open my door. "There are probably only ten or twelve human mates in all of Five Fangs."

He held out his hand and I grabbed it before I jumped down. *These darn SUVs are so high off the ground!*

"How many members are in our pack?" I asked as he led me into the cute little shop.

"About four thousand, give or take a couple of hundred."

I came to a stop, my hand still clutching his, and raised wide eyes to stare at him.

"Four *thousand?"*

"It *is* five packs put together, luna," he giggled down at me and squeezed my hand. "How big is your old pack?"

"Green River? Um, I guess maybe six or seven hundred."

"Tiny." He nodded. "Do you know what you want to get for a present?"

"Nope. I know she makes her own clothes, doesn't like lemon-lime flavor anything, and wears understated jewelry."

"What did the alphas get her?"

After I told him, I asked him if he had any ideas.

"She likes high-end things like Miss Dior perfume and Chanel bags," he murmured as his eyes softened, "but she also collects interesting rocks and minerals, prisms, kaleidoscopes, and stuffies. She's a perfect contradiction—"

He slammed his mouth closed, and the tips of his ears tinted as pink as his cheeks. He cleared his throat and opened the door.

"Anyway, luna, I'll probably just get her a gift card to her favorite fabric store."

"A gift card is practical, but seems so impersonal." I frowned up at him.

"I need it to be impersonal. If she finds her mate tonight, it wouldn't look good for me to give her anything too special, no matter how much I want to."

"Ty, you are still her friend, and you can remain her friend. Get her whatever you want and if anyone says anything, send them to me and I'll set them straight."

That made him laugh.

"Do you hang out together at school?"

"No," he said with a tone of finality that caught my curiosity. "She runs in a whole different circle at school. I wouldn't dare approach her outside of the pack."

"Then how do you know so much about her?"

"I pay attention. I notice everything about her—"

Again, he caught himself and stopped talking. This time, red flooded his face and spread to his neck, and I had to bite my lips together to keep from giggling.

#

At five o'clock, Mason, Cole, Tyler, and I piled into Cole's SUV with our gifts piled in the back. I was alive with nerves, and Mason reached over and untangled my fingers to hold my hands in his.

"Will your family like me?" I asked.

"They will love you." He kissed the tip of my nose. "Peri's been telling them all about you."

"Just stay away from our youngest two brothers," Cole teased from the driver's seat. "Their cute, chubby cheeks and big innocent eyes will steal your heart from us."

"Impossible," I assured him, although my smile was a little shaky with anxiety.

"Emerson's telling them about you, too," Cole continued. "He and the other betas and their mates are there already, and Mama and Mom are grilling them for information. You'll probably be mobbed as soon as you get out of the car."

I took a deep breath and let it out slowly.

You can do this, I told myself.

"I know you've had more social interaction in the past three weeks than you've had in the past six years, and it's probably exhausting." Mason squeezed my hands gently. "We can leave anytime you're ready. Just link one of us and we'll go home, okay?"

I nodded.

"We should start planning that beach vacation," he continued. "That would be relaxing for all of us."

"Best times to go to Bora Bora are November and April," Tyler piped up.

"Bora Bora?" Cole and Mason asked in sync.

"Oh, yes!" I brightened up and grinned at Mason. "Tyler told me about it and I looked up pictures on my phone! Can we go? *Please?* I want to stay in one of those bungalows over the water. I want to dip my feet in the water and watch sea turtles swim by!"

"Sure, baby." Mason brought my hands up and kissed the back of one, then the other. "If that's what's making your eyes sparkle like stars, then we are one-hundred percent going to Bora Bora."

"Yay!" I squealed.

"Take lots of photos for me, luna." Tyler turned around from the front seat to grin at me.

"What? You're coming along. All my beta are. I need my guards with me."

"Luna, you'll have your five mates with you." He rolled his eyes. "You won't need a guard."

"Yes, I will!" I pouted. "And they might as well bring their mates, too. Right, Mason?"

"Ah. Hmm. Well—"

"Thank you!" I leaned over as far as my seat belt would let me and smashed my lips on his in a quick kiss. "This is going to be so much fun! Oh, and I want Peri and Callie and Keeley to come along, too!"

"By the moon, you'll have the whole pack coming along in a minute," he muttered, but I noticed he didn't say no.

"We'll rent out one of the resorts," Cole said with a shrug.

Tyler and I exchanged wide-eyed looks, neither of us used to having the kind of money that my mates did.

"We'll figure it out." Mason tugged my hands to get my attention, and I saw a small smile on his lips. "Whatever you want, little flower, we will do."

"Thank you, Mason." Bouncing in my seat, I gave him a smile full of dimples, and his gray eyes grew soft.

"We're here!" Cole crowed and stopped the vehicle, and I tore my gaze away to look out the window.

A giant house made out of logs loomed before us, and my breath caught.

"It's so beautiful!" I whispered as I drank in the rich color of the wood, the handsome stonework, and the porch that ran all around the second floor.

"Thanks," Cole said. "Dad worked hard on it to get it exactly how he wanted it."

"Well, he did a good job. I can't wait to see inside!"

"Then come on!"

The betas and their mates were the first people I spotted when we went into the backyard. Then my eyes found the birthday girl talking with Callie and Keeley by the edge of the pool. She looked absolutely darling in her little swim shorts and matching top.

I sprinted over to my friends and wrapped Peri up in a hug.

"Happy birthday!" I squeezed her tight. "You look so cute!"

"Thanks! I'm so glad you're here! Let me introduce you to my family," she giggled.

"Hi, luna," the Breckenridge twins said in unison.

"Hi, twinnies! Your bathing suits are lovely."

"We bought you a suit, too," Peri said, then leaned closer to whisper in my ear, "but you don't have to wear it or go swimming if you don't want to."

I nodded, grateful for her consideration.

With the twins in tow, Peri took me around and introduced me to so many younger brothers that I forgot half of their names as soon as she said them. Only Winnie and William stuck in my memory because I'd already seen pictures of them and had heard so much about them.

And they were even more adorable than the boys had warned me they were.

"They're little devils behind those cherub cheeks," a deep, familiar voice came from behind me.

Whirling around, I saw Nathan Barlow, aka Dad, and I felt my cheeks turn pink.

"I can't believe that," I murmured and lowered my eyes.

"Oh, little luna, you will once you get to know them better!" he chuckled.

William and Winnie threw themselves at him, and he caught one under each thick, tattooed arm.

"Come on, little wolves," he said. "Let's swim before cake!"

"Cake?" William's little face lit up as he dangled under his father's arm.

"After swim?" Winnie asked in his adorable baby voice.

"Yeah, cake after swimming, my babies," Dad told them, and they both cheered.

As they walked away, Callie sighed and leaned on her sister's shoulder.

"Don't they make you want a pup?"

"Need a mate first, sissy," Keeley sighed.

"What about you, luna?" Callie asked. "Now that you're fully mated to the alphas, are you planning a pup at your first heat?"

Panicking, I held up both hands and waved them as my face burned like fire.

"I'm not ready for that," I stammered. "The boys aren't, either."

"Then it's good to wait until you all are," Keeley said.

"And there's no shortage of babies to play with in the pack," Callie laughed.

The three girls smiled at me, and I started to relax again.

Well, until Mama and Mom descended.

They were really nice and sweet, though, and dragged me to sit with them in a quiet corner as the rest went into the massive swimming pool.

"I haven't seen Mase so relaxed in a very long time." Mama suddenly sniffed, alarming me. "You've made him so happy, luna."

"I haven't done anything," I murmured and stared at my clasped hands. "And please, call me Posy."

"You are perfect for *all* our sons, Posy," Mom said. "Wyatt needs a mate to mature. Jayden needs a mate to help him with Quartz. Cole needs a mate to tame his temper. Ash needs a mate to keep him grounded. And Mase—"

She sighed and shook her head, then looked over at Mrs. Price.

"He needs a mate to remind him that life is worth living," Mama said. "The past few years have been overwhelmingly stressful for him. It's only eased up since the others came of age and could take their alphaships. For a year and a half, Mase was the sole alpha of five packs."

And the pressure Papa put on him didn't help one bit, I thought to myself.

You think she know how mean Papa is to Masey? Lark asked.

I hope not, I replied with a frown. *She seems too sweet, though, to support her husband behaving like that with their son.*

Then it was time for cake and ice cream, and my mates reclaimed me from their moms. After we ate, Peri began to open her presents. I didn't know what all the technology gifts were, but she made a fuss over everything she was given. When she got to my present, she stared at it for a long moment before looking at me with tears in her eyes.

Uh-oh! I messed up!

My heartbeat sped up and my breathing increased as she carefully set down the intricate kaleidoscope, then she flung herself at me and hugged me hard.

"How did you know I wanted this?" she whispered in my ear.

"Tyler took me to Stella's. She told me you've been obsessed with it since she got it."

203

"Posy, this is expensive! That's why it's been in her shop for two years."

She pulled back and gave me a worried look.

"Peri," I framed her face in my palms, "my mates are freaking billionaires. I can afford to spend a couple thousand dollars on my sister-in-law. Besides, I can't think of anyone else who will enjoy it and take care of it like you will."

Her face broke into a brilliant grin, and I hugged her.

"Happy birthday, Peri."

"Thanks," she giggled.

She went back to opening presents as Mom and Mama admired the kaleidoscope and kept the curious little boys away from it. Eventually, Dad carried it off, saying he'd put it in Peri's room away from "busy, destructive fingers."

Next, Peri opened Tyler's present, and her eyes sparkled with tears as she looked at him.

"Thank you so much, Tyler! It's beautiful!"

She held up a beautiful prism sun catcher, and the dying sun's last rays caught the crystals and hundreds of tiny rainbows suddenly danced all over us.

"I'm glad you like it," he said with a small smile.

They didn't hug, although we all knew they wanted to.

By the moon, I hope they're mates, Ash linked me and his brothers. *Per will be devastated if he isn't.*

Whoever her mate is, I don't want to see them kissing. Ever, Cole grumbled.

They'll be doing a whole lot more than kissing quick enough, Wyatt snickered.

Shut up, Wyatt!

As they bickered and Peri finished opening her gifts, I entertained myself by observing the two sets of parents.

Mr. and Mrs. Price's eyes found each other constantly if they weren't in touching distance. He held her in his lap, she played with his hair, or they held hands. Although he'd been a mean jerk to me and Mason, it was clear to see that Mr. Price was completely devoted to Mama and she to him.

It was the same with Wyatt's mom and Cole's dad, but the energy between the two was much more intense. Dad couldn't keep his hands off Mom, and Mom whimpered very quietly if he left her side for too long. It made me curious.

Is a chosen mate bond different from a Goddess-given one?

I mean, the boys were constantly touching me since we'd mated, which I loved and wanted, but they didn't smother me like Dad was doing to Mom.

And it doesn't hurt me if they aren't near me, but her whimpers say she's in pain.

I noticed Jayden watching them, too, which made me wonder if their behavior was new or unusual. I set my empty plate down and went over to him, smiling as his dragon eyes flashed up to mine.

"Want me to hold you?" he asked and opened his arms.

When I nodded, he put his hands on my hips and pulled me down so my bum was on his left thigh and my knees between his legs. My nose filled with the lovely scent of roses, and I leaned my shoulder against his with a contented sigh.

"Happy, sweetness?"

I nodded again. When he wrapped his arms around my waist, I closed my eyes and smiled. Then, I remembered what I came over here for.

"What's going on with Mom and Dad?" I asked in a soft tone. "Mason's parents are touchy, but those two are on a whole different level of clingy."

"Yep, but I think they don't want to steal Peri's thunder."

"What does that mean?

"They don't want their news to overshadow Peri's birthday." He chuckled. "They won't be able to hide it much longer, but they're safe for now. None of my knucklehead brothers are paying enough attention to figure it out."

I looked around at my other mates. They were all either eating, playing with the younger siblings, or, in Mason's case, simply sitting and staring at me.

Flapping my hand, I motioned for him to come join us. He dropped his eyes and didn't get up, which made me frown.

"He's so stubborn," Jayden muttered and dropped his arms. "Go get him, Posy."

Sitting up, I glanced at him over my shoulder and saw him grinning.

"You're not setting me up for something, are you?" I narrowed my eyes in suspicion.

"Of course not. If I were Wyatt, then yes. Don't trust him when it comes to pranking people. But Mase needs someone to shatter all that ice he's buried himself under, and that someone is you."

I hesitated, and Jayden booped my nose with his forefinger.

"Try to get him to loosen up a bit, sweetness. He shouldn't feel he has to be so stiff with his own family."

"Okay." I smiled, flashing my dimples.

I stood and went over to Mason, who looked up at me without a word.

"Don't you want to sit with us?" I asked.

He shrugged, his face blank as always, but I saw a different story in his gray eyes. He *did* want to join us. He wanted me to sit on his lap and snuggle into him, too, and he had no idea how to show or say that in front of his family.

In front of his *father*.

Things were awfully tense between them, and rightly so. No one, not even Mama, tried to force them to talk to each other, which was good. It would upset Peri if the two of them got into a fight on her birthday. Papa mainly talked with Mama or Dad, although I did see him tickling the two littlest boys with an actual smile on his face.

Maybe he only hates Mason? I asked myself.

As I stared at Mason, I thought about the look in his eyes earlier when the others asked him to play ball. He'd shaken his head, though I knew he wanted to join them. At the time, I thought he was worried that he'd accidentally hurt one of the younger boys, but now I realized he didn't want his father to see him having a little fun.

Does he feel as taut as a piano wire? Does he fear what might happen if he ever relaxes?

I knew all too well how grueling it could be to hold yourself so rigid day after day after day. To be afraid to move or to veer even a hair off the set path.

"Shatter all that ice he's buried himself under," Jayden had said.

I didn't like the thought of shattering *anything* about Mason, but maybe I could help him melt a little.

Without warning, I jumped on him and wrapped my arms around his neck.

"Oof!"

"Did I hurt you?" I asked with a smile, knowing I hadn't.

"Course not. Just surprised me."

He gently tugged me so that I sat on his lap facing him with my legs hanging over his. His hands moved to the small of my back and his fingers laced together over my bum.

My eyes widened at this position in front of others, but if he was fine with it, I was, too.

I slipped my hands around his neck to lay comfortably on his chest, and he buried his face in my throat and inhaled.

"Mmm. Cookies," he murmured, his lips brushing my skin.

I giggled.

"Mason?"

"Hmm?"

"I love you."

"I love you, too, little flower."

He raised his head and his eyes flicked to my lips. My heart tried to beat out of my chest.

Is he really going to kiss me in front of everyone? In front of his father?

Slowly, so slowly, his head came closer, our breath mingling. Then his soft lips were on mine and the whole world paused.

"Oh, they're so cute!" Mama squealed.

"I can't stand it! Nathan! Nathan, take a picture with your phone!"

Mason smirked against my lips, but I was embarrassed and hid my burning face in his throat. He chuckled softly, set his chin on top of my head, and ran his big hands up and down my back.

Thankfully, Jayden saved me.

"So, Mom and Dad," he said. "I believe you two have something to tell us."

I raised my head and looked at the older couple, curious to know what he knew that none of us did.

"As always, you are too perceptive, son," Dad chuckled.

Mom looked up at Dad, and he nodded. Taking a deep breath, she faced us again with pink cheeks.

"We're having another pup!"

"Yes!" Wyatt shouted as his arms shot up in victory pose. "Now you won't have time or energy to pester us night and day about popping out grand-pups! Good job, Dad. Just keep the little brothers coming for a few more years, okay?"

"Hey, it could be a girl this time," Dad pointed out.

"By the moon, you two are rabbits, not wolves," Cole groaned and shook his head.

Everyone laughed and began to congratulate the couple. Mama, however, went over to Wyatt and bopped him on the back of his head.

"Evie and I still want some grand-pups, so don't think you're getting out of anything!"

"Ow! Why does everyone always attack my *head*?"

"Because there's nothing to damage?" Cole suggested.

Of course, Wyatt tackled him with a growl, and they wrestled around on the grass. With war cries of their own, all the younger brothers dove on top of the two and quickly became a knot of tangled limbs.

"Big brothers! Big brothers!" William shouted as he and Winnie came running. "Us, too!"

Ash grabbed Winnie and Jayden grabbed William, then they rolled around on the grass with them, which I thought was such a nice thing to do. The babies got to play with "big brothers" without the risk of getting hurt in the dog pile.

And Mason, smart boy that he was, used everyone's distraction to kiss the breath out of me.

26: Swimming with Heathens

Peri Barlow

After I opened all of my birthday presents, I asked Posy to help me carry them up to my room. I appreciated her help, but what I really wanted to do was give her a gift of my own.

"I have something for you," I said as she carefully placed her armload of my presents on my desk.

"For me? But it's *your* birthday, silly!"

"A belated birthday gift for you." I grabbed the shopping bag out of my closet, then sat on my bed with it. "Come sit with me."

Once she was comfortable and turned to look at me, I gathered my courage and met her eyes.

"Cole told me about your scars." Yeah, I put it out there just like that. "I know you probably didn't want anyone to know, but he was so upset and needed to vent, and I guess I was just in the right place at the right time. Or the wrong place at the wrong time. Either way, he told me."

You're rambling, murmured my wolf.

Dove, you know I always do when I'm nervous.

"And I figured that was probably why you weren't interested in shopping for a swimsuit and haven't wanted to go swimming. Now, I'm not saying you need to do either of those things, but I think you should have options. Options are really important to me. Without options, I feel trapped, so I wanted to provide you with options so *you* don't feel trapped. What you choose to do is entirely up to you, and it won't hurt my feelings no matter what you decide."

She didn't say anything as she stared at me with wide eyes.

Probably waiting for your word vomit to stop, Dove snickered.

"Here's what I got you." I pulled out the suit I liked the most and held it up. "This is a one piece with good coverage on the front and lower cut legs, but most of the back is out. Cole didn't go into too much detail, so I wasn't sure exactly where your scars are or how much you want or need to cover."

I held it out to her, but she only looked at it with wide eyes. Laying it on the bed, I refused to give up and pulled out the next suit.

"This one's called a tankini." I held the top against me so she could see how long it was. "It has a scoop-neck tank top and shorts. It's probably the most coverage you can get outside of a surf suit."

I laid it on the bed, too, then reached for what I thought she'd consider the most risque piece.

"And of course, this is a bikini. I loved the blue and white pattern and the bows on the shoulders. The bottoms have a high waist

209

with moderate cut legs. The top has a scoop neck, so your girls aren't hanging out. I knew when I bought this one that you might refuse it outright because so much skin would be on display, but I wanted you to have the option to say screw it and let the world see the proof of how strong you are."

She stared at me for a long moment before tears filled her eyes.

"The scars show how weak I am, not how strong."

"No. You're wrong." I reached over and took her hands in mine. "You survived what tried to kill you. The scars are a testimony to that."

"They only show I was weak enough to be broken."

"We're all broken in some way, Posy." I squeezed her hands. "But broken doesn't mean failure. We only fail when we give up. When we don't piece ourselves back together after we break."

The sorrow and fear in her eyes hurt my heart.

Pushing too hard too fast, I scolded myself.

"Do you want me to get your mates?" I asked gently.

"No. They would just make it more—"

She searched for the right word, and I offered one after a long moment of silence.

"Complicated?"

"Yes. Complicated." She sighed. "Although I have a feeling that they're going to pick up on my feelings any minute and—"

Three thunderous knocks hit my door, making both of us jump.

"Posy! What's wrong, little flower?"

That's Mase.

"Can we come in, sweetness?"

Jay.

"Princess, are you okay?"

Ash.

"Who do I need to kill, cutie? Who upset you?"

Wyatt.

"Honey, are you in there alone or is Peri with you?"

And big brother Cole. Wow. The whole crew.

I rolled my eyes, then traded amused smiles with Posy.

"They each have a pet name for you?"

"Yes. I do, too, but I still need nicknames for Cole and Mason."

"Oh? What do you call—"

"Posy!" Cole half-shouted again, and two more knocks rattled my door.

"Oh, for the love of the moon!" I hissed. Turning toward the door, I yelled, "Stop shouting and leave us alone! We're doing girl stuff that you don't need to know about! And your precious mate is fine!"

"Posy, is that true?" Jay called. "Are you fine?"

"Yes." Her voice quavered as she raised it loud enough for them to hear her. "I am. I just got nervous about something."

"Can you open the door? We need to see you to make sure. Please, baby?"

Mase is begging? My eyes widened incredulously.

Only for his mate, Dove murmured.

"I should settle them down before they break something." Posy stood and went to the door, which she opened a crack. "See? I really am fine. Peri and I— Oh, my gosh! You guys are dripping water everywhere! What did you do, come straight out of the pool?"

"Um, yeah," Ash said, and I could just picture him rubbing the back of his neck. "We were worried about you when we felt your anxiety through the mate bond."

"Thank you for caring about me, and I'm sorry for worrying you. Peri and I will be down in a few minutes. Please clean up the water on your way back outside."

They each had to kiss her before they left, and Posy giggled as she shut the door and turned around.

"You are amazing." I slowly shook my head. "How do you manage those boys so easily? What's the secret?"

"I don't know." She shrugged, still smiling. "I ask them nicely and they do it. When they are good, I praise them. When they mess up, I tell them what they did wrong and how to fix it, and they do. Most important of all, I let them know that I appreciate how much they love me."

She has them so tightly wrapped around her fingers, it's amazing the circulation hasn't been cut off yet, Dove laughed.

Grinning, I agreed with her.

"I got you one more option." Reaching into the bag, I pulled out a floral-patterned robe with a tie in the front. "This is a cover up. In case you want the freedom of a suit, but don't want everyone seeing it. You can wear it right into the water if you want to."

She took the nearly sheer robe in her hands, testing out the smooth texture of the fabric between her thumb and forefinger.

"All right, luna. I'll leave you with the freedom of options. Stay dressed as you are, put on a suit, wear the cover up or don't. Whatever you choose, you won't hurt my feelings. You *will* come back down to the pool, though, right?"

"Yes." She nodded. "I told my mates I would. I can't lie to them, and I won't ever break their trust, even if it is over something little like that."

I had liked this girl from the moment I met her, even if our first shopping trip ended in disaster. The more I got to know her, the more I liked her - and the more relieved I was.

Each of my brothers had his own issues, and their mate needed to be a very special girl. A girl who had an open mind, a kind heart, a forgiving nature, a sense of humor, and patience.

Loads and *loads* of patience.

Before they found Posy, I'd worried that no such girl existed, but she proved me wrong.

She'd gone through hell, and I hated that for her, but the crucible of her suffering shaped her into the amazing woman she was today. The Moon Goddess had kept her promise to provide the exact right mate for my brothers, and I couldn't be more thankful.

#

Nathan Barlow

I watched with a grin as my daughter-in-law chased my two babies around, all three of them giggling like mad. While the others swam and played in the pool, the little luna had taken it upon herself to entertain William and Winnie, who could be quite a handful.

"She's great with them, isn't she?" Julia said as she came over and plopped on a chair next to Evie. "I can't understand why they don't want pups."

"They *do* want pups," I corrected with an eye roll. "The boys told you *twice* that they just want to wait a few years. They want to live a little now that the pack is settling into place and before pups tie them down, and I can't blame them for that."

"I know, Nathan, and I understand it." She sighed. "I just want grandpups so much!"

"Why don't you have another pup of your own?" Evie suggested, not for the first time. "You're only thirty-nine. You still have several more heats before they stop."

"I know. I've thought about it, believe me. I just—" She sighed again.

We knew. Evie and I both knew. Julia felt like she'd be replacing Willow, Mase's twin who died in the sickness. Grief was rarely logical, and Evie worried that her bestie would regret it in the end.

Royal joined us then and set a tray of drinks on the table. As he passed them out, I heard my two youngest letting out war cries that meant only one thing.

Uh-oh.

Alarmed, I turned in time to see Winnie jump on Posy's back right as William dove into the back of her knees.

The poor girl went down hard on the stone floor.

Anyone else, even Peri, and I wouldn't have been so worried, but the luna's physical fragility was obvious to anyone with eyes.

After we met her the other day, Royal wouldn't shut up about how she was bad news and would take the boys for every penny they had. My own opinion was very different, although I had a ton of questions. I wanted to meet with the boys and hear more about Posy, as well as what had happened at Tall Pines and why its former alpha was now in our pack, but they'd been up to their necks in work since their return.

I knew I could catch up with them later, but to satisfy some of my curiosity, I got Tyler alone after he arrived this afternoon and asked a few questions. He had no problem talking about Tall Pines, but he kept his trap shut about Posy, saying it was her story to tell. The only thing he *did* share was what my boys had told all the betas, which was that Alpha Kendall Briggs had not only kept her imprisoned in their house for six years, but also abused her.

I was not prepared to see the evidence of that abuse.

When the heathens tackled her, her flimsy cover-up came untied and slipped off, revealing her modest blue and white bikini, but it wasn't her swimsuit that made us freeze.

No, the obvious signs of starvation and the scars did that.

Her spine, ribs, and hip bones poked out like knobs. Long, thin lines of white ran down her back. Deeper, wider red gouges marred her upper arms and shoulders. A word was branded into her pale skin right above her waist band, and my eyes wouldn't give up trying to read the letters. The first one looked like a K and the last one might have been a B, but I couldn't be sure in the fading light.

"H-here, honey," Julia stammered. "Let us help you up."

As she and Evie put their arms around Posy and lifted her to her feet, more scars were revealed. Her stomach and upper thighs were littered with more white lines and red furrows.

Nathan, Evie whispered through the link. *Nathan?*

I know, baby. Hold it together for a few more minutes. Don't cry in front of her. Think about what you'll say to the heathens and how we should punish them.

She gave me a short nod, although I saw the tears glittering in her eyes.

I knew how she felt. My heart broke for this dear child. I'd only ever seen something like this once before, and that was when

Quartz discovered what Tyler's father was doing to him. My heart broke just as much then, too.

"Winnie! William! Why did you do that?" Evie scolded, and they got to their feet with shamed faces.

"Are you okay, Posy? Are you hurt anywhere?" Julia fussed. "Can I get you anything?"

"I'm fine," she whispered, her eyes wild as they darted around.

Is she looking for the boys? I linked the others.

For her cover up, I think, Evie replied, biting her bottom lip.

She probably feels so exposed, said Royal, of all people.

He hustled over, grabbed the thin fabric robe off the ground, and held it out to Posy. Curling in on herself, she looked at him with so much fear in her eyes that it made my chest ache.

"It's okay," he encouraged her in a gentle voice that I hadn't heard out of him in years. "No one here will hurt you. Please take it."

She began to knot her fingers together, and her breathing fractured into short, sharp pants.

Is she going to have a panic attack? Evie wondered.

I think we should get the b—

A stampede of elephants cut Julia off, and the boys surrounded her in a tight circle, murmuring soothing things. Mase snatched the cover up from Royal's hand with a venomous glare, then turned back to their girl.

I think we should give them some space, I said.

Not like they'd let us help anyway, Julia pointed out.

Retreating back to our table, I made sure to snag my two troublemakers on the way, tossing one over each shoulder.

"Daddy!" they whined, but not too loudly. They knew they'd screwed up.

I sat down, stood them before me, and gave them The Look to make sure they understood that this was serious.

"That was not a nice thing to do," I told them in a stern tone.

"We was just pwaying," Winnie tried, but William elbowed him in the ribs, and he snapped his mouth closed.

At least he hadn't tried to blame it all on William, which was his go-to for getting out of trouble.

Small progress, I thought to myself.

"You have to be careful," Evie told them. "You could have hurt Posy. She's not as big as your brothers, and doesn't play as rough as they do."

As Evie fussed at them, I looked over and saw Ash had Posy up in his arms, the cover up draped over her back as she clung to him like a koala. The other boys touched her arms, legs, or face and watched her with concerned eyes.

214

"What happened to Posy?" Peri came over, wide-eyed with worry.

"The heathens knocked her down," I told her.

"Did she get hurt?"

"Not physically." I looked up at my daughter. Something in her face made me suspicious, so I took a guess. "Her cover up came off."

Peri's hand flew to her mouth.

"Who saw?" she whispered.

"Just us four, and the heathens," I said. "You knew?"

She nodded.

"She's getting better." Peri wiped a tear from her cheek. "Cole and Wyatt swear she is. There's nothing any of them can do for the scars, though. They were made with silver and mercury."

"That's *better*?" I hissed. "She's nothing but bones!"

"She's only been with them for three weeks, Daddy. Cole said she's gained seven pounds since they brought her home. The pack doctor told Cole that slow weight gain is best, and not to push her to eat or it could make her sick."

Bile flooded my mouth, and I struggled to control Jet. He wanted to kill the one who hurt his luna, as did I. Knowing my sons already had was our only consolation.

While my daughter and I were whispering, Posy came over and stood in front of our little group, her mates looming behind her like avenging angels.

"Um, are the boys okay?" she asked.

"They're fine." I smiled at her, then raised an eyebrow at my heathens. "Little wolves, I think you have something to say to the luna."

"I'm sorry, luna." William dropped his chin to his chest.

"Sowwy, wuna," Winnie echoed. He blinked his big blue eyes at her and his bottom lip pooched out.

By the moon, that boy could melt a heart of stone!

Posy did *not* have a heart of stone. Quite the opposite, in fact. She looked as if she might cry at Winnie's pouty face.

If only she knew how often he uses his cuteness to get out of trouble, I linked Evie, who held back a giggle. *What are you laughing about? You're no more immune to it than our new daughter-in-law is.*

That made *her* pout, and her face looked so similar to our son's that I grinned.

"Oh, babies, it's okay! See? I'm fine!" Posy's eyes showed how frantic she was to cheer them up. "So, um, would you like to get into the pool with me?"

"Swim?" the little guys asked together with brightening faces.

215

"Yeah! Come on." She held out both hands.

With big grins, each of the boys grabbed one and tugged her toward the steps at the shallow end, closely supervised by five alphas who towered over their luna and probably wouldn't let her out of their sight for the rest of the night.

After they were all in the pool, Evie finally let the tears fall.

"Nathan, what happened to that poor girl?"

"Her father abused her," I said quietly and wrapped my arms around her, tucking her face into my neck as she cried.

"How do you know that?" Royal demanded.

"I talked to Tyler earlier today. The boys told the betas so they wouldn't do something dumb and trigger her when they met her." I paused to get the anger under control. "Her father kept her a prisoner in the alpha house for the last six years. She wasn't allowed to leave. Ever. He isolated her, starved her, and beat her."

Julia gasped, and Evie cried harder. Royal heaved a heavy sigh, and I looked over at him.

"I— I feel terrible. I misjudged her badly." Guilt shadowed his eyes.

"Royal?" Julia stared at him. "What did you do?"

"I ... said some things I shouldn't have." He took a deep breath and let it out slowly. "I'll apologize. To her and the boys."

"Mase, too?" I growled as I stroked Evie's hair. "It's high time you apologize to him, and *not* for insulting our daughter-in-law."

I'd learned long ago not to pull punches with Royal. Sometimes, he needed a hard hit to the head to get his thinking straight.

And even that doesn't always work, snorted Jet, my wolf.

"What did you do to Mason?" Jules narrowed her eyes at her mate.

"I said some things I shouldn't have," he repeated.

"On multiple occasions," I prompted, "and for no reason."

"Okay, okay! Nathan's right! You all tried to tell me so many times to ease up on him, but he was first alpha! He had to do it right. He had to be perfect. I wanted him to be a good, strong leader for the pack."

"He is, and he still would have been without your constant harassment and belittling," I bit out. "What Shawn, Jay, and I warned you about over and over again has finally come true. That boy hates you and wants nothing to do with you."

"Royal! What's Nathan talking about?" Jules demanded as she pulled away from him and planted her hands on her hips with a scowl.

He gulped. Say whatever you wanted about the man, but Royal Price loved his mate with all of his cold, selfish heart. When she found out what he'd been doing to Mase, she was going to be so hurt, and that was going to hurt *him* more than any words or wounds ever could.

He deserves it, Jet grumbled.

He and Al, Royal's wolf, had often tried to intervene on Mase's behalf over the years, but Royal wouldn't hear it.

Julia's voice turned into a hiss, demanding that he explain, and I let a small smile flit on my face as I swung Evie up in my arms and carried her away.

All hell was about to break loose in the Price household, and Royal had only himself to blame.

27: In the Doghouse

Julia Price

Royal and I left the party after a quick goodbye and best wishes to Peri. We didn't speak a word during the short ride home. I was too upset, and guilt kept Royal silent.

I'd known the man all of my life, been his mate for the last twenty-two years, and knew him better than he did himself. Whatever he'd been doing behind my back was nothing good, and now he regretted it.

Once we were home, I led him straight to his office and sat in his chair. Folding my hands on his desk, I waited until he sat down across from me.

"Tell me everything," I demanded baldly.

"I've been ... harsh with Mason." He dropped his gaze to the floor and clenched his jaw. "I've said some things I shouldn't have."

"For example?" I raised an eyebrow.

"When I went to his office the other day," he took a deep breath, then let it all out in a rush, "I questioned him about inducting those witches into the pack, then called him a disappointment and told him the pack would fail under his weak leadership."

"*What?*" I gasped.

"The day they came back from Tall Pines," Royal went on, "I said some things, then *he* said that he doesn't recognize me as his father anymore. Later, at his office, he told me if I'm such a disappointment, I had only myself to blame because I made him the way he is."

Angry and upset as I was, my son was only one half of the story. I wanted to know why Posy was so scared of my mate. Evie and I had picked up right away on how shy she was, and her eyes told us she'd been to hell and shaken the devil's hand, but that didn't explain the degree of fear on her face when Royal tried to hand her the cover up. I knew he never would raise a hand to her, so that could only mean his big mouth had gotten him into trouble.

Again.

"And what about Posy?"

"I, um, called her a scrawny, weak runt," he muttered. "Then I told Mase I could accept her as his whore, but not his mate."

"*Royal!*"

"I know, I know, okay? I knew I was wrong the moment she threw me out of his office after I said he was a disappointment. You should have seen her, Jules. She was quivering like a tiny rabbit, scared to death, but she stood there and defended her mate from me. I was too angry at the time to acknowledge it, but her courage was magnificent."

His eyes gleamed with either admiration or pride for a second, then dulled as he continued.

"When I saw her scars just now, I realized how badly I misjudged her. How wrongly I interpreted the information I'd been given about her."

"You ran a background check on her?"

"I wanted to keep the boys safe from a gold-digger, or at least that's how I justified it, but all I did was hurt an innocent girl who's already been hurt too many times in her life. And I hate myself for it, Jules! I wanted to slit my own throat when I saw that bastard's initials branded on her back!"

"They were initials? I couldn't tell much in the darkness."

"KAB. Kendall Allen Briggs. Nathan and I met him at an alpha conference a few years ago. I remember Nathan telling me he felt sorry for the man's family, and I agreed with him. We informed the king that we were concerned about Briggs' overly violent nature, but it was right at the time Magnus was abdicating the throne, and I think our report got lost in the shuffle. Now, I feel guilty that we didn't follow up on it. Nathan's kicking himself, too."

"Thank you for trying to give her the cover up, by the way."

"She was too scared of me to take it," he muttered. "I need to apologize to her."

"That's a great start. I'd like you to have a good relationship with our daughter-in-law. Now tell me more about what's been going on with Mase."

He dropped his head into his hands.

"At first, I was training him to become alpha the right way, but over time, I started acting more and more like my father. Harsh. Overly critical." His voice dropped to a whisper. "Verbally abusive."

I didn't need the details. I remembered Alpha JR Price and his methods very well.

"Jay and Shawn used to warn me to loosen up on the boy, but I didn't listen," Royal admitted, referring to Jay Carson and Shawn Black, his friends who died in the sickness. "In fact, I got worse. These past two years, Nathan and Al tried to tell me I'd drive him away if I didn't stop. Well, I didn't, and now their words are coming true."

I stared at him for a long time as I processed the information. I was angry - so very angry! - and had to work hard to control myself. I wanted to rage at him, pound him with my fists, throw him out of the house, anything to make him feel as much pain as I was.

Instead, I closed my eyes and took several deep breaths until I could say what I needed to without tears or shouting or both.

"Royal, if you had to describe your teenage self in one word, what would you say?"

"Bad." He rubbed the back of his neck. "In every way and on every level. You know that as well as I do."

"You're right. I do. That's why your father was hard on you and hounded you over every little thing. The whole pack knew you needed a heavy hand to shape all that wildness into a man worthy of becoming the alpha of Great Rocks."

"True. Without him, I would have been dead or in the pack's cells before I reached adulthood."

I nodded. It was the absolute truth.

"Now, how would you describe *me* as a teenager?" I asked.

"Also in one word? Perfect." He gave me a half-smile. "You were a straight-A student, polite and respectful to your teachers and parents, kind to everyone, even those who tried to bully you. Hmm. Did you know I beat Ferris Cargill to his knees that day he troubled you during gym class?"

"You didn't!"

"I did." His voice grew gruff. "I made damn sure everyone knew to leave you alone or they'd answer to me. We weren't mates yet, but you were mine, even if I wasn't worthy of the sweetest, loveliest girl in the pack."

More than twenty years, and this man still knew how to make my heart flutter.

You are mad at him, my wolf, Raven, reminded me. *He hurt your son.*

Right. Back to business.

"Royal, think back to when the twins were children. Who did our son act like more, you or me?"

"You, of course," he scoffed.

"Now, picture my father treating *me* the way your father treated *you*."

I saw the exact moment he understood. His skin lost all color and shock widened his eyes.

"I have no idea how you'll rebuild your relationship with our son." I got to my feet and laid my palms flat on the top of the desk. "If you want to keep your relationship with *me*, however, I recommend that you figure it out. Quickly."

"Jules—"

"We already lost our daughter in the sickness, which neither of us could control. I will not lose our son because you drove him away."

"Julia—"

"I'm heading over to their place, and I'm going to ask to stay the night. Don't follow me. Don't link me or call me. I'll let you know when I'm ready to talk."

"*Julia—*"

"I love you, Royal, but I don't like you very much right now. In all these years, I have never once been disappointed in you. Until now."

My heart shattered at the immense hurt that welled in his eyes, but I made myself walk past him and out the door.

\#

Mason

When we got home from the party, Posy gave us kisses, then went up to her special room.

The boys and I stood in the kitchen and looked at each other with helpless eyes, and I knew they felt as lost as I did.

Mase, my mother nudged the mind link. *May I please come over?*

You're always welcome, I told her, *but Posy's ... in a bad place, which means the boys and I are not doing so good, either.*

I can help her, honey. I need and want to help her. Please let me. And, she paused.

And? I encouraged her after a few seconds.

And I need a place to stay tonight.

Did he throw you out?! Outrage made my tone sharp.

No. I left. I ... can't be around him right now. He admitted some things tonight that I wish you *would have told me about a long time ago.*

I grimaced, wondering what exactly he'd admitted to.

Mama—

I don't blame you, Mase. Listen, I really would like to see you boys and Posy, but I can go to Evie's.

No, no. Come on over.

I'm already at the front door, honey.

Rolling my eyes, I went to let her in.

\#

Wyatt

"I don't know, Mama." I dropped my head on the table and banged it twice. "We were doing so well. Sure, there were a few speed bumps and we went back a step a couple of times, but I feel like we lost all our progress tonight."

"Back a step a couple of times?" Cole growled. "We make her panic all the time! We make her cry all the time! Who are we fooling? We're *terrible* at this! We're lucky she hasn't given up on us yet!"

"So are you calling it quits then?" Mama's voice was sharp, and I lifted my head. "Now that it's getting hard, are you washing your hands of her and walking away?"

221

"WHAT? NO!" Cole howled, Topaz glimmering in his eyes. "How dare you suggest we'd abandon her!"

"Calm down, brother." Mase put a hand on his shoulder. "Your temper is talking for you."

Cole took a couple of deep breaths, then nodded.

We really do rely on Mase for everything, don't we? I thought, disgusted with myself.

"You all need to remember that healing takes time, and there will be setbacks," Mama's tone turned gentle again. "You will have days you take two steps back for every one forward, and three or four forward for every one back. It's life. It's messy."

Looking at my brothers, I saw the same pain on their faces that was clawing at me. Cole was right; we had no idea what we were doing, and it *was* only luck that we still had her. I dug the heels of my hands into my eye sockets and groaned.

"Boys, what was she like the day you brought her here? What is she like now? Can you honestly say you see no difference? If you can't, maybe you're right and you *are* terrible mates. But if you can, then you're doing what you should be, and doing it well."

Mase had said something similar to me while we were at Tall Pines.

Maybe they're right.

They right, Granite insisted. *She getting better.*

"I'll go up and talk to her for a bit." Mama held up her hands when we started to protest. "If she doesn't want to talk, I'll respect that."

"It's her special room, her place to feel safe," Ash explained. "We don't want to cross that boundary, especially tonight, but it's killing us that she's isolating herself from us. We want to comfort her."

"Don't think of it as her not wanting you," Mama said. "Sometimes, your feelings are so big, you need time and space to deal with them. And for a girl who was isolated from everyone but her abuser for years, she's probably socially exhausted, not to mention emotionally and mentally drained, after the past few weeks."

I couldn't relate to the last part, but I understood all too well about needing time and space.

"A lot has happened in the short time she's been with us," Jay admitted. "It would have been difficult enough for a mate who *hadn't* been abused."

"All right, Mama," I said. "Go talk to her, but can you tell our girl that we love her and hope she—"

Hope she what? Feels better soon? Is that the right thing to say? I asked myself.

Know how much we need and want her in our lives, Granite came to the rescue.

222

"Knows how much we need and want her in our lives."

Good job, wolf.

And Granite rolled over with a toothy grin at the praise.

"I'm sure she knows, but I'll pass on the message." She cleared her throat and gave us The Look. "Depending on what she wants to do afterward, you boys and I need to have a talk of our own. Papa told me about how he's been treating Mase. I'm not happy you all kept that from me."

Oh, Goddess, I grimaced as we shuffled our feet.

We'd worried that one day she'd learn the truth, but Mase swore us to secrecy a couple of years ago. He'd convinced us by saying how badly it would hurt Mama, and none of us wanted to do that. He said he could handle it, and we believed him.

By the moon, we were dumb.

You were, Granite added his two cents. *Still are sometimes.*

Hush, wolf.

#

Posy

I heard a soft knock on the door and sighed.

I knew the boys were worried and upset, and I wanted to comfort them, but I needed to get myself together first.

They survive a few minutes without you, Lark said. *Nothing wrong with taking time for yourself.*

I know. I still feel guilty.

Taking a deep breath to see which of my mates was at the door, I was surprised to smell Mrs. Price. Or Mama, as she'd invited me to call her.

"Come in," I called and sat up on my bed, still cuddling Mr. Nibbles.

The door opened and Mama poked her head around.

"Hello, angel. You don't have to let me in or talk if you don't want to. You can say no," she told me.

"It's okay. I don't mind." I scooted to the edge of the bed and patted the space beside me.

She came in and sat next to me, then put her arm around me and hugged me. After kissing my forehead, she laid her cheek against the top of my head and rocked us a little bit.

As I sank into her soft warmth, I realized how much I missed the comfort only a mother could give.

"I love the boys," I assured her after a minute of sniffling. "I'm not shutting them out, I promise. I just needed room to breathe."

"That's fine. That's always fine, angel. Take all the time and space you need." She kissed the top of my head again. "I'm sorry that happened and upset you, but please know that none of us think any less of you. I know I'm not your mother, and I'd never want to take her place in your heart, but I already love you like my own daughter, Posy. Evie does too."

"That's the nice thing about hearts. They never run out of room," I whispered. "It would be nice to have a mom again."

"Then you have two."

I squeezed Mr. Nibbles and rubbed my cheek on his soft fur before I whispered, "Are my mates okay?"

"They're worried," she told me. "They're afraid you're going to give up on them. They feel like they're failing you because they make you panic and cry too often."

"What?" I raised my head and searched her brown eyes, but found only the truth. Shaking my head, I sighed. "Those silly boys."

"They are, aren't they? They love you so much, angel. You can't see it because you didn't know them before, but trust me. You have brought them so much happiness and peace."

"They've done the same and more for me." I smiled at her, then sat Mr. Nibbles beside me on the bed. "I'm ready to talk to them now."

"Would you like to change into your PJs first? I can arrange some snacks while you do. I'm staying here tonight, if that's okay with you."

"Of course it is." I bit my lip, then decided to go for it. "Can I ask you a question?"

"Anything, angel."

"Do you know that Mr. Price has been verbally abusing Mason? And do you know what he said about me?"

"I didn't until tonight. Papa told me everything. I promise you, Posy, if I had known..." She broke off and shook her head. "Royal isn't a bad man, and he would never raise his hand to you. He was always strict with Mase, but at some point he crossed the line, and he knows it, just as he knows he's going to have to work hard to earn Mase's forgiveness and rebuild their relationship."

Her eyes teared up and her bottom lip trembled. I could only imagine the hurt she was feeling after finding out the mate she loved was hurting their child. Wrapping my arms around her waist, I squeezed her in a tight hug.

"He also knows he hurt your feelings and scared you," she murmured. "Don't be surprised if he shows up tomorrow with a gift and profuse apologies."

I blinked. I didn't know the word profuse, but I got the idea. An image popped into my mind of the scary former alpha on his knees with a bouquet of flowers, and a little giggle slipped out.

"That's better, angel."

Julia

I came downstairs to hear bickering in the kitchen and wondered what the chaos twins were up to.

"No, wait. The recipe says a teaspoon, not a tablespoon."

"Does it matter that much?"

"Yes, *Ash-hole*, it does!"

"You know I hate it when you call me that, dickhead!"

"Guys, guys, you're losing focus."

Ah, my poor Jayden. The lone voice of reason.

"Sorry. I just want them to be perfect for our girl."

"Then follow the recipe!"

"Wyatt," I said as I walked into the kitchen, "why are you raising your voice? Ash and Jay have perfectly fine hearing."

"Sorry," Wyatt muttered. "Is she okay?"

"She's fine. She's changing into her PJs, then she'll be down." I went over to see what they were making. "Oh! Chocolate chip cookies!"

"Yep!" Ash beamed, bouncing on his toes. "For Posy. We wanted to make hot chocolate, too, but we're out of the instant stuff and none of us know how to make it from scratch."

"Recipes are precise for a reason. You don't want too much salt in your cookies, or that's all you'll taste," I explained. "How about you guys finish the cookies and I'll whip up some hot chocolate?"

They agreed, and Ash and Wyatt went back to work under Jay's watchful eye.

"Where are the others?" I asked while gathering my supplies.

"Cole let Topaz out for a run to blow off some steam," Ash said, "and Mase is in the home office doing paperwork, AKA hiding."

"He'll come out when Posy comes down," I said. "He needed some time and space, too."

"We didn't tell you because we knew it would hurt you," Jay said out of the blue.

"And Mase asked us not to," Wyatt chimed in. "He said he could handle it, and we stupidly believed him. We should have said something. I feel like a coward for staying silent."

"Oh, my baby boy." I put down the saucepan, went over, and pulled him down into a tight hug. "Children are not responsible for their parents' actions, and you are not a coward."

"I never realized how much responsibility we put on Mase until Posy pointed it out to me right after she moved here. He protects us too much."

Wyatt melted into me as his breath hitched, and I wanted to strangle Royal all over again. He knew better than anyone how actions have unintended consequences, and his behavior with our son had rippled into each of the boys, most of whom already had demons to battle. Of them all, Ash had the best mental health, which was surprising given that he lost not one, but two sets of parents.

"The only thing Mase would change in his life is his father," I whispered in Wyatt's ear. "He loves you so much, baby boy."

"I love him, too," he whispered back. "I just wish he'd let us protect *him* once in a while."

"He can't help it. It's his nature to throw himself on a live grenade. But he knows you're always there for him, Wyatt." I kissed his forehead. "Now enough sad talk. We got cookies and hot chocolate to make!"

#

Mason

When I was fourteen, our fathers set up a mini training school for me and my brothers to learn how to run a pack. One day, they assigned us a project to plan how we'd handle an attack similar to the one that wiped out Dark Woods and killed Ash's parents.

Cole and I each spent hours working on our individual plans, while the three musketeers slapped something together the night before it was due. They were only eleven and twelve, but Wyatt's dad still tore them a new one over it while the rest of our dads examined Cole's project, then mine.

"You have a few areas to improve on, such as your defense here and here," my father told Cole as he pointed to two different areas, "but your offensive plan is quite good."

Areas to improve on? I thought to myself as I looked over his plan, too. *He totally forgot the orphanage and safe house, the two most vulnerable areas!*

Alpha Nathan saw what I did and voiced my thoughts out loud almost for word. Alpha Jay recommended that Cole start with planning his defense first in the future as that seemed to be his weakest area.

Then the three alphas reviewed my work. I was really proud of it, to tell the truth - until my father began his critique. I'd forgotten to label the parking area at the alpha office building. The upper left corner was torn on one of the maps I'd sketched. I'd misspelled maneuver. And so on.

And on.

And on.

By the time he was done, I'd completely shut down. As I widened my eyes to hold back the tears, I saw Alpha Shawn take Papa aside. I couldn't hear what they were saying, but Wyatt's dad was pissed about something, and Shawn Black didn't get pissed easily.

Alpha Jay drew my attention away from them, though, when he patted me on the shoulder.

"It's a solid plan on both offensive and defensive fronts," he said. "This plan would save a pack, and that's what really matters."

"Don't worry about a torn paper or a misspelled word, okay, Mase?" Alpha Nathan put in his two cents. "You did good, son."

I jerked my chin up a little, afraid if I moved too much the tears would fall and shame me even more, and he let out a heavy sigh.

"Okay, guys," Alpha Shawn called out, "that's it for today. How about some ice cream?"

My brothers cheered as we packed up our stuff, and I watched Cole carefully store his plan back in his binder.

I threw mine in the trash.

Later that night, while my brothers were linking about their plans for the weekend, I sat at my desk in my room and looked up the word maneuver. Taking out a piece of notebook paper, I wrote it out at the top in big block letters. Then I wrote it again and again until the paper was full, front and back.

I never misspelled it again...

A soft knock at the office door drew me out of that grim memory, and I leapt to my feet when Posy's scent wafted to my nose. Throwing open the door, I looked down to find her smiling sweetly up at me.

"Come join us in the living room for hot chocolate and cookies," she said.

I opened my mouth to ask her how she was feeling, but Garnet stopped me.

Go with her current mood and don't remind her she was upset. Oh, and smile back at her, idiot.

Taking his unsolicited but welcome advice, I smiled, reached down and picked her up. She automatically wrapped her legs around my waist and her arms around my neck.

"I hope you don't mind, but I love carrying you," I murmured as I kissed the underside of her jaw. "We all do. If we could, we'd carry you everywhere all the time."

I hoped she heard more than the words.

"I don't mind." She sank her fingers into my hair and scrubbed my scalp gently.

"Mmm. That feels good, baby."

"Yours is the only hair I haven't had a chance to play with. Wyatt has soft fluff I like to pet, and Ash's curls are insane and get all tangled up in my fingers. Cole's is so long and silky, and Jayden's is super thick and bouncy."

"Yeah, we all like to pet Wyatt's fluff," I chuckled as I carried her toward the living room. "And you're always welcome to play with any part of me, little flower, hair included."

"Um, don't say things like that when your mom is here," she mumbled.

"Why? Does it give my little baby naughty thoughts?" I whispered in her ear.

Squeaking, she plunked her forehead in the middle of my chest to hide her hot face.

Grinning, I walked into the living room and joined Mama on the middle couch, Posy still clinging to me like a baby monkey. She only let me go and sat on my lap properly when Jay and Ash handed out mugs of hot chocolate and plates of chocolate chip cookies.

As Wyatt and Cole argued over what movie to watch, I drew in a huge lungful of Posy's lovely scent and looked around at my little family.

No matter how bad a day is, so long as it ends like this, I'm a happy man.

28: Sammiches

Royal Price

I stood on the front porch of the alpha house and waited until my hands were steady before I knocked.

A few seconds later, Beta Tyler James opened the door.

"Oh, hey, Mr. Price. The alphas are all out on jobs, if you're here to see them, and Mrs. Price went over to Mr. and Mrs. Barlow's early this morning. It's just me and the luna."

"Ty, how many times have I asked you to call me Royal? And I'm here to visit Posy."

Thank the Goddess he doesn't know what happened or he would never let us near her, I told Alabaster, my wolf. *We're also lucky that no one else is here.*

Al grunted. He was angry at me and had no qualms about letting me know that. Not that I could blame him. I was angry at me, too.

I followed Tyler into the kitchen, where Posy was washing her hands at the sink. I knew the second she smelled who the visitor was because her posture went rigid and her little body started to tremble.

Even though she wasn't in the pack yet, I could sense her panic and fear and knew that Tyler, as her beta, would feel it as keenly as if it were his own. He was beside her in a flash, and she dug her face into his side, gripping fistfuls of his t-shirt as she half-hid behind him.

"Oh, hey, luna, it's okay," he tried to soothe her. "This is Royal Price, Alpha Mase's dad. Didn't you meet him at the party last night?"

She knows who I am, Ty, I linked him.

Don't take it personally. It's because the alphas aren't here. She's less confident when they're not around.

That's probably some of it, but the truth is, I stuffed up and scared her.

Tyler's whole demeanor changed in an instant. He curled his arm around Posy and pulled her even further behind his body, and a low growl rumbled from his chest.

The bond between a beta and the luna is unlike any other bond in the pack. A beta becomes a fanatic about her safety and would protect her to his death, even from her own mate. So, while the man Tyler saw me as a friend and mentor, the beta Tyler saw only a jerk who'd hurt his luna.

Al scare luna? River's voice was far too calm.

Crap.

Not me, little one, Al answered, giving me a smirk.

229

Don't encourage his anger. We can't afford for him to come out right now, I scolded Al, then linked back with River and Tyler. *I did, but I'm here to apologize and make it right.*

No scare luna again, River said, still with that calm voice.

Double crap.

I won't, I promised.

Better not! River taunted in a sing-song, and Tyler's eyes flared with golden wolf light.

Shit.

The alphas have picked on her panic and are demanding to know what's wrong, Tyler linked me. *I told them she's fine and to give me five minutes before I explain. That's how long you have to fix this. Don't waste it.*

I gave him a brief nod.

"Luna Posy, I'd like a moment of your time, please." I kept my voice as quiet and gentle as I could. "I want to apologize and try to earn your forgiveness."

She peeked around Tyler, but her pretty blue eyes wouldn't lift above my chin and her fingers clenched tighter in his shirt.

Approaching her slowly, I raised my hand holding the bouquet of flowers.

"A small token of my regret. I am truly sorry for the cruel things I said about you." I laid the flowers on the counter when she made no move to take them. "I knew the moment you kicked me out of the home office that you were not what I thought you were. I'd already planned to apologize before last night, so please don't think I'm only here because I saw your scars."

I waited for some reaction, but not very hopeful that I'd get one.

"She says she accepts your apology and forgives you for your cruel words," Tyler said. His eyes still glittered with River's presence, and his face was set in a fierce scowl. "I expect better from you in the future, sir. She deserves to be treated with respect as both your luna and your daughter-in-law."

"I know. I will do better," I vowed. "Luna, I hope you will allow me to get to know you. I am excited to have a daughter-in-law, especially one who is not only lovely and kind, but also brave and strong."

She blushed heavily, and her eyes flicked to mine for a second.

"Mason," she murmured, and we both knew she didn't need to say anything else for me to understand what she was asking.

"I know I was wrong. So wrong. It took my wife reminding me that Mase isn't - and never was - anything like me before I understood just how stupid I've been. I'll apologize to him when he's ready to talk to me again, and I'm willing to work hard to earn his forgiveness and a place in his life, no matter how small."

Her eyes flitted to mine again, and I knew she recognized my sincerity when she nodded. Her fingers slowly knotted from Tyler's t-shirt and she patted him on the arm. He released his hold on her and stood at ease.

They move well together, Al commented.

I nodded in agreement. A stranger would think they'd known each other for years.

"I believe in second chances," she said softly, "but that's all you get. *One* chance. Don't screw it up."

"More than fair," I replied. "Thank you, luna."

She came close enough to pick up the bouquet.

"Thank you for the flowers." She buried her nose in them and inhaled. "They're beautiful. And call me Posy."

"Do you want to join us?" Ty asked me as she began to hunt for a vase. "We were about to learn a new game together."

Is that a good idea? I linked him.

You want to get to know her, right?

Yes, but she's still nervous. I don't want to spook her any more than I already have.

After the alphas, she trusts me the most out of her betas. Well, Em, too, but she's wary of Angelo, so they're keeping their distance for now. I don't think that's a good strategy. How can avoiding her help her feel comfortable with you?

He has a point, Al said.

"I'd like that, if it's okay with you, Posy?" When she nodded, I asked, "What game?"

"Monopoly," Tyler groaned. "The alphas want to start a tradition of having family game night with old-school board games and dominoes and stuff like that. Alpha Jay mentioned Monopoly, so she wants to learn it before then. She asked me to teach her, but I've never played before, either, so we were going to learn it together."

She doesn't want to look dumb in front of her mates, he added through the link.

Why would she look dumb? I frowned in confusion. *No one's born knowing how to play Monopoly.*

She doesn't understand how money works. Like, how to count it or anything, really. Earlier this morning, she asked me to help her with some cash she won in a bet, and she didn't understand that five tens are worth the same as one fifty dollar bill. She thought they'd be worth more because there were more of them.

Oh. I blinked. *And her mates are billionaires. Talk about irony!*

Tyler grinned, and River *finally* faded from his eyes.

"Monopoly?" I said aloud. "I'm surprised Cole didn't say anything about chess."

"He did, but he wants to teach her that himself."

"Chess takes a while to master," I said as I looked at Posy. "Cole's played for years and years, so he'll be a good teacher. Personally, I find it boring. Monopoly is much more fun! I'm going to teach you all the tricks so you can rob the boys blind!"

The little smile she gave me was a blessing I knew I didn't deserve, but one I'd treasure for the gift it was.

#

We set up the game on the dining room table, then I went over the rules and suggested I be the banker until they practiced a few times.

Now Posy and Tyler were arguing over who got to use the dog token. Posy wanted it because it was cute, and Tyler said River wanted it for the same reason. As if she knew a temper tantrum was approaching, Posy gave in with good grace and took the top hat.

Does she know about River? I linked Tyler.

No, he muttered. *I'd rather she didn't until she had to.*

Understood.

Then the sound of a vehicle coming up the drive caught our attention, but it was the smell of unfamiliar wolves that put us on alert.

"Stay with the luna, Ty. Do not leave her side."

"Yes, sir."

"What's going on?" Posy asked.

I stood and headed for the front door as Tyler explained to her. Going out onto the porch, I watched as a long-bed, extended cab truck pulled into the parking area. The boys had finally given in and gotten it and the long driveway paved.

Thank the Goddess. I was sick of all that dust.

As soon as the pick-up was parked, the driver's door opened, and a dark-haired shifter stepped out and came up the walk. When I recognized him, I had to hide my disgust behind a blank face.

*What is **he** doing here?* Al snarled.

I don't know, but I'm sure we're about to find out.

Three more shifters in the vehicle, my wolf pointed out.

I'm aware.

When the shifter came to a stop in front of me, I focused my attention on him.

"Alpha Bellamy Jones." I gave him a curt nod.

"Royal Price. It's been a while."

Neither of us held out our hands to shake.

"I take it this is a personal visit, since you didn't make an appointment?" Scowling, I crossed my arms over my chest.

He knew better than to just show up at an alpha's house. It was bad manners and could turn fatal in a heartbeat, especially if the alpha felt the stranger was a threat toward his mate or pups or both.

"It is," he said. "I heard your boys took Emerson in. Even made him one of their betas. I didn't take Five Fangs for a pack of bleeding hearts and rainbow lovers, but—"

"Whatever Five Fangs is, it's not an enemy Gray Shadows can afford to make," I bit out. "Now, get to the point so you can get out of here."

"I have something that belongs to Emerson." He raised his hands, palms facing me. "I'm only here to deliver it."

"Emerson is more than an hour away. Do you want to wait or leave it with me?"

"Rumor is that your boys found their luna. Is she available? I'll only entrust it to an official pack leader. Then I can say with a clear conscience that I did my duty."

Between Tyler and I, we could handle these four shifters if this was a trap, although it was a pretty dumb set-up for an ambush. Besides, Alpha Bellamy knew as well as I did that a war between our packs would end in the decimation of his.

Ty, I linked, *bring Posy out, but don't leave the porch. If things look like they're about to go sideways, get her back in the house and into the safe room, then link the alphas.*

Yes, sir, but I already linked the alphas and other betas. The betas are on their way, and the alphas are on standby.

That's fine, I told him. *Good thinking. I don't like being outnumbered with the luna here, even if the two of us can more than handle these jokers.*

Um, the alphas are not happy about this, sir.

I bet they aren't, Al snickered, and I rolled my eyes.

The front door opened, and Tyler came out with Posy hidden behind his tall frame. He held her hand and led her to the top of the stairs, where he stopped and drew her to the side so that he was still slightly in front of her.

"I'm Luna Posy Briggs of Five Fangs. How may I help you today?"

She clung to Tyler's hand with both of hers and trembled, but she spoke in a clear, calm voice and met the man's eyes.

I was so proud of her.

Alpha Bellamy spared her a glance, then studied Tyler for several moments.

"That *child* is what you're calling a beta these days?" He snorted. "Now your acceptance of Emerson makes sense. My, my, how your standards have fallen, Royal."

233

"You're not the first to dismiss him as harmless." I shrugged. "Don't piss him off or you'll discover how mistaken you are."

Oh, please, piss him off, Jet smirked.

I don't want to explain to my sons why my daughter-in-law is surrounded by dead bodies. Do you? I hissed, but he only laughed.

I'd known Tyler since he was a pup, worked with him at fighter practice every week since he'd gotten his wolf, and more recently helped train him for the role of beta. Harmless was the last word I'd use to describe him, and that was *before* taking his wolf into account.

In some ways, River was a very simple wolf. When it was time to go to work, he exploded into a killing machine. The instant the threat ceased to exist, he reverted to his baby self. Neither Nathan nor I had ever heard of any wolf with intermittent explosive disorder, but we figured it stemmed from the abuse Tyler had endured at his father's hands before Quartz ended the monster known as Seymour James.

I chuckled to myself, remembering a fight with rogues who'd strayed into our territory. River had ripped out the last wolf's throat, then turned to Nathan and I - blood and gore still dripping from his muzzle - and asked for ice cream. Aghast, we could only nod as his golden eyes blinked innocently up at us.

Don't get me wrong. When rogues attack, a whirlwind of fangs and claws is good to have on your side. It's damn disturbing, though, to watch that same berserker burst into tears when he realizes he ate all of his strawberry ice cream.

"Luna." Alpha Bellamy finally decided to get to the purpose of his visit. "This belongs to Emerson. I leave it with you to return to him."

He looked over his shoulder at his wolves and snapped his fingers. They went to the tailgate of the truck, dropped it, and dragged out a large travel crate like the humans used for their dogs. The men carried it over and set it on the grass about ten feet in front of me, then stepped back to flank their alpha.

Smells like a shifter, but I sense no wolf. Al's interest was piqued. *And why a crate like that? A violent shifter would tear that apart in seconds, and why else would you need to contain one?*

"Emerson made his mother promise we wouldn't kill the thing," Alpha Bellamy said, "or I would have done so long ago. Tell Emerson it is now his responsibility and he may keep or dispose of it as he wishes. I will bear this burden no longer and wash my hands of it."

With that, he and his men crawled back into the pickup and left as suddenly as they'd arrived.

"Mr. Price?" Posy's voice quavered. "Is there a shifter in there? I smell one, but neither Lark nor I can sense a wolf."

"Same," Tyler added.

"Wait there until I look," I told them.

I made sure they were both going to stay put, then cautiously approached the crate. I could hear soft whimpers, erratic breathing, and a racing heartbeat.

Hunkering down, I peered through the door grid and my eyes widened at what I saw.

"Oh."

"What is it?" Tyler demanded.

"A boy. He looks the same age as Archer and Wayne."

"Fifteen," I heard him tell Posy.

As they talked in hushed tones, I focused on the stone-colored eyes staring back at me through a tangle of dark matted curls. The child, trembling in fear, curled into a ball and pressed himself in the far corner.

"Hey, there, little buddy." Getting on my knees, I tried to make myself smaller and less intimidating, but there was only so much I could do. "My name's Royal Price. What's yours?"

He shook harder and stayed silent. Raising one hand slowly, I saw his eyes follow my every move as I lifted the latch and let the door swing open.

"It's okay," I told him. "You don't have to talk to me if you don't want to. Why don't you come out of there? We can get you something to eat. Would you like that?"

When he only huddled into a tighter ball, I started to crawl into the crate, intending to sit down next to him, but Posy's shout stopped me.

"No, don't do that!"

Popping my head up, I saw her running over with Tyler on her heels.

"It will make him feel crowded and trapped if you go in there with him," she explained when she reached me. "Let's sit on the grass and coax him to come out."

She wants to know if he looks like he's hurt, Tyler linked me as we all sat down a couple of feet away from the crate.

He's got bruises, and he's far too thin. I frowned. *I'm going to report this to the king when he returns from Tall Pines. Alpha Bellamy has a lot to answer for. No child should be beaten and starved, even if he's violent or did something wrong.*

Agreed, Tyler growled.

"Why did the alpha keep calling him an 'it'?" Posy whispered.

"Another way to torment, humiliate, demean," Tyler answered before I could, and River laced his voice.

"River, don't scare the luna," I murmured.

"Me sorry, luna," River said from Tyler's mouth, lighting the kid's eyes up like sunshine as he ascended.

"It's okay, River." Posy reached up and patted the top of Tyler's head, and I covered my grin with my hand. "This is upsetting for all of us, but don't worry. We'll take care of him."

"Otay." And River ceded control back to Tyler.

While we were talking, the boy had crawled to the open door and knelt just inside the crate. His eyes really were stone-colored, a silvery mix of not quite blue and not quite green.

"Are you hungry?" Posy smiled at him, but didn't move from her spot. "Would you like some food? Tyler can make us something."

"I'm not leaving your side, luna." Tyler rolled his eyes at her. "Mr. Price can do it."

"What should I make?" I asked. "I can't cook, but I can make sandwiches."

"Sammich? Peabutter jelly sammich?"

All our eyes turned to the boy who'd crawled out of the crate on his hands and knees and now sat perched on his haunches right in front of Posy. Tyler was on high alert, ready to tackle the kid, but it was obvious to us reasonable people that the boy was no threat.

"What would you like to drink with it?" Posy asked. "Apple juice? Orange—"

"Milk! Milk with peabutter jelly sammiches."

"Milk it is! All right, Mr. Price, that's our order. Milk and PB and Js. We'll have a picnic right here."

"Not PB and J." The boy's face screwed up into a pouty scowl. "Peabutter jelly sammich! You promised!"

"Oh, well, yes. Okay. My bad." Posy looked flustered, which made me chuckle. "What's your name, sweetie? "

"Row," he said.

"Row?" I asked. "Like 'Row, Row, Row Your Boat'?

"Gently down the stream!" the boy sang. "Mary, Mary, Mary, life is but a dream."

"Okay. Close enough." I chuckled. "Row, huh? Well, we have a Crew. Why not a Row?"

"Row, I'm Posy and these are my friends. He's Ty and he's Mr. Price." She pointed at Tyler, then me. "Can we be your friends?"

"Friends? I can have friends?" Row's eyes opened wide, turning almost as round as an owl's.

"Yeah, sweetie, you can have friends," Posy told him.

"I never had friends before. Only Bubba, and Mommy Daddy made Bubba leave."

"Oh, I'm so sorry! Maybe we can help you find Bubba. Is Bubba what you call your brother?"

"Yes, yes!" Row clapped his hands so energetically, he fell back on his butt.

The suddenness of Row's movement launched Tyler into protect mode, and the beta was crouched between Posy and Row before any of us could blink.

"Oh, come on, Ty," Posy complained. "He's an innocent kid."

"You don't know that. We don't know anything about him, luna. I'd prefer you kept your distance until we figure things out and get Emerson here."

"Emerson?" Row scrambled to his knees and slapped his palms on Tyler's cheeks. Leaning in *really* close, he stared into Tyler's eyes. "You know Bubba?! Where's my bubba?"

"He's on his way," Tyler mumbled and leaned back. "After you eat your sandwiches, okay?"

Row nodded, so I got off my duff and went into the house. I made a pile of PB and Js, loaded them on a tray with four glasses of milk, and carried it outside.

"Looky, looky, Row! Our picnic's here," Posy chirped, which made Row clap his hands again.

He's cute, Al grinned, which made me smile.

Row hummed contentedly while devouring 'sammich' after 'sammich,' then chugged his glass of milk. When he finished, he curled up half on Posy's lap and fell asleep.

By then, the four betas had arrived, and I linked them to approach slowly so the boy didn't get scared again. A tremor of shock hit the pack bond - *That was Emerson*, Al informed me, as if I couldn't guess - and then the big man himself stumbled toward Row and Posy.

"Thoreau?" he whispered.

\#

Posy

Curled into a ball, the boy had his head on my legs, his thumb in his mouth, and his eyes fixed on mine.

I moved slowly so as not to frighten him and laid one hand on his dark chocolate curls. They were thick with grease and mats and as dirty as the rest of him.

I began to hum a little melody my mother used to sing for me, my fingers gently stroking over his bruised forehead, and the boy's purple-veined eyelids drooped lower and lower until they closed.

Poor baby. What did they do to you?

"Thoreau?"

Emerson's whisper caught me by surprise. I'd been so focused on the boy that I didn't realize the other betas had arrived.

"He said his name's Row," I said.

237

Emerson dropped to his knees next to me and stared at Row as if he couldn't believe his eyes.

"It's short for Thoreau." Emerson sounded like he was about to burst into tears. "What happened to my baby brother?"

"Your father dropped him off and said he's your responsibility now. They brought him here in that crate," I explained. "He wouldn't come out of it at first. We fed him, then he crawled to me and laid down like this and just now fell asleep. His clothes are filthy and way too small for him, and look at how bony and bruised he is. I think they were very, very cruel to him."

"Bubba?" came a tired voice. "Bubba, I missed you."

"I missed you, too, Reau. So, so much!"

With a choked-off sob, Emerson grabbed Thoreau from me and wrapped him up in a tight hug. The boy hung limply in his arms.

"Will you kill me or will you keep me?" Reau whispered.

"What?" Emerson lifted his head to stare down at his brother's face.

"Mommy Daddy said you will kill me or keep me, and that is okay. Kill me or keep me, just don't send me back. Mommy Daddy are mean, Bubba. They give me ouchies because I'm retarded." Twisting his fists into Emerson's shirt, Thoreau began to cry. "I'm sorry I'm retarded, Bubba, but I will be a good boy if you keep me. I swear I'll be a good boy."

My hands flew to my mouth, and I stumbled back as an arrow of pain hit me right in the chest. Fortunately, Mr. Price caught me before I landed on my bum. I latched onto his forearms, my legs shaking too hard to hold me up.

Boys, are you almost here? I can't take this. I held back a sob. *He's so abused and neglected, it's breaking my heart.*

Cole and I are two minutes out, came Mason's clipped reply. *The three musketeers about twenty. Hold on, baby.*

"You are not retarded," Emerson said through clenched teeth. "That is a bad word. Don't say it ever again. And of course I'm going to keep you. You're my baby brother."

Thoreau's cries turned to sobs, and Emerson cradled him like a baby against his chest.

Angelo's here, Tyler linked me. *Just got out of his truck.*

Looking over my shoulder, I saw the feared Angel of Death racing toward us with a white face and panic in his eyes.

"Emerson!" he bellowed.

As he raced up the walk, everyone got out of his way, and he fell to his knees in front of his mate.

"Hey, hey, hey," he crooned. Reaching over Thoreau's head, he took Emerson's tear-streaked face in his palms. "Whatever's wrong, it's going to be okay. We'll figure it out."

"He's not— They *hurt* him! And I can't— He doesn't—" Emerson couldn't seem to *breathe*, let alone form coherent sentences.

"Shh, *orsacchiotto* (teddy bear). Shh." Angelo peppered Emerson's face with little kisses.

"I can't sense his wolf, Angelo!" Emerson whispered.

"While Mr. Price was making lunch, Reau told us that his wolf, Tanner, was sleeping," I said quickly to ease his anxiety. "I smell wolfsbane on him, so—"

Angelo cut me off as his eyes whipped over to stare at me.

"How do you know what that smells like?"

"Because I've been shot full of it before. Many times." I lifted my chin and stared back at him. "Anyway, I think someone gave it to him to put his wolf to sleep."

"Then we can give him some nightshade or foxglove to counter it," Angelo said as he turned back to Emerson.

As long as they didn't give him too much, I thought to myself and prayed they hadn't.

"Now, don't you think it's time to introduce me to this *piccolo cucciolo* (little puppy)?" Angelo smiled at Emerson, who nodded.

"Thoreau, meet my mate, Angelo del Vecchio. Angelo, this is my baby brother, Thoreau Ezra Jones. I call him Reau for short. He turned fifteen in March."

"Hello, *cucciolo* (puppy)," Angelo said with a gentle smile.

"My name is Reau, not cooch-low," Reau grumbled.

"Oh, I am sorry. It means puppy in Italian." Angelo grinned. "You are *cucciolo* (puppy) and Emerson is *orsacchiotto* (teddy bear)."

"And what are you?" Thoreau tilted his head in a very wolfy way.

"Emerson did not give me a nickname yet, but you can call me Gelo if you want."

"Jello! Jello is good. I love jello. Cook gives me extra jello on Wednesdays and Fridays. She is nice and—"

His ramble was cut off when the snot bubbling out of his nose finally dribbled onto his lip. Making a disgusted face, he lifted the hem of his t-shirt and wiped his face with it, and all of us gasped at what we saw.

He was as skeletal as I had been when the boys found me, and dozens of bruises in all stages of healing stood out like ink splotches on his pale skin.

"I'll kill that rat bastard!" Mr. Price snarled.

239

"Who needs killing?" Cole growled from somewhere behind me. "Because after the morning I've had, I'm more than ready to put down a wolf or two."

Whirling around, I saw him and Mason hurrying up the walk. They were covered nearly head to toe in whitish powder, and their eyes gleamed with their wolves.

Before I could blink, Cole picked me up under my arms and he and Mason squished me between them. Mason buried his face in my neck while Cole did the same thing on the other side.

Peals of laughter drew my eyes to Reau, who was pointing up at us.

"Posy sammich!" he giggled.

Hmm. Mason and I are starved for a Posy sammich, Garnet murmured.

Us, too, brother, Topaz said with a grin. *Yum, yum!*

"Papa, we're handing this matter over to you. You can give us a report later," Cole said. "Right now, Mase and I want to eat lunch with our girl."

You mean eat our girl for lunch, Mason smirked.

Squeaking, I buried my red face in the crook of Cole's neck and ignored everyone's chuckles as my mates carried me into the house and straight up to our bedroom.

Hey, wait for us! Wyatt blasted through the link.

Not a chance, Cole said smugly.

We're literally turning into the driveway!

Hurry up, then, Cole snarked as he smashed his lips on mine and laid me on the bed. *Or you'll miss her first orgasm of the day.*

Wide-eyed and gulping, I looked from Cole's smirking face to Mason's.

Too bad you no eat more of Reau's sammiches, Lark giggled. *Feeding five starving alphas going to burn through lots of calories!*

240

29: Loving Our Luna

Cole

After kissing Posy senseless, I lifted my head to smirk down at her - and a rain of debris fell out of my hair. She flinched and squeezed her eyes shut when minuscule pebbles bounced on her face, and I cursed myself out as I got off of her and stood next to the bed.

"Sorry, honey. I forgot how dirty we were." Grimacing, I rubbed the back of my neck and heard little plinks as dirt fell off me and onto the hardwood floor.

"Shower first." Mase grabbed my shoulder and pulled me toward our bathroom. "Posy, can I use yours?"

"Of course."

I grumbled as I walked towards the bathroom. The three musketeers were pulling into the parking lot, which meant they'd be up here in a few minutes to steal mine and Mase's alone time with our girl. That pissed me off, and I was already a little too angry to be safe with her.

Hey, boss! I have an idea! Topaz bounced around in my head like a jumping bean.

Once I heard what he was thinking, a broad grin stretched across my face and all my anger melted into mischievousness.

Mase, I linked, *come shower with me.*

What? Why? You're not going to touch me, are you?

No. I rolled my eyes, then decided to dig at him a little. *Unless you want me to.*

I don't! he snarled.

I snickered. Dude was always so uptight. He needed to play more often.

Whatever. Paz has an idea you're going to like.

After I explained Topaz's evil plan, Mase smirked, and I knew he was in, even though he wasn't too enthused about me ogling him.

The three musketeers came into the bedroom as we were stripping off our dusty, ruined clothes. Looking at each other, Mase and I nodded and stepped into the shower.

"I'll link first," I told him, and he nodded.

"Posy, are you okay?" Jayden asked her, his voice muffled by the closed door and falling water.

I opened my link with Posy and ran my eyes up Mase's body, lingering in certain areas I knew would interest her.

She gasped loud enough for us to hear, and Mase smirked at me.

"What happened?" Ash asked her, sounding concerned.

"Um, ah, nothing. I'm fine. I'll tell you about it later."

Cole, what are you doing? she linked me.

Making sure you don't forget about us while the three musketeers are taking our place.

I could never forget about you, she muttered, *and no one can ever take your place.*

Making sure you're wet and ready for us, then, I teased her.

I moved my eyes as Mase shampooed his hair, his arms raised so that his pecs and abs were on perfect display. Feeling her heartbeat begin to race, I lavished praise on Topaz for his brilliant plan.

"I want a Posy sammich, cutie," Wyatt giggled.

"Me, too!" Ash piped up.

"We're all hungry for one," Jay added.

Mase turned around, and I showed Posy his back muscles flexing, then followed the trail of water down to his ass. Her breathing picked up, and I chuckled.

"Princess, there's something about mating we've been meaning to bring up with you."

Ah, Ash. Not now! Wyatt whined in the alpha link.

It's fine, Mase linked them back. *She'll agree.*

Are you sure? Jay asked. *How do you know?*

I'm sure. Mase looked at me over his shoulder and winked. *Trust me.*

"What's that?" Posy asked in a breathless voice.

"Our wolves need to mate with Lark to solidify their bond with her. It isn't necessary, per se, but it would connect our wolves more deeply. And they'd find pleasure in it just like we do," Jay explained.

"My turn," Mase whispered as he turned around again.

Okay, boss, give our girl a show!

No pressure, huh?

No pressure, Topaz said solemnly, and I rolled my eyes.

I waited until Mase's eyes fogged over, then reached down and soaped up my dick and balls, taking my time.

"Oh!" Posy sounded on the edge of an orgasm already.

We are so doing this again, Mase linked me with a rare grin. *And no need to tell the trouble trio.*

Oh, yeah, I laughed. *Keeping it secret is the best part.*

"I know that sounds problematic with Lark's size," Jay hurried to say, probably thinking she made that sound out of worry, "but we have a solution. If you don't mind letting Lark have control of your body for a bit, we can let our wolves use ours to mate with her."

My balls started to draw up, and I debated whether to stop or come.

"She likes to watch it 'come out,' remember?" Mase murmured. "Finish off. You know you'll get hard again as soon as you see her lying naked on our bed."

Tipping my head back, I pictured Posy writhing under me and screaming my name and came so hard, I had to grab onto the wall to keep my balance.

Hearing her high-pitched whimper, I grinned.

"Posy!" the three musketeers called out in sync.

"Yes! I'm fine with that! But you all have too many clothes on!"

Mase laughed and jumped out of the shower, and I hurried to clean myself up. We dried off and wrapped towels around our waists before going back into the bedroom.

You two are bad, Posy linked us. *Very, very bad.*

You could have closed the link at any time, baby, Mase replied.

Which means you liked it, I added.

Her face should have caught on fire, it turned so red.

"You two showered together?" Jay's eyebrows flew up.

"Was it fun?" Wyatt smirked. "Can I join next time?"

"Is that why Posy is so flustered?" Ash asked.

Mase and I smirked at each other.

"We'll never tell," we said in unison.

"So a *Lark* sandwich," I murmured as I sauntered over to Posy, noting the way her eyes ran all over my chest and followed my abs down to my towel. "You sure you're okay with that? You know our wolves are crazy, right?"

"They're not crazy!" Her eyebrows drew together and she glared at me. "They're the best wolves in the world!"

Aw! Did you hear that, brothers? Topaz cooed.

Yep! Granite chirped. *We're the best!*

Me, too? Am I the best? Sid asked shyly.

"Of course!" Posy smiled at Ash, whose eyes already glowed green, then looked at Mase. "Garnet, you're the best, too."

What about Q? Granite asked.

"He already knows he's the best." Posy winked at Jay. "Don't you, love?"

Of course.

"If you're sure, honey, we'll try it, although it might turn into a disaster or a circus or a horror show—"

"Or the most marvelous, beautiful thing any of us have ever experienced," she cut me off with a bright smile.

And how do you continue arguing with that? I asked my boys.

You don't, Wyatt snickered.

243

I mean, what's the worst that could happen? Ash asked. *None of them can get her to climax? In which case, one of us will take control and satisfy her.*

The worst that could happen is that one of them hurts her, Jay said, gnawing his bottom lip.

None of our wolves would hurt our mate, I reassured him. *Not even accidentally. Relax, brother.*

And Garnet will be there if things look to be getting out of control, Mase said, which settled the matter.

Garnet was the most trustworthy wolf among us. If Topaz, Granite, or Sid got too silly, Quartz would probably knock them out. Garnet, on the other hand, would set them straight and help them try again.

"I'm giving Lark control now," Posy said. "You guys do the same with your wolves, and we'll see what happens."

#

Garnet

As Quartz and I predicted, the three pups make a hash of it at first. They were more interested in play-fighting and tickling Lark and each other, at least until they got her clothes off. Then their dicks stood at attention, and they changed their games.

Oh, not to more mature ones, of course. Oh, no, no, no. Not those pups.

First, they challenged each other to see who could make themselves come first, then who could shoot the juice the farthest.

Goddess, give me strength.

When they decided to see who could hit Lark's belly button while she lay in the center of the bed and they stood at the edge, Quartz's patience finally snapped.

To tell the truth, I was surprised he lasted as long as he did.

"Why are you three the way you are?" he snarled. "You're making a mess of this and getting semen everywhere but inside our girl!"

Too much jacking off must have fried Topaz's brain because he decided to tease Quartz.

To tease *Quartz.*

"Chill, Q! We're just playing. You should try it. It might get the stick out of your—"

Granite slapped a hand over Topaz's mouth, and Sid tackled them both to the far end of the bed, where the three of them wrestled around in a tangle of limbs and giggles.

Growling deep in his chest, Quartz's eyes blazed, and I knew he was a second away from attacking.

244

As annoying as they could be, I loved my brothers enough to save their silly butts.

"How about we take care of our mate?" I suggested. "I think it's time to please her, don't you?"

That caught his attention like nothing else could have. His posture relaxing, he looked at our mate, who giggled as the pups wrestled themselves over the edge of the bed and landed on the floor with a loud *thump!*

"Lark," he said in his alpha tone.

Her silver eyes jerked to his face as goosebumps raised all over her skin.

Ooh, she likes that, Q, I linked him with a smirk.

Good thing, he linked back with a dark smile.

"Come here, little girl. Crawl to your daddies on your hands and knees."

He didn't use his alpha voice - even the pups knew that wouldn't be right to do during intimate moments - but kept his tone stern, and Lark obeyed in an instant, her hips swaying from side to side and making me harder than I already was. She was gorgeous as she was; once she filled out a little more, she was going to kill us with her curves.

When she reached us, he wrapped one hand around her throat and guided her up until she was standing on her knees before us, then took her little fingers and laid them on his chest. He ran his hands up her arms, over her shoulders, and around her neck to cup her jaw in his palms.

"Granite and I want to try taking you at the same time," he rumbled softly. "Do you know what that means we would do?"

She shook her head and bit her bottom lip, but her eyes never left his.

"I would put myself here." He ran one hand down her body and between her thighs.

She shivered and a little moan parted her lips. Taking the opportunity, I leaned down and kissed her hard, my tongue thoroughly plundering her mouth. The rich scent of her arousal floated to my nostrils and nearly made me come right then and there.

"And Garnet would put himself here." Q ran his other hand down her back and between her soft, smooth cheeks.

I knew the second he touched her back hole. She jerked in surprise and pulled her mouth away from mine. Her pretty breasts jiggling as she panted, she stared up at me with wide eyes that burned with want.

"Are you okay with that, my love?" Quartz asked. "You can say no if you're not comfortable with it. We're just as happy to make love to you one at a time."

"The boys gave us the idea while they were talking about a Posy sammich," I explained.

She laughed and tilted her head back so the smooth line of her throat was bared to us. Q and I groaned, then attacked, kissing and sucking and marking her as we pleased. When we stopped and raised our faces, she was red-faced and mewling with need. A drop of drool slipped from the right side of her lips, and I wiped it away with my thumb.

"Yes," she moaned. "I want to try it."

"Ask your daddies nicely," Q demanded.

"Please, daddies, make me your sandwich," she whimpered.

I'm going to come right here and now, I groaned.

Get the lube, he said with no sympathy.

While he stripped out of his boxers and climbed onto the bed, I went to one of the nightstands and found the lube. After a *very* awkward conversation with Dad, all of us - man and wolf - knew how to use it and why, but learning about it and doing it were two very different things.

I was a little worried to be first, but the pups wouldn't be able to control themselves, and Quartz was ... Quartz. *I* didn't doubt him, but he doubted himself. He feared he'd get too rough taking her pussy, never mind the patience that would be needed to take her sweet ass.

Closing my eyes as I settled my nerves, I listened as Q asked Lark if she needed to use the bathroom, and her reply that she didn't need to pee. He explained in a little more detail, and she again said no.

I turned back to the bed and saw Quartz was already flat on his back with Lark lying on top of him. He played with her breasts as he kissed her, his hands dark against her creamy skin, and my dick hardened painfully. Dropping the towel, I crawled into bed, dropped the lube next to us, and began to kiss Lark's shoulders and back.

Check if she's wet enough for me, Quartz linked me.

Gently biting her left cheek, I slipped my hand between her thighs and dipped my fingers into her wet warmth. Her responding moan sent a jolt straight to my groin.

Oh, yeah. She's a dripping mess.

That was all he needed to hear before he told her to sit up. Grabbing her hips, he lifted her up enough for her entrance to hover over his dick. Then he thrust up into her at the same time he pulled her hips down, and she squealed as her eyes rolled back in her head.

"Ride your daddy, little girl," he rasped.

After she caught the rhythm he wanted, he moved his hands to spread her soft cheeks and put her back hole on full display.

I don't know, Quartz, Mase. I grimaced. *Like everything else about her, it's small!*

You can do it, Mase encouraged me. *Just remember what Dad said.*

Stretch slowly, use lots of lube, and be gentle, Quartz and I recited together.

She's pretty distracted right now, so it would be a good time to start, Mase added.

I glanced at our girl, and I had no idea how Q hadn't come yet just from watching her fingers play with her nipples as she bounced away on him.

Drawing a deep breath, I reached for the lube and smeared some all over my finger, then her hole. She didn't seem to notice until I circled it and gently pressed on it. Instead of tensing or telling me to stop, she threw her head back onto my shoulder and groaned.

Encouraged, I worked my finger in as slowly and gently as I could and gradually worked up to two. She came while I was stretching her, and Quartz took over their mating, ramming up into her as she collapsed on his chest. That angle actually made it much easier for me, and I carefully scissored her open and pressed my thick tip in.

She gasped and her body stiffened.

"Don't tighten up, little girl," Quartz warned her, slowing his pace a little to make it easier for her to accept me. "Be good for your daddies and trust us. Your daddies are going to make you feel real good, little girl."

"Yes, daddy," she moaned and relaxed her muscles.

Going as slowly and gently as I could, I eased all the way into her.

"Such a good girl," Q panted, still hammering into her. "Taking both your daddies like the queen you are. Our good little girl."

She whimpered at his praise and started to move her hips, trying to find a rhythm between us.

It'd help if you moved! Q snarled at me.

I wanted to make sure she's okay, I defended myself, but calmly.

Out of all us wolves, I was the most powerful, with Topaz a close second, and if a real fight broke out between Quartz and me, we both knew who would win. I still tried hard not to set him off, and especially not anytime our mate could be hurt in the crossfire.

And right now, I was feeling *way* too mellow to bother putting him in his place.

247

Holding onto Lark's hips, I lowered myself onto her back, then planted my fists next to Quartz's head to keep most of my weight off of her. We both slid in and out of her in sync and had her on the edge of another orgasm in no time. I could tell Quartz was close, too, if his frantic thrusting was anything to go by, and it wouldn't take much more to send me over the edge, either.

"You want to come, little girl?" Quartz taunted her.

"Yes, please, daddies!" she begged.

"Come, little girl. Come hard for your daddies."

With a scream, Lark clamped down on my dick, and that was all it took. I shot my load balls-deep in our mate's ass, my loud groan rumbling through the room like thunder.

I was brought back to my senses by enthusiastic applause, and I rolled my eyes as I carefully pulled out of her. Quartz did the same, and we turned to see the three pups lying in a row on their stomachs, clapping and grinning at us.

"Our turn!" they said together.

"We want to do that, too," Topaz said.

Quartz dropped his head back on his pillow with a groan, and I rolled off of them.

"Give Lark a minute," I murmured.

I lay on my side and Quartz flipped them onto his, snuggling our girl tightly between us.

"Are you okay, my love?" I asked her.

"That was amazing, Daddy."

"Are you sore? Did I hurt you at all?"

"I thought I died," she whispered, then buried her face in Quartz's throat.

Worried, I looked over her head and met Q's eyes, but he only smirked.

She's fine, he assured me. *It was an intense amount of pleasure for her, that's all.*

Satisfied, I glanced at the pups, two of whom looked impatient and jealous while Sid just looked curious.

She needs to rest, then you can take your turn, I linked them. *Are you sure you want to try that? You have to be super careful and gentle.*

Granite gets the back, Topaz decreed, *and I get the front, but we don't know where to put Sid. Does he just have to wait for a solo turn?*

How did you determine who—

Rock-Paper-Scissors, they chorused.

No, they didn't! Mason hissed.

Of course they did, I chuckled as I dropped my face in Lark's neck.

You have a couple of options, Quartz told them as he petted her hair. *You can ask her to take you in her mouth and suck you off, or she could give you a hand job. Either of those might take too much balancing and concentration, though, since Gran and Topaz will have her ... distracted.*

Raising my head, I looked at Sid to see what he was thinking, but his eyes only reflected distress and fear.

Unlike Quartz and me, none of the three pups had matured. They lingered around a kindergartner's level of development, which wasn't that unusual in wolves. Most either matured along with their humans or stayed in a juvenile state, and there wasn't much in between.

Topaz and Granite were fearless and mischievous devils just like little Winnie and William Black. Sid, on the other hand, could be the twin of River, Beta Tyler's wolf. They were innocent babies who got scared and worried and overwhelmed - when they weren't killing machines, that is.

It was an interesting dichotomy that a human psychologist would have a field day with. To us, they were just Sid and River.

"Listen to me, Obsidian. You can make love to her however you want," I said. "You don't have to do anything fancy or new to impress her or make her happy, right, Lark?"

"Right." She lifted her arms and made grabby hands. "Sid?"

He walked over on his knees, his dick slapping his stomach with each move, and Lark sucked in a sharp breath as her cheeks flushed pink.

See? She wants you already, I linked him. *You're going to do fine.*

He nodded as he scooped her up and freed her from our sweaty embrace, and I immediately felt the loss of her soft, warm body. From his deep sigh, Q felt the same way, but we knew the pups had waited as long as they could.

"But it's our turn," Granite whined.

Did you Rock-Paper-Scissor turns or just positions? Quartz asked him.

Positions, he admitted sullenly.

Then let Sid go first. It will give her ass time to rest before you tear it up.

You better not tear it up! I snarled. *You better not give her so much as a tiny bruise!*

I would never! Granite sounded on the edge of tears. *I would never hurt our mate, Garnet!*

For the love of the moon, it's just an expression, Quartz sighed. *It means to do something with a lot of enthusiasm. Don't cry, Gran. We know you wouldn't hurt our girl.*

Knowing Sid might need support, I sat up against the headboard and rested my arms on my drawn-up knees. Quartz joined me a few seconds later, and we waited to see if he'd be okay. Gran and Topaz cheered him on in the link until we told them to shut up because it was making Sid even more nervous.

I don't know what he was so worried about, Q said on a yawn as he stretched his arms up. *He's doing great.*

He was, too. He touched our mate as if she were made out of spun glass, all the while whispering words of praise and encouragement. When he kissed her, he savored every millimeter of her mouth and jaw and neck in super slow motion. He entered her just as slowly, as if he had all the time in the world, and gave her long, leisurely thrusts that made her whimper and clutch his shoulders.

And Lark responded to him with the same passion she'd given me and Quartz, only quieter and with soft sighs and whispers instead of screams.

It was Sid being his normal, sweet self, but his unhurried lovemaking was erotic as hell to watch, and I felt myself growing hard again.

When she came, Sid kissed each of her nipples tenderly and thanked her with child-like innocence, and she cried, her tears glittering on her cheeks like diamond dust.

She's crying because she's emotional, Quartz hurried to assure Sid when he started to panic. *That was intense in a different way than it was with us. Just hold her for a bit to help her calm down.*

Acknowledging Quartz with a nod, he cradled our girl to his chest and stroked her hair and dotted her face with little kisses.

"Did you come, Sid?" I asked quietly.

"Yes. Inside her. Ashy said that was right." His eyebrows lifted in question, as if he wanted me to confirm it.

I nodded and gave him a thumbs up, and he beamed with happiness and pride as she rested in his arms.

Over the past few minutes, Topaz had slowly worked his way across the bed to sit next to me, his eyes on my dick, and I caught his wrist before his hand made contact.

No touchy, I grumbled at him.

But it needs it!

Not from you. I'll do it myself later if I have to.

But Garnet—

Why don't you three ever pester Q? When you get tired of playing with each other, you always make a beeline for me. He has a dick, too, you know! Masturbate him!

Are you kidding? Topaz squeaked. *He would break every finger and hand that touched him!*

How do you know I won't do the same? I growled softly.

Because you're Garnet. He shrugged and gave me a cheeky grin. *And we don't get tired of playing with each other. We just don't want you to feel left out.*

Trust me, I'm happy to be left out, I deadpanned. *I love being left out. I treasure being left out.*

Before he could argue more, Lark was unfolding herself from Ash's arms and reaching for Granite. That was Topaz's cue, too, and he eagerly shuffled over to the two of them.

As Lark practically tackled Topaz to the bed, Granite nudged me with his elbow.

"You're going to help me, right?" he whispered.

I nodded in resignation, and he fist-pumped the air. Cutting my eyes over at Quartz, I saw him close his eyes and pinch the bridge of his nose.

After watching Quartz earlier, Topaz didn't need much help getting himself and Lark into position, although Granite got in the way when he wouldn't leave her breasts alone. I grabbed his shoulder and pulled him back and slapped the container of lube in his hand. My eyes went from the lube to his hand to Lark's ass, and he just blinked at me a few times.

Hearing Lark and Topaz begin to pant and the steady slap of skin on skin, my balls began to draw up without anyone even touching my dick.

"Let me help you—" Granite began.

"No!" I howled. "You have something else to do."

"Yeah? What?"

I lifted my face to the ceiling.

Goddess. Me again. More strength, please.

"Put the damn lube on your fingers, Gran," I said through gritted teeth, "and start prepping her!"

"Oh. Right!" Grinning like a fool, he opened the container and did as I said.

She was probably still wet enough from the earlier lube and my semen, and I saw she was still fairly well stretched, but I made him go through the steps anyway. He needed to learn how to do it on his own if he wanted to repeat this in the future.

Finally, everything was ready. Topaz had Lark calling out his name as she came, and Granite was positioning his tip at her back hole.

251

Be gentle, I warned him when it looked like he was going to slam into her.

He gulped and nodded, then super carefully pushed into her half an inch at a time until he was fully seated. His head turned to stare at me, and the wonder in his wide eyes made me chuckle.

Looking back at our mate, he rubbed his hands all over her bum and up her back, his fingers lightly tracing her scars and making her shiver. She began to ride Topaz hard and fast, chasing another orgasm, and Granite used her movements to guide his own, rocking in time with her and going at her pace.

Good job, I told him, although I doubted he was listening.

"That was the most nerve-wracking thing I've ever done," I grumbled as I collapsed flat on my back between Sid and Quartz.

"Your dick's standing up again," Sid pointed out ever so helpfully.

Strangling in frustration, I ground the heels of my hands in my eyes and groaned.

"I can rub it, if you want?"

"No thanks, Sid."

Quartz, that bastard, burst into laughter, and I shoved him off the bed.

#

Posy

"I don't— I don't have words for what just happened," Jayden stammered.

"I don't think there *are* words for what just happened," Mason sighed.

"Maybe not, but we need to do that again," Wyatt smirked. "Like once a month or something."

"Oh, thank the Goddess you didn't say once a week," Ash blew out a breath in relief. "Sid's nerves couldn't take it."

I met Wyatt's eyes, and we giggled so hard that we snorted. I blamed it on my extreme exhaustion. I felt like I could sleep for a week.

"By the moon," Cole groaned, "they are the gayest straight wolves in the world. Granite and Sid *cannot* leave each other's dicks alone, and Topaz wanted so badly to play with Garnet's."

"You're that strict daddy," Wyatt said, "who doesn't let his kid have fun at the playground while the rest of the heathens destroy everything around you."

"Hey, if Posy wants to call me Daddy, I am not opposed," Cole grinned.

Quartz and Garnet had liked it when Lark called them her daddies. I thought it was … unsettling, but didn't ask questions since she seemed fine with it. Looking at Wyatt now, I burst into giggles with him again.

"No more sex today for you two," Jayden teased. "It's rotted your brains and now you need to regrow them."

That made us giggle even harder and Ash joined us. Tears rolled down Wyatt's red cheeks, my stomach hurt, and Ash caught the hiccups. Then, Cole and Jayden started giggling because Ash was hiccuping non-stop. Poor Mason closed his eyes and pretended to be asleep.

This was the best day of my life, Lark yawned as she curled up in a worn-out heap at the back of my mind.

"Lark said - *giggle* - this was the - *giggle* - best day of her - *giggle* - life," I wheezed, my eyes so heavy that I couldn't keep them open anymore. "Mine, too!"

"Mine thr— *hiccup* —ee!" Ash said. "Even with the hic— *hiccup* —cups!"

That sent all of us, even Mason, into another round of giggles, and for the first time ever, I giggled myself to sleep.

30: Luna Ceremony

Posy

One good thing about having Julia and Evie for moms was how quickly and enthusiastically they could organize things.

Friday morning, I called Peri to see if she wanted to come over and help me plan my luna ceremony, but she was catching a ride into the human city with Callie and Keeley. The twins had summer jobs there as lifeguards at a community pool, and Peri needed to pick up some supplies for a 'secret project.'

"No worries. Maybe another day," I said.

"Actually," she drawled the word out, "Mom and Mama would love to come over and help you plan. They've been waiting for you to ask them."

"Oh! I didn't realize that."

So she put the moms on the phone and I talked with them and, before I knew it, they were standing at the front door.

"Are you here by yourself?" Mama asked as she hugged me. "After Alpha Bellamy's surprise visit the other day, I thought our sons would go into hyper-protective mode and have someone with you twenty-four seven."

"They tried, but I know where the safe room is, and I can link them and my betas anytime." I giggled a little. "They wanted to Rock-Paper-Scissors who would ditch his job to stay with me, but I told them to stop being silly."

She laughed at that as she stepped back so Mom could smother me in a bear hug.

"Archer, Wayne, and Wade went to work with Dad today, but Peri isn't free to babysit Wesley and the heathens, so we brought them along. Sorry in advance for whatever they break."

Mom's smile was bright, but I could see the tired lines around her eyes. Winnie and William were busy boys and, on top of being pregnant, she probably tired out quickly.

"Wait! I think I can find us a babysitter," I chirped.

"Oh? Who?"

I held up my index finger as I linked him.

Tyler, what are you doing today?

Just hanging out with Rube, he linked back right away. *You need something, luna?*

Rube?

Reuben Ford. Alpha Wyatt's gamma, he clarified.

Oh. Well, Mom and Mama are here to help me plan my luna ceremony, but we need a babysitter for Wesley, William, and Winnie. If you're busy, I can ask someone—

No, we'll do it, he linked back. *Rube needs something to occupy his mind, anyway. He's still on sick leave and is getting bored, even though he doesn't really feel up to doing much.*

Will watching the boys be too hard on him? I worried.

Never fear, luna. I have a great idea that will work for everyone. We'll be there in about ten minutes.

Smiling, I thanked him, then told Mom what was happening. She was fine with Tyler and Reuben babysitting. Tyler had watched the babies before, she said, and Wesley didn't need much watching. All he wanted was companionship and attention, which William and Winnie often stole from him.

As promised, within ten minutes, the doorbell rang and I went to let Tyler in. Throwing open the door, I found him and who I took to be Gamma Reuben on the porch.

"Thank you so much for this," I told them both.

"Never a problem, luna. Have you two met?"

"I haven't met any of the gammas yet." I twisted my fingers together and my eyes dropped to the floor.

"We'll have to fix that. For now, though, this is Reuben Ford, Alpha Wyatt's gamma. Rube, this is Luna Posy Briggs."

"It's nice to meet you." I leaned closer to Tyler and looped my arms around his, hoping to avoid a handshake.

"It's an honor and a pleasure to finally meet you, luna."

I forced myself to look up at him.

He was covered in tattoos - he even had a pretty lotus flower on his neck! - stood about Jayden's height of six foot three, and was obviously of Asian heritage with his thick, straight black hair and deep brown eyes. Those eyes were underscored with dark shadows, though, and never reflected the smile his mouth was trying to make.

My mates hadn't told me details, but whatever this man had endured while imprisoned at Tall Pines had hurt something deep inside him.

Does he have a mate? I linked Tyler. *He looks old enough to find one.*

No, and he's nineteen.

A mate would help him recover faster. I bit my lip. *I hope he finds one soon.*

The witches are helping him as they can, but, yeah. Tyler sighed. *He's better than he was, luna, and that's all we can ask for, right?*

Right.

255

"So what was your great idea for the kids?" I asked as I led the two of them into the living room.

"We're taking them to Bounce."

"What's Bounce?" I tilted my head as I looked up at Tyler.

"An indoor playground and trampoline park."

"Bounce?!" Wesley heard him and came running. "We're going to Bounce, Beta Ty?"

"Yep! Go fetch your baby bros, little dude."

Squealing with delight, Wesley went to do as he was told, and Mom and Mama came over to hug Tyler and Reuben. The moms fussed over both of them, telling them they needed to eat more because they were wasting away, which made me giggle.

Before they left, I tried to give them money to pay for their adventure, but Mom shook her head and told me to put my cash away.

"They're my kids, Posy." She dug her wallet out of her purse. "It's my responsibility to pay for them."

"But it's only because of me—"

"Hush, honey. To keep the heathens busy for a couple of hours is worth every dime." She patted her stomach and grinned. "Nathan and I are happy with whatever gender we get so long as he or she is healthy, but I really do hope this baby is a calm one."

"Mrs. Barlow, there is no chance of that," Tyler giggled. "From Alpha Wyatt down to baby Winnie, none of your children are calm."

"Oh, hush, Ty! Let me dream a little before reality crushes me."

"Beta Ty! Gamma Rube!"

Screaming at the top of his lungs, William ran into the room at full speed. Winnie was hot on his heels and yelling just as loudly.

"What have I told you boys?!" Evie thundered and the little ones came to a screeching halt and stared at her with big eyes. "Inside voices!"

"Says the woman shouting at them," Tyler said out of the side of his mouth, and I had to put my hand over my mouth to hide my grin.

"Dude, you're really going to poke a pregnant bear?" Reuben raised an eyebrow. "Not wise."

I giggled as Tyler rolled his eyes.

Then the kids followed Reuben out to his car and Tyler told Mom and Mama to enjoy the quiet while they could.

After the boys left, the moms descended on me.

One minute we were discussing decorations, and the next Mom and Mama had the whole ceremony planned and wanted to schedule it for Monday.

Monday.

And today was Friday.

"What will I do for a dress?" I freaked out. "And food. And tables for the food. And tablecloths for the tables for the food—"

"Relax, angel." Mama squeezed me in a hug. "We've both done this before, and we helped Jay's mom and Cole's mom with their luna ceremonies, too. We've got this."

"As for your gown, Peri would be honored to make it," Mom added. "That is, if you trust her enough to do a good job."

"Of course I do!" I clasped my hands under my chin. "I've seen some of the clothes she's made for herself. She's very talented."

"I'll pass along your compliments." Mom looked pleased. "She dreams of opening her own shop after she graduates. She'd like to specialize in formal gowns."

"Good thing she knows some brothers who would finance it," I grinned, then realized they'd need clothes, too. "What about my mates? Do they have nice clothes to wear?"

"Yes, baby," Mom giggled. "They have dress clothes. And trust me, getting Wyatt and Cole fitted for a suit is an experience I never want to repeat. Mase stood there in his usual stoic silence, and Jay and Ash wanted to look good, so they behaved, but Cole and Wyatt squirmed around and whined more than little boys getting their first hair cut."

I laughed.

"Wait til you see them all dressed up." Mama nudged me with her elbow. "Sharp doesn't begin to describe it. Your jaw will drop."

"Unfortunately, you won't get Wyatt to stay dressed up for long." Mom shook her head with a sigh. "He'll be stripped out of the coat and tie as soon as the ceremony's over. And be prepared for sneakers. We demanded, cried, threatened, bribed, and begged, but we couldn't make him buy dress shoes."

"Sounds like my boy," I laughed. "Will Peri have enough time to make a gown by Monday?"

"Oh, honey, she's already started it." Mom bounced up and down in her seat. "Wait until you see the design! She went with Callie and Keeley into the city to look at some fabrics. If you have a color preference, text or link her now."

"It doesn't matter. Whatever she thinks will look good on me." I bit my lip and knotted my fingers together in my lap as I admitted in a whisper, "I need to look good enough so I don't shame the boys."

"You could never do that," Mom assured me. "You could show up in ripped jeans and a tank top, and they'd be just as proud to stand at your side."

"You'll look like the angel you are." Mama reached over and untwisted my fingers. "Trust me, Posy, those boys are going to take one look and fall in love with you all over again."

#

Wyatt

Three times since Friday, Mom had threatened me - *me!* her firstborn son and her alpha! - with a sudden but painful death if I screwed up our girl's special day.

Which was why I was out of bed and showered by eight a.m. Monday morning, devouring breakfast in a freaking suit - most of a suit, anyway - and wishing I could have caught another hour of sleep.

The moms wanted to take the photos before the big event, wise enough to know none of my brothers, except maybe Mase, would look good for long after the ceremony. I for one planned to ditch my suit coat as soon as we stepped off the stage.

My brothers and I had finished eating, wondering where our girl was and why she wasn't down here with us, when Mama came into the kitchen and clapped her hands.

"All right, boys, I hope you're ready for this!" She beamed. "Put on your suit coats and go wait in the living room."

"What's going on, Mama? And why didn't Posy eat breakfast?" I frowned as I stood and grabbed the wretched coat from the back of my chair. "She can't afford to miss any meals."

"She ate in your room as we were getting her ready." Mama made shooing gestures. "Go, go! She'll be down in a second so we can take photos, and the quintet needs to be in place for her grand entrance."

Women get so worked up over this kind of thing, I grumbled to my boys as we shuffled into the living room.

It's important to them, Jay linked back. *The least we can do is cooperate.*

Yeah, yeah. I rolled my eyes. *Mom said if I mess this up, she'll tell Dad I took the Lamborghini for a spin the other day.*

The one he just finished restoring for the Russian king? Ash squeaked. *The one that's worth two million?*

Yep! I grinned. *And I am so getting one. If I knew how much fun they were to drive, I would have bought one as soon as I had my license.*

Boy, you best behave today, Cole said. *Dad will skin you alive if he finds out.*

He'll find out, anyway. You're lucky he hasn't already, Jay snickered.

258

How would he? Other than Mom, you're the only ones who know, and you'd better not tell him. I shot them dark looks.

And how did Mom find out? Mase asked.

I may have passed her on the highway. I scrubbed the back of my neck with one hand.

And how fast were you going?

She says she was going seventy and I passed her like she was standing still. I shrugged. *I highly doubt she was going seventy. She was in the minivan with Wesley and the heathens.*

How fast were you going, Wy? Papa Bear demanded.

One-fifty. I looked at my shoes. *Or so.*

Wyatt! he growled. *Not even a shifter could survive a wreck at that speed! You could have been—*

Mom ran into the living room and interrupted him.

"Gentleman, I am pleased and proud to present your beautiful luna!"

Mom held her arms out like a game show model displaying a prize, and all our eyes went to the doorway.

Four tiny fingers gripped the door frame, and half of Posy's face slowly appeared. The one blue eye that I could see was wide with anxiety, and her teeth sank into her bottom lip.

I wanted to send her words of encouragement, but she wasn't opening the link with any of us, and I was afraid that speaking aloud would ruin the moment.

And I was trying hard to not do anything that would make Cole slap me upside my head. I had my hair just the way I wanted it for the photos.

Come on, baby, I whispered in my head, trying to will her forward. *You can do it. You're our strong, brave girl.*

A foot clad in a pink ballet flat came around the corner, followed by a smooth leg, then a knee under a pink frou-frou skirt.

Pretty, pretty! Granite chanted. *Our mate is so pretty!*

We haven't even seen all of her yet, wolf. I rolled my eyes at him.

What I see so far is pretty enough.

True, I gave him that one.

Then the rest of Posy ever so slowly moved into view and my breath caught in my throat.

See?! Pretty, pretty Posy!

Hush, wolf.

My brothers must have been as stunned as I was. No one said a word or moved or even seemed to be breathing.

I could hear the clicking of a camera and Mom and Mama giggling, but ignored it all. How could I give even a sliver of attention to anything or anyone other than the ethereal creature standing uncertainly before us?

"Posy," Mase whispered, the first of us to come out of our stupor. "I have no words to describe how lovely you are, little flower."

"It's the gown Peri made." She held her arms out to her sides and looked down at the dress. "It's gorgeous, isn't it?"

"No, sweetness. It's the girl wearing it who's gorgeous." Jay took two long strides and grabbed one of her hands in both of his, then bent over it to kiss her knuckles.

A pink blush colored her cheeks and she cast her eyes to the floor.

"Such a shy little baby," Cole murmured as he walked up to her. "We're proud to be your mates, honey. You are so precious to us."

Taking her other hand, he copied Jay, and we had the pleasure of watching her blush darken.

"Even though I didn't get to do your hair today, princess, it looks amazing." Ash joined them and leaned down to kiss her forehead. "Simple but elegant, just like you."

Now her whole face turned red, making the three of them smirk at each other.

"Brothers, step back for a second," I requested and came closer. "Give us a slow twirl, cutie."

A dimpled smile flashed on her face, and Jay and Cole let go of her hands so she could do what I asked.

"Again," I demanded in a husky tone when she came to a stop.

Grinning, she slowly spun around a second time, her pretty dress flaring at the knees.

"Baby, you are as pretty as a picture."

So in love with mate! Granite swooned with heart eyes. *Our special girl.*

He howled in happiness, which drew the attention of his brother wolves, and they all sang out an *a-roo!* as if we were running under the full moon. Lark joined in with an adorable baby howl, and Posy giggled.

"All right, people!" Mama clapped at us again. "We have photos to take before the heat wilts us all and Wyatt loses his suit coat."

"I'll still look better than everyone except for our cutie," I smirked and met Posy's laughter-filled eyes. "I mean, have you seen how good my hair looks today?"

"Your fluff is very cute, baby." Mom leaned up and kissed my cheek.

I scowled and wiped it off with the back of my hand.

"Sorry, Mom. I know I'm a handsome devil, but these cheeks are only for Posy's kisses."

"Is that right?" Her eyes turned ice-cold as she leaned closer and whispered, "Lambo."

"Okay, okay! Sheesh. You're scary when you're pregnant." Turning my face, I lowered my cheek and let her give me another kiss.

#

Posy

We finished taking the last of the formal photos outside and headed back to the house. As we walked, the boys started horsing around, although carefully. Mom and Mama had warned them to keep their suits immaculate - I didn't know what that word meant, but I could guess - and they were trying, but I could see they were getting bored and antsy.

Five competitive alphas with free time and nothing to do was just asking for trouble. Fortunately, Dad trotted up to us before they found it.

"Posy," he said, leading me off to the side, "your brothers are here."

All the air rushed out of my lungs and my heart stalled before it kicked into high gear.

"They are?" I gasped.

I knew they were coming; I'd called and invited them myself - the first time I'd talked to them since I left Green River. So why was I reacting like this?

Dad raised one hand as if he wanted to touch my shoulder, then caught himself, clenched his fingers in a fist, and let his hand drop.

"I put them in the living room. Is that okay?" he asked.

Swallowing on the hard knot of emotion in my throat, I nodded.

"Posy? What's going on?" Mason was suddenly at my side, his big hand spanning the small of my back.

I opened my mouth, but nothing came out. Closing it, I stared up at Dad.

"Her brothers are here," he said for me.

Mason's body stiffened and a low growl rumbled out of his chest.

"You didn't know they were coming?" Dad frowned, his eyebrows drawing together.

"We did," Mason bit out.

"No one seems happy about it," Dad pointed out.

"I am," I disagreed quietly. "Just ... scared. Nervous. I wasn't very nice, not talking to them for three weeks. What if they hate me again?"

261

"Little flower," Mason gathered me in his arms, careful not to mess up my fancy hairdo, "you did nothing wrong."

"And how could anyone hate you?" Jayden said from behind me, and his fingertips brushed against my neck.

Turning my head, I saw concern in his beautiful eyes and couldn't stand it. This was supposed to be our happiest day, yet I was messing up already, and it wasn't even ten o'clock in the morning.

"Okay. I'm ready," I said, squaring my shoulders and walking forward, determined to at least see them and say hello.

"See, Dad?" Ash whispered, which he wasn't very good at, and I heard every word. "I *told* you that our baby was a badass bitch."

#

James and Aiden looked horrible.

Sure, their suits were high quality and their hair nicely styled, but their faces were pale and haggard with bags as dark as bruises under their eyes. Neither one looked as if they had much sleep recently, and I was sure they'd both lost weight.

"Are you sick?" I asked, concern welling up in me.

I sat on the couch across from them and my mates arranged themselves around me. Jay sat on my right and Ash on my left with Wyatt next to him. Cole and Mason stood behind the couch, one on either side of me.

"Sick at heart." James' smile was sad. "We can't get over how badly we failed you, Posy."

Oh. *Oh.*

"We were using some unhealthy methods to cope with Father's abuse," Aiden admitted. "Not just us, either. An alpha's actions ripple through the whole pack, and our pack had - and still has - a lot of ripples to work through. Beta Roy, for example, committed suicide three days after you left."

Shocked, I let my jaw fall open.

"What?" I gasped and squeezed Ash's hand.

"He ... he left a note. Saying he couldn't live with the guilt. He set you up that morning, Posy."

"Aiden—" James tried to interrupt him.

"No, James, she has a right to know."

"Know what?" I demanded.

As if sensing Aiden was going to tell me something terrible, Jay picked up my free hand and brought it to his mouth so he could drop little kisses on the back of it.

"Father specifically told him to have you make waffles that morning. Roy knew if you didn't, Father would beat you. Roy timed everything so the king's representatives would see it as soon as they arrived."

Shock. Betrayal. Disgust. Anger. Sorrow. So many emotions rushed through me at once, I couldn't process any of them.

I suddenly remembered Father storming into the kitchen, demanding waffles, and me wondering if Beta Roy had set me up.

"Did you know? At the time, did you know he set me up?" I whispered.

Both of them shook their heads.

Their wolves say no, Lark confirmed. *Slate and Agate sad and so worried about their boys.*

If what my brothers had said at Green River was true, Father had hurt them, too. Unlike Mason's papa, who only targeted him, Father hurt everyone.

I wonder if he hurt my mother?

Loosening my hands from my mates, I went over and sank to my knees in front of James and touched my fingers to one of his clenched fists.

"You asked me before I left Green River if I thought you had hurt me by choice, and I did," I admitted with a sniffle. "I didn't know. I didn't know he was hurting you both, too. To be honest, I think Lark hid a lot from me, and I was so fogged by pain most of the time, I really didn't understand what was going on."

James dropped his head, not meeting my eyes, but Aiden stood, took off his suit coat, and pulled up the back of his shirt. Amid all the scars, the one that drew my eye was a set of initials - KAB - that had been brutally branded in the center of his spine right above his waistband.

It was a twin to mine, right down to the location.

"Father didn't want us to forget who we belonged to," Aiden whispered, fixing his shirt and sitting down again.

"We've hired a couple of therapists to work with the pack." James lifted his face to look at me again. "They have everyone doing art therapy to get our mental health to a better place. I've been painting, and Aiden's learning to knit. No therapy can ever erase what we did to you, though. We'll go to our graves with that guilt on our souls."

"James—"

"And rightly so," Aiden interrupted me. "We deserve it, Posy. We deserve every lash of our conscience, every sleepless night, every word your mates said. We ourselves don't even deserve mates. We've already agreed that, if we find them, we'll ask them to reject us."

"Not that it will be hard to convince them," James snorted. "No one would want to be stuck for life with a pathetic bastard who sacrificed his baby sister to the monster just to save his own skin and sanity."

263

I cut my eyes to my silent and stone-faced mates. Mason *did* tell me that they'd had 'a talk' with my brothers before we left Green River. I hadn't asked questions, but I could guess what had been said. I knew my mates. I was just glad that they hadn't hurt or killed my brothers.

It broke my heart, though, to think they may have made James and Aiden believe they were unworthy of mates.

Shifters needed mates to have purpose and happiness in their lives. Mates could heal each other, and not just physically. Sometimes, a mate was all that kept a shifter sane.

"I don't believe that," I told my brothers in a firm tone. "No one is beyond forgiveness. Anyone can redeem themselves. Everyone should have a second chance. You *do* deserve mates, and if you find them, I forbid you to make them reject you as some form of punishment you've given yourselves."

They hung their heads, and I could see my argument wasn't making an impact, so I switched tactics.

"Don't you understand that you would be punishing two innocent girls, too?" That got their attention. "Two girls who've dreamed their whole life of finding their mates, and you'd deny them that out of a sense of guilt? If the Goddess sees fit to give you her best gift, who are you to refuse or reject it and hurt two more people?"

They both looked at me, hope at war with despair in their eyes.

"I can't forget what happened. I *can't*. But I forgive you," I murmured. "James, Aiden, I forgive you."

"You're too sweet, baby sister." James shook his head with a tiny smile. "You'd forgive the devil himself."

"And invite him in for lemonade and cookies so he could tell you his life story," Aiden added, also with a tiny smile.

"You have no idea," Wyatt chuckled. "Remind us to tell you about her 'interrogation' of Leo Halder sometime."

"That was an *interview,* not an interrogation!" I pouted. "And it worked, didn't it?"

James raised his eyebrows, and Aiden giggled, something I hadn't heard in years. It was amazing how much the happy sound lightened my heart.

Whether my mates agreed with me or not, I knew I'd done the right thing in forgiving my brothers.

Now, I had to work on getting them to forgive themselves.

#

Cole

Mom and Mama did a great job planning the ceremony.

After we'd told them about Posy's anxiety in big crowds and panic-inducing fear around strange men, they'd modified the traditional reception into more of an all-day buffet luncheon and got rid of the receiving line part all together.

That would have taken hours and hours, and I think both Mom and Mama knew *we'd* never make it that long, let alone our dear girl. With a pack of more than four thousand members, we would have been shaking hands until midnight.

This is much better, I thought to myself.

We sat at a long table on the stage at the front of the community hall with waiters bringing us food and drinks. Everyone could see and approach us for congratulations, but Posy still had a modicum of distance and security up here.

She'd been plenty nervous, but after Queen Lilah took a seat next to her, Posy loosened up and the two chatted away happily while we talked with the king, who told us what Ranger was doing to reshape Tall Pines.

After that, we alphas had to mingle with the masses, as did the king and queen, their pair of betas trailing them while holding hands. We played Rock-Paper-Scissors to create a rota so one of us was always with Posy here at the table. Jay got to stay first, so the rest of us kissed our girl and headed into the crowd.

There was a small stir of excitement when Callie and Keeley Breckenridge entered the hall and almost immediately scented their mates.

On one hand, I was happy. The twins were the last of their family after their older brother, Everett, was killed three months ago. They had always feared their mates would be in different packs and they'd be separated, and that fear became worse after Ev's death. They'd also been struggling to support themselves, although my brothers and I stepped in when we realized that. The poor kids were still in high school, for Goddess' sake! They shouldn't have had to worry about full-time jobs.

On the other hand, James and Aiden Briggs were not who I would have wanted for their mates. I knew better than anyone that they didn't have the best track record when it came to taking care of those they were supposed to love and protect.

Where are you going? Mase linked me as I walked toward the small knot of people near our parents.

In Ev's honor, I have to give the older brother talk to the Briggs boys, I told him with a little smirk.

Keep a tight hold on your temper.

You going to ground me if I don't, Papa Bear? I sneered.

You don't answer to me, Alpha Cole.

He sent me the image of our girl's face as she clapped her hands with gleaming eyes and an excited smile, happy that her friends and brothers were mates.

Well, hell. My mouth twisted into a grimace.

Exactly.

Sighing, I pinched the bridge of my nose with my thumb and forefinger.

You can still scare them, boss, Topaz said and drew his lips up in a pretend snarl that was actually cute enough to make me laugh.

#

Jayden

More shifters than I'd anticipated came to see our luna and the new members inducted into the pack.

Of course, some came just because King Julian was there with his new queen, and they wanted to get a glimpse of her.

Thank the Goddess that Mama and Mom knew what they were doing and had everything running as smooth as glass, efficiently managing a reception of thousands of shifters from five packs in a staggered rotation, although the few remaining Dark Wood wolves were folded in with special guests and outside visitors.

Dad and Papa helped, too, by arranging photographers and media for the event so that it was broadcast live on the pack's private channel and recorded "for posterity," according to Papa.

After officially making Posy our luna by inducting her into the pack, we exchanged rings with our girl, and our wolves puffed with pride to see how she incorporated their namesakes into our platinum bands.

When Wyatt slid our set on her finger, her bottom lip trembled and a couple of tears skated down her cheeks, then a beautiful smile brightened her face, and we all breathed a sigh of relief.

Wyatt kept telling us she'd love it, and he was right.

Finally, we welcomed the new members into the pack: the del Vecchio flock, Zayden and Zayne Maxwell, Leo Halder, and Thoreau Jones, who had a small breakdown when we had to cut his thumb. Emerson was ready to storm the stage, but Leo, of all people, gave the kid a hug and turned his face away from the blood until it was done.

Later, Angelo told us that Leo had bonded in a big brother-way with Thoreau, and both of them were thriving under Emerson and Angelo's positive attention, which was good news.

As we were being seated at our table, two unmated shifters muttered a few crude comments about Posy. Unfortunately, Tyler happened to overhear them, and River flew into a fury. We linked

266

Emerson to contain Tyler before River broke free, and it was a struggle to control *him* after he found out why River was mad.

By then the other betas were aware of what was happening. Matthew grabbed the offending shifters by the backs of their necks and dragged them out of the hall with his usual subtlety - which meant not at all - and Tristan and Crew held Emerson back and joined Angelo, who was wrestling Tyler out the door on the other side.

River's fierce roar and Cove's deep growl shook the windows in their frames, and everyone in the hall cowered. However, when no further threat came and they saw their alphas not reacting, they stood again and carried on with their conversations and eating.

"What's going on?" Posy's eyes were huge and her hands had started to shake.

"Tyler's wolf got angry about something someone said," I told her. "Then Emerson's wolf found out and lost his temper, too."

"River and Cove? Should I go—"

"No, baby." I took her trembling hands in mine. "The other betas and Angelo have it under control. Don't worry. Tyler and Emerson would feel terrible if they knew they upset you on your special day."

"I don't want them to feel bad, but I'm worried about them." She bit her bottom lip.

I raised our joined hands and nudged her lip out of her teeth with my knuckles.

"No more worrying." I smiled. "I know nurturing others is your nature, and being luna will magnify that, but not today, sweetness. Today, focus on yourself and us. We're being selfish today, okay?"

She stared at me in silence for a second, then smiled, showing her pearly teeth. I bent down and kissed her cheek, and she took the opportunity to cup her hand around my ear.

"How much longer until we can go home?" she whispered.

Pulling back, I looked at her carefully. She'd been holding up so well, but now I could see she was exhausted. Whether from stress or nerves, she needed a rest and cuddling.

"Soon, baby." I dropped a kiss on the tip of her nose and rubbed one hand up and down her back.

She nodded and laid her head on my shoulder with a soft sigh.

This sort of thing is inhumane, Quartz grumbled. *It's wearing on our mate, and I'm bored to tears.*

Unlike us, at least you can take a nap, I retorted. *We're the ones stuck shaking hands and smiling and being sociable.*

Good thing, too. His eyes glimmered for a second before he closed them and rolled over with a huff. *I'd have eaten half of these people by now.*

267

Ash

Our girl was drooping.

We all were, really. Only Mase looked as sharp as he had this morning. Cole had shed his suit coat, vest, and tie. Jay and I had ditched our coats and loosened our ties, but we stuck with the vests, mainly because Posy thought they were sexy. As for Wyatt, who hadn't bothered with a vest or tie to begin with, he'd stripped out of his coat almost immediately after the ceremony. By the time we were done eating and mingling with pack members, he had the sleeves of his dress shirt rolled up to his elbows and the top three buttons undone - two more than he'd started with.

Ashy, Wy going to lose that shirt in a minute, Sid giggled.

You may be right, buddy.

At long last, Mom and Mama realized how exhausted Posy was and agreed that I could take her home.

While my brothers stayed to chat with a few people, I led her from the community hall and out to my SUV and got her home before she could fall asleep. While I carefully hung her gown up, she changed into one of Mase's t-shirts, then we propped ourselves up against the headboard with all of Wyatt's pillows.

"I want to see my brothers again before they go home," she slurred, not quite awake anymore.

"Okay. We'll go see them tomorrow sometime."

" 'Morrow? They're staying?"

"Yeah. At the twins' house."

"With their mates," she giggled sleepily. "Love you, waffle."

"I love you, too, cupcake."

Getting her tucked in under the covers, I kissed her forehead and watched her nod off before falling into the darkness myself.

#

Mason

After the reception dwindled to nothing, I looked around for Angelo. I wanted to check in with him about how the pack bond and link were working for him since he didn't have an animal spirit.

To be honest, none of us knew how much or little he'd be affected by the moon magic. Tyler had done some research in the alpha library and found that it was a crap shoot. There weren't too many cases to study, maybe fifty animal-less shifters in the whole of our recorded history, but it looked like about half of them had links and bonds only with their mates while the other half got the full pack experience.

I found him, Tyler, and King Julian chatting about bird shifters, which seemed like perfect timing.

"So you're the one who told Lilah about the shifter my grandfather kept in a cage?" The king raised an eyebrow at Tyler.

"Uh, yes, your majesty." Tyler's cheeks and the tips of his ears glowed fire red.

"Are you talking about Menno?" Angelo chimed in. "I met him once."

"I don't know his name," Tyler said. "The book I read didn't go into much detail. It was sort of a side note."

"Menno got stuck in bird form," the king explained. "A very unusual situation. No one could figure out why or how, but he was never able to transform back to his human body. He wasn't happy, and Grandad offered him mercy, but he wanted to live. So Grandad took him in, and he became the advisor no one knew about until he finally passed away, oh, maybe four years ago now."

"Speaking of unusual situations," I butted into the conversation, "Angelo, can you feel the pack bond? Are you able to link anyone other than Emerson?"

I can and I am, he linked me with a grin.

Oh, that's great! I said.

"I take it that's a yes?" King Julian snickered, and I nodded.

The talk turned more general after that, and Emerson came to claim his mate, saying Thoreau was asking if they could go home now. Tyler asked if he could catch a ride, seeing as the O was on the way, and left with them. Then the king's attention shifted to his queen, who was chatting with Gamma Rio and his mate, a human girl named Emmeline.

"She wants me to meet them," King Julian said. "She's curious about how a human is fitting into a werewolf pack."

"Then I'll catch you tomorrow, your majesty." I nodded. "I think I'm going to head home now, too."

"See you tomorrow, Mase."

I turned and started walking toward the door when the *last* voice I wanted to hear called my name.

"Alpha Mason? May I please have a moment of your time?"

269

31: Discoveries

Mason

"Is it official pack business, *Mr. Price?*" I spat, not even turning to look at my father.

Let him talk to my back.

"I want to congratulate my son and alpha on finding his mate and luna."

His voice was calm and even, which threw me off. I was too used to the harsh, biting voice he used to criticize me.

"Thank you." I nodded my head curtly and figured even that was more than he deserved.

"I'd like you to come to my home office, please, if you have time," he said before I could escape. "I have something to show you as well as something to say to you."

I hesitated. I did not physically fear him, but the little boy in my heart still feared his disapproval and belittling words. I didn't want to hear any more of them. Add in the explosive rage he'd stoked to an inferno over the past couple of years, and I wasn't sure that I could hold back if he began to poke and pick at me in the privacy of his office.

On the other hand, what I felt toward him was a heavy and exhausting burden. It stewed in my gut constantly, and I had better things to focus on now that Posy was in our lives. I couldn't forgive him like she forgave her brothers, but I couldn't carry on like this, either.

Of course, that didn't mean I wanted to rebuild a father-son bond like we had when he taught me to ride a bike on my sixth birthday. What I wanted, what I *truly* wanted, was to move forward into a bright future with my mate and brothers, and I couldn't do that so long as I stagnated in the past, draining my energy to feed the anger and hate I had toward my father.

"All right, Mr. Price," I told him, glancing at him over my shoulder. "On one condition. After this, we will talk only when and if *I* want to. You don't approach me again on a personal level, only for pack business. And no more stunts like that 'urgent and dire' appointment."

"I'm invited to the same family functions you are, and what if Mama invites you to dinner? We're going to have to interact with each other."

He didn't sound happy, but I was past caring what he felt. He never cared how I felt when he denigrated me in front of his friends or my brothers.

"I'll be as civil as you are whenever we're around our family," I said. "The second you overstep, so will I."

Oh, I am looking forward to what we'll do if he oversteps, Garnet muttered.

"Very well," he agreed, surprising me again. "I accept your terms with the hope that we can renegotiate them in the future."

So instead of going home to our girl, I got into my truck and linked Cole to let him know I was going AWOL for a while.

For how long are we talking? he demanded. *Hours or days?*

Maybe an hour or two.

Is everything okay? he wanted to know. *Do you need us? Ash is asleep with Posy, but the rest of us are just playing COD. We can—*

My father wants to talk. I don't know how long it will take, and I might need a run afterwards, depending on what he has to say. I'll be back when I get back.

Dude, let me come with you.

I'd rather you stay with our girl. I didn't want to tell him I might be a mess afterwards, and none of my brothers needed to see me like that. *He's been decent so far, and it's not like he'll do anything to me.*

Except say things to hurt you! Cole blasted through the link.

Nah. Nothing he can say will hurt me, I lied. *I've decided I don't value his opinion enough to care anymore.*

Mase, I can tell your ly—

Look, if I need you, I'll link you.

You always say that, but you never do. We want to support you, brother. You need to let us. It hurts us to know that you'd rather suffer alone than trust us to be there for you.

It's not like that. I shook my head as I turned onto my parents' street. *It's not about trusting you; it's about burdening you when you all have your own issues you're working through.*

You are not a burden, Mase! he growled. *How many times have you said that to Wyatt? Or Jay? Or me? Hear your own words. Stop bottling everything up and shutting us out. We want to help you. We need to help you. We're in this together, brother.*

All right, I said as I parked along the curb. *I'll try. This time, I promise I'll link you if I need you. Fairs?*

Fairs.

Closing the link, I got out of my truck and followed my father into the house and back to his home office. As soon as I entered, my eyes flicked around to see nothing had changed in the three years since I'd moved into the alpha house.

Well, wait. That's new.

My gaze stopped on a large easel that held a black frame full of professionally matted documents.

It stood out in this plain room. Royal Price was not one for trinkets, knick knacks, or any kind of decoration, really. His desk held a PC, keyboard, and mouse, and that was all. No toys, photographs, or even a cup of pens. Likewise, the walls were bare save for a simple clock.

What was so important to him that he'd have it framed and displayed in his minimalist workspace?

My curiosity getting the better of me, I walked over to see what it was - and came to a sudden halt, my body turning into a statue.

I recognized that handwriting. The torn corner of the one map. The unlabeled spot. The misspelled word.

"I threw that away," I whispered.

"While Shawn, Jay, and Nathan took you boys for ice cream that night, I stayed back to clean up and found it. All these years, I saved it because it was a damn good plan. It was only after Peri's pool party that I understood why you threw it out. I had it framed yesterday so I will never forget."

"Forget what?" I sneered. "That I didn't know how to spell maneuver when I was fourteen?"

"Mason, I cannot apologize enough. Everyone, even my wolf and Nathan's, tried to tell me, but like the pigheaded man I am, I wouldn't hear them. I was so convinced I had to make you strong that I never saw how my words were killing you. I am so sorry, son, and I will spend the rest of my life trying to make it up to you."

I still didn't turn around, although I kind of wanted to. My poker face was solid, but I knew my eyes would give me away to anyone who knew me well.

Like Posy. She always watches my eyes for the truth.

"Mason, I want you to know three things. One, it was never your fault. It was never anything you did or didn't do. You were a kind, honest, hardworking boy who grew up to be a kind, honest, hardworking man. I was too blind to see that and too insensitive to appreciate it."

Okay. Wasn't expecting that, I told Garnet.

Me, either.

"Two, I am proud of you. I never should have called you a disappointment. You were right. You're not the disappointment. *I* am. You are a great alpha, a great brother, a great son, and a great mate to your girl. Five Fangs will only grow stronger and better with you and your brothers at the helm."

Wasn't expecting that, either, I admitted.

Garnet stayed silent, and I wondered if he was as shocked as I was at all these confessions.

272

"Three, and most important of all, I love you. I can't remember the last time I told you that. Can you? I should have told you that every day of your life. You'd think, after everyone we lost in the sickness, I would have learned that you don't always have another day with someone. I wish I could have told Shawn and Jay and Willow that I love them just one more time, but I'm sure they died knowing I did. Yet here you are, my living son, convinced I don't love you because of my own stupidity."

My father's voice grew hoarse and thick as he continued, and I wondered what I'd see in his face if I turned around.

"I am so sorry I made you think that. I love you so much, Mason. You're my boy. Whether you can ever forgive me, whether you can ever think of me as your father again, you will always be my son, and I will always love you."

My eyes stung and my nose clogged up, but I forced myself to ignore it and not sniff. My moment of weakness with Posy the other day was as close to crying as I'd come in years, and I wasn't going to start now.

Especially in front of *him*.

"I understand if you can't or don't want to talk," he said, apparently wrapping up his speech. "All I can do is thank you for listening. If you ever want to talk, any time of the day or night, link me or call me or just come over. I am willing to do whatever it takes to earn your forgiveness and a place in your life again. For now, I'll leave you to your thoughts. I'm sure you want to get home to your brothers and that beautiful, sweet mate of yours."

I nodded once, then heard his footsteps walk out of the room and grow quieter as he headed down the hallway.

I don't know what to say to any of that. Garnet sounded as bewildered as I felt.

Yeah.

In a daze, I wandered out of my parents' house and walked down the driveway towards my truck.

The sound of running feet caught my ear, and I swiveled my head to see what was going on.

The boys came to save us, Garnet informed me with an amused huff right as my brothers' scent went up my nose.

The four of them raced up and came to a breathless, sweaty halt right in front of me. I frowned as I studied them. They'd at least had the chance to change into shorts and t-shirts. I was dying out here in my suit on this sultry summer evening.

The dry cleaning bill is going to be outrageous, I thought with slight annoyance.

"Sorry." Cole bent over and braced his hands on his knees as he panted. "We would have been here sooner, but we couldn't leave our sleeping girl without a guard, and Crew was the only beta still awake."

"Or not engaged in ... activities ... with his mate," Jay said tactfully.

My eyebrows shot up and I fought back a grin.

"You know it takes a while to get from Crew's place to ours," Ash continued the explanation while yawning, "and Sara wanted to come along, so that added a few extra minutes."

"Are you okay, Mase?" Wyatt's eyes glittered with worry.

"I'm fine. And you ran instead of drove because?"

Wyatt rolled his eyes at me.

"You can ask that after being cooped up all day at that dumb reception?"

Slinging an arm around his neck, I pulled him in for a noogie.

"Hey! My hair!"

"Oh, the photos are over and it's pitch dark out. No one can see your perfectly coiffed fluff," I teased him.

As he wrestled around, trying to get out of my hold, I linked Cole.

Do you remember when our dads first started that alpha training school? They gave us an assignment to make a plan that would have saved Dark Woods.

Yeah, I remember. He sent me a confused look. *What did you do with your plan?*

Huh? Oh. Well, I was pretty proud of it. He smirked a little. *I mean, for a thirteen-year-old, it wasn't bad. I revised it as the alphas suggested, then filed it in my dad's office under A.*

A? Why A? I let Wyatt go as I wondered about the organization of Dad's filing system.

A for Assignment. It's probably still there. He tilted his head. *Why?*

No reason. Just wondered.

What did you do with yours? he asked.

Threw it away.

What?! It was so good! Alpha Jay said it would have saved Dark Woods!

My father had nothing but bad things to say about it. Why would I keep it? I shrugged. *Anyway, that's what he wanted to show me. He fished it out of the trash that night and had it framed. It's in his office. What do you think that means?*

I think, Cole said slowly, *it means he messed up, knows he messed up, and would do anything to fix what he messed up.*

I nodded, jiggling my keys in my pocket. I wasn't going to forgive my father, at least not any time soon, but I wasn't going to waste another minute grieving for our broken relationship or invest another erg of energy into hating him.

For now, I decided, I would pretend he was an acquaintance and treat him as such until I could process everything I was feeling.

"Mase?"

"Pile in the truck, boys," I said when Jay's voice penetrated my thoughts. "Let's go home."

"Home to our bed," Ash said on a mighty yawn.

"Home to a shower," Cole grumbled.

"Home to a snack," Wyatt said.

"Home to *our mate*," Jay corrected them all.

"Our heart and soul," I agreed.

"Yes," my brothers all said at once, and our smiles were bright ones.

End of Book Two